"I am not a little girl anymore," huskily.

"No, but you are still fool."

"Is this so foolish?" ggling closer. His efforts to tr way were of no avail. But he wa longer trying very hard. Her head bent lower, her golden hair cascading over him, brushing against his cheek as she dared to steal a kiss from the taut line of his mouth. It was barely a whisper, shy and tremulous, but enough to break what remained of Max's self-control.

Instead of pushing her away, he crushed her hard against him, taking possession of her lips with a ruthless fervor. He caught one hand in the silky tangle of curls at the nape of her neck. Holding her captive, his mouth greedily devoured hers. . . .

Books published by The Ballantine Publishing Group
are available at quantity discounts on bulk purchases
for premium, educational, fund-raising, and special
sales use. For details, please call 1-800-733-3000.

MISTRESS MISCHIEF

THE LADY WHO HATED SHAKESPEARE

Susan Carroll

FAWCETT CREST • NEW YORK

A Fawcett Crest Book
Published by Ballantine Books
Mistress Mischief copyright © 1992 by Susan Coppula
The Lady Who Hated Shakespeare copyright © 1986 by Susan Coppula

Library of Congress Catalog Card Number: 95-90433

ISBN 0-449-22397-3

Manufactured in the United States of America

First Edition: December 1995

10 9 8 7 6 5 4 3 2 1

Contents

MISTRESS MISCHIEF

Chapter 1

Leon Auguste Barry, the Viscount Raincliffe, was not yet cold in his grave. His lordship had been laid to rest among the family tombs upon a Sunday afternoon. By the following morning, his eldest son and heir, Sir Wilfred Barry, prepared triumphantly to evict his stepmama from Dunhaven Manor.

For two long years, Sir Wilfred, his thin, sharp features twitching with disapproval, had endured the presence of *that woman* polluting the halls of his ancestral home, that yellow-haired strumpet, that fortune-hunting minx who had so beguiled his father, making a complete fool of the old viscount.

But when the will had been read out after the funeral services, it appeared that the late Lord Raincliffe had finally come to his senses. Not a single mention had been made of his second wife, not so much as a pound note left to her. Sir Wilfred, who had lived in expectation of seeing over half his inheritance bequeathed to the scheming wench, had been hard put not to burst forth with an unseemly "huzzah."

The new Lord Raincliffe had wasted little time in informing his stepmama that her presence at Dunhaven was no longer welcome. Now, as he paced the great hall, consulting his pocket watch, he impatiently awaited her departure.

The manor was draped with black crepe in memory of its late master, and the atmosphere at Dunhaven was unusually somber as Frederica Eleanor Barry, now the Dowager Countess of Raincliffe, emerged from her bedchamber.

Struggling with the weight of her portmanteau, she closed the door. The youngest footman, John, would have darted forward to her aid if he had dared, because for a wicked adventuress, Lady Raincliffe possessed a remarkably sweet countenance. Her delicate, heart-shaped face was framed by

3

a halo of golden ringlets. Her complexion cream and roses, she might have looked all softness and innocence but for the strength to be found in her stubborn chin and the naughty sparkle to be discovered in her deep blue eyes.

But her expression this morning was subdued, far more so than her apparel. With her diminutive frame garbed in a pelisse of bright apple green, her straw bonnet trimmed with artificial cherries and tied with a coquelicot ribbon, no one had ever appeared less like a grieving widow. Any sorrow she felt had to be detected beneath the lush sweep of her gold-tipped lashes, and that was no easy task. At the age of twenty, Freddie was already a most accomplished actress, having learned a long time before how to guard her more tender emotions from the scorn of the world.

Switching the heavy portmanteau to her other hand, she mustered all her dignity and set forth down the long gallery that connected the east wing with the main part of the house. Gray morning light filtered through the tall, latticed windows, revealing the vast chamber to be a hive of bustling footmen. Most of them averted their gaze as Freddie passed by, refusing to meet her eyes.

Trust servants to always know when one was no longer a person of any account, she thought dryly. She watched as the men busied themselves, carting away some of her late husband's prized possessions, the heavily carved Jacobean chairs that like a pair of thrones had flanked the fireplace, the brassplated torchère, the quaint old fire screen.

Sir Wilfred was apparently wasting little time in making his ownership felt, altering Dunhaven to suit his own mundane tastes. Freddie noted with some amusement that her portrait was already gone, leaving a rectangular shadow in the empty space along the dark oak wainscoting. Doubtless her stepson had burned the painting. Not that she much cared, having thought that the likeness had made her look wretchedly fubsy-faced.

She was far more disturbed to see that the footmen were removing the portrait of Leon as well, likely to consign it to one of the rooms at the far back of the house with the rest of the unwanted furnishings.

Painted upon the occasion of their marriage, it was a full-length pose of the late viscount, ever the gallant in his satin knee breeches, his frock coat frothing with lace at the cuffs, his white powdered wig pulled back into a neat queue reminiscent of another era. But Leon had never apologized for his old-fashioned attire.

As he had once told her, "Not even for you, babe, will I make a cake of m'self, aping the fashions of these young sparks, tricked out in yaller breeches, m'hair cut to resemble some dead Roman."

And although Freddie had often teased him about it, she had quite agreed with him. Leon had been magnificent in his powder and patch, always the grand seigneur. The French artist had captured that regal bearing. Monsieur Le Brun had done nothing to soften or flatter Leon's advancing years, but there had been no necessity. Despite the lines that time and the devil had carved in Leon's aquiline features, the roguish light in his eyes had been unquenchable.

A faint sigh escaped Freddie. She would have gone down on both knees and begged Wilfred to let her have the painting if she thought that would have done any good. As it was, all she could do was watch the footmen cart it off to gather dust.

She turned away, slowly recommencing her final journey through the manor that had been her home for the past two years, the one place in her misbegotten life where she had almost been happy. But Freddie refused to allow herself any sentimental memories about Dunhaven. After all, it had been a man she had loved, not a place. And he was gone.

When she reached the top of the grand staircase, she glanced down to the marble-tiled hall below. At the foot of the stairs stood her stepson, some fifteen years Freddie's senior, a stick of a man with pinched nostrils and small, close-set eyes. Behind him stood two unmarried sisters equally scrawny and self-righteous. To his left hovered his meek wife, Harriet, nervously wringing her mittened hands.

Sir Wilfred had not as yet deigned to bring any of his children to Dunhaven. Doubtless to the last, he feared having his offspring contaminated by Freddie's presence. The supposition did not pain Freddie. Assuming Sir Wilfred's heirs to be molded in his own image, she had never desired to make their acquaintance. Indeed, at the moment she rather wished she had never been introduced to the rest of the family.

The elder generation of Barrys were all attired in unrelenting black, reminding Freddie of a flock of beady-eyed crows come to pick over her bones. She might have been daunted to face such a disapproving throng, except that she could hear the echoes of her late husband's voice in her ear, Leon lamenting

5

in that droll way of his: *Stap me, m'dear. Just look at 'em. How did an old rip like me ever come to father such a sanctimonious bunch of prigs? I would suspect I had been made a cuckold, but m'first wife was so stuffed with virtue, I don't even have the comfort of that notion.*

Despite the grimness of Freddie's situation, the memory caused her lips to quiver. She sauntered down the broad stairs, achieving a deal of grace despite the awkwardness of balancing the valise. Wilfred's gaze raked her up and down, regarding the bright folds of her pelisse with a thunderstruck expression.

"Madam!" he said. "Fie upon you. You could at least have had the decency to put on the semblance of mourning for my father."

Setting down the portmanteau that was causing her arm to ache, Freddie smiled sweetly. "I saw no occasion for it. You and your sisters seem to be doing more than an adequate job of that. Besides, milord never liked me to wear black."

And the whisper of Leon's voice came to her again, some of his final instructions to her as he had lain dying.

And don't you dare be decking yourself out like a magpie lest you want me coming back from my grave to haunt you. You be sure to wear that bonnet I like, the one with the saucy ribbons. It will give me something pleasant to think on when I am down trading quips in hell.

The memory this time of that familiar, raspy voice became a little too poignant, and Freddie felt a thickness gather in her throat. She swallowed hard, determined not to think of Leon again until she was clear of this house. She would perish herself before she gave these smug fools the satisfaction of seeing her weep.

She noted Wilfred moistening his lips, his thin chest filling with air, and realized that he could not let the occasion pass without delivering one last diatribe against her.

"Madam—"

Freddie cut him off with an airy wave of her hand. "Oh, pray, my . . ." No, she could not do it. She could not accord him the dignity of Leon's title.

"Sir Wilfred," she continued, "let us part for once without quarreling. I trust you have had the carriage brought round."

"You trust wrong, madam," he sneered. "It is but a short walk to the crossroads. If you hurry, you may contrive to catch the afternoon stage."

Like a Delphic chorus, his sisters murmured their satisfied

6

agreement while Freddie was momentarily shaken. Curse him! The crossroads was nearly ten miles away and the skies already threatening rain. Freddie would not have thought that even Wilfred could be such a toad as that, but she managed to conceal her dismay. Not so his wife Harriet, who paled and faltered, "Oh, n-no, my lord. Surely we could at least offer Frederica the use of the old brougham—"

"No, we could not," Wilfred snapped. "Let this strumpet leave as she came, sneaking through the gates."

"Actually," Freddie said, "I arrived in a coach and four with gilt-trimmed wheels and peacock blue cushions. Six outriders and two postilions. But I know what pain such an outlay of money would occasion you, my dear Wilfred, and I would not want to leave you suffering from an attack of biliousness."

Sir Wilfred's face washed a dull red. In a spirit of pure mischief, Freddie could not resist adding, "So I suppose that nothing remains but for you to come kiss your mama goodbye."

Wilfred looked as though he would strangle on his own neck cloth. He became nearly incoherent as he spluttered, "I'd—I'd sooner box your ears."

"Would you?" Freddie inquired amicably. "I confess, I would think the better of you if you did. But you have always been naught but a bully, all bluster."

It was a melancholy prospect, to think of this mean-spirited scarecrow of a man stepping into Leon's shoes. But Freddie refused to dwell on what she could not remedy. Gathering up the burden of her baggage once more, she swept past her affronted stepson.

She paused to press Harriet's hand and murmur loud enough for Wilfred to hear, "Take heart, my dear. With such spleen, he's bound to be taken off with a fit of apoplexy someday. That, at least, will give you something to look forward to."

Harriet gave a shocked gasp, and Sir Wilfred thundered out, "Why—you—you wretched woman. 'Tis you who will come to a bad end one day."

"So I have been told since I was eight years old," Freddie said. "It is hardly a novel prediction, Sir Wilfred."

"Be gone, you Jezebel!" He swept one finger, pointing toward the front door.

But the melodramatic gesture was entirely wasted, for

Freddie was already heading in that direction. Chawton, the old butler, stepped forward to open the door for her, his gaze fixed rigidly ahead.

Freddie thought his eyes looked slightly reddened. It was not surprising that even this stiff-necked manservant should have been weeping for his late master. What did astonish her was the low whisper that followed her out the door.

"God keep you, milady."

Startled, Freddie half looked back, but the door was already being closed in her face. It was far easier to pretend that she had never heard the words. Insults and disapproval she knew how to deal with. Any show of kindness always proved her undoing.

Turning her back on Dunhaven, she stepped out from the shelter of the portico onto the gravel drive leading away from the house, cheerfully consigning Sir Wilfred and all his kind to the devil.

But beneath her spirit of bravado came the first flutterings of panic as a gust of October wind penetrated the unlined silk of her pelisse, the muslin gown she wore beneath. Shivering, she stared down the lane that wound past Dunhaven's broad lawns, the stately line of sycamore trees showing their first hintings of autumn gold. The drive looked bleak and empty, a road leading to nowhere.

For one deemed such a hardened fortune hunter, she had little to show for being the widow of one of the wealthiest peers in England, only a small cache of jewels and what little she had managed to save out of her pin money. She had no notion of where she was going or even how to get there.

"What am I going to do, Leon?" she murmured, racking her brain for some of the worldly wisdom Leon had dispensed to her so freely over the brief course of their marriage.

On one of those rare occasions when he could be induced to be serious, she recollected, he had said to her with a melancholy sigh, "Ah, the time has ever been out of joint for us, my dear. If only you had been born forty years sooner or I much later. But there is little sense repining over that. I have been selfish enough to rob you of a brief portion of your youth. But when I am gone—"

She had tried to hush him, ever hating to hear him talk of his dying or even to think of it. But he had insisted, continuing on to say, "When I am gone, don't bury yourself in the country. Life was not meant to be such a dull affair. Find

8

yourself some gaiety, some laughter, some adventure. London is the best place for that. And then find yourself some handsome young buck who will make you a proper husband."

Freddie frowned at the memory. It had always troubled Leon that he had been no longer capable of being what he had deemed a "proper" husband to her. Any visits to her bed at night had been only to tuck her in, to plant a chaste kiss upon her brow. Not fully understanding the allure of the physical aspect of marriage, Freddie had not found anything lacking in Leon's behavior. But she comprehended enough to realize it had been a source of deep humiliation to him and she had vowed even after his death to keep his secret forever.

Missing Leon, grieving for him as she did, the prospect of finding "some handsome young buck" held no appeal for her. But she was still young enough to long for the gaiety and adventure that Leon had spoken of.

London is the best place, Leon had said. And so to London she would go.

Valiantly squaring her shoulders, Freddie started down the drive. Setting out on an adventure might have been a great deal more appealing if one didn't have to carry one's own bag, or if the lane ahead was not so infernally long. But she was not about to waste time complaining.

When she finally saw the park gates and the lodgekeeper's house looming up ahead of her, she heaved a sigh of relief, trying to forget she had yet another eight miles to go before she reached the crossroads. At least it was not raining yet.

But her relief faded when she observed a tall figure garbed in a drab brown cloak step away from the shelter of the lodge's whitewashed stone walls. Freddie's heart sank. No, it could not be. But it was. There was only one woman in all of Somerset, perhaps all of England, with a pair of shoulders so broad, she could have been a prizefighter— Miss Theodora Applegate, Leon's niece by marriage, a poor relation of his first wife.

As Freddie approached, the middle-aged spinster regarded her through reproachful dark eyes, the breeze tossing strands of her lank brown hair free of her prim bonnet. Her mournful expression served only to accent the leanness of Theodora's features, her long chin, her even longer nose. As Leon had been wont to remark, "Dora would have been a handsome filly if only she had been a horse."

Freddie cringed, damning herself for a coward, but she had

9

tried to avoid taking leave of Dora. The woman was the one person at Dunhaven besides Leon who was sincerely attached to Freddie. There was nothing Freddie hated so much as tearful good-byes, and she had hoped the letter she had slipped beneath Dora's pillow last night would have spared her this one. But it seemed she was not to escape so lightly.

As she came to a halt in front of Miss Applegate, Freddie did not give her a chance to speak, but immediately began to scold. "Dora, what are you doing here? Did I not beg you in my note to spare us both a parting that can only be painful?"

"And so I am." Dora shuffled her feet, looking sheepish, but there was a most dogged light in her eyes all the same. "There won't be any parting. I am coming with you."

"What!" For the first time, Freddie noted that beneath the cloak peeked the hem of Dora's best traveling gown and stacked behind her was a neat pile of bandboxes.

"My dear Dora," Freddie said. "Of course you are doing no such thing."

"You don't want me?" Dora faltered.

"It isn't that at all. But where I am going . . . 'tis just not possible to take you with me."

"Oh," Dora's shoulders slumped. "You are going back to your uncle's house, then."

"Good Lord, no!" Freddie shuddered at the mere thought of the cheerless, unloving home in which she had spent her childhood. "That is the last place where I would go even if my aunt and uncle would have me back. No, I am entirely on my own now, with scarcely a feather to fly with."

"I know. I heard the terms of that infamous will." Dora's stolid features darkened with a rare flash of anger. "I cannot believe that Uncle Leon would have treated you so shabbily."

"It was not his fault, but mine. He spoke of changing the will many times, but I always diverted him. There were so many more pleasant things for us to do than closet ourselves with a bunch of musty solicitors." Freddie's lips curved into a wry smile at what had been perhaps her greatest folly, but she still could not bring herself to regret it. Leon had had Wilfred to flap about him like a great black buzzard, reminding his father of death. Freddie had only ever wanted him to think about living.

Even at the end, when Leon had begged for the attorney to be fetched, Freddie's main concern had been sending for the doctor. By the time the solicitor had arrived, it had already been far too late.

Dora gave an indignant sniff. "Wilfred should have done something. He must know his papa always meant to have provided for you. If my cousin has a generous bone in his body—"

"If he has, he broke it a long time ago," Freddie interrupted. "But you see how it is with me, Dora. I would gladly take you with me, but I have no home to offer you. I must live now entirely by my own wits."

"Then that is why you need me," Dora persisted. "I will be your companion, lend you an air of respectability."

"I don't intend to be respectable anymore," Freddie said recklessly. "For once, I may try to be just as bad and wicked as everyone has always thought me."

"Oh!" Dora appeared momentarily daunted, then said stoutly, "Well . . . well, good! That shall suit me. I have always wanted to be a wicked woman myself."

When Freddie broke into a reluctant laugh, Dora added fiercely, "Truly!"

"My dearest friend," Freddie murmured. Touched more than she cared to admit by the woman's loyalty, she gently tucked back some of the straying tendrils beneath the rim of Dora's bonnet. "You cannot know what you are saying. Your home has always been here at Dunhaven, your family . . ."

Dora's large brown eyes filled with tears. "You are my family, the only one who truly ever cared for me."

Freddie wanted to assure her that was not true, but found she could not. Even Leon had sometimes been less than kind to poor Dora, introducing her in that teasing way of his as "m'inheritance from my late wife, along with the silverplate and some odd bits of china."

"I am sure Sir Wilfred will insist you continue on here at Dunhaven. You are his cousin," Freddie said lamely.

"Oh, aye. Wilfred has already told me that he understands his obligation toward me." Dora's tears brimmed over, trickling down her sallow cheeks. "He hopes that I will be properly grateful and continue to make myself useful. *You* more than anyone should understand what that means, what it feels like to be an unwanted poor relation."

Freddie winced, struck to the heart by Dora's words more than her tears. Because she did understand, only too well. Freddie had only to close her eyes to summon up her aunt

11

Jameson's cold voice, speaking as though Freddie were not even present.

"Oh, yes, the child is a sad trial to us, wild to a fault. My late brother's daughter, you know, left on our hands when she was only eight. Quite a financial burden considering we have four girls of our own. One would not mind so much if Frederica would contrive to be more obliging. But still, one must do one's duty."

God preserve her forever, Freddie thought bitterly, from people who did their duty. And preserve Dora, too.

Digging out her lace-edged handkerchief, Freddie mopped at the woman's tears. "There now, please don't cry anymore, Dora. You know I cannot bear waterworks." And though she thought herself quite mad, she heard herself adding, "If you truly wish it, you may come with me."

Dora blew her nose gustily into Freddie's linen. "Oh, F-Freddie, do you mean it?"

Freddie could do no more than nod her head before she was enveloped in a huge bear hug. Dora lit up with a beaming smile that rendered her face quite appealing. Spinning on her heel, she called out to the bushes at the side of the lodge.

"Everything is all right. Her ladyship says we can go with her."

"We?" Freddie repeated faintly. Before she could question Dora or even protest, two more figures popped out from behind the shrubberies, an elderly man with rheumy eyes and age spots on his balding pate, accompanied by a pert girl with round apple cheeks and flyaway curls. Freddie had no difficulty in recognizing Dunhaven's old coachman and the upper-story housemaid, but she shifted uneasily.

"Dora, whatever is going on here?"

"It's that horrid Wilfred," Dora said, dragging the bashful coachman forward. "Can you believe it? He has already pensioned off poor Stubbins."

Freddie had no difficulty believing it. Mr. Stubbins was half blind, and some of the more recent outings she had taken with him at the reins had left Freddie thinking she should have paid more heed to making out *her* will. It had been inevitable that the old man would have to give up his position.

"That is too bad, Stubbins," Freddie said, "but surely you will be glad to retire to a cozy cottage."

"Not on the miserly pension Sir Wilfred has given him,"

Dora said. "Such a paltry sum would not keep a beggar alive."

Freddie's gaze turned from the wistful old man to the housemaid. "And Till?" she asked with a sinking heart. "Never tell me she has also been dismissed."

Dora nodded vigorously. "Turned off without a character because . . ." As she leaned forward to whisper in Freddie's ear, Till cast down her eyes, blushing bright red.

"Oh!" Freddie said, unable to keep her gaze from drifting to the girl's thickening middle.

"But everything will be fine now," Dora said. "I knew with your kind heart you would never turn them away. And we will need servants in our new household."

Freddie rolled her eyes. Dora did not seem to comprehend they might consider themselves fortunate if they managed to have a house, let alone a household. She tried to find a polite but firm way to explain this. It was all but impossible, not with Till bobbing curtsies and crying out. "God bless your ladyship," and Stubbins blubbering and attempting to kiss the ring on her left hand.

With some dismay, Freddie watched as her three newly acquired charges gathered up their various belongings.

"So," Dora said happily, "where are we going?"

"To London, I guess."

Freddie's doubtful announcement met with approval all around, Stubbins declaring he'd allus had a desire to see furrin' parts. He insisted upon carrying Freddie's portmanteau. All she had to do was make sure that he did not walk into the gates.

She heaved a deep sigh. For the first time in her life, she was entirely on her own, the mistress of her own destiny. Yet she seemed to have lost control of everything before setting foot off the estate.

She was on her way to the vast and strange city of London with scarcely a guinea to her name, having assumed the responsibility of an elderly spinster, a half-blind manservant, and a pregnant housemaid.

And the truly awful thing was that of all of them, only she seemed to possess enough wits to be terrified.

13

Chapter 2

The sun had the temerity to peek into the breakfast parlor before the Honorable Maxmillian Warfield took his first sip of coffee. But even the rays of morning light seemed to tiptoe past the powerful figure in the burgundy-colored dressing gown seated at the head of the dining table. His legs, encased in tan breeches, were stretched out in a negligent attitude, his broad shoulders nestled against the back of the chair. All that was visible of Mr. Warfield's head was the top of his close-cropped black hair as he perused the latest edition of the *Morning Post*.

He sipped his coffee and returned the delicate Sèvres cup to the table. The parlor maid skittered in to place Mr. Warfield's breakfast before him, one beefsteak, medium rare, two eggs cooked precisely three minutes, never less, never more, and several slices of toast, thinly buttered, absolutely no jam.

Mr. Warfield never even glanced up, and the maid slipped out unobtrusively. It was a fact completely understood by all the staff at Warfield House that no one, not even royalty, was permitted to disturb the master with a word of conversation before he had finished his breakfast.

That was why the youthful footman who entered the parlor trembled, his throat so dry with nervousness that he could do no more than cough. The sound, slight as it was, sounded like gunshot in the chamber, silent except for the muted sounds of carriages clattering by on the London street outside.

Warfield slowly lowered the paper. He had a lean, handsome countenance with an uncompromisingly square jaw, his complexion inclined to be dark. His heavy lids gave him an expression of perpetual boredom, but when he looked up, there was no mistaking the piercing intelligence to be found in his keen

14

gray eyes. His full lips were of a sensual cast and seemed formed to accommodate his own sardonic brand of humor.

Max stared at the footman long enough to convey the full weight of his displeasure, then barked, "Well, Bartholomew?"

The footman started and nearly dropped the silver-plated salver he carried. He clutched at the rectangle of vellum balanced on the tray, then stammered, "Th-there is a c-caller to see you, sir."

"A what!"

"A caller," Bartholomew repeated more faintly, now so pale, the freckles stood out on the bridge of his nose. "Mr. Crispin desired me to come in to tell you."

"I'll wager he did," Max said dryly. His butler was an inveterate coward.

" 'Tis a lady, sir," the footman continued. "Th-the caller, I mean."

A lady? Max arched his brow in surprise. Most of his acquaintances were familiar enough with his rigid dislike of being disturbed by anyone before noon. He could not imagine which lady might be so bold. Not even his former mistress, the tempestuous Mademoiselle Vivani, would have been that foolhardy.

"The lady is most insistent upon seeing you, sir." Bartholomew added, "She has brought a child with her."

"Indeed? Is she claiming it is mine?"

The footman looked much shocked. "Oh, no, I shouldn't think so, sir. That is, I don't know." The boy went from pale to bright red.

Max took pity upon him at last and suggested, "I presume that is the lady's card you have there. Perhaps it would behoove us to read it?"

"Oh? Oh, yes, sir!"

Max cast down his paper and straightened in his chair as the footman crept closer, proffering the tray with one trembling, gloved hand. Max steadied the salver himself before taking up the card.

He gave the inked line a cursory glance—*Lady Arthur Bentley*.

Max grimaced and tossed the card back on the tray. "That is no lady. It is only my sister. Tell her to go to the deuce."

"Sir?"

"You heard me." Max vented an impatient sigh, then

15

amended, "Inform Lady Bentley that I do not receive in the morning."

"Mr. Crispin already tried to tell her that, sir," Bartholomew said unhappily. "But the lady—your sister is most persistent. I do not think she will go away without seeing you."

"No, she won't!" A sharp feminine voice agreed.

Max stifled a curse as Caroline, Lady Bentley, swept across the threshold, even the feathers on her fashionable bonnet quivering with indignation as she towed by the hand her youngest offspring, a girl of three. Both mother and daughter were remarkably alike in their matching pink muslin pelisses, their dusky curls, upturned noses, and truculent expressions.

Lady Bentley pointed one finger dramatically at the footman, who cringed. "Maxmillian, I demand that you dismiss that creature from your service at once. And your beastly butler. Never have I been treated so shabbily. Being obliged to send in calling cards to my own brother and kept waiting in the hall as though I were some sort of tradeswoman."

Max shoved back his chair and rose lazily to his feet. "You need not blame my staff, Caroline. They were only attempting to carry out my orders. You know how I detest being disturbed before noon, and it is now . . ." He consulted his pocket watch. "Only ten forty-seven."

"But of course such an order does not apply to me! Your own sister."

Max started to assure her that it applied most particularly to her and any other of his relations, but Lady Bentley's attention had been claimed by the moppet at her side, the little girl tugging impatiently at her mother's sleeve.

While Caroline bent down to catch her daughter's lisping words, Max took the opportunity of dismissing the footman. Bartholomew backed out of the room, looking grateful to escape, and Max would have been happy to have done the same.

He had once had an old nursery governess who had told him that no matter how heartily he disliked Caroline, when he was quite grown-up, he would be very fond of his older sister. It was one of the few times that the redoubtable Nurse Roberts had ever been wrong.

Far from being pleased to see Caroline, he could only wonder what had brought her abroad at an hour when she was usually still abed sipping chocolate or fussing with her toilette. Lady Bentley never called upon him at all unless she wanted something, and whatever it was, it was generally something he would find disagreeable.

Whatever favor she desired this time, he had no intention of granting it. But he also knew there would be no getting rid of Caroline until she had her say. Eyeing his breakfast, which was getting cold, he started to demand what she wanted, but Caroline was still attempting to soothe her daughter.

"There now, Felicity love. Don't fidget so. I told you I would buy you a sweetmeat, but you must be patient while we visit Uncle Max."

"Don't want to." Felicity pouted. "Don't like Uncle Max."

"Nonsense. Now, come bid him good morrow and make your prettiest curtsy."

Max uttered a protest, but Caroline was already propelling the glowering Felicity toward him. He did not believe that he was fond of children and his niece had never done much to convince him otherwise.

But as Felicity sullenly spread her skirts, sinking into a wobbly curtsy, Max offered his hand to steady her. He was rather amused when the little girl drew his fingers toward her lips.

"You are a trifle confused, Miss Felicity. It is the gentleman who is supposed to kiss the lady's—" He broke off with a gasp as a sharp pain pierced his knuckle.

Max snatched back his hand and stared in disbelief at the raw red indentations on his finger. "She bit me!"

"Naughty Felicity," Caroline cooed. "You promised Mama not to do that anymore. Now I must scold you."

"Scold her? A good caning would be to more the purpose. She nearly drew blood. The little vixen!"

"Oh, don't make such a fuss, Max," his sister said airily. " 'Tis only a passing habit. She will outgrow it."

"Hmmph!" Max said, still nursing his injured finger. Himself, he had dark visions of Felicity someday making her debut at Almack's and sinking her fangs into Lady Jersey or one of the other patronesses of that hallowed assembly.

Caroline called upon her daughter to apologize to "dear uncle Max," but the child had already wandered off to inspect with an unholy gleam in her eye some of the china and crystal displayed upon the sideboard.

Max's unease was divided between watching Felicity's progress around the room and observing his sister stripping off her gloves and bonnet as though she intended to make a rather lengthy stay.

"And to what do I owe the honor of this invasion—I mean visit?" he demanded.

"I need to speak to you on a matter of some urgency."

"You might have just sent a note asking me to wait upon you."

"You would have ignored it."

Max was unable to refute that, and Caroline continued. "So I came when I would be sure of catching you at home. I had to venture out, in any case. Felicity has been fussing so lately that I am taking her to visit the tooth drawer."

"What a good idea," Max muttered. His niece by now had reached atop one of the pedestal cupboards and fixed her grubby little hands upon the basaltware water urn. She was in imminent danger of toppling it upon the Axminster carpet, and Caroline showed no signs of intervening or even noticing. She merely rattled on. "Of course, Nurse would choose just this moment to contract a bad cold. Really, servants are so unreliable these days."

With a mumbled oath, Max strode across the room and pried Felicity away from the urn. She set up a howl, but he ignored it, seizing his niece around the waist and transporting her bodily out of the room.

In the main hall beyond, Max looked about for the parlor maid, but saw only his butler. The dapper Crispin was as ever being quite useless, lounging about, admiring himself in the pier glass.

Max strode over and thrust the screeching, kicking bundle of fury that was his niece into the man's arms. "Here. Take care of this."

Crispin's imperturbable features crumpled into an expression of dismay. "B-but, sir. What am I to do with her?"

"Stick her into the linen cupboard," Max snapped. "I don't know. Just keep the child occupied until I have managed to dispose of—to deal with her mother."

As Max strode back toward the parlor, he heard Crispin's frantic shushing noises break off into a howl as Felicity's teeth found their mark. He closed the breakfast parlor door behind him with a certain grim satisfaction. It served the cowardly butler right for letting Caroline get past him and for sending in a footman to do his job.

But his satisfaction in getting rid of his niece was fleeting. Caroline remained, and unfortunately there was no prospect of scooping her up under his arm. She had removed her pelisse and appeared undisturbed by his summary disposal of Felicity. But then, Max had frequently observed that his sister played the doting mother only during those rare half-hour intervals when her children were immediately before her.

Now she settled herself at the table and informed him in lofty accents, "You had better sit down, Max. Your breakfast is getting cold."

Max glared at her but did as she suggested, scraping back his chair with a gesture of unnecessary force. As he plunked himself down, Caroline studied his plate with a shudder. "How you can eat so much is beyond me. I am unable to choke down a morsel in the morning. It would quite upset my delicate constitution. But you might offer me a cup of coffee."

"I might," Max said. "But I won't. It would only encourage you to linger."

Caroline pouted, but then rustled over to the sideboard to the silver coffee service and helped herself, all the while complaining. "I do not know why you must ever be so surly in the morning, Max."

"I don't know either, but I am. So I wish you would simply state your business and be on your way before your she-cub causes my butler to hand in his notice."

But Caroline moved at that frustrating leisurely pace that had aggravated him ever since their nursery days. After ruining her coffee by ladening it with an inordinate amount of cream and sugar, she resumed her place at the table.

Apparently quite forgetting her delicate stomach, she plucked a piece of the toast from Max's plate and nibbled at it before getting around to explaining her latest crisis. She remarked at last with a gloomy sigh.

"Frederica has moved to London."

This portentous announcement conveyed nothing to Max.

"Frederica?" he repeated. "Am I supposed to know her?"

"Of course, you are. *Frederica Barry*," Caroline mumbled around a mouthful of toast.

When Max continued to regard her blankly, she said, "Before her marriage, she was Frederica Jameson, that wretched girl Cousin Margaret took in after she was orphaned. Major Alex Jameson's daughter."

"Oh. You mean *Freddie*."

Caroline pulled a face. "Yes, though I believe only you ever called her that. I am relieved to hear that you at least remember something of her."

Max remembered a great deal more than he cared to. His brow creased into a slight frown. He did not always keep a clear accounting of his various and sundry relatives. Indeed, he generally did his best to forget most of them. But Major Alexander Jameson and his daughter formed one of the better remembrances of Max's youth.

For a glorious week one autumn, this dashing major, a second cousin, had come to visit at Courtland, the principal country estate of Max's father. Although many years Max's senior, the major had not been too toplofty to bestow a great deal of attention on a young boy who often felt ignored and insignificant, being only the third son of a marquis.

For seven halcyon days, Max had hunted, rode, and fished with his great strapping cousin with the booming laugh. It had almost been enough to make Max forget his own disgrace. He had been sent down from Eton at that time, for what hellish piece of mischief Max could no longer recall.

Max's acquaintance with the major had been brief, but he had still felt a real sense of loss when several years later he had learned of the death of Alexander and his young wife in a coach accident.

Max had been but seventeen when he had journeyed down to Dorchester for the funeral. He recollected little of the service, more of what had transpired afterward when the family had gathered at the home of his Dorchester cousins. The major's now-orphaned eight-year-old daughter had been fetched there as well. But the little girl had balked at entering the mansion that was to be her new home, insisting upon being taken back to the lodgings where she had lived with Mama. Papa would never be able to find her here.

Cousin Margaret had smiled that thin smile of hers, laced with feigned indulgence. She had said, "Very well, miss. Have it your own way. But there is a storm brewing. I imagine you will be glad to come in soon enough."

But she had quite mistaken Frederica's character. Even when the rains had broken, the child had stood outside on the drive, soaked to the skin, shivering like a wet puppy. The thunder cracked, but she merely turned her small face up to the skies in defiance.

Watching out the window, Max had been inspired with a grudging admiration. When he heard Margaret bidding the governess fetch the stubborn chit inside and give her a sharp smack besides, Max had protested and gone to fetch the child himself.

Bolting down the steps of the Georgian manor, he had rolled up the collar of his greatcoat, but to no avail. He was in a fair way to being soaked himself by the time he reached Freddie.

She was a picture of abject misery, her blond curls plastered to her cheeks, the rain dripping off her chin. But when she glanced up at him, the lightning itself seemed caught in her very blue eyes.

"Are you a footman sent to carry me in?" she had demanded before he could even speak.

"No, I'm of even less importance than that. I'm a younger son, Miss Frederica." His bitter jest only caused the child to scowl.

"My name is Fred," she said stoutly, thrusting our her thin chest. "My papa named me after the Duke of York, who was a great general."

"Well, I am Max, named after nobody in particular. I suppose I am your cousin of sorts, thrice removed."

She glared and said, "I don't care who you are. I am not going inside. Leave me alone."

"I'd be glad to do that, Fred, but I am supposed to fetch you. You might not mind being wet, but I am getting drenched, too, and I don't like it."

"Then go away. My papa will fetch me." Despite the fierceness of her tone, beneath it Max caught the threading of fear, almost desperation. Her delicate features were etched with a grief far beyond her years.

He hunkered down beside her, brushing back his rain-slicked hair. He said as gently as possible, "Freddie, I think you know that's not true. It is very sad, but your papa has had to go to heaven. That is a place quite far away. But wherever he is, I am sure he is still watching you. He would not like you being out in a storm."

She digested this in stony silence. Then her lip quivered. "But I can't go inside. I don't want this to be my new home. No one in there loves me."

"I love you, Freddie," he said solemnly, holding his arms out to her. "Come in out of the rain."

Her blue eyes searched his face earnestly for a moment. When the next boom of thunder sounded, she suddenly crumpled and flung herself into his arms, sobbing against his shoulder. Max raised her up and carried her back into the house.

21

He had gone to visit her many times after that day, taken her out riding in the pony cart, allowed her to hold the reins of his curricle, showed her how to climb an apple tree. It had been after that that Cousin Margaret had complained, insisting he keep his distance from the child. Margaret was doing her best to rear Frederica as a proper young lady, and a wild seventeen-year-old lad was decidedly a bad influence. Max was prepared to defy the old crone, but he had become neck deep in trouble of his own. . . . It all seemed so long ago. But it astonished him how well he still remembered Frederica, and with an unexpected stirring of tenderness.

I love you, Freddie. Come in out of the rain.

What an extraordinary thing for him to have said to the child. At the time, he had really meant those words. But he had been a much more sentimental sort of fellow in those days.

Now such feelings only made him uncomfortable, and he was quick to shrug off the memory, snap himself back to the present. He discovered that while he had been woolgathering, his sister had made further inroads upon his toast. He was alerted in time to rescue his last piece.

Unperturbed, Caroline picked up a fork and started on his eggs.

"Yes, so I do remember Frederica Jameson," he said at last. "What of it? It has been years since I saw her. She must be nearly . . ."

"Twenty-one. And already a widow."

"No one ever bothered to even tell me she had been married."

"It scarce matters now, for Frederica's husband died last autumn and she moved immediately to London," Caroline said. "She must have lived quietly for a while, for I did not know she was here until I returned to town myself in January for the Little Season. Then I discovered she had already set aside her mourning and seems bent on kicking up quite a dust."

"Is she? Good for her."

Caroline paused in consuming his eggs to eye him reproachfully. "That is hardly the reaction I would have hoped for, Maxmillian."

"Isn't it? I always seemed doomed to disappoint people." Max removed his plate out of her reach. But as he picked up his own fork, he saw there was scarce enough left of the eggs to bother. With a grunt of resignation, he shoved the plate back toward his sister.

She finished off the eggs, waxing even more indignant as she detailed Freddie's further iniquities. "People are starting to say she is *fast*. Frederica has been wearing the brightest of gowns and her husband only gone these six months. She has been seen walking alone at St. James, already attending parties, playing deep at whist and—and—heaven only knows what else."

"She sounds like she is having a remarkably good time. I am glad to hear it."

"Oh, aye, *you* would be, with never a care for what gossip she might be stirring. You have raised quite a few eyebrows yourself. Though I suppose it is indelicate of me to mention it." Caroline paused to give a discreet cough.

Max had never known delicacy to prevent Caroline from saying anything she chose. He was right, for she continued. "As your sister, I ought to warn you. I know all about that infamous wager being laid, how the gentlemen are all taking bets at White's as to who your next mistress will be."

"Truly?" Max drawled. "I was not aware you were a member there. I prefer Brook's myself."

She glowered at him. "Don't be tiresome, Max. Of course I have never been inside White's. I heard about the wager when I was taking tea with Lady Ormskirk, who had it from her youngest son."

"A rattle-pated youth if there ever was one. Glad as I am to have afforded you ladies some entertainment over your tea, my dear Caroline, I feel obliged to remind you we were not discussing my peccadilloes, but Freddie's. I assume that eventually you are going to get to the point of this visit."

"The point *is* that there is every danger Frederica will create a real scandal, prove an embarrassment to the entire family."

Max grimaced. "Heaven forfend we ever cause embarrassment to the family."

"I am quite serious, Max. Any sort of bumblebroth stirred up by Frederica could prove a disaster. Have you forgotten that Elizabeth is bringing her second daughter out this season?"

"I cannot say I have been losing much sleep over that fact." Max liked his eldest sister, Eliza, even less than he did Caroline.

"And I have planned several routs and a ball of my own," Caroline said. "We simply cannot ignore Frederica. Everyone knows she is a relative of sorts. It will look most odd if she is not invited, and yet we cannot have her disgracing us all either."

"Well, what the deuce do you expect me to do about it?"

Caroline adopted that sweet, coaxing expression that Max had ever learned to mistrust. "Why, you could persuade her to return quietly to the country or go to Bath and take the waters. I hear that it is very pleasant there for widows. The Bentley family even owns a house on the Crescent that she could use. It is standing empty anyway. You could mention that to Frederica."

Max regarded his sister with patent disbelief. "You must have more maggots in your head than I ever supposed, if you think I will attempt such a thing. What makes you think the girl would listen to me?"

"Why, I believe she was once quite fond of you."

"She was eight years old then! Now she would be more likely to tell me go to the devil and mind my own business. *And* she would be in the right of it. If someone must reason with her, what is wrong with those dratted Dorchester cousins that raised her?"

Caroline sighed and proceeded to carve up the beefsteak. "Do not think that Cousin Margaret did not try. She journeyed all the way to London just for that purpose. But Frederica was positively rude to her. So ungrateful after the way the Jamesons took her in when she was left orphaned, penniless. They raised her up like one of their own daughters, arranged a brilliant match for her."

Max felt a rare stirring of curiosity. "Whom did she marry, by the by?"

"Max, you are quite impossible. Don't you ever know anything that is going on? Oh, but I forgot. You were out of the country then, still living in that barbaric place."

"The West Indies."

"Yes, just so." Caroline said vaguely, looking uncomfortable. The members of his family always did at any mention of Jamaicatown, the place where Max had acquired his fortune. They had no compunction in trying to help him spend his wealth, but none of them liked to consider the mercantile interests that were its source. It smacked too sordidly much of trade.

Caroline hastened back to the subject of Frederica. "Well, precisely two years ago, she was wed to the fifth Viscount Raincliffe."

Max, who had been taking a sip of his coffee, choked. "Raincliffe! The fifth viscount! That elderly rakehell. My God, he was an old rip back when I was just a lad. He must have been ancient enough to have been her grandfather."

"I suppose there was some difference in their ages," Caroline conceded. "But Freddie was still quite fortunate. A dowerless girl with little besides a pretty face to recommend her! She could have done far worse."

"Far worse than being forced to marry some gout-ridden old rascal?"

"Far worse than to marry wealth and a title. And the viscount must have left her well off, for she has been spending money like mad. I would sell my soul for the diamonds she wore to ... Oh, it is entirely too vexing. She is not behaving in the least as a dowager viscountess should. You must stop her, Max, before she ruins the season for all of us."

"You would do far better to appeal to our revered brother, Harry. He is the head of the family."

"Harry!" Caroline gave a delicate snort. "He never comes to London. Such a country bumpkin! He might as well be some odious squire instead of a marquis."

"Well, Edward, then. He's the bishop in the family."

"No one can listen to Ned for more than five minutes without falling asleep. No, it has to be you, Max. No one is better at bullying people than you—when you bestir yourself to do so."

"Thank you."

"I meant bullying them for their own good. I heard what you did for young Tom Harker, getting him out of that sponging house, forcing him to give up gaming and join a cavalry regiment. His mother declares that you quite saved Tom's life."

"She quite exaggerates. I never put myself to that much trouble for anyone, although I do actually like Tom Harker. Despite his wild streak, he is a young man of great merits, his chief one being that he is no relation of mine."

Caroline pouted. "You take such delight in vexing me. Does this mean you utterly refuse to do anything about Frederica?"

"Your understanding, my dear sister, is, as ever, acute."

"And so our family is to be humiliated by her antics, the season ruined, and you will not care a jot! In all my twenty-nine years, I have never known anyone as selfish."

"Twenty-nine? But I was thirty-three last Michaelmas. That should make you—"

"Never mind," Caroline said, turning an angry shade of red. "I should have known you would be disobliging."

"So you should have. It would have saved us both a deal of bother, and I might have gotten to eat my own breakfast."

She shoved back her chair and huffed to her feet.

"What! You are going?" he mocked. "There is still half the beefsteak left."

"Don't be horrid. I told you I cannot eat in the mornings. And with all this upset over Frederica, I am likely to become quite ill. Indeed, I feel a spasm coming on already."

But since she made this announcement in very hearty accents, Max saw no cause for alarm. She flounced over and jerked on her pelisse, gloves, and finally her bonnet.

Max, who had also risen, reached out to help her straighten it but received a sharp rap across the knuckles for his pains. Seeing how agitated she was, Max relented enough to offer some rare brotherly advice.

"You need to cultivate a thicker skin, Caro. If the old tabbies want to wag their tongues over Freddie, let them."

"That is all very well for you to say." She sniffed. "When that dreadful girl creates a scandal and people start to cut us, I daresay you won't even notice. But what if I send out the cards to my ball and no one comes?"

"Then the devil with them. Close up your house and take a holiday. I have it on excellent authority that Bath is a very nice place."

His sister shot him such a look, Max felt glad she no longer had the carving knife within reach. Turning on her heel, Caroline stormed toward the door, spurning him with an imperious wave of her hand.

"Do not attempt to accompany me out, Maxmillian. I am seriously displeased with you."

"I shall endeavor not to be crushed."

She entirely missed his ironic bow as she slammed the parlor door behind her. The last she heard of her was in the front hall, demanding that Crispin unhand her darling child at once.

Max grinned. He supposed he ought to be ashamed for baiting his sister. Ought to be, but wasn't. Caroline deserved whatever she got for bursting in upon him with her brat at this hour.

And what she had gotten had been a damn fine breakfast, Max thought ruefully, observing what little remained on his plate. He sank back down in his chair to the comforts of half a beefsteak and a cold cup of coffee.

26

He thought of summoning Crispin and ordering up a fresh plate, but he found he had little appetite. That was always the way of it whenever his routine was interrupted.

The devil take Caroline anyway for disturbing what had been an otherwise peaceful morning, and all to no purpose. She should have known he would never agree to her ridiculous request. Perhaps he was as selfish as she said, but then, he never pretended to be otherwise.

He had long ago arranged his life entirely to his own satisfaction. That was the great reward of being both wealthy and a confirmed bachelor. His family often took a different view of the matter, but his acid tongue kept most of them from badgering him for favors. Most of them except for Caroline. What cork-brained notions she was always entertaining, and this latest one topped them all! Expecting him to meddle in the doings of little Freddie Jameson.

Although, he supposed, she was not that little anymore. In spite of himself, he could not help wondering. What sort of woman had she grown up to be, that stubborn, spirited child? He tried to picture her as a lady, a wife, a widow, but his mind refused to make the leap. He could envision her only as that wistful-eyed moppet clinging to his hand whenever he had to turn her over to the Jamesons' governess after one of their outings.

He had promised her he would continue to visit her often. But it had been a promise he had been unable to keep. He remembered he had tried to write her a letter explaining. But how did one explain to an eight-year-old child a tale of passion gone awry, the youthful madness that had brought him dishonor and a perhaps well-deserved exile to a land both foreign and far away? He had torn the letter up before he had written more than the greeting.

Not that it signified. Doubtlessly Freddie had forgotten him swiftly enough. Without her wild cousin Max to corrupt her, she had likely grown to be an accomplished young lady, captivating enough to secure for herself a viscount, though it still disturbed Max to think of her marrying that disgusting old roué.

In any case, she was well off now, a wealthy widow, a position that gave her some measure of freedom if only she had the good sense not to take it too far. And if she didn't?

Then perhaps someone ought to shake some sense into the young woman. But, thank God, it was not his place to do so.

Simply because he had been kind to her once, made her some half-baked promises in the sentimental folly of his youth, there was no reason he should feel responsible or even guilty for never having inquired after her in all these years. In the interval, he had learned a great deal of wisdom, most particularly to avoid anyone likely to disturb his comfortable existence.

Leaning back in his chair, he unfolded his newspaper and attempted to dismiss all thoughts of Freddie, recapture the peace and solitude he had been enjoying before Caroline had burst in upon him.

But it was the most aggravating thing imaginable. He could not seem to focus on the inkprint. Having resurrected Frederica's memory, he could not restore it to the ashes where it belonged. As stubborn as Freddie herself, the image persisted in swimming through his mind.

The image of a little girl swallowed up by a threatening sky, her tears mingling with the rain.

Chapter 3

The mansion beyond the high screen wall glowed like a bright beacon, candlelight spilling through the windows upon the press of carriages lining up on the winding drive. The vehicles paused in turn before the imposing Palladian-style manor, depositing their occupants at the doorstep. Ladies whose jewels winked in the moonlight, gentlemen in their high crown beavers all drifted up the stairs toward the lights and music.

To Freddie, they looked like a parcel of giddy moths fluttering through the darkness toward a beckoning flame. Huddling deeper in the satiny folds of her cloak, she peered between the bars of the iron gate. She could feel the tension between her shoulder blades as she judged the chaos of the arriving guests, awaiting the right moment to make her move.

Dora crowded close behind her, the tall, ungainly woman easily able to see over Frederica's head.

"Oooh, 'tis just like fairyland," she breathed in a hiss loud enough to have done credit to a stage villain.

"Shhh!" Freddie said, placing a cautioning finger to her lips.

Dora nodded, but even in the shadows Freddie could see the way the woman's brown eyes shone with excitement. After six months of struggling to survive in the vast, cold city of London, it still all seemed like a grand adventure to Dora. Nothing daunted her. Not the creditors beating upon their door, nor that their money was nearly gone, nor that the larder was practically empty.

They had dined that evening upon boiled cabbage and tough chicken. Dora had made merry jests about how the poor thing had sacrificed its life in vain. With a hungry rumble yet sounding in her stomach, Freddie wished she found their situation equally amusing.

As the two women studied the distant mansion, it was Dora who tried to crowd closer to the gate, Dora who nearly trod upon Freddie's toes in her eagerness.

" 'Tis all so grand." She sighed. "Lord and Lady Channing must be quite rich."

"Yes," Freddie agreed.

"The ball is going to be wonderful, quite the event of the season."

"Yes," Freddie said.

"What a pity you weren't invited."

"Yes."

"It would be so magnificent to be able to go in through the *front* door."

"Yes," Freddie repeated glumly. Of course, if her scheme went awry, she might be seeing the front door far sooner than she wished. For a moment, she desired nothing more than to be able to walk away and forget the whole thing. But propelled by a combination of desperation and determination, she stepped back from the gates, whispering, "All right. The house appears crowded enough to risk it. Let's go."

Freddie set off without looking back. Clinging close to the wall, she rounded the corner, staying well out of the lamplight spilling on the pavement. It would not do for any of the other arriving guests to see the Dowager Viscountess of Raincliffe creeping about the streets like a footpad.

That might entirely put an end to the rumors that she had been left a wealthy widow, convenient rumors that had secured her a great deal of credit. Tradesmen who thought she was merely forgetful about paying her bills might not be nearly so forbearing if the truth were bandied abroad.

But as she slipped along, following the stone wall, she noted that her stealth was entirely wasted. Dora, hard on her heels, lumbered along, crackling twigs beneath her feet, panting a little from the exertion of keeping up.

When they reached the back of the mansion, the wall became lower, closing off the gardens from the bustle of the London streets. Dora reached out to pluck at Freddie's cloak, the woman trembling now as much from nervousness as excitement.

"I—I have been reconsidering, Freddie. Perhaps this is not such a good idea. It would be so humiliating if you were caught. Perhaps the Channings might even send for the constable and—and after all, we were invited to Mrs. Pomfret's. Such a very sweet lady. We should go there instead."

"I've already explained to you, Dora. We are getting nowhere with me playing at whist with old ladies for a penny a point. If we are even going to pay the rent this month, I need to sit in on a game of higher stakes."

"But you have never been to the Channings. Perhaps they don't game at all."

"Nonsense. That is all they do at affairs like this, play cards, waltz, and eat."

"Oh, waltzing! That would be so agreeable."

"So would eating," Freddie said tartly. "But I am afraid we have other business to accomplish first."

A sparkle of sudden tears glinted in Dora's eyes. For such a stolid-looking female, she was an excessively emotional creature. She sniffed. "It should not be this way, you so young and left a widow to fend for yourself. Why, you are not much older than the young ladies making their debut this Season. You should be attending the ball tonight, going in by the front door, all gowned in white like an angel, with me as your chaperone, a grand lady . . .

"A grand *married* lady," she added with a quiver in her voice. "I would be bringing you out in society, introducing you to eligible partners. You would be the toast of the season, so carefree with all the gentlemen flocking around you. You would flirt, sip champagne, and then that certain one would appear far more handsome and gallant than all the rest, and you—"

"Oh, please, Dora," Freddie interrupted. The wistfulness in Dora's voice touched off an unexpected answering chord in her own heart. She had almost become caught up in Dora's vision, and that seemed somehow disloyal to Leon to be having such dreams, regrets, wishes that her life had proceeded upon different lines.

"It would be dreadfully boring," she said. "I fear I have always been destined to be more of a hell-born babe than anyone's angel. Besides, the pair of us came to London to be wicked women, remember?"

"Oh, yes." Dora sighed. "I keep forgetting."

"Being respectably invited to the Channings' party would be so tame. This way will be infinitely more exciting."

But Freddie was not certain whom she was trying to convince, herself or Dora, as she gazed at the wall looming before her. It was not so high as in the front and the brickwork un-even enough to afford her a toehold. But the challenge would be to get over it unseen or without arriving in a totally dishev-eled state.

Compressing her lips, she stripped off her cloak and handed it to Dora. As Freddie straightened her mameluke turban adorned with white ostrich feathers, she noticed Dora regard-ing her with a frown.

"What is the matter? Do I not look all right?" She spread out the folds of her India muslin gown, the gilt spangles shim-mering even in the semi-darkness. Although the strings of her stays might be a little frayed, at least outwardly she was the picture of elegance, owing to the services of a little modiste who was too flattered by the patronage of a viscountess to worry about dilatory payments.

Though of late, Freddie often felt as if she would have traded all the silks on her back for a good roast beef dinner. The butcher and greengrocer had not proved near as tolerant as her seamstress.

Pacing closer, Dora continued to study the new gown and scowl. "It's that turban," she pronounced at last. "It's too *old* for you, and the skirts of the gown are far too full for the cur-rent fashion."

"Oh, *that.*" Freddie shrugged. "My dear Dora, you know the necessity for the turban and the full skirts as well as I do."

Dora nodded her agreement, but looked none too happy about it. "What if someone notices when you try to— Oh, dear, I wish you would let me come with you."

"That would only increase the chance of detection. If this goes awry, there is no sense both of us ending in Newgate." Freddie gave her a quick smile, feeling vaguely guilty as she of-fered this excuse. Dora was a perfect dear, but the truth was, Freddie found the woman something of a detriment when she was playing cards. Dora had a tendency to hover at Freddie's shoulders, her candid eyes lighting up when Freddie drew a good hand, biting her nails whenever Freddie attempted to bluff.

Before Dora could argue with her, Freddie took the woman by the arm, urging her on her way. "Now, we have stood here whispering long enough. Get along with you before someone comes. Secure a hackney cab and wait for me at the corner over there. I will meet you in a couple of hours."

She gave Dora a nudge, hustling her on her way, but not so

briskly that she failed to call softly after her. "And, Dora . . . have a care for yourself."

"Pooh!" Dora said stoutly. Grinning, she produced a pearl-handled pistol from beneath the depths of her shawl and waved it recklessly about. "Don't worry about me. I am more than a match for any rascal lurking in the dark."

"For heaven's sake," Freddie hissed. "Watch where you are aiming that thing."

But Dora had already plunged off into the shadows, her attempts to slink along all but ludicrous. With a mixture of amusement and anxiety, Freddie watched her disappear. There could be no more naive woman in all of London than Theodora Applegate. She was so trusting, she would surrender her pistol to the nearest footpad if he but politely asked to admire the handle.

Freddie wished that Dora would have stayed safely at home, but there had been no way to compel her to do so. Dora could be amazingly obstinate. In truth, it was the height of foolhardiness for either one of them to be skulking about the streets at night, even in London's elegant Mayfair district. But necessity, Freddie had often found, frequently obliged one to act the fool.

Keeping to the darkness, she stood close to the wall, trying to summon up the final burst of courage that would carry her over it. A night breeze wafted to her the scent of roses from the garden, the heady perfume seeming somehow bound up with the distant lilt of violins. But rather than enticing her, the sound of a waltz filled her with an odd melancholy.

She never had learned to perform the modern dance. Her aunt had not approved of it, and Leon had preferred the stately minuets and spritely cotillions of his own youth. The waltz seemed so much more daring, so romantic. But after all, she had not come here for the dancing.

Shivering a little in the night air, Freddie nervously fingered her necklace. Her diamonds were long gone, cleverly copied with paste imitations, likewise the sapphire aigrette affixed to her turban. The only thing that seemed genuine about her was the hollow feeling in the pit of her stomach.

Leon had always declared it possible for a man to live handsomely by his wits alone in the vast city of London. But Freddie was coming to the conclusion that she must not possess as much of that particular commodity as her late husband.

She had begun to feel wearied, a little overwhelmed by the mounting list of her creditors, weighed down with her responsibilities. Sometimes she longed to give up and just flee, though she scarce knew where. She was always restrained by the knowledge that she no longer had just herself to consider. For the first time in her life, she had people dependent upon her, people who actually believed in her abilities to accomplish miracles; dear, foolish Dora, the nearsighted Stubbins now elevated to the position of butler, fiercely proud of his keys to the wine cellar, although they scarce had a single bottle to rack there. And Till, that sweet, timid housemaid who had been seduced and abandoned, had given birth to the most darling baby girl only two months before.

They all, even the babe, seemed to regard Freddie with misplaced adoration, as though she were some sort of heroine, Joan of Arc and Lady Bountiful rolled into one. Their blind faith in her both touched and terrified Freddie.

What if she let them down? What if she got them all arrested for debt or worse? What if—

No, she could not continue this line of thinking or in another moment she would lose heart altogether and flee from the Channings' mansion like the veriest coward.

She must be calm, harbor only optimistic thoughts. What if she won a fortune at the tables tonight? It had been known to happen, especially at these sort of wealthy parties where people frequently played for high stakes.

Men had also been known to retire from these events utterly ruined and go home to blow their brains out. The thought crept in unbidden. Seeking to quell it, Freddie was only partly successful.

She felt a fluttering beneath her rib cage, but she stripped off her gloves, slipping them into the pocket concealed by the folds of her gown. Stepping close to the wall, she listened intently, trying to discern if any one of the Channings' guests might have attempted to take a moonlight stroll in the gardens.

She heard nothing but the gentle rustling of leaves, the distant sounds of music and laughter spilling from the house beyond. She drew in a deep breath. It was now or never.

"Ah, well, champagne and roses tonight," she muttered. "Disgrace and debtor's prison tomorrow. If all else fails, we can flee to the Continent. I daresay Dora would like to see Paris."

Freddie examined the wall, feeling for her first toehold. It was time to see if all those years of defying Aunt Jameson's injunction against climbing were about to pay off.

Chapter 4

The hostess of one of the most highly attended routs of the season should not have been stealing into the garden with any man, let alone one not her husband. But Lady Lavinia Channing had always been a little reckless with her reputation.

Yet the lady was well over thirty, Max Warfield thought as he ducked to avoid a low-hanging branch. She was experienced enough to be fly to the time of day and certainly old enough to look out for herself. It was more likely he who should be wary, Max admonished himself with a wry crook of his lips as he followed his hostess to a sequestered spot behind some of the rosebushes.

Perhaps he should not have chosen to attend this particular affair at all. He rarely ever attended such balls, finding the throngs of people, the fluttering debutantes, the empty conversation, all rather tedious. Yet the Channings' parties were certainly livelier than most and the hostess most charming.

But his presence here was only giving Lavinia Channing ideas, and Lord knows, the lady already had enough of those. He had welcomed her suggestion to step outside for a breath of air. It had been infernally hot in the ballroom and he had hardly expected Lavinia to be bold enough to attempt a tryst with him in her husband's own gardens.

But his hostess had clearly selected Max for the role of Adam in this Garden of Eden. And this particular Eve was quite tempting, possessed of a most lovely set of apples. Having put a respectable distance between them and the French doors leading out from the ballroom, the light pooling onto the garden walkway, Lavinia turned to face him.

Her lush breasts seemed to strain against the confines of her low-necked gown, the gauzy fabric almost scandalously transparent. Moonlight haloed her crown of dark curls, outlining the sensual cast of her slanted eyes and full lips.

Max knew that Lady Channing was the odds-on favorite to be his next mistress ever since he had parted company with that temperamental virago Vivani. And he could scarce deny Lavinia's full-blown attraction. She was exactly as he preferred his women, with no pretensions to innocence and possessed of a lusty sense of humor.

Yet for all that, even when her lips parted invitingly, he made no move to fulfill her expectations by taking her into his embrace.

Rather, he folded his arms across his chest and quirked one brow in mocking fashion. "Well, so now we have had our little stroll. Shouldn't we be getting back?"

She smiled. "Do not be so provoking, Max. You cannot believe I brought you out here to admire my hydrangea bushes. Kiss me."

He bent forward and obliged, bestowing a light peck on her cheek.

She pulled a face. "I could have gotten that much from my brother."

"Or your husband?"

"Ah!" Her face lit up with sudden comprehension. "Is that all that has been restraining you?"

"One of my trifling scruples, my dear. I admit I don't have many of them, but I rather stick at involving myself with a married woman. Jealous husbands are the very devil, full of the most annoying suggestions, such as pistols at dawn. And I do hate having my morning routine disturbed."

She gave a tinkling laugh. "You need have no fear of my George. I doubt he has ever bestirred himself to see the sunrise in the whole of his life. Besides, he takes little notice of my— er—social activities. He is a most complacent sort of husband."

Max only shrugged. He found the complacent ones worse than the jealous sort and far more difficult to comprehend. "I am flattered by your interest, my lady," he said, "but I have my own peculiar code. Never to drive my high perch phaeton when I am foxed, never to trade fisticuffs with anyone half my weight, and never to bed a married lady."

"Then what do you expect me to do?" Lavinia pouted. "Poison poor George and bury him 'neath the delphiniums?"

"Given the size of Lord Channing, I doubt he'd fit so tidily in a flower bed. Alas, my lady. I fear there is little to be done but return discreetly to the ballroom."

Max stepped back, sweeping her a mock gallant bow, waiting for her to glide past him. But discretion was not one of Lavinia's strong points. Nor was giving up so easily.

Instead of skirting by, she brushed provocatively against him, her closeness affording him a full view down the front of her bodice. She murmured, "Maybe I don't wish to return to the house so soon. And maybe you don't want me to either." She ran one finger lightly against the sensitive skin beneath his eye, touching upon a recent bruise that was still tender. He winced.

Her lips curved in a sly smile. "I heard about what happened at Gentleman Jackson's yesterday when you were taking your sparring exercise. The great Max Warfield, so noted for his ability at fisticuffs, allowing a greenhorn to slip in a hit past his guard.

"What happened to the famous Warfield concentration?" she teased. "Could it be you were thinking of me?"

Max scowled. No, he had been thinking about an eight-year-old girl, but he was not about to confess that to Lady Channing. He was annoyed enough by the remembrance of the incident at the sparring salon, even more annoyed to hear it was being bruited about. His concentration *had* slipped. Little Freddie Jameson kept leaping into his head at the most damnably inconvenient times ever since Caroline's intrusion at his breakfast table yesterday morning.

After he had had his eye clipped by a raw youth, Max had nearly decided to go see the girl after all, if for no other reason than to exorcise Freddie from his thoughts. But something had held him back. Perhaps it had been a fear of what he might find. He cherished so few of his memories, but he did rather have a fancy for the one of that sprite of a girl, her liveliness and quick wit reflected in her dancing blue eyes. It would be cursed disappointing to discover that she had been molded into just another fashionable female with cotton for brains.

But perhaps the stronger motive holding him back from calling on Freddie was a vague sense of guilt, which was both irritating and ridiculous. Why should he continue to feel any sort of responsibility just because he had once plucked the girl out of a storm?

"Pure foolishness," Max muttered. He did not realize he had

spoken aloud until Lavinia Channing responded in purring tones. "Do you really think so?"

Max snapped back to his surroundings with a start, realizing that Lavinia had taken advantage of his inattention to wrap her arms around his neck, insinuating herself close against him.

"Ah, Max, you were woolgathering again." She chuckled. "This is getting to be a dangerous habit. I fear that now even I can pop a hit past your guard."

So saying, she tugged his head down, her lips crashing against his own. Her mouth was hot and accomplished enough that Max felt an inevitable stirring of masculine response. He caught himself kissing her back, and there was no saying where this idiocy would have led him, when he was startled by the crackling of a twig. Contrasted to the soft hush of the garden, the distant lilt of music from the ballroom, it had about the same effect as the snap of a whip.

Max's head jerked upward. As he strained, listening, peering into the darkness of the trees, a loud rustling caught his attention, coming from the opposite end of the garden near the wall.

"What the—" he exclaimed, his startled gaze focusing on the shadowy form that was taking on a more distinct shape.

"Mmmm," Lavinia murmured, snuggling closer, her hands creeping beneath his frock coat to caress his chest through the fabric of his white silk waistcoat.

"Behave yourself, Lavinia," he hissed, trying to still her busy hands. "We are not alone."

"Don't be absurd, darling. Of course we are." She pressed hot, hungry kisses along the line of his jaw.

"No!" he insisted, though he could scarce credit his own eyes. "There—there appears to be a dowager in a turban scaling your garden wall."

"What!"

He succeeded in capturing Lavinia's attention at last. She broke off in mid-kiss and whipped about to peer behind her.

Moonlight shimmered on the folds of a spangled gown, two white slippers flailing the air for a second, until the strange woman dropped down with a soft thud, staggering to keep her balance.

Max dodged farther back behind the bushes, pulling Lady Channing with him.

"Oh, bother," she whispered. "I bribed my footman heavily to make sure no guests came out through the garden doors to spy upon us. Who would have thought that one of the old tabbies would possess enough enterprise to climb the wall?"

"I doubt this is one of your guests," Max said. He tensed, peering between the branches of the leaves. The conduct of the strange woman was no less furtive than his own. She looked quickly from side to side and began creeping forward along the cobbled path.

"Be still, Lavinia," he said when Lady Channing shifted restively at his side. "I think we are about to capture a most daring thief."

"A thief? Wearing diamonds?"

As the woman tiptoed through the garden and glided within yards of where he hid, Max had to admit there had never been a less likely-looking burglar. He still could not obtain a clear view of her face, but something about her caused him to assess his initial estimate of her age. Her figure was far too lithe, her step too quick for an old woman.

She paused just outside the circle of light spilling through the French doors to calmly pull on her gloves. Then, bold as any West End doxy, she headed for the house. Max caught just a glimpse of a youthful countenance, a hint of golden curl wisping from beneath the turban before he started forward, intending to apprehend her.

He was surprised when Lady Channing restrained him.

"No, Max. Let her go."

"Let her go? You're going to permit some stranger to enter your house? Diamonds or not, she might still intend to walk off with your silver."

"I don't think so." Lady Channing smothered a soft trill of laughter. "I recognize her. It is the Merry Widow."

"Who?"

"The Merry Widow. That is the nickname everyone has been giving the Dowager Viscountess of Raincliffe."

Dowager Viscountess of— Max felt as if he had taken a sudden swift kick to the gut. That very odd female scrambling over the wall, slinking through the garden had been . . . Frederica Jameson?

He whirled around, staring at the spot where he had last seen her, but of course she had already disappeared, vanished as though she were as much of an apparition as those phantom memories that had been plaguing him of late.

"That's absurd," he told Lady Channing uncertainly. "What

39

would Freddie—I mean, what would Lady Raincliffe be doing sneaking through your garden?"

"Trying to find a way to get into my party, I suppose. Poor dear. She need not have gone to such trouble. I would have invited her, but your sister, that is, Lady Bentley, told me not to bother."

"Did she, by God!"

"Yes. She said the viscountess is far too sickly to be accepting so many invitations. That Lady Raincliffe would likely be departing for Bath very soon."

Max grimaced. Either Caroline had placed too much faith in her abilities to coax Max into interfering, or his sister had devised some plan of her own to send Freddie packing.

He said, "You should know better than to place much confidence in anything Caroline might say."

"Obviously." Lavinia's eyes twinkled with amusement. "Not only does the viscountess appear quite hale, but excessively athletic."

"Indeed," Max agreed without really paying much heed to what she was saying. Frowning, he paced toward the house.

Lavinia fell into step beside him. "She is a cousin of yours, isn't she, this little widow? At least that was what Caroline led me to believe."

"Frederica is a relative of sorts," Max said slowly. "I have not seen her for years, since she was a child, in fact."

"Then I suppose I had best take you inside and see that you become reacquainted. You appear far too distracted to resume what we were doing. Ah, well, perhaps I did choose my moment unwisely. But you are a difficult man to catch alone."

She looked up at him, flashing her glinting smile. "Another time, another place, perhaps?"

Max knew he should set her straight about that at once. He never made the mistake of letting the same opponent get past his guard. But instead, he made some noncommittal reply. Lady Channing was quite right. He was distracted. Freddie's sudden and startling appearance had unsettled him in a way he could not explain.

All he knew was that having earlier decided that he did not want to see her, he now felt afire with curiosity, impatient to rush into the ballroom and have a good look at the Dowager Viscountess Raincliffe.

He took such long strides, Lavinia had difficulty keeping up with him. But by the time they emerged beneath the arch of the blue and gilt ballroom, she had managed to link her arm through his in a possessive fashion.

He should have discouraged the gesture, but he was too busy scanning the assembled throng for some sign of Freddie, mentally cursing the fact that Lavinia had seen fit to invite so blasted many people.

The crush was so complete, there was scarce room for dancing. Couples moving through the measures of a quadrille nearly trod the toes of the stately matrons attempting to keep an eye on their charges.

Max began inching his way forward through the press of people. Lady Channing clung to his arm, firing off gracious remarks to some of her other guests.

She still managed to find time to whisper to Max behind the screen of her fan. "Of course, you realize this little cousin of yours has been causing quite a stir, having put off her mourning and begun amusing herself a little too soon."

So Caroline had already said. As usual, Max had assumed that his sister's reports were greatly exaggerated. But what he had seen of Freddie's behavior so far was hardly reassuring.

Craning his neck, he spotted her bare yards away, holding court in the shadow of one of the ballroom's tall marble pillars. Freddie had wasted little time in making herself at home, sipping a glass of lemonade. She was surrounded by a throng of gentlemen in their black evening coats. They buzzed around her like a hive full of drones guarding a honey pot.

Max's first impression was that she seemed very much the little girl he remembered, gotten up in Mother's clothes, that turban too large for her. Upon closer inspection, he noted the plump peach of her cheeks had faded to a complexion of flawless ivory, the snub nose had somehow taken an aquiline turn, the babe-soft face molded into one of delicate and dazzlingly feminine proportions.

The once-stubborn little mouth curved into generous berry red lips. And her figure . . . If the turban was large, the gown was not, hugging to perfection the high, pert outline of her breasts. There was no trace of the girl-child left in her willowy form, only the evidence of a woman grown.

Max stared, shot through with an unexpected pang of melancholy. Lavinia bent close to him to murmur, "Ah, I see the viscountess has attracted her usual court."

Max managed to wrench his gaze from Freddie, taking note

of the males clustered around her. Stanway, Whitby, Fremont, and Burke.

He frowned. "Good God. She seems to have gathered up every fortune hunter within a fifty-mile radius of London."

He moved purposefully forward. Most of the gentlemen bore the sense to clear a path for Max and Lady Channing, but he was obliged to elbow his way in front of Mr. Burke. The slick, sandy-haired fop emitted a protest which Max ignored.

Freddie had been laughing at something the portly Lord Stanway had said. But she straightened, glancing in Max's direction. Her eyes were still that same perfect shade of blue, though the gold-tipped lashes seemed more lush. Yet she looked out at the world with the same expression, that mingling of boldness and wariness, as though she expected to be hurt but defied anyone to try to harm her.

Max wondered if it was possible she would recognize him after all these years. For a moment he thought she did, for some of the color ebbed from her cheeks. Then he realized her gaze had shifted to the woman pressed so close to his side. It was not he who caused Freddie's hand to flutter nervously, toy with her necklace, but Lavinia.

Then Frederica seemed to rally. She sank into a graceful curtsy, forcing a broad smile to her lips.

"Why, Lady Channing, there you are at last. I—I have been looking for you. So rude you must be thinking me, not even to greet my hostess. But I arrived late owing to the press of carriages. This London traffic, my dear! Too dreadful. I declare, it gets worse all the time."

It was the most brazen performance Max had ever seen, Freddie's fear betrayed only in the candid depths of her eyes. He was sore tempted to break into applause, but he was a little tense himself, uncertain what Lavinia meant to do.

But Lavinia also smiled brilliantly, slipping into her own part with equal ease. "My dear viscountess, there is not the least need to apologize. I am only too delighted to see you here. I had greatly feared my invitation to you might have gone astray."

Frederica did have the grace to blush a little at that. "Your ladyship is too kind."

Apparently relieved of her apprehension of being escorted to the door, Freddie turned her attention back to Max. She studied him more earnestly this time, a faint crease appearing between the delicate arch of her brows.

42

"Dear viscountess," Lavinia cooed. "I am placed in the awkward position of introducing you to someone you already know. The Honorable Mr. Maxmillian Warfield."

Freddie half extended her hand, and Max took it, waiting, for he scarce knew what. A flicker of something—perhaps recognition at last—appeared in Frederica's eyes. Her fingers trembled. But then she lowered her lashes, withdrawing her hand. Her smile was so distant, he was left to wonder if he had imagined any other response.

"Good evening, Mr. Warfield," she said. "Yes, I am acquainted with some people by that name. Distant cousins, I believe, of the Marquis of Huntley branch of the family. Principal estate, Courtland Park in Derbyshire. Would you be one of those Warfields?"

"One of those?" Max echoed, strangely irritated. She made it sound as if she were reading out of the social register. "Yes, I am. In fact, I am the cousin who used to call upon you when you lived in Dorchester. I took you out riding in the pony cart."

"Did you? Why, how handsome of you. You must forgive my not remembering. It is so difficult to recollect events that happened when one was only eight years old."

She turned aside to wave to an elderly gallant who approached, his bristling mustaches every bit as gray as the rows of curls on his old-fashioned tye wig.

"Ah, here is the gentleman I have been waiting for. I am promised to General Fortescue for the next dance. I do trust all of you will excuse me."

And before Max could say another word, Frederica glided away on the arm of General Sir Mordant Fortescue, oblivious to the grumblings of all her younger gallants left in the lurch.

And Max was disconcerted to find that he was as disappointed as any of them. So that was all there was to his meeting Freddie Jameson again after all these years! She didn't even remember him. Of course, he assured himself that he had never been unreasonable enough to expect otherwise. Then what was he making such a bother about? Just because he had thought perhaps some sort of special bond had existed between them. What rubbish!

She had been only a child. Indeed, when he had gone away, he had hoped that she would forget him. Why then did he feel so piqued that she had done just that? Piqued and even though he was loathe to admit it, a little . . . hurt?

Hurt! Maxmillian Warfield? Never! He was long past anyone being able to accomplish such a thing. He gave himself a sharp mental shake to clear his head. If he indulged in any more such fuddled notions, he might even be drummed out of the care-for-nobody society of which he considered himself a member in good standing.

He became aware that Lavinia was trying to claim his attention, telling him that it was his dance. Whether it was or not, waltzing with her seemed as good a way to pass his time as any.

Resting one hand lightly on her trim waist, clasping her hand with the other, he set off down the ballroom. Max knew he was not the most inspired dancer, but at least he kept good steady time. He felt better now that he had seen Frederica. His curiosity had been satisfied. He could stop thinking about her.

Having come to this conclusion, he spent the next several twirls about the ballroom trying to see which of the other couples might be Frederica and General Fortescue.

He continued to do so without success until Lavinia complained, "Max. Halloo! I am down *here*, Max."

"What?" He frowned, glancing down at her, not even certain what she had just said. "Oh, yes, certainly. Your ball is going quite splendidly. You have outdone yourself as usual, my lady."

Then he went back to looking for Frederica, twisting his head in various directions, half dancing, half pulling Lavinia along with him.

"She isn't dancing, Max," Lavinia said, more loudly this time to be sure of claiming his attention.

"I—I beg your pardon?"

"I said, your pretty little cousin isn't dancing. She and General Fortescue appear to have decided to sit this one out."

Max was mortified, partly because Lady Channing should so easily have guessed what he was doing and partly because his lack of concentration caused him to tread upon her toes.

"My apologies," he said gruffly, but other concerns crowded uppermost to his mind. "Where on earth could Freddie and that old roué have gone? A fine set she appears to have taken up with. Fortune hunters and then a miserable loose screw like Mordy Fortescue. One would think she would have had enough of that sort of thing with her late husband."

"One would think," Lavinia replied in accents of long-suffering patience.

Max whipped her around in a dizzying circle as he tried to scan all sides of the room at once. "Surely Freddie has better sense than to slip off alone with an unconscionable rogue like that."

Lavinia sighed. "Does she? I don't know. But if you are going to continue looking like a stern papa who has caught the footman tweaking his daughter's garters, perhaps you had better go look for your Freddie."

She came to a stop and began to ease herself out of his grasp. Max suddenly realized what an ass he must appear. He tightened his grip and apologized, making an effort to take some heed of his partner.

"I am sorry. Of course, I don't want to go look for her. It is just—" What was it just? Damned if he knew himself what was causing him to behave so oddly. He finished lamely, "Frederica is a relative of sorts. One feels a little responsible."

"Maybe *one* does, but not Max Warfield." Lavinia glanced up at him through narrowed eyes. "You are the only person I have ever met who wishes he was born an orphan. 'Fess up, Max. What is your real interest in the girl?"

"I already told you."

"Oh, yes, you used to know her when she was eight years old. Well, she obviously isn't eight anymore. She's grown to be a beautiful woman with a handsome figure and a complexion that makes me want to hate her. And you . . . perhaps you are harboring some notions like Burke and those others of dangling for a rich wife."

Max gave a snort. "I am not dangling for a wife, rich or otherwise."

"Good." She smiled. "Not that it matters to me. I assure you, I have no scruples about forming liaisons with married men. But you might be severely disappointed in your widow. I have heard something, just a rumor, mind you, from a dear friend who knows the Raincliffe family intimately. She believes that far from being left wealthy, Frederica was cut out of the old man's will, and that his heirs promptly turned her out of doors."

"Foolish gossip," Max growled. "I trust you will not go about repeating it."

"Oh, no," Lavinia said, lowering her lashes demurely. "It would not at all amuse me to do so. At the moment."

Max started to demand what she meant by that. But the

45

dance ended and it became her parting shot. She rustled away to be claimed by her next partner.

With a mighty scowl Max watched her go. There was no real harm in Lavinia. But she could be teasing, exasperating, with claws as sharp as any female. If there was one thing he had no patience for, it was petticoat intrigue. He fervently wished he had spent his evening in far more sensible fashion, in the totally masculine world of his club.

It only added to his aggravation that he was doing the very thing he had sworn to his sister Caroline he would not do, take an interest in the affairs of Frederica Jameson. He determined anew to put her out of his head and succeeded rather better this time.

He located Mr. Leith Garson and Sir Pollack Sprague by the punch bowl, acquaintances of his from the Corinthian set he favored. He was soon lost in a conversation regarding the curricle race Mr. Garson was slated to run the next week. Max's humor improved enough that he even pledged himself to Sir Pollack for the next morning. Sprague was thinking of purchasing a new hack, and he desired Max's opinion of the beast.

Pleasantly occupied, it was nigh on midnight before Max caught another glimpse of Freddie. He paused to peek into the parlor, which had been set aside for cards. He looked in with no real interest. He always found both cards and the dice too sedentary an activity. Any wagering he did involved more active sport, a prizefight, a horse race, a cricket match.

Besides, the players gathered around the green baize tables at the Channings appeared a most uninteresting lot, mostly the older gentlemen and a few dowagers who were avid whist players.

And Freddie.

Max halted in mid-step, taking a second look into the room. There was no missing that turban, even though Freddie was seated all the way across the room, in front of the velvet-covered windows.

Max crossed the threshold with assumed casualness, but he could have leapt in hooting, performing a Scottish sword dance for all the attention he would have aroused. Everyone was far too intent upon their cards.

The parlor was decorated according to the Channings' passion for the classics. Max had always found the painted frescoes rather amusing, bacchanalian revelry with gentlemen in

46

tight curls swilling down wine, leering centaurs carrying off naked maidens.

But he felt strangely uncomfortable with Freddie present, for once wishing those ladies' abundant charms were adorned with some tastefully placed flower garlands.

But Freddie seemed oblivious to her surroundings. Bent over the cards splayed in her hand, she was seated at a table with General Fortescue, Lady Diedre McCaulay, and Mr. Horace Canterfield.

Judging from the pile of coin, Fortescue appeared the big winner, a fact he did not much regard, being possessed of a large fortune. Lady McCaulay seemed a trifle put out, but it was well known that she was the Duke of Portnoy's latest mistress and he always made her losses good.

As for Canterfield, he was a hardened enough gamester merely to look bored. What he lost tonight he would attempt to recoup tomorrow at hazard or the faro table.

But Freddie . . . Max wished he could believe it was only the candlelight making her look so pale. He had seen that look of desperation too many times not to recognize it, the moisture beaded on the brow, the fretted underlip, all signs of a gamester about to be run off his, or, in this case her, pretty legs.

She was taking so long over her discard, it seemed her life depended upon it. Maybe it did..

But she was supposed to be quite wealthy, Max thought. Yet Lavinia's recent words kept echoing through his head. *Cut out of the will . . . Turned out of doors.*

Surely if she had been left penniless, the woman ought to know better than to be playing so deep. He hesitated, reminding himself it was none of his concern. For heaven's sake, the girl did not even remember who he was. But at that moment, Freddie chanced to glance up from her table and see him. Even from across the room there was no mistaking the look of mute appeal she flashed at him before bending back over her cards.

So the chit was in over her head. Max gave a faint sigh of resignation. Well, he supposed it would not take that much effort on his part to extricate her. But when he had, he would make it clear to her he was no longer in the habit of rescuing damsels in distress.

Smoothing his sleeves, he strode across the room, coming to stand just behind her chair. Freddie had folded her hand. She was signing her name to a vowel and gloomily shoving it across the table to Fortescue.

47

"So unfortunate, milady," the general commiserated. "But perhaps you will have better luck next hand."

"There won't be a next hand," Max said.

All heads at the table turned toward him except Freddie's.

Max summoned up a benign smile, touching her lightly on the shoulder. "You promised to dance with me this evening, Cousin Frederica, remember?"

She raised her head slowly. Max expected gratitude, at least relief. He was not at all prepared for the cool way her fine brows arched upward. "I don't recall doing anything of the kind."

"I fear you suffer from a faulty memory, milady," Max said, still smiling but now through clenched teeth.

"My memory is excellent, Mr. Warfield," she said.

Max wondered if he had been mistaken when he thought she had silently beseeched his aid. What the deuce was the matter with her—did she want to be rescued or not?

"Then damn it—er, that is, I am asking you now. Will you have the next waltz with me?"

She turned her shoulder on him, gathering up the cards to reshuffle the deck. "You can see that I am otherwise engaged. You are disrupting our game."

Max stood thunderstruck, feeling something of a fool and not much enjoying the sensation. He was uncertain what to do next, but Frederica's opponents at the table decided the issue.

"Oh, I believe I have had enough." Mr. Canterfield stifled a yawn and stood up. He held Lady McCauley's chair as she also rose.

"But—but we have only just begun," Freddie said.

Her protest went unheeded as Canterfield complained good-naturedly to the general. "I suppose we might as well all pack it in, curse you, Fortescue. The luck's been with you all evening."

Fortescue fingered the ends of his mustache, preening. "Alas, I feel the luck is more with Mr. Warfield. He comes to bear off the fairest prize of all."

"No, I am not going to dance, General, I assure you," Freddie said. "Pray, let us continue—"

But Mr. Canterfield was already escorting Lady McCauley back to the ballroom and the general began scooping up his pile of coin and paper. Freddie watched with a look of sick dismay as her vowels were stuffed heedlessly into his waistcoat pocket. She bit down hard to steady her trembling under-lip.

Beneath his irritation, Max could not help a stirring of un-ease. Curse it all! How badly dipped was the little fool?

The general shuffled to his feet, taking Freddie's hand, the old devil carrying her fingertips to his lips with one of those leering glances that made Max long to kick the backside of his breeches.

"If you will excuse me, m'dear. I must take m'leave. Prom-ised Lady Marlborough to have a look in at her rout, though 'tis bound to be a deadly dull affair." He clapped Max jovially on the shoulder. "Enjoy your partner, Warfield. Possesses more than mere charm, you know. Such a solidly sensible sort of gel."

Max would have liked to favor him with a pithy opinion of what *he* thought of Frederica's good sense. But he contented himself with a curt bow, managing not to curl his lip with dis-dain as the general swaggered on his way. Freddie affected to forget that Max stood waiting behind her chair, continuing to play with the cards, shuffling them in wooden fashion. But he could tell how aware she was of his presence by the stiffness in her shoulders.

It would have served her right if he had just stalked away and left her. But even if he was a most reluctant knight errant, he could also be a stubborn one.

"I believe the orchestra has struck up the next waltz, mi-lady." Max extended one hand to her almost in the manner of one flinging down a gauntlet.

She ignored it. "I did not come here tonight to dance, Mr. Warfield."

"No?" He plunked down into the chair the general had va-cated. Her lips formed a slight pout that was soft and adorable, but the storm brewing in her eyes was pure Olympian goddess. She began to lay down the cards in a row before her, preparing for a game of solitaire. With the flush mounted high in her cheeks, her golden ringlets escaping from beneath that ridicu-lous turban, she looked more like a half-wild Gypsy than a dowager viscountess.

"So what are you planning to do?" Max asked. "Tell my fortune?"

"Oh, I don't need cards for that." She slammed down the king of hearts with a vengeance. "You will come to a violent end, Mr. Warfield. That is what usually befalls people who go about meddling in someone else's business."

"You intend to call me out simply because I asked you to dance?"

"You are not interested in dancing either. At least not with me. I strongly suspect you came and broke up my card game merely to ring a peal over me. So you might as well get on with it. Tell me, sir, what is your lecture to be about? My improper behavior as a recent widow, or the evils of gaming?"

"I'm not in the habit of giving lectures," Max snapped, forgetting that he had been planning to do just that.

"What a novelty. Everyone else in your family appears to do so." Freddie tossed her head, a rather too-bright sparkle in her eyes. "I received a lengthy sermon from Lady Bentley only this morning. Your sister, I believe?"

"I do my best not to acknowledge the connection, but yes, I fear she is." He added gruffly, "You should not let anything that Caroline might have said distress you."

"I didn't. She was most diverting. Lady Bentley merely hinted that it might be better for all concerned if I took myself off to Bath. She even offered me the use of her own house there. I rather think she hopes that I might drown taking the waters."

"No! Be poisoned perhaps, but not drowned."

This did not even cause her lips to twitch, but as Max recalled, it never had been easy to coax a smile from Freddie when she had determined not to do so.

"And you, Mr. Warfield—" she began.

"You used to call me Max."

She ignored the interruption. "Is that what you wanted to tell me, Mr. Warfield. That you also wish I would go away to Bath?"

Max's gaze roved over the lovely sculpted planes of her face down to the generous curve of her bosom. He started to assure her that her going away was the last thing he desired, when he brought himself up short. This was his little cousin, Freddie Jameson, after all. Damnation. He hadn't sat down to flirt with her.

"I have no opinion on the matter," he said with a shrug. He suddenly felt as though he had gotten himself into deep waters here, no longer exactly sure what he was doing. Beyond stopping Freddie from hazarding so much at cards, he had given no thought to what else he might have to say to her.

He was not accustomed to dealing with young women. They either irritated him by blushing and stammering or attempting to play the coquette. But Frederica did neither. She treated him in that same offhand fashion she had as a little girl.

But she wasn't little anymore. That realization kept stabbing at him again and again, making him curiously awkward. To keep his eyes from straying to her more seductive curves, he focused on her hands instead. Gone were the stubby, childlike fingers, replaced by ones long and graceful.

Her game of solitaire was already going awry, and he watched as she deftly rearranged the pattern of the cards to suit herself.

"Do you always cheat?" he asked with a slight frown.

"Only myself, Mr. Warfield," she said. A flash of rare, sweet sadness appeared in her eyes, quickly shuttered away. "And so if you haven't come to lecture me or to advise me which hotel to put up at in Bath, what do you want, sir?"

"Just what I told you—to persuade you to dance with me."

"I am more interested in dining than dancing." She began to gather up the cards. "If I am going to the devil, I am determined not to do it on an empty stomach."

"And are you?"

"Am I what?"

"Going to the devil." After the barest hesitation, he demanded, "Exactly how much did you lose to Fortescue tonight?"

"Only a trifling sum of—" she began in defensive tones, then broke off, glaring at him. "Really, sir. I thought you did not mean to lecture."

He countered her complaint with another question. "Can you afford to pay this *trifling* sum, Freddie?"

She looked down the length of her nose at him. "I am accustomed to being addressed as your ladyship."

"Very well, then," he said irritably. "Can *your ladyship* afford to pay?"

She rose slowly to her feet. He could tell the gesture was meant to be one of icy dignity, but she was flushed and trembling too much. "I suppose you mean well, Mr. Warfield, but I am a woman grown and a widow. Tend to your own business and stop troubling me with—"

"Whoa! Hold up there a moment. I would never have 'troubled' you at all but for that look you shot in my direction."

"Look? What look?"

"The big blue eyes, the beseeching lips."

She looked a little flustered by the accusation, but was quick to recover herself with a shrug. "You have a fanciful imagination, sir. I—I did nothing of the kind. I don't beg. I am a lady of wealth and independence. I can wager any sum I choose and—and I am tired of being quizzed and badgered by—by a parcel of elderly, doddering relatives!"

"Elderly, doddering—" Max gasped. "Why, you little shrew!"

But before he could say anything more, she slapped down the deck of cards, then turned on her heel and flounced from the room. By the time Max had gotten to his own feet, she was well on her way out the door.

He could feel a faint hint of color in his own face and half expected to find himself the cynosure of all eyes. But Frederica had not shouted at him. It only seemed as if she had.

None of the other whist players raised so much as an eyebrow, and Max was relieved that their avidity for cards prevented anyone from noticing that the imperturbable Mr. Warfield had just received a stinging setdown.

"Elderly, doddering relative, indeed," he muttered, Freddie's words having stung more than he cared to admit. Was that how she saw him now?

He was annoyed, but less with Freddie than himself. And Caroline. Had he not told his sister this would be the likely outcome of any effort on his part to interfere with Frederica? And knowing that, he had proceeded to do so anyway and gotten the exact response he had predicted and so richly merited.

Stupid! And most unlike himself. He was many reprehensible things, but he had always flattered himself that being an idiot did not number among them. Now he was not so sure.

You ought to know better, Warfield, he thought grimly. Never go around saving damsels until you are sure they want to be rescued. He would require the next one to submit her request for help into writing, and then he would cheerfully rip it up and settle back comfortably at his own fireside. Let some other poor sot play the hero. It was not his style.

Feeling that he had made enough of a fool of himself for one evening, Max resolved to seek out his hostess and take his leave. He would have been just as pleased not to encounter his cousin again. But having lost sight of Freddie for most of the evening, it seemed inevitable that now he would trip over her wherever he went.

He was but passing through the mahogany dining room, where an elegant buffet had been laid out on the white linen surface of a massive table. The branches of the silver candlesticks cast an inviting glow over chafing dishes filled with pastries, lobster, oyster pâtés, and steaming hot rolls.

But the chamber was as yet deserted except for the young woman with the cascade of blond curls standing at the far end of the table.

Max froze in the shadows of the doorway, watched as Freddie slipped along the length of the table, glancing nervously around her. She had removed that foolish turban and he could not but applaud the effect—that is, until he realized what she was doing. Quickly scooping something off the table, she dropped it into the depths of the turban, then balanced the headgear rather clumsily back on her head. Without a backward glance she scurried out the French doors. Like the ones from the ballroom, these also led into the garden.

Max stood, stunned for a moment until the full significance of what he had just witnessed sunk in. Freddie . . . Freddie had just stolen some of the Channings' silverplate!

He had not been mistaken earlier when he had observed her play at the tables. He had guessed she might be desperate, but desperate enough to resort to thievery?

Max's lips set into a taut line. He had resolved to stay clear of the young woman, to seek no further involvement. He preferred to remain oblivious to his relatives' peccadilloes, but this was too much even for him to ignore.

Damnation, if the girl were caught at this! Likely she would not be sent to prison. The Channings would never take it that far. But the resulting scandal would ruin Frederica forever. Had she grown up to have no sense whatsoever?

Cursing Freddie for her folly and for once again forcing him to intervene, Max started after her. He bolted through the French doors, plunging into the rustling foliage of the Channings' garden for the second time that night.

The place seemed silent, a place of hushed moonlight and shadows, even the music from the ballroom at a temporary lull. Max had hoped to intercept Freddie before she scaled the wall again and reached the street, but he saw that he was already too late.

Disgruntled, he raced forward and tackled the wall himself. As he struggled for a foothold in the crumbling brick, he wondered how the deuce Freddie had cleared it, and her in skirts.

Cursing at some thorny vine that snagged and tore the sleeve of his black evening coat, he managed to gain the top of the wall, marveling that Freddie could have done it so much more swiftly.

It was not until he dropped triumphantly to the other side that he realized the reason. This time she had employed the simple expediency of unlatching the garden gate and letting herself out. She was halfway up the street heading toward a coach that awaited her on the opposite corner.

Swearing, Max tore after her. His footfall must have alerted her of his approach. She cast a startled glance over her shoulder and started to run. But Max seized her by the arm and spun her around.

She shrank back, striking wildly out at him. "Let go of me or I shall scream to— Oh, it's you, Max. I—I mean Mr. Warfield." The light from the street lamp played over her delicate features. Her look of fear dissolved into one of indignation.

"You frightened me to death. Now what do you want? You cannot be this desperate for a dance partner that you need chase me through the streets."

Max paused to catch his breath. She tried to catch pull away, but he refused to ease his grip on her arm.

"No, I would not seem to be the one who is desperate. You little fool!" He gave her a brisk shake. "I saw you back there."

"So you did! When you were busy ruining my evening—"

"I am not talking about the cards. I realize you must be in a great deal of trouble, but there is no need for you to resort to this."

"Resort to what? So I cannot afford to own a coach and have to slip away to take a hackney. It is not against the law."

"But other things you have been doing are. Come on, Freddie. We are going to have to put it back."

"Put what back? I have no idea what you are talking about," she said loftily, but her eyes shifted, unable to meet his.

"I am talking about this." Before she could protest, he wrenched off her turban.

"Are you mad?" she spluttered. "Give me that back."

But as Max gave the garment a good shake, something wrapped in a napkin tumbled to the paving stones. He nudged the cloth with his foot, expecting to reveal the gleam of silver. Instead, a half-dozen maids of honor tumbled into the gutter, the small cakes leaving a trail of crumbs.

He blinked, then stared uncomprehending at Freddie. Shamefaced but still defiant, she cried, "Very well. I suppose you might as well have the rest of it."

Groping in the folds of her skirt, she produced several more cloth bundles from concealed pockets. She thrust the parcels into his hands, a delicious spicy scent carrying to his nostrils, a splash of some rich sauce dampening his cuff.

"Lobster? Chicken aspic?" he muttered, feeling like the greatest idiot this side of Bedlam. He hardly knew what to say or do next, when a shriek rent the night air.

He heard the click of heels approaching from behind him, saw Freddie tense, her eyes widening in alarm.

"No, Dora," she called. "Stop. It is all right—"

Max had little time to make sense of these cryptic words, but enough to guess he stood in some sort of danger. He whipped around to see a large female bearing down on him, like something out of legends of the Valkyries. With his hands full of Freddie's supper, he was too slow to react. The butt end of a pistol swung out, clipping him on the side of the head.

Max reeled dizzily for a moment, then pitched to his knees, falling into the gutter as darkness claimed him.

Chapter 5

Max lay sprawled upon the red velvet chaise longue in Frederica's front parlor. Even with the combined efforts of herself, Dora, and Stubbins, that had been as far as they could get the still-unconscious Max, his hard-muscled frame weighing a good deal more than at first had appeared.

The chaise was one of the few pieces of furniture in the parlor, the elegant Grecian-style sofa having been bought in a moment of rash enthusiasm one long-ago time when Freddie had actually *won* something at lottery tickets.

Dora had had to fetch a candlestick from the dining room. She held the taper aloft with a trembling hand, its soft glow seemed to cast a harsh light upon Max's pallid features. Freddie hovered over him anxiously, applying a cold cloth to the knot upon his temple. She felt a little relieved when Max emitted a low moan.

"Thank heavens, I think he may be coming to his senses."

"Oh, dear, oh, dear," Dora said for perhaps the thousandth time since Max had first collapsed into the street. "You know I never meant to, Freddie—That is, I thought he was a footpad. I never imagined he was someone you knew. Your cousin, you say? Are you quite sure?"

"Quite sure," Freddie murmured, her gaze skating over the familiar line of rock-hard, stubborn jaw, the glossy ebony hair, the full curve of those mocking lips.

"He is called Max, after nobody in particular." A rueful half smile tipped Freddie's lips at the remembrance. For a long time in her childhood innocence she had really believed that was his surname. Max After-Nobody-in-Particular. She had thought it quite grand.

But she was quick to shrug off the memory, as she had

earlier that evening when she had first suffered the shock of meeting Max again after so many years, then feigned not to know him. It had astonished her just how well she did remember him, though in her mind's eye, his features had not been cast so harsh. But her memories had been those of a child, rose-colored visions confused with notions of knights in shining armor and princes riding white chargers. She hated to think how much of her childhood she had spent with her nose pressed against the glass, waiting for this particular errant knight to come riding down the drive to rescue the princess from the ogre's castle.

But Prince Charming had never kept his promise, had never come back, and in the end the princess had had to rescue herself. Freddie thought she had put aside all recollection of Max and his defection. To admit that she still felt any hurt because of it would be the same as admitting she could be vulnerable, and she was not about to do that. She patted the compress upon his brow, her hand a little rougher than she meant it to be.

Max groaned again and flung up one arm as though to fend her off. He shifted on the chaise and moved his lips as though trying to speak, but his eyes remained closed.

"Perhaps we should fetch a doctor," Dora said.

"Where would we find a physician at this hour of night? Or pay for one if we did." Freddie frowned, lifting the cloth long enough to peer at Max's injury. The swelling had gone down considerably. "I can't understand it. The wound does not seem that great. I thought he would be roused by now."

"I did not mean to hit him so hard," Dora said.

"I am just thankful you did not shoot him."

"Oh, I couldn't have done that. I know only how to aim the pistol, not load it." Dora started to wring her hands and nearly dropped the candle, spattering hot wax everywhere.

"Take care, Dora. Let us not burn him as well," Freddie admonished. "No doubt he already will be eager to haul us up before the nearest magistrate."

"What will we do if he dies?" Dora wailed. "I shall be hung for murder."

"Nonsense. You know I should never let such a thing happen to you. I'd—I'd stuff his body up the chimney first."

"No!"

Max's sudden rebuttal was little more than a grunt, but it startled both Freddie and Dora as much as if he had bellowed.

"Not . . . chimney," he muttered, his eyes flickering at last. "Won't draw properly. Best weight me down . . . drop in Thames."

Freddie started to laugh, but her relief at this sign of his recovery was tempered with indignation. "Exactly how long have you been conscious?" she demanded. "Have you been lying there listening to us fret over you the whole time? Why didn't you say something?"

"Didn't sound to me . . . as if doing much fretting. Been trying to decide if it would hurt to talk."

"And does it?" Freddie asked anxiously.

"Like hell." With an irritated motion, he brushed away both her hand and the compress. "Stop slopping water on me." He managed to shove himself up onto one elbow. "And do we need to . . . have so many blasted candles."

Freddie cast one look at the single wavering taper in Dora's hand, then placed her hands gently on Max's shoulders. "I think you better lie back down."

But he resisted her, struggling to a sitting position. He blinked, seeming to focus on Dora, a dark scowl setting over his features.

"Ah, the Valkyrie."

"N-no, sir. Actually, I'm Miss Applegate, Frederica's companion." Dora dropped a nervous curtsy. "And I'm so very sorry."

"Not as sorry as I am." Max gingerly felt the lump swelling just at his hairline. He stifled a curse.

"It looks much better than when we first brought you here," Dora said. "Doesn't it, Freddie? I daresay, if he combs his hair over the other way, no one will even notice."

Max shot Dora such a black look, Freddie made haste to suggest, "Dora, dear, why don't you fetch Mr. Warfield a glass of brandy?"

Dora's eyes went round. "But Freddie, we don't have any."

Freddie groped in the concealed pocket of her gown and produced a small flask, some of the spoils she had forgotten to hand over to Max earlier.

Max's eyes narrowed. "Lord Channing's French stock. I am glad to see you at least had the wit to steal the very best."

Freddie felt her cheeks flood with color, but she compressed her lips, saying nothing. She took the candle from Dora and lit one of the tapers mounted on the wall near the fireplace, then dispatched Dora on her errand to fetch a glass. But the older woman hesitated upon the threshold, her broad, honest brow knit with concern.

"I am not sure this is proper, Frederica. Leaving you alone with a gentleman at this hour."

Freddie stifled an urge to break into hysterical laughter. Considering some of the risks she had already taken that evening, Dora's sudden concern for the proprieties was ludicrous.

Before Freddie could reassure her, Max spoke up, saying rather sourly, "There is no need to worry about me, ma'am. I'm only one of her elderly, doddering relatives."

Dora looked far from convinced, but went on her way. Freddie bit back a satisfied smile. Max Warfield always seemed so cool, if not mocking, at least aggravatingly teasing. It was good to know that she had managed to nettle him a little.

But her satisfaction was marred when she noted how pale he looked. He forced himself to stand, then reeled a little on his feet. Freddie hastened over to clutch at his arm.

"I don't think this is wise, Mr. Warfield. You should lie down. You don't look at all the thing."

But he shook her off, resisting her attempts to ease him back onto the chaise, seeking the support of the fireplace mantel instead.

Candlelight played over his drawn features as he studied his surroundings. "Where the deuce am I?"

"In my town house in Cheapside."

She thought his brows rose a little at that, and added defensively, "It may not be Grosvenor Square, but it is still quite a respectable neighborhood."

Max paced off a few steps. Freddie watched him with bated breath, but he seemed steady enough now. He continued to inspect the chamber, his scowl deepening. Freddie had always been rather proud of her front parlor. It had the loveliest hand-painted French wallpaper, to say nothing of the elaborate carvings on the ceiling.

But Max's footsteps seemed to echo very loudly off the uncarpeted floor, the near-empty parlor smacking more of a house for let than a lived-in residence.

She should have had him laid out in the dining room. It was a little better furnished than this room with its solitary chaise, scattering of mismatched Hepplewhite chairs, and sofa tables. Before he could make any remark, Freddie summoned up a brazen smile.

"Do you like my decor, Mr. Warfield? Simplicity . . . it is all the dernier cri these days. The uncluttered look."

The door connecting to the study had been left ajar, and he stole a peek inside before remarking dryly. "How very fashionable the next room is. You have nothing at all in there."

Freddie lifted her chin. "If you came here to criticize—"

"I did not come here at all," he reminded her in rather testy accents. "You brought me."

"I suppose you would have preferred it if I had left you lying in the gutter. It would have been far simpler to have done so. Dora and I had a dreadful time getting you into the hackney. If the driver had not taken pity upon us and helped because he thought you were bosky, we never would have managed it." Freddie smiled a little. "He said, when you came round, I should give you a dreadful scold for being so ungentlemanlike as to get foxed when you were escorting ladies."

Max did not return her smile, his thick brows coming together like black thunderheads.

"I can see plainly that you have no sense of humor about this entire affair. It was all an honest mistake. Dora thought you were attacking me. But go ahead," she said, drawing herself up into a dramatic pose, holding both hands out as though waiting to be shackled. "Send for the constable. You can have me and my poor companion clapped up in Newgate before cock's crow."

"Please. Enact me no Cheltenham tragedies." He rubbed the back of his neck, wincing. "My head is already aching fit to burst."

"Then I should summon a hackney and have you taken home," she said eagerly. "Bed is what you need."

"I would be very happy to be home in my own bed, but I have a few things I need to say to you first, Frederica."

That had an ominous sound to it. She turned stubbornly away. "I cannot imagine anything so important that will not keep until—"

"Sit down, milady."

"I wonder what is keeping Dora. I should go help her to find the glasses."

"I said sit down!"

She whipped to face him, her cheeks heating. "I do not like being bellowed at."

He clutched his head. "Believe me. I am not going to bellow again. Now, please. Sit down."

60

She complied, sinking reluctantly onto the chaise, spreading out her skirts to conceal how ill at ease she was. He stalked over and sat down beside her, letting go his breath in a long sigh. When she had been a child, Max had always seemed quite large to her, a towering giant. She would have thought that the passage of time and her added inches would have diminished that effect.

But if anything, she had a heightened awareness of how tall and broad-shouldered he was, the way his skin-tight breeches molded the muscular outline of his thighs. Her heart set up a peculiar fluttering at his proximity. She tried to put a little more distance between them on the chaise longue, but scoot one more inch and she would end up on the floor.

Freddie expected a tongue-lashing. It had been humiliating enough, Max witnessing her losses at the card table, but then to also catch her behaving like a pickpocket, pilfering food from the Channings' buffet! She had to fight down the urge to blush with shame. Max would likely have quite a few caustic remarks to make about her behavior. He had a very cutting wit, and being coshed over the head was bound to render any man a little surly. Freddie braced herself for the worst.

She was a good deal surprised when his hand reached out to cover her own, his callused palm chafing her skin. Her gaze flew to his face. He looked quite disreputable, dark strands of hair tumbled across his brow, the spectacular bruise upon his forehead, his cravat disheveled, the very picture of a rakehell after a wild night on the town.

But his gray eyes were somber, his expression grave as he asked, "Freddie, how long have you been going on this way?"

She moistened her lips, and said brightly, "Goodness, I don't know what you mean, Mr. Warfield. What way?"

He indicated the room with an expressive frown. "Living so—so uncluttered. Do you even have any servants?"

"Yes! I have a very fine butler and a housemaid, which quite suffices for my needs. There is not much to dust."

"Just how badly off did your late husband leave you?"

"Merely because I choose to live simply is no reason for you to assume—"

"Cut line, Freddie. You know I can always find out the terms of the viscount's will just by checking with the family solicitors."

She withdrew her hand from his grasp. Freddie struggled a moment more with her pride before replying. "Very well, if

you insist upon prying into my affairs, sir, I will tell you . . .
I was left practically penniless and soon after the funeral, my
stepson turned me out of doors."

"That bastard!"

"Yes," Freddie agreed. "That is a very accurate summary of
Sir Wilfred's character."

"I was not speaking of Sir Wilfred, but your late husband."

"I beg your pardon," Freddie said, stiffening.

Max was treading upon dangerous ground, but appeared
quite unaware of it. "That old bounder! To wed an innocent
young girl, then leave her unprovided for! How the Jamesons
could have forced you to wed a demi-rep with one foot in the
grave—"

"Mr. Warfield." Her hands knotted into fists. "If you want to
keep all your teeth, I strongly advise you not to say anything
more about Leon."

"Leon?"

"Lord Raincliffe." She felt a hot stinging behind her eyes
and blinked furiously. "He—he was magnificent, and I won't
let anyone abuse his memory. Not even you."

He regarded her with a puzzled frown, then remarked
slowly, "I am sorry if I said anything to distress you. Apparently I misunderstood about your marriage. I spoke only out of
concern for you. How do you contrive to live?"

"I manage well enough," she snapped.

"Were tonight's activities supposed to be a sample of that?
Wandering the streets alone, losing large sums at cards, being
obliged to steal your supper?"

"I took only what I would have eaten if I had stayed to
dine."

"Or if you had been a starving waif who had not had a decent meal for several days."

Freddie glared at him. "Well, I had Dora to think of, too,
didn't I?"

He shoved abruptly to his feet, like a man who has reached
some resolution, one he found unpleasant. He started to rake
his hand back through his hair, but winced, checking the motion. Pacing back toward the fireplace, he said, "Much as I
hate to admit it, my sister Caroline was right."

"Right about what?" Freddie asked suspiciously.

"Something has to be done about you before you break your
neck scaling walls, get arrested for theft, or assault some other

hapless fellow whose head may not be as hard as mine. You are badly in need of a strong hand at the reins, my girl."

"Indeed, Mr. Warfield. And just whose strong hand did you have in mind?"

"Little as I relish the prospect, the task seems to have fallen to me." He gave vent to a weary sigh. "To begin with, I shall, of course, have to pay your gaming debts with the understanding that I will not see you with a deck of cards in your hands again. Then the lease on this house will have to be given up. Temporarily, you will have to move in with one of my sisters."

Freddie shot to her feet, outrage rendering her momentarily speechless.

"Most likely it should be Lady Bentley," he continued. "It would serve Caroline right for attempting to drag me into this business to begin with."

"Mr. Warfield!" Freddie gasped, finding her own voice at last. He regarded her with upraised eyebrows, as though surprised that she should have anything to say in the matter, a fact that only added fuel to her mounting anger.

"How dare you!" she spluttered. "What makes you think that after all these years I will permit you to charge back into my life again and start ordering me around? You always were infernally high-handed."

"*Always?*" Beneath his heavy lids, those keen gray eyes seemed to bore into her. "I thought you said you did not remember me."

Freddie started guiltily, then made haste to recover her error. "I—I don't. I meant that—that you were high-handed tonight, the way you interrupted my card game, persisted in following me, and now this. Standing there calmly planning my future. I cannot even think why you would trouble yourself. I doubt that you suffer much from any great sense of family duty."

"I don't."

"Then why come bothering me?"

He gave a careless shrug. "Call it a whim, if you like. I must be growing sentimental in my dotage. You still remind me so much of that wayward little girl I once knew."

"Perhaps you should take a closer look," she said tartly.

"Oh, I already have," he murmured. He stepped toward her, Freddie experienced a sudden wild impulse to retreat. But she stood her ground as his lean, strong fingers cupped her chin, tilting her face up to the light. He subjected her to a lingering inspection that caused the blood to fire into her cheeks.

Leon had often done the same, teasingly catching her chin when he wanted to be assured of her full attention. But Leon's touch, she was forced to admit, had never sent her heart pounding so madly.

She wanted to draw away, but found herself strangely unable to stir. She returned Max's gaze as though mesmerized, her eyes drawn to the full shape of his mouth. He was smiling slightly, the movement of his lips so enticing, it took her a moment before she could concentrate upon what he was saying.

". . . and you have grown to be a beautiful woman."

She wanted to tell him she did not care for his compliments, but she was surprised to discover she did. She blushed like any simpering debutante, stammering, "Th-thank you."

"A pity you have not acquired some wisdom to match that lovely profile." He gave her chin one final playful flick.

The dismissive gesture as much as the mockery of his words restored Freddie to her senses. She stepped back from him and grated, "I am wise enough to know one thing, sir. That I will live as I choose with no help or hindrance. And if you think otherwise, you may go and be damned."

"Likely I will," he drawled. "But first I intend to make sure you don't follow suit."

Although amusement glimmered in his smoke gray eyes, his jaw set in a manner that matched her own stubborn resolve, and Freddie regretted that she had never been able to afford any china to adorn her mantel. She longed for something to throw at him, a plate, a vase. It didn't even have to be Sèvres.

It was at that moment that Dora rustled back into the room, bearing a tray and glasses. She beamed at both of them, as ever oblivious to any undercurrents of tension.

"Oh, Mr. Warfield," she trilled. " 'Tis such a relief to see you on your feet again. And the color back in your face, too. I am sorry I took so long. I had difficulty finding any clean glasses. Poor Till has been so busy with the baby, and when Stubbins does the washing up—Well, you know what his eyes are!"

Max didn't, and Freddie was not keen to have him enlightened any further about her unorthodox domestic arrangements.

"I am sorry you were put to such bother, Dora," Freddie said. "Mr. Warfield was just on the point of leaving.

"And he will not be coming back," she added, low enough that only he could hear.

"At least not tonight," he murmured.

Looking crestfallen, Dora set the tray down upon the sofa table. "But—but, oh, dear. Do you really feel well enough to go, sir? If you should collapse again . . . I feel so responsible. You will never forgive me."

"On the contrary, madam. There is nothing to forgive." Max strode over and took Dora's hand, the offhand kiss he brushed on her fingertips nonetheless leaving the elderly spinster blushing and flustered. "Take care of my wayward cousin until I return. She seems to need a great deal of looking after."

"Oh, I am. I—I mean I shall."

"Good-bye, Mr. Warfield," Freddie said pointedly.

"Au revoir, my dear." Max gave her one of his infuriatingly languid grins. "Don't bother to ring for the butler. I can find my own way out."

"A good thing, too," Dora said. "For I doubt if Stubbins could."

Luckily Max was already slipping out the door and he did not seem to hear this frank if imprudent remark. The door was left ajar and Freddie rushed across the room and slammed it closed as though she would bar it against Max's threatened return.

Dora sighed. "Such an abrupt man, your cousin. He is not at all handsome, but likely he looks better when he has not been hit over the head." She added wistfully. "I hope he does come back. It would be so pleasant to have a gentleman calling upon us. I could act as chaperone and pour out the tea."

"If Mr. Warfield calls upon us again, we are not going to be at home."

"Why, Freddie." Dora regarded her with a mixture of mild reproach and surprise.

"Don't you understand?" Freddie asked impatiently. "He is as bad as any of my other cousins, as bad as Lady Bentley or Aunt Jameson, scheming for a way to be rid of me. You should have heard him before you came back into the room, calling me a nuisance, saying how he would have this house closed up, send me to live with his sisters."

Dora went quite pale, her lower lip trembling. "That means I should have to return to Dorchester, to live with Wilfred and his family."

"No, it doesn't. For I won't let it happen. I shall send Mr. Max Warfield to the right just as I have all the others. We want none of his meddling."

"No." Dora gave her a wobbly smile. "And I am sure with

all you won tonight, we will be able to snap our fingers at the entire world."

Freddie found herself unable to meet Dora's hopeful gaze. "You—you did win, didn't you, Freddie?"

"No, Dora. I didn't. I fear I lost quite a dreadful sum."

She sank down upon the chaise while Dora swallowed hard with disappointment, then tried to put a brave front upon it.

"Oh, well. I am sure you will win next time."

Freddie only shook her head. "I am beginning to realize I am not cut out to make a living as a gamester. I always thought I was so brilliant at cards. I fear all those times Leon must have been letting me win."

She propped her elbows on her knees, allowing her chin to droop upon her hands. "The truth is, Dora, I don't quite know what we are going to do."

It had been a total disaster of a night, between her losses at the tables and that humiliating episode that had resulted in Max Warfield's intrusion back into her life. What else could possibly go wrong?

It was a question that unfortunately was answered the next morning. Despite her pressing worries, Freddie had been exhausted enough to sleep soundly. She had roused herself, slipped into a morning frock of sprigged muslin, and was in the process of arranging her hair beneath a lacy cap when Till barged into the room.

"Oh, madam, you must come at once." The winsome housemaid gasped. "There must be some great trouble. Stubbins is at the front door, arguing and trying to bar admittance to somebody."

"Another bill collector!" Freddie groaned. Could they not even have the decency to wait until after breakfast. She was tempted to dive back beneath the covers and pull them over her head.

But she could not leave poor Stubbins in the lurch, manfully but singlehandedly attempting to guard the castle. The erstwhile coachman was far more accustomed to dealing with recalcitrant horses than people.

Her hair tumbling in a golden sheen around her shoulders, her lace cap still askew, Freddie bolted from her room. She was nearly all the way down the stairs leading to the front hall when she paused.

For the first time, it occurred to her, it might not be a bill collector at all, but Max making good on his threat to return.

Freddie raised one hand and started to self-consciously smooth back the wild disarray of her tresses. She stopped almost at once, angry with herself. What did she care what Max Warfield might think about her appearance?

As she hesitated on the last step, she could see the agitated Stubbins attempting to close the front door. He said in querulous tones, "You must come back later. Her ladyship is not even out of bed yet."

"Stubbins?" Freddie called out.

"Eh?" The old man whirled around, squinting in her direction. "That be you, milady? Beggin' yer pardon. Did not mean to rouse you with this fracas."

"Who is out there?"

"Hanged if I can be sure, milady. Can't get any sense out of the fellow. Says his name is Wilfred Raincliffe."

Frederica paled. "Wilfred! Here?"

"I didn't say any such thing, you old fool," an impatient young voice piped up. "Let me pass."

The next instant, the door was shoved wider, and a short, stout boy of about ten dodged past Stubbins and into the hallway. He appeared a sturdy lad with ruddy cheeks and a shock of sun-streaked blond hair. He was attired in tan trousers and a navy blue short jacket, and his apparel looked dusty from traveling.

Spying Freddie, he made her a magnificent leg which was all that was elegant and polite, but the devil fair danced in his sparkling blue eyes.

"Your servant, milady," he said grandly, sweeping a soft-brimmed cap from his waving locks.

Astonishment warred with amusement in Freddie at such a courtly display from so youthful a gallant.

"Sir," she said biting back a smile, managing to curtsy with perfect gravity. "What means this intrusion? What sort of tale have you been foisting off upon my butler about being Sir Wilfred?"

"Faith, milady," he trilled. "Your pardon, but I told the muttonhead no such thing. I said Lord Wilfred Raincliffe was my father."

"Your f-father?" Freddie faltered.

"Indeed. I am St. John Bartholmy Barry." The sunny features darkened for a moment. "B'God, did you ever hear anything so awful. I prefer to be called Jack."

"How do you do, Master Jack," Freddie said, her mind

whirling. Of course she knew of the existence of Sir Wilfred's children. But during the entire course of her marriage, her stepson had never suffered her to meet any of his offspring. It made no sense that with Leon gone and Sir Wilfred well rid of her, the dour man would now choose to relent.

Thoroughly bewildered, Freddie let her gaze flutter toward the door Stubbins had closed with a disgruntled shake of his head. She feared to see Wilfred come striding in, his long nose twitching as ever with disapproval.

She glanced back to the boy, asking doubtfully, "Your papa brought you here to call upon me?"

" 'Course not, milady. Have you maggots 'neath your cap? I am supposed to be at school."

"Then—then what—"

"I ran away." He gave her an engaging grin. "To you. You are my *grandmama*, are you not?"

Chapter 6

Freddie sank into a chair behind the pine worktable in the kitchen, feeling she had of a sudden aged considerably beyond her twenty-one years. Perhaps the acquisition of a grandson did that to one, she thought with a wry smile. She stared in bemusement at the boy seated opposite her, licking a drip of honey from his fingers with great relish. Master Jack had already devoured half a loaf of bread and now darted eager glances to where Till stirred a pot of porridge over the open range, all the while rocking her baby's cradle with her foot.

Freddie had not so much as touched her own steaming cup of chocolate. She was still reeling with the shock of the child's announcement. Her first impulse was to discredit it entirely. How could a lively imp with such an engaging smile have ever sprung from Sir Wilfred's scrawny loins? And yet when St. John looked up at her, those devils dancing in those vivid blue eyes, there was something sweetly familiar about him that brought a lump to her throat.

No, not so much Sir Wilfred's son, but very much Leon's grandchild.

Freddie swallowed thickly and glanced quickly away to hide her tears. She had a notion that young Master Jack would not take too kindly to being wept over.

But she soon discovered that she had not entirely given the lad his due. Along with that spark of mischief, he appeared to have inherited his grandfather's innate sense of chivalry. Moments later when Dora skittered into the kitchen, having heard of the boy's arrival, she swept him into her arms, tears pouring down her cheeks.

Jack bore it stoically, merely crinkling his snub nose and

murmuring, " 'Faith, lady, have a little mercy on all that remains of a fellow's best shirtfront."

"Oh, Master St. John. I—I never thought to see you again," Dora sobbed. "How—how you have grown."

"I don't see why that should make you cry," Jack said with frank bewilderment. "I could not help it."

This only provoked Dora into a fresh spasm of sentimental tears and several more hugs until Freddie thought it time to rescue the poor lad. Dora was full of questions regarding Jack's sudden appearance on their doorstep, but Freddie refused to allow the child to be badgered until his appetite had been appeased.

Two bowls full of porridge later, he settled back in his chair with a satisfied sigh. Rather hopefully he requested a mug of ale to wash it all down, but settled for a glass of milk.

After a long draft at his glass, he emerged with a milky mustache that was all boy, but the tidy way he applied his napkin would have done justice to the most elegant courtier.

Freddie said gravely, "And now, Master Jack, perhaps you would be so good as to explain what brought you here."

"Why, the stage, madam," he said, the wide blue eyes much too innocent. "Lots of fellows travel that way."

"That is not what I meant, as you perfectly well know, sir. I want to know what induced you to run away, come to London in this fashion."

"Oh, I had been planning this for some time. Of course I would have come much sooner if I had realized what a fetching grandmama I have."

Dora gasped at this piece of audaciousness. Jack regarded Freddie through the thickness of his lashes, shooting her the most heart-melting grin. What a charming devil he was already. Give him ten more years and—Freddie suppressed the amused thought behind a quelling frown.

When she sternly demanded that he stop offering her Spanish coin and proceed with his explanation, Jack became more subdued, though there was no way to entirely douse the twinkle in those blue eyes.

"I had simply had enough of school," he said indignantly. " 'Tis not even a good school like Eton, where a fellow could learn something important like cricket. Nay, 'tis all Latin and Greek, from morn till night, until a man's brain is fit to burst. But then, Cliveden gave me the happy notion of running off to London."

"Cliveden?" Freddie asked.

"Sir Wilfred's oldest son," Dora explained. "He must be nearly sixteen by now."

"Seventeen," Jack added gloomily.

"And the very image of Sir Wilfred."

Freddie grimaced. As far as she was concerned, Dora did not need to describe Sir Wilfred's heir any further. The name Cliveden alone was enough to conjure up a most unwelcome vision.

"If your brother is so much like your papa," Freddie told Jack, "I cannot imagine this Cliveden suggesting you do anything so audacious as run away."

"That slow-top. 'Course he didn't. But he *inspired* me." Jack's broad grin faded. "Clive sometimes visits me at school. Oh, not like the other fellows' big brothers who come to slip one a guinea or take one out for a ride. No, Clive comes only to prose at me or to find out what mischief I have been about so that he can squeak beef to Papa.

"The last time Cliveden came"—Jack paused, a slight quiver in his voice—"it was to bring me black armbands because of—of Grandpapa dying and all."

The child's grief-stricken expression matched the sense of loss Freddie still so often felt. She could not resist reaching across the table to squeeze his hand. Although Jack looked embarrassed, he made no movement to draw away.

Swallowing hard, he continued. "Cliveden was so smug, telling me what had happened after the funeral, how you had just been sent away. It was the shabbiest thing I had ever heard of. I decided that very day to come to London as soon as I could to visit you."

Jack went on to describe how he had attempted to save coach fare from his miserly allowance. After months of failing in that, he had formed a new plan. He had faked illness to be confined to his bed, then slipped away, managing to sell his watch, then catch the stage.

"But however did you find us?" Dora asked, obviously as enthralled at hearing the tale of this daring escapade as Jack was to be telling it.

Jack sat up straighter, swaggering a little. "That was easy. I simply made the rounds of all the fashionable shops where they sell fripperies for ladies until I found one that had heard of the Dowager Viscountess of Raincliffe and was able to give me your address."

71

"How did you persuade the clerk to tell you—" Freddie began, took one look into those outrageous blue eyes, and stopped. "Never mind," she muttered. "Foolish question."

"Oh, how very brave and enterprising you are," Dora cooed.

Recalling what courage and resource it had taken to get herself to London, Freddie was inclined to agree. But she held her tongue. The boy was becoming puffed up enough with Dora's admiration.

"Aye." Jack gloated, looking well pleased with himself. "It was clever of me, wasn't it? Perhaps I shall become a Bow Street Runner when I am grown."

"Yes, er—that is all very well, Master Jack," Freddie interrupted at last. "But one thing still puzzles me. Why did you decide to come to me? You had never even met me."

"No-ooo," he said. "But if Cliveden and my papa said you were such a horrid person, I was certain you had to be wonderful. I thought we could have the most bang-up holiday together. We could go see the Royal Menagerie and Astley's Amphitheatre, have ices at Gunther's and—"

"That would be lovely," Dora cried.

"Dora!" Freddie shot her a repressive frown. Young Jack needed no further encouragement in this folly. Freddie saw that it was her unhappy lot to point out to the boy how reckless his actions had been. When she thought of the things that might have befallen a young boy traveling alone, wandering the shops of London, it was enough to chill her blood.

"Jack," she began gently. "I am quite delighted to make your acquaintance at last, but you must see that you have behaved very badly. Your mama and papa will be quite worried when they find you have gone—"

"No one will even notice," Jack interrupted with a rebellious sniff.

"Of course they will. If you wanted to come to London, the proper thing to have done—" Freddie paused, wincing a little at her own tone. She was beginning to sound like someone's maiden aunt. How dreadful. But she continued doggedly. "The proper thing would have been to ask your papa to bring you to the city."

"He wouldn't. I never have holidays, not like all the other fellows. Biddington's uncle took him to the races at Newmarket once and Stokely went to the seaside. And at least most of the boys get to go home once in a while."

"You—you don't get to go home?" Freddie faltered.

"Papa says it is better for me to stay at school and have extra lessons."

"Oh, you poor boy," Dora cried, close to tears again.

Jack shrugged, his display of defiance doing little to conceal the wistfulness in his eyes. "Oh, I don't mind so much. I am far too old to be missing my mama or anything like that. But every fellow needs a holiday once in a while."

He angled a beguiling glance at Freddie. "We could have such a splendid time together, and you could tell me all about my grandpapa. I don't really remember him, you see. Is it true that he once fought a duel?"

"Yes, I believe that he did—"

"Good. You can tell me all about it while we are off visiting the Tower."

Freddie took one look at his smile, so bright with hope, and struggled to steel herself against it.

"I am afraid that is impossible, Jack. You cannot stay here."

"Oh, Freddie, no," Dora said.

But Freddie ignored this outcry. It was far harder to ignore the way the child's face fell.

"Sir Wilfred . . . your papa would be furious if he ever learned you had come to me," she said. "Goodness knows what he might do. I am sorry, Jack, but you will have to go back to school."

An awful silence descended upon the room after her announcement. Freddie braced herself for a barrage of pleading, perhaps even tears. But although the boy's lip trembled, he rose to his feet with great dignity.

"I understand perfectly, milady," he said in a small voice. "Of course, I have no wish to get you into any trouble. Thank you for a fine breakfast. I'll just be on my way."

Freddie suppressed a sigh, feeling like the greatest beast in nature. But she needed no more trouble laid at her door. She would escort him to the stage herself and see that he got on it. It was all for the best.

The forlorn figure retrieved his hat and shuffled past her, his shoulders bent. "I suppose I shall never see London, now. I shall likely be caned and locked into a closet until I am twenty-one. 'Course you must not worry about me," he proclaimed in accents that would have done credit to Edmund Kean.

These melodramatic pronouncements were enough to send Dora diving for her handkerchief, but Freddie remained proof against them. Yet she could not help but be touched by the way he strove to take his disappointment like a man, the attitude at odds with the still-babelike softness of his cheeks. What proved her final undoing was the very real misery in the boy's eyes as he sketched her the most heroic little bow.

She sighed, saying gruffly, "Don't be a wet goose, Master Jack. Of course, I did not mean for you to leave immediately. You must be tired from your journey. You will need to rest up a bit."

"A bit?" Jack's head came up sharply, as though he could scent her resolve weakening.

"At least for a day?" Dora said pleadingly.

"Or several days perhaps?" Jack cried. "I am *really* tired."

Freddie made one more futile struggle with her common sense. But at his appealing glance, she could do no other than nod. She said, "But then I absolutely will have to find some way to get you safely back to school."

But in the midst of the exuberant hugs she received from both Dora and Jack, Freddie was not certain that anyone was listening to her.

By the time she had dispatched Till to show the boy abovestairs, where he might wash up and rest, Freddie was berating herself for her folly. As if her life were not already on the brink of ruin, what must she do but assume responsibility for a child, a boy, moreover, with an appetite hearty enough to eat the pantry barer than it was now?

And God help her if Sir Wilfred ever found out she had housed his son, even briefly. He might have her arrested for abduction. Well, Freddie thought wearily, Newgate clearly seemed destined to be her fate. That is, if Bedlam did not claim her first.

Dora, as ever oblivious to the prospects of fresh disaster hanging over their heads, followed Freddie cheerfully as she returned to her bedchamber to finish her interrupted toilette.

"Dear little St. John," Dora chattered on. "Only fancy. I had not seen him since he was in leading strings. He has grown up so delightfully. Oh, I do wish that we might keep him."

"He is not a stray puppy, Dora," Freddie said irritably. She wished the woman would leave her alone for a while. She badly needed time to think. But Dora showed no signs of leaving, plunking down to sit upon the edge of Freddie's bed while Freddie removed her lace cap and finished the task of brushing out her hair.

She continued to lecture Dora, thinking it best to disabuse the woman of any foolish notion that Jack might ever become a permanent guest.

"He must be sent back as soon as I can arrange it. Even someone as cold-blooded as Sir Wilfred will be bound to feel anxiety at the disappearance of his son."

"Anxiety indeed!" Dora said hotly. "You heard how he abandoned the poor child at that horrid school. It affected you as well. I could tell."

Freddie paused in the act of dragging her brush through a particularly stubborn knot. She stared into the mirror and saw her own troubled eyes gaze back at her. "I fear I was thinking more of Leon," she said. "What delight he would have taken in young Jack. It—it was my fault Leon never got to know his own grandson. If Wilfred had not detested me so—" Her image shimmered before a gathering of crystal tears. Freddie bowed her head.

"Oh, no, my dear, pray don't." Dora leapt up from the bed, seeking to comfort her with little distracted gestures, patting her awkwardly upon the back. "You are not to be thinking such things. My lord and Cousin Wilfred were at odds long before Lord Raincliffe ever married you. You are not in the least to blame for the fact that horrid Wilfred never brought his children to wait upon their grandfather."

Freddie drew forth a handkerchief and mopped at her eyes, ashamed of her momentary weakness. She said briskly, "In any case, it is far too late now for any regrets. I must think about the present. Much as I loathe the notion, I will have to dispatch a note to Wilfred, assure him the boy is safe."

"Perhaps he will be so angry with Jack, he will say that we may keep him."

Freddie shot Dora a look expressive of what she thought of the absurdity of that notion. "I don't know how I would keep Jack, or anyone else for that matter."

Master Jack's unexpected arrival had been a momentary diversion, distracting Freddie from her more pressing problems—the enormous gaming debt to the general, how she would stave off the creditors who would inevitably come knocking, how she was even going to order up tonight's dinner, especially when she now had a new mouth to feed, a ten-year-old boy with a lusty appetite.

When she expressed this concern aloud to Dora, the woman frowned a moment, then said, "You have been invited to another party tonight. I can get your turban ready, cleaned up as good as new. I only hope Mr. Warfield will not be present this time to spoil things."

"Whether Max is present or not, I fear the turban will no longer answer," Freddie said with a tired smile. "I needs must find a more permanent solution."

"Permanent? What do you mean, Freddie?"

Freddie was not precisely sure herself. "I only know we cannot continue on as we have been. I suppose I am going to have to seek out some sort of a position."

"A position!" Dora was aghast. "Do you mean like—like a cook or a lady's maid."

"Or a governess."

"Perhaps I could get hired on as someone's companion," Dora suggested timidly, "but Freddie, my dear, I fear that no one would ever engage you as a governess."

Gazing at her reflection in the mirror, Freddie was bound to concede that Dora was right. With her golden hair tumbling about her shoulders, she looked absurdly youthful, a chit straight out of the schoolroom.

"I should not care for being a governess, anyway," Freddie conceded with a toss of her head. She reached behind her to squeeze Dora's hand. "Nor will I have you hiring out to be a slave to some horrid old woman. No, that is all too drearily respectable for us. We must think of something more daring."

"The stage?" Dora proposed dubiously.

The idea had a momentary appeal for Freddie, but she shook her head. "Even if I could be engaged as an actress, I don't know if I should make enough money at it to pay the staggering sum I so stupidly lost last night."

She added in disgruntled accents, "Of course, it was nothing compared to what Lady Deidre McCaulay dropped at the table, and she never turned a hair. It must be a fine thing to have a rich duke in one's pocket. Perhaps I should acquire myself a wealthy protector."

Freddie spoke only in jest. She was astonished when Dora paled, apparently taking her quite seriously.

"Oh, no. That would be a little too wicked, Freddie. And after all, you are a grandmother now."

"Only temporarily."

"And besides, your cousin Max would never permit it. He struck me as being a most forceful man. I don't believe he would at all like your becoming someone—someone's protected person."

"It would be none of Max's business," Freddie said.

"I fear he would make it so. Recollect, he did promise to call upon you again soon and he said you were to stay out of mischief until then."

"Max Warfield's promises are not always to be trusted," Freddie said bitterly. "And as for Mr. Warfield *presuming* to give me orders—" She broke off, flushing, an evil demon seeming to stir within her breast. "You truly think Max would mind my seeking a wealthy lover?"

"Most definitely," came Dora's emphatic reply.

Freddie's lips parted into a slow, hard smile. "Well, I find it an excellent notion. I wonder that I did not think of it sooner. Such an arrangement can even be respectable if managed discreetly. Lady Deidre is still received everywhere although it is well known she is the duke's mistress. She rides in an elegant carriage, drips with jewels, and has a wealthy man dancing attendance upon her every whim. What more could one want?"

"I don't know," Dora said, fretting her lower lip. "To be loved—loved *honestly* perhaps? Surely you could always marry again. You have acquired so many admirers. Young Mr. Whitby, Lord Fremont, Mr. Burke . . ."

"Fortune hunters! I doubt any of them would be so enamored of me if they realized how poor I was."

"Your lack of dowry never bothered Cousin Leon."

"Ah, but there will never be another Leon," Freddie said sadly. "No other man could be so generous, so understanding, so—" She swallowed, then firmly shook her head. "No, Dora, I am not at all interested in marrying again."

"But yet you would engage in an illicit liaison with some—some . . . oh, Freddie, my dear. Do but think. Could you truly be happy under such circumstances?"

"Why not? The wickedest people always seem to be the most happy. I have quite decided, Dora. Find me a wealthy rake and our problems will all be solved."

Dora said nothing, but her eyes spoke volumes. Freddie was accustomed to seeing nothing but unqualified admiration on the woman's plain, open features. Dora's troubled gaze unnerved her. Perhaps she had gone too far this time. She was not sure herself what she really meant by all this wild talk. She knew only that she felt more weary and frightened than she ever had in her life, completely at wit's end.

Unable to bear any more of Dora's disapproving expression, Freddie glanced away. "I did warn you not to come with me, didn't I? That I meant to lead a life of mad debauchery? If—if you chose to write Sir Wilfred and ask him if you can return with Jack, I would quite understand."

Freddie waited, for what she scarce knew, perhaps for Dora's usual reassurances. She was stunned when none came. In subdued tones, Dora merely asked to borrow some of her scented paper.

" 'Tis there, beneath the lid of my writing desk," Freddie said.

Frowning, Dora located the vellum and bustled out of the room, leaving Freddie feeling strangely bereft. So she had finally succeeded in disgusting and shocking even her devoted Dora.

She tried to shrug. Perhaps it was right for Dora to go, even for the best. The sort of mad, uncertain life Freddie proposed to lead, *was* leading, had never been right for an elderly spinster. Yet until this moment Freddie had not been aware how much she had come to depend upon Dora's loyalty and devotion.

It seemed to be her fate in life to always lose the people she came to care about. Perhaps the trick was to stop caring. Bleakly, Freddie turned back to the mirror to finish arranging her hair into a smooth topknot of curls. She was usually so clever at such things, but this morning her fingers were quite clumsy.

She had barely finished the task when Dora returned as unceremoniously as she had left. She looked more composed although her brow was furrowed in concentration. She approached Freddie, holding out a sheet of paper that Freddie could see was covered with Dora's neat, slightly crabbed handwriting.

Freddie's heart sank, but she rallied, saying with forced lightness, "Goodness! Finished so soon? I hope you set aside your pride enough to insist that Wilfred send the carriage for you or at least coach fare."

Dora regarded her blankly. "Wilfred? What has this to do with him?"

"I assume that letter is for him. . . ."

"Certainly not. Whatever would I be writing him for? This is our list."

"List? List of what?"

"Why, of all the most eligible rakes in London. If you are determined upon this course, I thought we should go about it properly." Dora beamed proudly. "A capital notion, is it not? I have grown to be so sensible and efficient since we have moved to London."

Freddie stared at her a moment. Then tears misted her eyes. She thoroughly confounded Dora by seizing the older woman in a strong, fierce hug.

Dora gasped in astonishment. "My—my dear, Freddie. What is all this?"

"Nothing." Freddie sniffed. "Only I do not think I fully appreciated you until this moment, my very dear friend."

Dora looked equal parts flustered and pleased, as she always was by any compliment. "Well!" she said. "I did not realize I had been that clever."

"It has nothing to do with—'Tis only that I thought—" Freddie hesitated with a shaky laugh. "Never mind. Sometimes I am a great fool. Come, show me your list."

Dora regarded her anxiously several moments longer as if she feared Freddie might be losing her reason. But pride won out and she presented her paper to Freddie with a grand flourish.

The heading at the top of the page read: A Compilation of the Most Eligible and Wealthy Rakes in London.

The very notion of such a thing tickled Freddie's sense of the ridiculous, but Dora looked as solemn as a member of Parliament presenting a new bill. With a valiant struggle, Freddie composed her features not to laugh.

Peering over Freddie's shoulder, Dora pointed to the first name on the list. "Now, there is Sir Alston Walcott. Very handsome and well set up. But there is a nasty rumor about that he suffers from the pox.

"Next I listed General Fortescue. He is a little—ah, mature, but extremely well heeled. And after all, you are already in debt to him. But he does take snuff, a most disagreeable habit. Then there is Mr. Petries. He prefers dark-haired opera dancers, but you are so lovely, he might make an exception. However, he is reputed to snore loudly in bed."

Freddie no longer felt any desire to laugh. She could only stare at her friend in complete astonishment. "Dora, where in heaven's name did you ever come by such information?"

"Oh, from the housekeeper two doors down, the seamstress who does your clothes, the milliner who sold you that darling hat." Dora preened herself a little. "If I ever possessed any talent, it is for gleaning gossip. And it is all so much more interesting here in London than it ever was buried in Dunhaven."

Freddie could only shake her head. She was constantly underestimating Miss Dora Applegate. She tried to concentrate on the names that Dora continued to rattle off, the attributes and failings of the various gentlemen.

But to her dismay, she experienced a strange and uncomfortable fluttering in the pit of her stomach. It had been one thing to indulge in such bold talk of finding herself a wealthy rake. Dora's earnest concentration and her list were all making it seem somehow nerve-rackingly real.

Freddie was not quite so naive that she did not realize there was a little more to becoming a man's mistress than accepting his admiration and expensive presents. Rakehells were noted for expecting something more in return than a lady's smile.

Leon had never been able to teach her anything of a man's physical needs, but Freddie bore a vague and discomfiting notion of what would be required of her. She could already feel a knot of tension forming in her chest, but resolutely she sought to ignore it.

She was familiar, at least by sight, with most of the gentlemen Dora listed. But the thought of any of these men caressing her in intimate fashion left her feeling cold, her palms clammy.

Paying no heed to Dora's reading or comments, Freddie scanned ahead, hoping to find the mention of at least one whose touch she might be able to tolerate. She neared the bottom of the list when she drew up short.

"Dora! You have my cousin's name listed!"

"What? Oh, you mean Mr. Warfield? Well, you did say he was only a very distant relative. And he is perhaps the most eligible rake in all of London."

"Is he indeed?" Freddie asked, even the sight of Max's name enough to bring heat flaring into her cheeks, whether through anger or some other reason, she could not be sure.

"Oh, yes! They are laying bets at White's this very minute as to who his next mistress will be."

Freddie crinkled her nose in disgust. "How vulgar and crude men can be."

"Distressingly so. I did hesitate to list Mr. Warfield. The competition for his favor seems to be great. Although he did show much interest in you last night, it seemed so—so avuncular."

Freddie nearly choked. "He said I had grown to be beautiful. He—" But she broke off in mortification, remembering that Max had also said she still reminded him of a little girl.

"Truly," Dora said. "I can see I have distressed you. I don't know what I was thinking of. Indeed, I am certain he would be as horrified at the notion as you."

"Horrified?" Freddie repeated. "Yes, I suppose Max would be." She thought of Max's arrogance, how after years of neglect he had barged back into her life, lectured her as though she were still a child, the bored way he had declared it his duty to make "arrangements" for her. If the man was so determined to come to her aid, perhaps it was time to show him she had a few notions of her own, show him beyond all doubt what sort of woman she had grown to be and pay off an old score at the same time. By the time she had done with Mr. Max Warfield, she doubted he would ever seek to interfere with her again.

Despite the fire that now seemed to be racing through Freddie's veins as well as flooding her cheeks, a taut smile curved her lips.

Dora greeted Freddie's long silence with increasing nervousness. "Perhaps I had just better mark Mr. Warfield off the list." Dora extended her hand to take the paper, but Freddie held it out of her reach.

"Don't be so hasty, Dora," Freddie purred. "I think you may have had an excellent idea. In fact, if Max is so sought after, I should not leave the matter to chance. I should call on him as soon as possible."

Dora made a faint sound of protest, but as usual Frederica paid her no heed. Her dear friend was such a headstrong young woman, but for once Dora thought she had been remarkably clever. Freddie's plan of seeking a wealthy lover had appalled Dora, but she knew how Freddie was once she got an idea into her head.

That is why the list had seemed an inspired notion, rattling off the names of all those gentlemen, but pointing out their most disagreeable features. Freddie would be bound to be discouraged from pursuing this any further.

If only she had not listed Mr. Warfield's name. But who would have guessed that Freddie would have reacted so? Dora had been certain that she had a most pointed dislike of the man.

Now Dora could only watch Freddie's actions with mounting horror, the substitution of a girl's demure muslin for a dress with a scandalously lower neckline, the dabbing of perfume between her breasts, the application of a tiny hint of rouge to Freddie's already flaming cheeks.

Despite these alarming preparations, Dora could not help but note that Freddie did not look in the least like a young woman about to go seeking a lover. No, there was a militant sparkle to her eyes, a hard set to her chin. She looked more like a duelist about to blast some poor fellow right between the eyes.

"Oh, dear. Oh, dear," Dora murmured. But short of locking Freddie in her room, she did not know what else to do. She could only wring her hands and set up a fervent prayer that when Freddie called, Mr. Max Warfield would not be at home.

Chapter 7

The morning had begun badly for Max. He had overslept, an unusual occurrence for one accustomed to waking precisely at seven-ten, no matter how late he had been abroad the night before. Rising past noon, destroying his routine, was always a guarantee that the rest of the day would proceed on disastrous lines.

And Max noted grimly that this particular day did not seem likely to prove an exception to that rule. He could not locate his favorite dressing gown, he stubbed his toe against the doorjamb leading into his dressing room, there was no fresh soap, and his French valet was nowhere to be found.

Max stripped off his nightshirt and stumbled over to the washstand. Georges had at least fetched up the bathing water, though by now it was tepid. Squinting at the flood of sunlight pouring through the latticed windows, Max scraped up what was left of the soap and proceeded to lather his arms and neck. He winced as he did so. Every muscle in his body was stiff and aching, a headache throbbing behind his temples.

He felt just like—like— His mouth quirked into a sardonic grimace. He felt just like a man who had been bashed over the head last night and knocked down in a gutter. Freddie's companion, friend, *dragon*, whatever she was, Miss Dora Applegate possessed quite a hefty right arm.

Max closed his eyes, longing for nothing more than to drag his battered frame back into bed. But it was already approaching the hour of one, and he recollected the promise he had made to Sir Pollack Sprague to ride out with him to see about the purchase of that horse. Max did not know what misplaced burst of good fellowship had induced him to make such a pledge. Sir Pollack was a most congenial fellow, but Max well knew he was not in the mood to tolerate that much cheerfulness.

And after finishing with Sir Pollack, Max was going to have to call upon his sister. That in itself was enough to dampen the prospect of any day. But he was placed in the awkward position of admitting that Caroline had been right. Something did need to be done about Freddie. Max hoped that Caroline would have enough sense not to look too smug over his capitulation, but he doubted it.

She would not gloat for long when Max informed her that he had decided Freddie was about to become her houseguest. Caroline would be less than pleased with his decision, but Max would take great pleasure in reminding her that his interference in this matter had been *her* idea.

With a low growl, Max groped for the towel to dry himself. He needed to make arrangements to have Freddie moved to Caroline's as soon as possible. A rather daunting task, he was forced to admit, because he had taken enough of Freddie's measure last night to know that she would not tamely acquiesce.

She had as good as told him to get out and not come back, to mind his own business. That was something Max was normally very good at, and he would have been happy to oblige except—

Except he could not forget how she had looked when she had squared off with him, the fragility of her features at odds with the mulish set of her chin, that spark of desperation in her blue eyes, as volatile as a fuse burning too near its end. God knows when she "went off" what mischief she might get into next time.

And what damned contradictory feelings the girl aroused in him. He had been irritated by her antics, gaming and flirting with the likes of General Sir Mordant Fortescue. And yet when he thought of her circumstances, cast off penniless by her late husband's family, living in that practically empty house with only a dithery spinster for company, forced to steal her own supper . . . his heart melted. Poor Freddie, once more his abandoned little orphan girl. He wanted to scoop her up in his arms and cradle her against him. He wanted to seize her fiercely and shake some sense into her.

Max felt a surge of anger at this Sir Wilfred Barry whom he had never met, anger at Freddie for being too damn proud to let anyone know how badly off she had been left. He was also angry at his sisters Caroline and Elizabeth, at his cousin Jameson, all of them so concerned about the family reputation, none of them having the wit to perceive Freddie's plight.

And, yes, he was angry with Max Warfield, callous bastard that he was for not inquiring after Freddie sooner, perhaps years and years sooner. Guilt was not an emotion he was comfortable with. Scowling, he raged over to his wardrobe, muttering under his breath because he still could not find his favorite dressing gown.

He was obliged to shrug into one of dark blue wool, the fabric further irritating him by abrading his skin. He cursed again when he discovered that Georges had not yet appeared with hot water for shaving.

"Rise late one morning," he muttered savagely, "and the entire damn household decides to take a holiday."

Georges knew Max did not like to have to speak to anyone before breakfast, let alone bellow for his valet. Max strode impatiently from the dressing room back into his bedchamber, only pausing in front of the glass mounted upon the wall. He wondered if he looked as hellacious as he felt.

He did. A night's growth of beard grizzled his jaw, dark circles cast shadows under his eyes, and the knot on his temple had formed into a bruise the most alarming hue of purple. Recoiling in disgust from his own reflection, Max did not glance up when he heard the door glide open softly.

"Bloody well about time, Georges," Max growled.

His valet had enough sense not to reply. As he heard Georges creep farther into the room, Max snatched up a comb and dragged it through his disheveled black hair. He experimented, attempting to plaster the strands across his temple, covering up the bruise.

"Dreadful," a voice purred, startling Max into dropping the comb. Those sultry tones definitely did not belong to Georges. "Leave it alone. I like the bruise. It makes you look like a prizefighter."

"What the deuce!" Max whipped around, staring at the apparition leaning up against the frame of his four-poster—a golden-haired angel gowned in white, a crimson shawl draped around her shoulders. Her blue eyes glinted at him through the thickness of downswept lashes in a manner calculated to fire his blood.

He caught his breath, still unable to credit his eyes, wondering exactly how hard he had been hit over the head last night.

As he stood gaping, the angel eased her shawl away, letting it drop to the floor, and Max felt an involuntary shudder rack through him.

No. Certainly no angel. No respectable cherub ever had a robe that clung like that sheer muslin over the swell of delectable curves. But he was obliged to admit, momentarily distracted by the low neck of the gown, the view was heavenly.

Then he gave himself a brisk shake, bringing his wayward masculine senses to order with a snap. "F-Freddie," he croaked. "What—what the—"

"Hullo, Max." She offered him a crooked smile, her offhand words overbright and a shade defiant.

"What the devil are you doing here!"

His explosive greeting did not appear to disconcert her. If she was at all nervous, the only sign of it was the way she played with one lock of hair, twisting it until it became a curl, lying tantalizingly along the ivory column of her neck.

"You said last night you were coming to call upon me. I thought I would save you the trouble."

"Have you lost your mind?" Max asked.

"I don't think so. How about you?" Freddie's head tilted, regarding him with unabashed curiosity.

Max suddenly recalled that he was clad in nothing but his dressing gown. It was strange. He could have paraded in the buff before the likes of a Lavinia Channing without a blush. But Freddie's innocent regard afflicted him with a rare attack of modesty.

He caught himself fumbling with the belt, drawing the folds of the robe tighter as he blustered, "You—you little idiot. Have you no notion of propriety? You cannot come calling upon an unmarried man in this fashion."

"Oh?" Freddie dimpled into a mischievous smile. "Would it be all right if you were married, then?"

Max glared at her. "How did you get past Crispin?"

"Your butler? I merely told him I was your—um—very dear cousin and that you were expecting me. I could find my own way up."

"That useless popinjay." Max swore under his breath. "He'd make a better man milliner or dancing master than he does a butler."

"I thought he was very sweet."

"Then you are a remarkably poor judge of character as well as everything else. I cannot believe you were stupid enough to

86

come here. Calling upon a single gentleman alone would be bad enough, but—"

"I am not alone," Freddie interrupted. "Dora is with me."

"The Valkyrie? Wonderful! That is all I need. I'd best go don my armor at once."

"The armor won't be necessary, but some breeches perhaps."

Freddie had the effrontery to laugh when Max felt the red creep into his cheeks. She said, "You need not worry about Dora, in any event. Mr. Crispin is serving her tea belowstairs."

"Which is where you should be." Max strode purposefully forward, but Freddie evaded his grasp for her arm. To his complete horror, she flopped back on his unmade bed, stretching out upon the sheets with a languid sigh.

"Why are you making such a fuss, Max? We are cousins, after all. I remember once after one of our outings, you even stayed late enough to tuck me in at night. You tickled me so unmercifully that I fell off the bed and I was not the least bit sleepy. Aunt Jameson was furious."

"You are now too old for tickling games, so I would appreciate it if you would get off my bed and—" Max pulled up short, frowning. "This is the second time you have let something like that slip. Are you still going to insist you don't remember me?"

Freddie's teasing smile faded, her lashes fluttering down to conceal the expression in her eyes. "Ah, well, I suppose memories have a habit of coming back to one like—like bad dreams."

Max stared at her hard. He had a strong suspicion that nothing had come back to Freddie, that she had remembered him quite well all along. So why had she pretended otherwise? And what was all this nonsense this morning? After their parting last night, he had half expected he would have to go in search of her. Instead of indicating any desire to see him again, she had fairly told him to go to the devil.

What, then, had induced her to turn up in this startling manner? Far from darting scorn and fury, she was almost playful. She was up to some mischief, that was certain, but what it might be, he could not think.

That might be because of her perfume. As he leaned over the bed, he caught a whiff of it, the sweet odor of violets seeming to curl around his brain, threatening to steal his reason.

He gazed down at her, her golden hair tumbled against his pillow. Her breasts strained against the fabric of her dress, so damned thin she might well be in her nightgown. Sprawled upon his bed, a faint flush colored her cheeks, her eyes as blue as a crystal clear sea. A man could get lost in their depths, Max thought. She was both innocent and seductress, a lethal combination if ever there was one.

He felt his throat go suddenly dry, the stirrings she roused in him neither cousinly nor gentlemanly. But inevitable. Damnation. Whatever devilment she contemplated, she should have had more sense. She had been married. She ought to know what behavior such as this could do to a man. But then, Freddie did not think of him that way. He was just Cousin Max, one of her old, doddering relatives. And he needed to get her the deuce out of there before he was tempted to show her otherwise.

Reaching down, he seized her by both wrists and hauled her roughly to her feet. "All right, I have had enough of this nonsense, Freddie. Tell me what you are really doing here, and I warn you not to trifle. I am in a very dangerous mood."

"So am I." Her eyes glinted up at him, hard and bright as sapphires.

Max discovered that in dragging her off the bed, he had pulled her closer than he had intended. The soft, appealing curve of her mouth was barely inches away. He forced his gaze from the tempting outline of her moist lips, his eyes drifting lower—a mistake. He found himself looking down the front of her bodice, contemplating the satiny swell of her breasts. A shaft of fire spread through him, and he released her as though he had been scorched.

Snatching up her shawl, he attempted in clumsy fashion to arrange it back around her shoulders. She made no effort to help.

"You must be mad," he groused. "Running around dressed in a damned bed sheet."

"White muslin is all the rage," she said sweetly. "Very proper for morning wear."

It might have been if she had worn some lace to fill in the bodice, and if she had not, as Max strongly suspected, dampened her petticoats to make them cling with a shocking transparency.

He started to express further disapproval of her apparel

when he was interrupted by a soft footfall outside the door, a brief tap at the wood. It was most definitely Georges this time.

Cursing, Max wheeled to the door to intercept the man.

"Good morning, m'sieur," Georges piped cheerfully. Attempting to step across the threshold, carrying a pitcher of hot water and a towel, he looked puzzled to find Max barring his path. "*Mille pardons* for my tardiness. I—"

"Never mind. I'll take that." Max grabbed both the pitcher and the towel from him. "I can shave myself this morning."

The little Frenchman actually paled at the prospect. "But, m'sieur—"

"Do you think I cannot?" Max asked fiercely.

"No, m'sieur! Er—ah, well, perhaps. Er—yes."

The valet was still babbling as Max slammed the door in his face. Max cringed at his own guilty behavior, slinking around as though something were going on in this bedchamber, as though there were something to hide. It was ridiculous in any case. Georges might not have been aware of Freddie's presence, but he soon would be. Some of the other servants, Crispin at least, would know she had come upstairs.

Max's idea had been to preserve her reputation, not to help destroy it. He turned angrily, then emitted a groan. Freddie had used the interval to discard the shawl again and her sandals as well.

She had curled up on an upholstered armchair near the fireplace, her legs tucked beneath her, her bare toes peeking out from the hem of her dress in a way that was both childlike and incredibly alluring.

"Get out of here," he roared. "Downstairs now! Until I am finished dressing."

Any of his servants would have flown to obey when he spoke in that tone. Freddie merely yawned, stretching her arms with the lazy contentment of a drowsy kitten.

"I thought I could stay and help you shave."

"I wouldn't trust you anywhere near me with a razor," he said. Stalking to the dresser, he slapped the pitcher down with such force, some of the hot liquid spattered up at him. Muttering curses, he dabbed at himself with the towel.

She straightened as though preparing to rush to him. "Oh, did you hurt yourself?"

"No! You—you just stay where you are."

She subsided back into the chair with a tiny shrug. "You

89

seem very edgy, Max. One would think you were not accustomed to having women around."

"Women, yes. You, no!" He flung down the towel, then swiveled to face her, fists propped against his hips. "Of course, I have an idea what this is all about."

Her brows rose a fraction. "Do you indeed?"

"Yes. I annoyed you last night by pointing out some home truths, that the notion you could take care of yourself was madness and that I intended to put a stop to your recklessness. I believe this absurd visit is simply a way of getting some of your own back, of tormenting me. But you should take care, Freddie. Such amusements have a way of backfiring."

A flash of anger appeared in her eyes, a sudden rise in color in her cheeks. Max figured his accusation must have hit somewhere near the mark. But she kept her smile fixed firmly in place.

"Why, how astute you are, Max. I will admit you did . . . irritate me a trifle. But I have been thinking—"

"God save us all!"

She ignored his interjection. "You were right. I cannot continue on as I have been. But the suggestion you put forward, that I go live with your sister, did not please me. I have come up with a plan of my own."

He flung up his hands in exasperation, then drew up a wingback chair and plunked himself down opposite her. "Well," he said impatiently. "Let's hear it. What is it?"

She did not answer immediately, but dropped her gaze as though suddenly transfixed by the pattern on the carpet. When she finally raised her eyes, she drew in a deep breath, saying almost diffidently, "I heard they are laying bets at White's as to who your next mistress will be. That Lady Channing is the odds-on favorite. Is that true?"

For a moment, Max was utterly confounded by this abrupt change of subject. He scowled. "That's none of your affair. Respectable women are not even supposed to know about such things."

Freddie rolled her eyes and sighed. "Men are so naive. And I am not in the least respectable."

"So it is true?" she persisted. "Are you looking for a mistress? Would you be willing to consider someone else besides Lady Channing?"

"I am hardly planning on taking applications for the position, but—" He broke off, annoyed. "This is a damned outrageous conversation, and I don't see what this has to do with you. I thought we were discussing your future."

"So we are. I was wondering if you might be interested in—" She paused, fretting her lower lip.

"Interested in what?"

"Interested in having me as your mistress," she blurted out.

Max was glad he was sitting down. Feeling like he had just taken an unexpected blow to the gut, he roared out, "You! My mistress! I'd sooner stare down the mouth of a loaded cannon. Where did you get such a bacon-brained notion?"

She flinched a little at his harsh words, but lifted her chin stubbornly. "It is obvious I have no talent for cards and you seem to think I need a protector."

"I didn't mean that sort of protection. Good God, when I offered to help you out of your difficulties, you cannot think that I intended . . . that you—"

"Why not?" she said softly. She shoved to her feet and glided toward him, her step a little unsteady but determined. Before he could divine her intent, she eased herself onto his knee, draping her arms around his neck.

"Don't you find me at all attractive?" she whispered.

Attractive? A bolt of lightning seemed to have shot through him at the close contact of her body against his. He could feel the warmth of her thighs pressing upon his lap, even through the layers of muslin and wool. He took a shuddering breath. If she knew anything at all about men, she would soon have no doubt about the level of his attraction to her. It was rising beneath his robe this very minute.

Squirming, he sought to pry her arms away. "Behave yourself, Freddie. Before I put you over my knee and give you a sound spanking."

"I am not a little girl anymore," she said huskily.

"No, but you are still very much a little fool."

"Is this so foolish?" she asked, snuggling closer. His efforts to thrust her away were nonavailing. But he was no longer trying very hard. Her head bent lower, her golden hair cascading over him, brushing against his cheek as she dared to steal a kiss from the taut line of his mouth. It was barely a whisper, shy and tremulous enough to break what remained of Max's self-control.

Instead of pushing her away, he crushed her hard against him, taking possession of her lips with a ruthless fervor. He caught one hand in the silky tangle of curls at the nape of her neck. Holding her captive, his mouth greedily devoured hers. Never had he felt a rush of desire, so hot, so intense, so sweet. Never had a kiss left him so profoundly shaken, hungering for more.

It was Freddie who brought him to his senses. He became aware of her hands pressed against his chest, fluttering like some delicate moth struggling to be free. He released her enough that she drew back her head with a tiny gasp. Through the mist of his own passion, he saw her eyes, wide, innocent, stunned. For all her bravado, she was nothing but a little girl playing with fire. And he had come damned close to accommodating her.

A ripple of disgust for himself tore through Max. Angry, ashamed, he thrust her away, standing up so abruptly, she tumbled to the carpet. He stepped past her, not trusting himself to touch her again.

He stalked to lean against the dresser, gulping in cleansing breaths, seeking to regain his composure, his mind reeling. What the blazes had happened to him? He had nearly allowed himself to be seduced by his cousin. By his poor, orphaned, *helpless* little cousin, he thought mockingly.

When he turned back, Freddie was getting shakily to her feet. She was pale, two spots of color branding her cheeks, but she looked a damn sight more composed than he felt at the moment. She smoothed out her skirts, saying with forced cheerfulness, "Well! Does—does this mean you found me satisfactory or not?"

"Satisfactory?" Max nearly choked, giving his anger free rein. It was far safer channeling the fire that yet coursed through his veins into fury. "Damn it, Freddie! Stop talking that way, do you hear? You provoke me beyond endurance. What sort of man do you think I am that I would take advantage of my own cousin?"

She raised her hand proudly. "No one takes advantage of me. If you insist upon thrusting your help on me whether I want it or not, I simply thought to make it a more fair arrangement for both of us."

"By offering yourself to me like some Haymarket doxy? I wasn't looking for that sort of repayment, Frederica."

She flinched, but shot back, "I don't accept charity anymore, Max."

"It wasn't that either, blast you. I insisted upon helping you because . . . because . . ." Max rubbed his throat, near strangling on the admission, the sort of words he ever found hardest to say. "Because I care about you, damn it."

A glitter of angry tears sparkled in Freddie's eyes. "Yes, I recall you once saying something along those lines to me. What was it now?"

"I love you, Freddie," she mimicked. *"Come in out of the rain."* She swallowed hard. "I can get myself in out of the storm these days, thank you very much, Mr. Max Named-After-Nobody-in-Particular."

Her words stunned him. He was not surprised so much that she remembered. He had already suspected that. But the depth of bitter unhappiness that obviously accompanied her memories of him disturbed him greatly.

Ducking her head, she tried to head for the door, but he barred her path, catching hold of her shoulders. "Freddie, I—I did mean those words when I said them."

"Yes." She sniffed, the tears coming freely. She averted her head, trying not to let him see. "Then you just went away and never came back."

He frowned. "There were . . . circumstances beyond my control."

His excuse sounded lame and far too vague. Her accusing glance told him that she thought so, too. But even after all this time, Max was astonished to find the memory of his youthful folly, his subsequent exile, raw and painful, difficult to share. As he struggled for some way to explain this to her, she waved him aside.

"Never mind, Max. The past is no longer important to me. I do not know why I bothered to mention it. And as to you refusing my offer . . ." She shrugged. "You are not the only rake in London."

Despite her tears, there was a hard, determined light in her eyes that made him uneasy. "And just what the devil is that supposed to mean?"

"Only that Dora made me up a whole list of wealthy gentlemen who might be interested in acquiring a mistress. General Fortescue, for instance."

"Fortescue!" Max hissed. "If you set one foot near that old rip again, I'll—"

He never had the opportunity to finish his threat. He and Freddie were both startled by a frantic rapping at the bedroom door.

Max swore and Freddie turned away, mopping hastily at her

93

damp eyes. As the hammering continued without ceasing, Max strode toward the door and flung it open, preparing to tell Georges or whoever to go to the deuce.

He was nearly knocked over as Miss Dora Applegate barreled into the room. "G-good morning, Mr. Warfield," she stammered, absurdly polite under the circumstances. Her greeting broke off in a gasp as she fully took in Max clad only in his robe. In her shock, she left the bedchamber door standing open behind her.

Wrenching her attention to Freddie, Dora cried, "Oh, my dear. Calamity! We must get out of here. One of Mr. Warfield's friends has come calling. Mr. Crispin is trying to get rid of him, but he is being quite insistent."

"Sir Pollack." Max groaned. "Come about the horse. What damnable timing."

Dora clutched at Freddie's sleeve. "We must not be seen here. Think of your reputation, my dear."

Freddie gave a shrug, at once listless and defiant.

"What of it?"

Dora eyed her with reproach. "You said that even wicked women must be discreet."

"Yes, it would be better for both of you—" Max began. But he never finished, for Sir Pollack's cheerful voice could be heard, carrying up the stairs. " . . . cannot believe the lazy fellow is still abed. 'Tis most unlike Max. Don't worry, Crispin. I am not afraid to beard the lion in his den. I'll roust your master out myself."

Thunderation, Max thought, ready to tear out his own hair. The fellow was already on his way up. Thinking quickly, Max rapped out a command to Freddie and her companion, "Both of you just stay here. I will intercept Sir Pollack and get rid of him."

"Oh, that won't be necessary," Freddie said. "I have met Sir Pollack before. I look forward to renewing my acquaintance with the gentleman."

She started toward the bedchamber door, her hurt and anger not quite masked by her tight-lipped smile. She looked reckless enough to do or say anything that would whistle her own reputation down the wind.

Max saw he had no time to argue with her. He did not think, did not hesitate, but overtook her in several quick strides. Before she could even cry out, he seized her around the waist.

94

Hustling her toward the dressing room, he shoved her through the door and turned the key in the lock.

The doorknob rattled with the force of Freddie's fury and indignation. "Damn you, Max. Open this door at once, do you hear?"

"*Damn you,* Freddie. Be quiet, or I'll come in there and box your ears."

"Ohhh, yes, Freddie," Dora cried. "Do be still. Sir Pollack is almost here. We've got to hide."

Max stiffened. He had been so concerned about dealing with Freddie, he had forgotten her companion. He saw that Miss Applegate was waxing frantic to the point of hysteria. She glanced wildly around for another place of concealment, then made a dive for Max's bedstead, struggling to conceal her large frame behind the bed curtains.

"Miss Applegate!" Max said sternly. "Don't be absurd. I will unlock the door and you must go into the other room with Freddie. Miss Applegate?"

But he might as well have been talking to himself. Dora had a death grip on the curtains and would not come out. Max felt himself rapidly losing control of the situation, a sensation he hated. At least, thank God, he could be grateful for one thing. Freddie had finally shown the good sense to lapse into silence.

Max moved to haul Dora out by force and send her into the dressing room, when he froze at the sound of his friend's cheery voice.

"Max?"

Sir Pollack Sprague hesitated on the threshold, peering through the open door, a broad grin spreading over his good-humored countenance. There was nothing for Max to do but position himself in front of the bed with assumed casualness, trying not to look like a schoolboy who had been caught kissing the parlor maid.

"I trust I am not intruding?" Sir Pollack said.

"Oh, no," Max muttered. "The amount of traffic coming through here, my bedchamber might well be a turnpike. I am thinking of charging tolls."

Sprague laughed, bringing up a quizzing glass to inspect Max's attire. "Stap me, but it is true. Crack-of-dawn Warfield still in his dressing gown and 'tis near mid-afternoon."

Max rubbed his unshaven jaw, self-conscious. "You will have to excuse me. I had rather a bad night. If you would wait below, I—"

But Sir Pollack only stepped farther into the room. "I should say you did have quite a time from that knot on your head. You left the Channings early enough. It must have been one devil of party you went on to. And you didn't take me!"

Max managed a stiff smile for his friend's raillery. He was trying to act natural, but it was difficult since he had just realized the edge of Dora's petticoats and the tips of her serviceable countrystyle boots were showing beneath the bed curtain.

"You can be thankful you were not with me," Max said, moving to take Sir Pollack's arm and guide him firmly back into the hall. "I will tell you all about it sometime. I am sorry I forgot our appointment. I should have sent word, but I must further crave your pardon and beg off. Something has come up."

"Or down, as the case may be." Sir Pollack emitted a soft whistle. Max did not know what Sprague meant until he bent to retrieve something from the floor. Freddie's shawl, the telltale scent of her perfume lingering in its folds. Sir Pollack gave an appreciative sniff.

"Beg pardon, old man," he said jovially. "It appears I truly have interrupted something."

"Nothing at all," Max growled. "That belongs to—to my sister. She left it the last time she was here."

Unfortunately at that moment, a loud sneeze issued from the bedstead. Sir Pollack's gaze traveled to where he could no longer miss the quivering bulge behind the curtain.

He smirked. "Your sister appears to have caught a chill."

"A highly contagious one." Max tried again to steer his friend from the room, but Sir Pollack shook him off playfully. He regarded Max with a mock wounded expression.

"Max, you cannot mean to be so uncivil. Would you send me away without presenting me to your—er—sister?"

Max gave him a killing glare, but Sprague only grinned.

"After all, I wagered a handsome sum myself upon whom your next light o' love would be. I laid my blunt that you would reconcile with Mademoiselle Vivani. You have to tell me. I know I must be right. There could not be another female so tall in all of London."

"You should not bet on that. Now, come along, Sprague."

To Max's dismay, Sir Pollack skittered over to the bed, his eyes full of mischief. "Mademoiselle," he called. "Remember me? Sir Pollack Sprague. We met at a supper one evening after the opera." He reached out to tweak at the curtain. "Don't think me rude, but if I could have but one glimpse of your enchanting face to confirm . . .

"Sprague!" Max snarled out a warning, but it was too late.

Sir Pollack had already peeked behind the curtain. Dora's pale face emerged, the feather on her drab bonnet bent down so that it tickled her nose, causing her to sneeze again.

Sir Pollack's eyes popped. He glanced toward Max with an expression of ludicrous dismay, then back to Dora, who was earnestly puffing at the feather, trying to get it off her face.

Red-faced Sir Pollack moved away, nearly stumbling over his own feet. "I—I beg your pardon, madam. Uh, Max, I thought—this is . . . I didn't—Perhaps I had—had best call again at a more opportune time."

"Perhaps you had."

"Right." Pollack nodded, half sketched Dora an awkward bow, then bolted from the room.

"Oh! Oh, dear," Dora moaned, sagging down on the edge of the bed.

"That sums up the situation quite aptly," Max said dryly.

She pressed her hands to her face. "What that man must have thought! I really am a wicked woman now." She did not look distressed so much as awestricken. "Whatever has this done to my reputation?"

"I don't know. But I can imagine quite clearly what it has done to mine." Max grimaced. He was fond of farce. But he preferred it confined to Drury Lane, not running rampant through his bedchamber.

"I am sorry, Miss Applegate." He apologized gruffly. "I will find Sir Pollack and explain."

"Truly. What are you going to tell him?" Dora asked with genuine interest.

Max hadn't the damnedest notion. "I will think of something. Meantime, you'd best collect Freddie. Take her home and keep her there until I straighten out this damnable coil."

Dora nodded. Still flustered from her encounter with Sir Pollack, Max was not sure she was even attending him. He moved to fetch Freddie himself, unlocking the dressing room door. Freddie was being amazingly quiet, but she still might be furious enough to fly at him like a mad cat. Cautiously, Max thrust his head into the room and called her name.

There was no response, the room silent and undisturbed, except for his wardrobe door propped open, his clothes tumbled out from his previous search for his dressing gown.

97

Max's eyes narrowed. He did not recall having left that great of a mess. It had to have been Freddie. Now what mischief had she been about and, more to the point, where the deuce could she have gone?

The only other way out was— Max felt a chill pass through him, his gaze focusing on the window. One of them stood open, a makeshift rope of his own white shirts knotted together, trailing over the sill.

No, impossible. This was the second story. Freddie wouldn't. She couldn't have.

Max hastened over to the window, his heart pumping as he looked out and down. He expected he scarce knew what, Freddie clinging perilously to the side of the house or worse yet, her slender frame broken on the garden walk below. But nothing stirred beneath him except for Thornton, the gardener, hunched over to weed the flower beds.

Max started to call out to him, but thought better of it. The old man was half deaf. Besides, when Thornton was absorbed with his precious roses, the sky could be raining golden-haired young women and the gardener would not notice a thing.

Freddie had obviously made good her escape. Drawing up the precarious rope which had aided her flight, Max could only be grateful he had spared no expense upon his shirts, that the linen had been sturdy enough to withstand bearing Freddie's weight.

The little idiot, Max thought savagely. She could have snapped her neck. However had she contrived to knot the shirts so tightly together? As if that were of any importance.

All that mattered was that Freddie was gone, leaving so much between them unsettled. Feeling frustrated and strangely bereft, Max yanked the window closed, silently cursing the day he had ever taught that girl to climb.

Chapter 8

Whatever dignity was left to Freddie after her encounter with Max she was obliged to part with upon the following day. It was hard to be dignified struggling with someone over the possession of a ham.

Bracing herself upon the threshold of her kitchen door, Freddie barred entrance to the butcher's apprentice, who balanced the large slab of meat in his muscular arms.

"I told you," Freddie snapped for the third time. "You have the wrong house."

The burly youth only grinned at her, handsome in his way despite the shaggy lengths of brown hair tumbling across his eyes. His gaze was bold, the apron knotted around Freddie's waist obviously deceiving him as to her position in the household.

"And I told you, sweeting," he said. "Been born and raised in London. Bill Tolliver never mistakes an address. Now, why don't you scoot your pretty self upstairs and ask your mistress? I'll wager she knows how this order came about."

"I am the mistress of this house," Freddie said icily. "And I assure you I know nothing whatsoever of any ham, nor can I—er—nor do I intend to pay for it."

The lad assumed a somewhat more respectful stance. "Beg pardon ma'am. But this here ham is a gift, courtesy of one o' your gentleman admirers."

"A gift? From whom?" Freddie demanded, although she had a sinking feeling she already knew the answer.

"A Mr. Maxmillian Warfield." The young man retained enough impudence to wink at her. "A most practical sort of gent. A good slab of bacon's better than posies, eh?"

Freddie felt her cheeks flame. She bit back the urge to inform the youth that Max Warfield was no "gent," and as for the rest, she very much doubted Max had any admiration left for her after yesterday's scene in the bedchamber.

She wanted to step back and slam the door in the lad's smirking face, but that was a little difficult considering that the rest of her household had already gathered in the kitchen. Dora, Till, balancing the baby on her hip, even the squinting Stubbins, all regarded the ham with varying degrees of wistfulness.

The matter, however, was decided when Master Jack whooped into the kitchen, exclaiming, "Ham! Stap me, of all things my favorite!"

Freddie thought she had no pride left, but she felt a large lump of it gather in her throat. Nonetheless, she swallowed and stepped aside, grudgingly allowing Bill Tolliver to enter.

The butcher's apprentice was hard followed by a poulter bearing a large dressed goose and, after him, the greengrocer. All courtesy of Mr. Maxmillian Warfield. Freddie found herself thrust aside in the hubbub of excitement these deliveries occasioned.

While Tolliver flirted with Till and admired the baby, Jack helped to cart in the crates of fresh fruits and vegetables with a deal of boyish enthusiasm, already crunching down upon an apple.

It astonished Freddie how quickly the boy had fit himself into their rather topsy-turvy household, cheerfully turning his hand to tasks that most noblemen's sons would have considered far beneath them. But Jack possessed a zest for any activity, a lively curiosity that led him to try anything from helping Stubbins sweep the front stoop to aiding Till in the kitchen, rattling the copper pans until they were all nigh driven to distraction.

Despite her chagrin at being forced to accept Max's latest act of charity, Freddie managed to spare the boy a brief smile before slipping quietly out of the kitchen.

Only when she passed into the dining parlor did she permit her frown to return. Absently, she stripped off the apron, soiled from her morning's efforts, trying to help Till bake two loaves of bread out of only one cup of flour.

Thanks to Max, they would not now have to worry about such shortages. But Freddie did not want to be offering any thanks to Max. Not now, not ever.

A restless night of reflection and fretting had done nothing to soften yesterday's humiliation for her. She felt her face might burn forever at the mere thought of how she had thrown herself at Max's head and been summarily rejected.

She still smarted as she recollected his blunt outburst. He would rather face a loaded cannon than have her as his mistress. But truthfully, what had she expected him to say? Had she really thought for one moment he would ever take her up on her outrageous offer?

Looking back, she did not know what madness had possessed her to approach him with such a suggestion. Perhaps Max had been right when he had questioned her motives, hinted that she had been acting partly out of a need for revenge. Never one to shrink from examining the dark corners of her own soul, Freddie was forced to admit there might be some truth in Max's words. In some perverse way, she had been trying to shock him, hurt him as he had hurt her so long ago.

Aye, that truly was the worst of it, far worse than making herself ridiculous attempting to play the role of seductress. She had let down her defenses, revealed to Max just how well she remembered him, how important those memories were, how much they still had the ability to wound her. She had let him see beyond the brittle gaiety of her careless smiles, shown him just how vulnerable she could be.

She had actually cried. Freddie winced. Good Lord, how long had it been since she had done that, wept in front of anyone? No wonder Max still viewed her as a child, and an idiotic one at that.

After that mortifying contretemps in his bedchamber, it would be gratifying never to have to see the man again. Even after her successful escape from his house, Freddie had been a bundle of nerves yesterday evening, fearful that Max would turn up, demanding to see her.

When he hadn't come then or this morning, she had told herself that she must have succeeded in disgusting him enough to leave her alone. But the ham certainly put paid to that notion, Freddie thought glumly. She obviously was not quit of Mr. Max Warfield yet. Sighing, she rubbed her temples, feeling the nigglings of another headache coming on.

The London air did not seem to agree with her. Perhaps Lady Caroline Bentley had been correct. Maybe Freddie should retire to Bath with the other elderly widows and invalids.

Realizing that she had lingered too long in the dining parlor, Freddie moved briskly forward. She hoped to steal away unnoticed, have more time to brood alone in privacy. But Freddie had waited too long to make good her escape. The parlor door swung open and Dora came bustling over to her.

"Well! If that wasn't the most provident thing in the world, the arrival of all that food," Dora exclaimed. "Like manna from heaven. I was certain we were going to have to resort to the turban again. Wasn't it simply too thoughtful of Mr. Warfield?"

"Quite," Freddie said with a grimace.

Dora's brow knit in a puzzled frown. "Though I do not quite understand it. I thought you said that Mr. Warfield had most definitely turned down your—ah—suggestion?"

"He did. This morning's bounty is charity, Dora, pure and simple." Freddie gritted her teeth. "And I shall pay him back if it takes me until the end of my days."

"Oh, dear, oh, dear! And I was hoping Mr. Warfield might call. For all his gruffness, he truly is a nice young man. But if you intend to quarrel with him again—"

"Don't fret, Dora. Perhaps Mr. Warfield will content himself with playing King Cophetua from a distance. Gentlemen do not care for scenes either, and I certainly enacted him a memorable one yesterday."

The bitterness in Freddie's voice only seemed to add to Dora's distress. Her lower lip trembled. "You must not blame yourself, Freddie. It was my fault. As your older and wiser companion, I never should have let you go to Mr. Warfield in the first place. I am so very sorry."

The notion of Dora's wisdom would have at any other time provoked Freddie with a desire to smile, but she was too overcome with shame, a sense of her own guilt.

She caught hold of Dora's hand, saying, "Don't you dare take on so, Dora. We both know full well it is I who should be apologizing to you."

"But you already did—"

"But not enough. I shall never be able to tell you I am sorry half enough. When I think of how I ran off and left you there—I always knew I was many things, but I never thought a coward was one of them."

"You aren't! You are the most courageous, brave, and loyal friend anyone could have."

Freddie only shook her head darkly, recalling how she had fled from Max's town house. At the time, she had considered herself as acting out of defiance, determined to show Max she would not tolerate being locked in like a naughty child. But in truth, she had had but one selfish thought in her head, that she could not bear to face Max again at that moment. She had not even considered what Dora might be left to deal with. Later, when Dora had described her encounter with Sir Pollack Sprague, Freddie had been and still was horrified.

She stroked a stray curl back from her older friend's brow, murmuring, "Oh, my Dora, whatever have I done to you? You led such a quiet, peaceful life at Dunhaven, and I have brought you nothing but chaos and worry, perhaps even cost you your reputation. I should not blame you if you had come to quite detest me."

"Never!" Dora cried, the ever-ready sentimental tears starting to her eyes. "What you have done for me is wonderful. Don't you see? Back at Dunhaven, I was nobody, just poor, dull, respectable Cousin Dora. I never turned any man's head, not unless one tripped over my feet."

The woman smiled mistily. "But yesterday I was actually mistaken for a wicked woman. Oh, I know it won't last. Mr. Warfield will find Sir Pollack and explain everything. He said that if Sir Pollack dared to impugn my honor, Max—that is, Mr. Warfield, would call him out even if he was his friend.

"But of course Sir Pollack will believe Max, because after all, I am not the sort of woman a gentleman would—well, but at least I shall always have the memory."

She drew herself up proudly. "For at least one afternoon in my life I was the center of a most delicious, scandalous adventure."

Freddie stared at her somberly. Until that moment, she felt she had never fully understood how bleak, how barren Dora's life must have been.

"Someday, Dora," she vowed, "I'll give you a truly grand adventure, one that will last longer than an afternoon. I'll give you—"

But she broke off, as ever haunted by the realization of their circumstances. Deflated, she concluded, "What I will most likely give you is debtor's prison and disgrace."

"Oh, no, Freddie. I am sure Mr. Warfield will not let that happen. Even though he was not so obliging as to accept your offer, he must still mean to—"

"Mr. Warfield is not the solution to our problems, Dora."

"Then what is, my dear Freddie?"

Freddie already knew the answer, and although the thought left her feeling bleak, she managed a smile and a careless hunch of one shoulder. "Oh, I suppose I must now simply make another choice from our list of rakes."

Dora's eyes widened immediately in alarm. "Oh, Freddie, now what are you planning to do?"

"I fear I have already done it," Freddie said with a sad smile. "General Fortescue sent an invitation this morning and I have accepted it. I am riding out with him this very afternoon."

Three o'clock was not the fashionable hour to go riding through St. James. The paths of the sprawling park were by and large devoid of company and it was the perfect time to arrange a clandestine meeting or a lover's rendezvous.

Freddie thought she might have had great success in making her intentions obvious to an experienced rake like General Sir Mordant Fortescue. But any flirtation was impossible, not with her companion wedged on one side of her in the open carriage, her grandson on the other.

Freddie still was not sure how it had come about that Dora and Jack had been included in the outing. If she had not known Dora to be completely without guile, she might have strongly suspected her of maneuvering it thus.

As it was, Freddie supposed it had to be put down to General Fortescue's gallantry. For all his foolish little vanities and blustering manner, there was an underlying core of kindness about the man. He appeared genuinely fond of children and liked the company of women, taking a roguish delight in quizzing even the stolid Dora, putting her to the blush.

As the carriage rattled along the park's shady lanes, the general entertained them with tales of his army days, campaigns he had fought in, battles won and lost.

Freddie placed one gloved hand to her lips, trying not to yawn. Dora and Jack, however, were enthralled, Dora's admiring murmurs in particular causing the old man to puff out his chest like a pouter pigeon and continue to drone on.

Freddie supposed she should feel annoyed to find her plans so disrupted. There would be no casting out lures to the general this afternoon. Instead, she felt a half-guilty relief, like a prisoner receiving a temporary stay of execution but knowing the hanging must come eventually.

Yet today she could relax a little, even enjoy the breeze tickling her curls, soft and warm as a lover's caress. It was a perfect spring day, as though, weary of the drabness of winter, nature had become like an artist run wild, splashing the grass vivid green, streaking the sky breathtaking blue, running a rainbow riot through the flower beds.

General Fortescue commanded his driver to pull up so that they could all alight and walk along the edge of the lake. Jack insisted upon handing his "grandmama" down himself with a quaint courtliness that amused the general.

The next instant the lad charged toward the lake with a cry of heartfelt boyish delight, his arms flung wide, as though he would embrace the entire scene. He skipped along the edge, his antics causing no end of consternation among the ducks who waddled there.

The general was nearly as bad, showing the boy how to skim stones across the lake's rippling surface, make raucous noises that would set the prim swans aflutter. Dora followed after them, clucking her tongue.

"Take care, Master Jack, you will fall in. Mind where you step, General Fortescue. You will get the toes of your Hessians wet."

Her gentle scoldings filled Fortescue with a chortling delight. He laughed and slapped his thigh, saying, "We'd best heed the lady before she tweaks our ears, eh, lad? Such a solidly sensible sort of a gel." With the rest of her party so obviously entertained, Freddie was content to lag behind, absorbed by her own thoughts. She intended to proceed more subtly with the general than she had with Max. Fortescue had certainly offered her far more encouragement, enough signs of his admiration. Her experience with Leon had taught her how to get on with gentlemen of a more mature persuasion. She and the general should deal quite comfortably together.

True, the thought of their relationship assuming a more intimate nature roused no enthusiasm in her, indeed left her feeling a little cold. But surely that was better than being unnerved as she had been by Max—

Freddie felt her cheeks warm and wished she had remembered to bring her parasol. The small poke front of her bonnet was not enough to keep the sun off her face. Yet, as she moved into the shade of a towering elm, she was obliged to admit, it was not the sun heating her countenance, but a memory.

The memory of Max's kiss. Leaning up against the tree, she had only to close her eyes and she could still recall the taste, the rough, warm texture of his lips, the ruthless passion of his embrace which should have terrified her but hadn't. It had only succeeded in arousing something hot and equally hungry in herself.

And it had been *that* that had frightened her, the waking of some part of her that had been slumbering inside of her all these years, the stirrings of a hidden sensuality she had heretofore never suspected.

Leon had often laughed and warned her it would be thus one day. When he had embraced her, Freddie had once shyly admitted she found kissing sweet and very pleasant. Strangely enough, her compliment caused a momentary flash of hurt to cross his age-lined features.

"If I were twenty years younger," he had growled, his eyes lightning with a wry self-mockery. "Ah, but someday, little girl. Someday we shall see if you find kissing 'very pleasant.' " His words had been laced with sadness, resignation, and something of a tender amusement.

Freddie had never understood exactly what Leon had meant. Now she wondered if he had known that someday there would be a man like Max who would teach her.

No! Freddie tensed, digging her gloved fingers against the tree bark. She had learned all from Max that she cared to, and he certainly was interested in offering no more lessons. It still seemed disloyal to Leon to be thinking such things, and yet every instinct she possessed told her that Leon would have liked Max, approved of him.

And would Leon approve of her present plans for the future regarding General Fortescue? She doubted her late husband would have been pleased by the necessity of them. But unlike Max, Leon would have understood.

Freddie sighed, a shout from Jack disrupting her reveries. Shading her eyes with one hand, she squinted along the length of the lakeshore, half expecting to find the boy had tumbled in at last. Scarce noticing her absence, her party had moved a considerable distance ahead.

Jack wasn't in the lake, but only the general's grip on the boy's coattails appeared to be restraining him. What occasioned Jack's excitement was a vehicle moving at a smart pace through the park.

Jack pointed back in the direction of the road, calling loudly enough for the whole park to hear. "Damme! What a sweet pair of goers!"

The boy was correct. Even Freddie knew a pair of perfectly matched bays when she saw them. They were hitched in the

106

traces of a high-perched phaeton, and for a moment Freddie forgot her more troubling thoughts, lost in admiration for the way the driver handled such a spirited team.

That is, until the carriage drew close enough for her to glimpse the face of the man at the reins.

Max.

Cursing the perversity of fate, Freddie shrank back farther behind the tree. But she realized it was to no avail. Fate was not to be blamed for this particular mischance. Max appeared to be scanning the depths of the park as much as keeping an eye on the roadway. Freddie knew instinctively he was looking for her.

She also knew the instant he spotted her. Max drew back abruptly on the reins, bringing his team to a halt. Turning over the ribbons to his groom, Max had vaulted to the ground in a trice and was striding across the grass, heading purposefully in Freddie's direction.

She knew a strong impulse to run, cover the distance along the lake to catch up with the others, obliging Max to greet her in the safety of company. But if she kept giving way to these craven impulses where Max was concerned, she would end by despising herself.

She forced herself to wait, boldly watching his approach. Leon had been wont to mock the uninspiring apparel of the modern young man, prefering the flamboyant silks and brocades of his own era. But the present styles became Max well, the close-fitting dark jacket seeming designed to call attention to the power of his shoulders, the breadth of his chest. The skin-tight buckskin breeches outlined his legs so well, Freddie could tell Max had no need to resort to padding to fill out the muscular shape of his thighs.

Ashamed to be ogling him, Freddie lowered her gaze but fixed her impudent smile in place like a shield of armor. The best defense was ever a good attack, so as soon as he was within hearing range, she called out with forced merriment.

"As I live and breathe, Max Warfield. What an unlucky chance—I mean, what a coincidence. What brings you abroad at such an unfashionable hour."

But one look at the grim set of Max's mouth told her he was having none of it. He drew up alongside of her, saying, "Your butler told me where you had gone."

"I've always told Stubbins he can be forthcoming with my *friends*. But the poor man is nearsighted. I daresay he did not recognize it was *you*."

Max flinched at this jab, and Freddie was half ashamed of making it.

"We did not part on the best of terms yesterday," he said, "but you should not have run away like that."

"I suppose you were not amused by the use I made of your shirts. I trust your laundress was able to—"

"This is not about my shirts, Frederica. There were other things I badly needed to say to you."

"Truly? I suppose that is why you half beat my door down last night."

It was Max's turn to look a little ashamed. He colored slightly beneath his layering of tan. "I wanted to come last evening, but I thought better of it. It seemed wise to allow—to allow emotions some time to settle."

She angled a mocking glance from beneath the brim of her bonnet. "What, were you afraid I might make another attempt to ravish you? I suppose you need have no fear meeting me here in the park. Your cries for help would surely be answered by someone."

"It was not *your* lack of self-control that worried me." He whipped off his high-crowned beaver, jamming his fingers through his hair in a gesture rife with frustration. "Damn. I might have known you were not going to make this easy."

"A gentleman of intuition. How rare," Freddie drawled. Then she sighed. "I don't think there is anything more we have to talk about, Max. We both made our feelings plain yesterday afternoon. Now, if you will excuse me. I am not here alone. My companions will soon tire of disturbing the swans and be looking for me."

At her words, Max also turned and regarded the trio at the far bend of the lake. He peered more intently at the distant figures.

"That's Fortescue with Miss Applegate."

"I believe it is," Freddie said pleasantly.

Max eyed her with hard suspicion. "What the deuce are you doing with here with him?"

Freddie smiled sweetly. "I told you about Dora's list of eligible rakes, did I not? Well, his name came after yours."

She gasped aloud as the next instant Max seized her upper arms in a bruising grip and pressed her back against the elm.

"Are you mad?" he grated. "You cannot truly be thinking of offering yourself to that old roué."

"My plans are none of your business." She raised her chin in defiance, but somehow found herself unable to meet his piercing gaze. She murmured, "You are hurting me, Max. Let me go."

He eased the pressure of his fingers, but still did not release her. "Freddie, believe me, I understand the desperation that is driving you, but there is another way. I have been talking to both of my sisters about the way you have been neglected by the family, convincing them that something must be done."

"Just doing your duty, Max?" Freddie sneered.

He ignored her interpolation. "I have told them—that is, we have all agreed you should be brought out properly in society, given another chance. You are a young and beautiful woman. Even without a great dowry you could surely achieve a respectable marriage."

Freddie squirmed, managing to wrench out of his grasp. "I don't want to be married!"

"Forgive me, but from what you hinted about your late husband, I thought you did not find marriage a disagreeable experience."

"No, it . . . it was wonderful."

"Then why not marry again?"

"Because I cheat at solitaire, not hearts!"

Her passionate response clearly puzzled him. She tried to explain. "I find what you are proposing quite cold-blooded, the idea of marrying a man for security and not affection."

Max's dark brows arched with incredulity. "And yet you talk of finding a lover by going down a list of names. If that is not cold-blooded, I scarce know what is."

"That is different," Freddie said stubbornly. "No one expects undying devotion in a mistress. It is more of a business arrangement."

"Most people would say the same of marriage."

"Well, I am not one of them. Marriage is for a lifetime, based on vows of love and fidelity. I may be flippant about many things, Max, but *I* take *my* promises very seriously."

He looked away, saying gruffly, "That is another reason I needed to speak to you. You mentioned something yesterday about broken promises, the way I once left you without ever saying good-bye."

"I was being silly." Freddie waved him off with a dismissive gesture. "There is no point in raking over old coals. It was not important."

"Obviously I hurt you very badly and you are entitled to an explanation."

"Your explanation comes years too late. I am not interested." Freddie tried for an air of icy dignity, but her voice came out sounding petulant, even childish. What was it about Max that could reduce her to the state of a hurt little girl again?

"Besides," she added, "I already know why you went away. Aunt Jameson told me."

"She did?"

"She said you had gone off to make your fortune in Jamaica."

Max essayed a hard laugh. "That was half true. But unfortunately there was a little more to it than that. I did not go. I was banished by my father, asked never to return during his lifetime."

"Good God!" Freddie exclaimed in involuntary horror. "You could not have done anything that dreadful . . . could you?"

He didn't answer, merely stared into the distance, absently shredding one of the elm leaves. Even after all these years Max was obviously very reluctant to talk about what he had done to so alienate his father.

Wild thoughts of theft, sedition, even murder chased through Freddie's brain. She half dreaded to ask, "What terrible crime did you commit?"

"I fell in love." Max turned to offer her a wry half smile. "Your memory of that summer is obviously incomplete, Frederica. Seen through a child's eyes, you recall only pony rides and tickling games. You don't remember me wandering about like a moon-calf, sighing over the flowers, telling you ridiculous things like when I was married, I would take you to live with me."

"Yes, I—I do remember some such faradiddle."

"Aye, faraddidle is the word, and what's more I believed it myself. I truly thought by some miracle I would acquire enough of a fortune to build a mansion for me and my bride. And you. You were to come and be our little sister."

Freddie crinkled her nose. Once she would have been entranced by the thought of being Max's little sister. Now the notion struck her as extremely displeasing. At the outset she had assured herself she would be interested in nothing Max could have to say. But now she could not refrain from asking him, "And who was to be the bride, this lady who had so bewitched you?"

"She was the daughter of longtime friends of my father. A lovely, gentle girl. An heiress in her own right."

"She sounds perfect. So what was the difficulty?"

"Jane was already betrothed, her match arranged to a man of title and property. But that did not deter me. I fear I was infatuated beyond reason."

Max spread his hands in a helpless gesture, as though groping for the words to explain. "Jane admired me. And she seemed delicate and vulnerable. She made me feel so wise, the great, strong male. That's heady stuff when you're a gawky lad of eighteen, brought up to think of yourself as a person of no importance. I was special to her, not just an insignificant younger son."

You were special to me, too, Max, Freddie wanted to cry out. But pride kept her silent. She was dismayed to feel the jealousy curling inside her over a female she had never met, a lady long gone from Max's life. Gone perhaps, but from the shadows that touched his eyes, clearly not forgotten.

Sighing, Max continued. "As the time drew near for her wedding, she promised me to cry off. But with each passing day, she found some excuse, and I realized she would never have the courage to stand against the wishes of her family. In desperation I took matters into my own hands. I—I abducted her."

When Freddie stared at him, Max drew himself up defensively. "I was so certain Jane loved me. I thought once her initial fear and apprehension passed, she would see that eloping was the only way, perhaps even find some romance in the notion."

His lips drew back into a derisive smile, sneering at his own folly. "As it turned out, my love was not that romantic, nor was she that much in love with me. As I watched her lash herself into hysterics, I realized what I mistook for gentleness was naught but weakness. Oh, she was very fond of me, enjoyed my attentions, but not enough to sacrifice her future for me. Did I not understand? Jane was not made for a life of poverty and scandal. She had been brought up to be a marchioness. That was what she wanted and I ruined everything."

Even after so many years that ages-old disillusionment seemed to weigh down upon Max, the heavy, carved lines around his mouth becoming more prominent as he concluded, "By the time her father caught up to us, I was ready to hand her back and gladly. Of course, my father came as well, so furious, I thought he would have a fit of apoplexy. He said I had disgraced my family for the last time, that he would make arrangements at once to send me to my uncle in Jamaica. At that

111

moment he could have sent me to the devil and I would not have cared."

Freddie did not want to feel sympathy for Max, but she trembled with indignation for him all the same. "It seems a little excessive to have sent you so far away forever. I suppose it was dishonorable, trying to steal another man's bride. But you were very young, hotheaded. Surely after your lady went back and wed her lord, you could simply have stayed away from her and—"

"Ah, but you do not fully comprehend the extent of my villainy. My lady love did indeed return to her lord, who has since succeeded to his title. She is now the Marchioness of Huntley."

When Freddie furrowed her brow, still uncomprehending, he added softly, "My brother's wife."

"You had to endure losing the woman you loved to your own brother! Oh, Max." Unable to stay the impulsive gesture, she reached out, resting her hand on his wrist. "Why did you not tell me all these years ago?"

"You were only a child. You thought me some sort of blasted hero. How could I tell you such a sordid tale?"

"It was not sordid so much as very sad. And you were exiled to Jamaica all this time?"

He turned her hand over, capturing her fingers, kneading them lightly as though grateful for the contact. "More or less. Don't look so pitying. It was not that bad. I finally discovered something I was good at. I have a real head for business concerns, eventually made my fortune in shipping. I returned to England only two years ago, when my father died. I had been pretty much ignored by the entire family until then. But when I came back, well juiced, they all magnanimously forgave my past transgressions, including the fact that I had made my money in trade."

"Then I suppose you saw your brother's wife again?"

"Inevitably."

"I daresay she had grown plump, quite matronly," Freddie suggested hopefully.

"No, the years have changed Jane very little. She is as lovely as ever."

"Oh." Freddie was unable to account for the sinking feeling in the pit of her stomach.

Max continued cheerfully. "Jane is still the same flighty little ninnyhammer she always was. I expect I am the one who changed. I know you perceive me as doddering, but I assure you that the advancing years have rendered my mental perceptions only more acute."

A laugh escaped Freddie. For a moment she felt lightheaded with relief. She sobered immediately, trying to ignore the fact that Max had now taken possession of both her hands.

"You could have written to me, Max. At least once in all those years. I was a very precocious child, you know. I learned to read when I was only five."

"Precocious and impertinent." He started a smile, but it faded before it ever reached his eyes. "I didn't expect that I was ever coming back to England, Freddie. I thought you would soon forget me and just as well. I was no proper companion for a little girl. I did not believe my going away could have mattered so much to you."

"It did. For a long time I did not believe Aunt Jameson when she said you would visit me no more. I watched out the nursery window, waiting every day, expecting to see you come riding down the drive." To her dismay, she felt a lump rise into her throat. She finished in a whisper, "I felt as though I had lost my only friend. It—it was as bad as when Mama and Papa had died."

Max reached out to brush the moisture from her cheek, a tear that Freddie was scarce aware had escaped.

"Forgive me," he murmured. He turned her palm upright and bent to brush a kiss upon the area of her wrist exposed by the edge of her glove. A tingling warmth shot through her, and her heart did a crazed flip-flop.

"Forgive me," he repeated, "for I will never be able to forgive myself."

Once Freddie had thought she would have given much to see Max stricken with guilt, but now her only desire was to drive the shades of remorse from his eyes.

"It was not so great a matter," she said, attempting to disguise her breathlessness, her desire to run her fingers through his crisp ebony hair as he once more caressed her throbbing pulse with his lips. "You scarcely left me a homeless waif. My uncle's estate was one of the most prominent ones in Dorchester."

"I should have made inquiries," he insisted. "Found some way to make provision for you."

"The Jamesons were very generous. I had all the advantages their daughters did, the same dolls, gowns, tutors." Freddie could not help biting down upon her lip, observing ruefully. "How-

113

ever, it would have been a deal more pleasant if Aunt Jameson had not always been reminding me how grateful I should be, pointing out the new pianoforte or sofa that they could have gotten if so much did not have to be spent on my support."

Max muttered something about her aunt under his breath. But Freddie was certain she could not have heard him right. No, he could not have called Aunt Jameson anything like *that*.

She shrugged. "Oh, I expect that I was the ungrateful, wicked wretch that Aunt Jameson always said. I even upset the marriage plans she had taken pains to arrange for me."

"I thought you had been quite dutiful about accepting Raincliffe."

When Freddie realized his misconception, she laughed. "Aunt Jameson never arranged my match to Leon. She thought him the most utter reprobate despite his title and money. He absolutely horrified her and took great pleasure in doing so. No, the Jamesons attempted to pair me off to a man of the utmost respectability, a sallow-faced squire with the meanest, squinty little eyes. Leon rescued me.

"I had known Leon for a long time. One of his lesser estates bordered the Jamesons'. He kept a hunting box there. I was always trespassing, stealing the apples off his trees, setting my pup into his coveys, stirring up his birds.

"I hid in his orchard the day I realized I would have to marry that dreadful squire or run away. Leon found me sitting in one of his apple trees, crying. He lifted me down and swore that he would never know another day's decent shooting again if he didn't marry me himself and teach me to be a lady."

Freddie grew misty-eyed at the memory. She became aware that Max had released her hands. His gaze was fixed on her, his expression unreadable as he said hoarsely, "You must have loved him a great deal."

"I was very fond of him. How could I have been otherwise? He pampered me, made much of me, treated me like a princess."

"In fact, behaved just like a doting grandfather," Max said eagerly.

Freddie chuckled. "There was never anything the least grandfatherly about Leon. He used to tell me stories about his youth that would make your hair stand on end."

Max's brows knit into a heavy scowl. "Doubtless that is where you acquired all your information about mistresses and discreet arrangements."

"I certainly did not learn it from Aunt Jameson."

"It seems to me that your late husband imparted a great many notions that were improper for an innocent young bride."

"Leon was always a gentleman, but certainly not ruled by conventional behavior. In many ways he was like you, but of course, not nearly so stuffy."

"Stuffy!"

Freddie thought Max would choke on the word, and her lips parted in a self-satisfied smile. "Aye, for a rakehell, Max, I find you incredibly prudish."

"Only where you are concerned."

"I think I liked you better in the days of your wild youth," Freddie mused teasingly. "You taught me so many useful things."

Max quirked one brow. "Such as how to climb out second-story windows?"

She had the grace to blush. "I suppose I ought to apologize for my—er—precipitous departure yesterday. But I don't take kindly to being locked in."

"I only wanted to keep you—" He broke off ruefully. "I seem to make so many mistakes where you are concerned. And you have never yet said whether you will forgive me or no."

Freddie stared deep into the mists of his gray eyes. If he persisted in regarding one in that bone-melting way, a woman would be apt to forgive him anything. No wonder he was styled as the most eligible rake in London.

She held out her hand to him in what she hoped was casual fashion. "Gracious, I am not the sort to hold a grudge, Max. From herein, I do hope we can be friends again."

He shook hands with her, retaining possession longer than was necessary. His eyes lit with amusement. "I should warn you about that. I no longer give my friendship lightly. But when I do, I am told that I can be high-handed and damnably interfering."

"You already are."

Max had no opportunity to reply to this riposte, for they both became aware that they no longer stood alone beneath the elm's spreading leaves.

Jack came tearing up, his round face red and perspiring with excitement. "Faith, lady, look what I have found." He held up one hand, an ugly specimen of a caterpillar inching along his stubby finger.

"Ugh. How perfectly charming." Freddie grimaced.

Max looked a little irritated at being interrupted. He flicked a glance over the boy. "And who might this young rogue be?"

Jack returned Max's frown, his own deepening to a scowl when his gaze slid pointedly to where Max still retained Freddie's hand.

"More to the point, who are you, sir?" Jack said, forgetting the caterpillar as he drew himself up. "I believe I must request you to unhand my grandmama."

"Your grandmama?" Max relaxed to a stance of wary amusement. When Jack glowered, Freddie stepped quickly into the breach with introductions.

"Jack, this is Mr. Warfield, the owner of that bang-up rig you so recently admired. Max, this is my grandson, St. John Bartholmew Barry, otherwise known as Jack."

"Mr. Barry to you, sir," Jack said with a stiff bow.

Max's lazy grin had slowly faded as he whipped to face Freddie. "What! You don't mean Sir Wilfred's son."

"Yes, his youngest, in fact."

"Frederica! I heard rumors in my club only this morning. A search has been set up for that boy since he turned up missing from school."

"I am not missing," Jack growled. "I am with my grandmama."

Freddie laughed, but Max did not look in the least diverted. Dark lights of annoyance sparked into his eyes, his lips setting in a determined clamp, all signs which Freddie had come to recognize as heralding trouble.

"By God, Frederica," he said. "When I locked you in yesterday, I should have thrown away the key and boarded up the windows. You are insane. Abducting Sir Wilfred's son."

"I didn't," she cried. "He came to me."

"Then you should have had the sense to—never mind," he ground out. " 'Tis clearly one more coil for me to untangle."

Something in the tone of Max's voice caused Freddie to encircle her arm protectively about Jack's shoulders.

"And just what do you think you are going to do?" she challenged.

"First, I am seizing Master Jack here by the collar and marching him back to school." Max leveled a grim look in her direction. "And then, by God, madam, I shall return to deal with you."

Chapter 9

Max realized he was not the most popular fellow at the moment. As he paced the confines of Freddie's parlor, he scanned the faces of his companions. Friendlier countenances were more likely to be found on the faces of a mob crowding around the base of a guillotine.

Dora perched on the chaise lounge, sniffing into a handkerchief, pausing only long enough to glare balefully at Max. The hand that Freddie had so recently extended in friendship was now clenched into a tight fist. Even General Fortescue looked as though Max had just kicked his favorite dog.

Frowning, Max drummed his fingers on the mantelpiece, waiting for the boy to make his reappearance. Master Jack had been dispatched abovestairs to make himself ready for the journey. Max had had some qualms about trusting the feisty youth out of his sight, but the boy had swept him a scorn-filled glance, saying, "You have my word that I will not attempt to run off, sir. And *I* am a gentleman."

There was something touching about the way the child squared his shoulders, managing a certain dignity despite the snub nose and dusting of freckles. But Max steeled himself against any softer feelings, refusing to give way to the spell that young Jack appeared to have cast over the rest of the household.

The silence in the drawing room stretched out to the point of being unbearable until it was at last broken by Dora, who cried, "Oh, Mr. Warfield, I simply do not understand how you can be so cruel."

"Cruel, madam?" Max shot her a look rife with impatience. "Call it, rather, common sense, and you should be thankful that I, at least, have some. You are lucky that Sir Wilfred has not

117

swooped down upon all of you, bringing the authorities with him. There are laws against keeping a boy hidden from his father. The only reason you have not been discovered is that Sir Wilfred has been so cautious, keeping his inquiries after the boy most discreet."

The general pulled a face of disgust. "Aye, that in itself shows what sort of father he is. B'gad, if it had been m'lad who had gone missing, I would have upended all of England searching for him."

Privately, Max agreed with him, although he said aloud, "I daresay Sir Wilfred hopes to avoid stirring up any gossip."

"I daresay he does," Freddie said tartly. "Wilfred would hardly want the world to know that he neglected his own son so badly, the child felt obliged to run away. That would be quite a nuisance, so troublesome to poor Wilfred."

Max frowned at her. "Trouble that, as usual, appears ready to land on your doorstep."

"I have a penchant for it, which you obviously do not. I will say to you the same thing I did when we left the park, Max. Stay clear of this. Let me handle the problem with Jack."

"You have yet to make any effort to do so and you have had the boy with you for two whole days."

Freddie flushed. "I—I will write to Sir Wilfred this very day. I promise."

"No, Frederica. I think not. The boy goes with me."

Freddie eyed him with complete frustration, but it was the general who thrust himself forward, blustering. "See here, Warfield. I fail to see how this concerns you. The boy is no relative of yours."

"No, but Lady Raincliffe is. She is my cousin and I feel some obligation to keep her out of mischief. A most thankless task." Max lowered his voice, putting an edge of steel into his words. "In fact, sir, you may find me interfering with her a great deal from now on."

General Fortescue's thick gray brows drew together in bewilderment, but Freddie clearly took Max's meaning, for she blushed. Max knew a sense of relief. So the seduction plans thus far were all on Freddie's side and her flirtation with the general had not yet proceeded onto dangerous ground.

Fortescue had no chance to demand any explanation of Max's remark, for at that moment Dora rose dramatically to her feet.

"Well, I for one cannot bear to sit here and see that p-poor boy dragged off to his doom." With a mighty sob she buried her face in her handkerchief and rushed out of the room.

"Now see what you have done." Fortescue glowered at Max. "You have greatly distressed Miss Applegate, and her such a solid, sensible sort of gel. B'gad if there was not a lady present, I would deal you a leveler." Still spluttering his indignation, Fortescue spun on his heel and went charging after Dora.

Left alone with Freddie, Max shifted uneasily. He knew she was every bit as upset as Dora, but he did not think she would render him uncomfortable with a bout of weeping. Far more likely, Freddie would pursue the general's suggestion and attempt to hit him.

Max could have dealt with either response. But he was not prepared for the pleading way she looked at him, fixing him with those wide blue eyes.

"Max, if you could just try to understand about Jack," she began.

"I understand quite well what mischief a boy can get up to. I once enjoyed any number of scrapes myself."

"All the more reason you should sympathize with Jack. Do you know why he ran away? He's been abandoned at that school. He never leaves there, not even to go home."

"That is a great pity, but—"

"He is a younger son, Max, considered of no importance by his father. Jack is so spirited, so lively, the image of his grandpapa. I daresay Sir Wilfred despises him for that. Leon and Wilfred were ever at odds with each other."

A younger son, of no importance. The words caused Max to wince inwardly, like Freddie had raked sharp nails over old memories, clawing at hurts Max had long glossed over. He sighed.

"I could say I do understand, even sympathize. But that doesn't change things, Freddie. Jack is Sir Wilfred's son. You cannot think that you could keep him here forever."

"No, all I am asking for is just a little longer. The child never had a proper holiday. That is why he took such an absurd risk, running away. He wanted to see the sights of London. If you could allow me one more day to take him around—"

"That would be madness, Frederica. I'm trying to avoid having you caught with the boy in your company."

"I would be very discreet."

The notion of Freddie being discreet was enough to make Max snort aloud. But before she could press her argument further, Jack appeared at the door of the parlor.

He was scrubbed clean, his hair brushed, his stocky frame garbed in a fresh jacket. Yet he still presented a forlorn figure with his small bundle of possessions clutched in his fists. He avoided acknowledging Max, his gaze directed wistfully at Freddie.

"I am r-ready to go back, Grandmama." Jack blinked fiercely.

Max knew well the effort that took, striving at all costs to avoid babyish tears, to be a man when one was not quite.

When was the last time he had allowed rein to feelings of misery, permitted himself an unmasculine display? Oddly enough, it had been only two years ago when word had reached him of his father's death. He had sat, his brother's letter gripped in his hand, a hot tear escaping down his cheek as he had grieved for the loss of an affection that never had been.

As Freddie moved to wrap one arm around Jack, Max turned away from the pair of them. He hardly knew what had happened to himself this past week. He had cultivated such a hard shell during his years of exile. Cast off by his family, he had formed the selfish determination to remain aloof, never burden himself with anyone else's cares. It was bad enough that he was already embroiled in the chaos that was Freddie. He was not about to be drawn into young Jack's woes.

And yet, as though from some great distance, he heard himself snap, "Oh, very well, Frederica. I will take the boy back day after tomorrow. You may have your excursion with him around London.

"But—" he added sternly before she and Jack grew too boisterous in their rejoicing, "I am going with you."

The next morning it took Freddie more than a few tries to adjust the ribbon strings on her bonnet. She seemed to have more thumbs than fingers, and the strange flutterings she experienced beneath her rib cage did nothing to help. Although delighted by Max's capitulation, she had a good many qualms about him accompanying her and Jack.

The talk she had had yesterday in the park with Max had been wonderful, lifting aside a veil of ancient misunderstandings. But she did not fool herself into thinking that the years would suddenly melt, that she and Max could slip back into the same easy camaraderie they had known when he had been her childhood hero. For one thing, she was obliged to admit he had changed.

She saw little trace of the reckless youth who had once been so marvelous about entertaining a hoydenish little girl. The years had cast Max into a mold of adult stiffness. He no longer seemed to know how to unbend to children.

As Freddie scooped up her shawl, she could not help recalling Max's gruff reactions of the day before. He had been on the point of leaving when she had displayed to him Till's darling baby. Max had kept a wary distance, his only remark, "Does it bite?"

Even being assured that the babe had as yet cut no teeth did nothing to dispel his unease. But many men were uncomfortable around babies. It should be much easier for Max to deal with a lad of ten.

But Jack, for obvious reasons, had taken a dislike to Max. He not only saw him as the enemy, but, Freddie feared, in some strange way her courtly young gallant perceived Max as a rival as well.

Thus it was with some trepidation that Freddie joined the two gentlemen where they awaited her in the parlor. She had prolonged her dressing, hoping they might get to know each other better in her absence. If nothing else, they could join together in bemoaning the dilatoriness of females. But as Freddie crossed the threshold, her heart sank. Jack and Max stood at opposite ends of the room as stiff and stubborn as the pillar supports holding up the roof.

Max consulted his watch, his attitude one of impatience, a decided let's-get-this-blasted-thing-over-with. Although outwardly polite, Jack's bright eyes clearly conveyed the message, we-would-do-just-as-well-without-you-sir.

Gritting her teeth, Freddie maintained a manner of determined cheerfulness and shepherded both of them out of the house. Max's carriage stood waiting at the curb. It would have been a great help if Max had brought his high perch phaeton, such a delight to Jack's boyish soul.

Instead, Max had chosen a more sedate traveling gig that caused Jack to growl under his breath. "Humph. Fit for nothing but old ladies to go racketing about the park on Sunday."

He did brighten a little to see a spirited chestnut hitched in the traces. Jack scrambled up onto the seat of the vehicle himself while Max offered Freddie his hand.

"May I take a turn at the ribbons?" Jack asked eagerly.

"Certainly not," Max snapped. He assumed his own seat and gathered up the reins, giving the nod to the groom to stand away from the horse's head. With an expert flick of Max's wrist, the chestnut started down the cobblestone street with a jaunty step.

Wedged between Max and Freddie on the narrow seat, Jack heaved a disappointed sigh, which made Freddie long to remind Max that he had once let a little girl much younger than Jack hold the reins of his precious horses. But as Max eased the carriage into the flow of London traffic, his countenance was so dark and forbidding, Freddie kept silent.

The three of them would keep company together only this one day. Freddie supposed they would all survive it. She did not know why it seemed desperately important to her that Jack and Max learn to like each other, that this outing be a shining success.

Perhaps it was because that on the morrow Jack had to leave and Freddie knew she would never be permitted to see him again. She had grown fond of the young scamp for his own sake as much for the fact that he was Leon's grandson and reminded her so poignantly of her lost friend. And perhaps it was because in some odd way she felt she was about to lose Max as well.

A temporary truce existed between them because of Jack's holiday. But Freddie had no doubts as to what would happen when Jack left. She remembered Max's terse warning that after Jack was back in school, Max would return to "deal with her." He fully intended to interfere with her own plans to remain independent, likely still wanted to foist her off onto the charity of his sisters.

Freddie brought herself up short, attempting to cast out such gloomy thoughts. This was no time for her to lapse into a fit of the blue devils and ruin Jack's holiday. Max's surly humor was bad enough.

She slipped her arm around Jack's shoulders. The boy continued to stare with disgruntled longing at the prancing chestnut.

"Cliveden never lets me drive either," Jack grumbled.

"Cliveden?" Max asked with a frown.

"His eldest brother," Freddie filled in.

"Aye." Jack's chest swelled with indignation. "He thinks he's top of the trees simply because he's going to be a viscount someday. He says I don't need to learn to handle a team 'cause I will be naught but a country parson joggin' about on an old mare."

"Does he indeed?" Max's jaw clenched. He might already have begun to be irritated by Jack's chatter, but somehow Freddie did not think so, for a moment later Max added with gruff but genuine interest, "And what do you say about that?"

"Not a great deal." Jack propped his chin on his hands, his expression gloomy. "Cliveden is always far too ready to carry tales back to Papa or my tutors. The time I put the raspberry jam in his beaver hat only earned me extra Latin lessons. And as for milling him down, I tried that, too. Clive only shoved me away and thrashed me with his riding crop. He is nearly seventeen, so much taller than me."

"He won't always be. Someday when he comes thrusting his nose into your affairs, you'll be able to draw his cork." Max spoke these words with such grim satisfaction, Freddie wondered at what point he must have punched his own elder brother in the nose. Max added, "From the size of your shoulders, you're likely to grow up to be quite a bruiser."

"Do you truly think so?" Jack asked anxiously.

At Max's staunch affirmative, the boy's eyes lit up. Max's words must have conjured up an agreeable vision of the future for Jack, for he stretched back, a beatific smile lighting his features. The tension between him and Max eased just a little.

By the time they reached their destination and Max escorted them into the vast arena of Astley's Amphitheatre, Jack was bubbling over with as much excitement as any ten-year-old. Lustily Jack cheered the pony races, calling particular encouragement to one little dappled gray until he was hoarse. Some of her own anxiety eased, Freddie was able to gasp along with Jack in amazement at the skill of a conjurer and laugh at the antics of the clowns.

If Max was bored, he gave no sign of it, regarding both Freddie and Jack with a kind of avuncular amusement. He placed a hand on Jack's shoulder, gently easing him back in his seat when the eager boy leaned too far over the partition, showing every sign of being about to land headfirst in the ring.

Although Jack had been delighted with the ponies, he was absolutely enthralled by the grace and agility of the acrobats. His ambition to be a Bow Street Runner quite forgotten, Jack cried, "Now, that is what I should like to do when I am grown. That would be something dashing."

123

Freddie and Max exchanged a smile over the boy's head, though Max's was a trifle wistful. "Poor little chap," he murmured. "He may as well dream while he can. They'll likely have him stuffed into a clerical collar before he knows where he's about."

"Never. Not Jack," Freddie whispered.

"The army or the navy, then. Or he'll be obliged to marry an heiress. Younger sons must be gotten rid of somehow." Max pulled a wry face. "I've often thought if the eldest and heir is healthy, the rest might as well be drowned at birth like a parcel of unwanted pups."

"I would never favor such a practice. I am decidedly fond of younger sons." Freddie tipped her chin to a challenging angle, her gaze locking with Max's. For once his expression was not sheltered beneath those hooded lids. He stared straight back at her, a glow akin to gratitude in his eyes, gratitude and something more. A warmth stole in her heart and at the same time caused her to shiver, tingling with awareness of that powerful masculine presence.

She realized that Max had not changed with the years nearly so much as herself. She had grown from a child to a woman, and Max's nearness, the appreciation simmering in his steel gray eyes, made her glad of it. When she had made the offer to be his mistress, she had done so mainly to torment him. Now she could not help thinking that it was too bad that he had refused.

Freddie blushed hotly, shocked at her own wayward thoughts. She quickly looked away, reminding herself why she was there. She was, after all, a grandmama on an outing with her grandson.

Yet when they exited the amphitheatre and Max tucked her arm within his own, she made no effort to pull away from him. The protective gesture seemed so right, so familiar. Perhaps for one afternoon, she, too, could take a holiday from her fierce pride and lean a little on Max, reveling in the aura of strength, of pure male possessiveness that emanated from his lean, hard frame.

While the groom brought Max's carriage around after the performance, Jack practiced a few handsprings until he was red-faced and panting with exertion. Max growled at Jack to settle some of his wild spirits before he spooked the horse. As ever high strung, the chestnut was pawing in the traces, impatiently tossing its mane, resisting the groom's efforts to calm it. Jack crept toward the horse's head himself.

"Jack!" Freddie protested, starting forward to drag the child back from those restless equine feet, those flashes of large teeth, Jack's small hands seeming in danger of being snapped from his wrists.

But to her astonishment, Max stayed her, watching intently as Jack stroked the horse's velvety muzzle, murmuring soothing words. The chestnut quieted all at once, as though some sorcerer's wand had been waved above its head.

The groom stepped back respectfully, remarking to Max. "Young master's got the way about him with the beastie, eh, sir?"

"Yes," Max said slowly. "Yes, indeed he has." The light in his gray eyes grew almost hazy, like the mists that rolled over London in the early morning. He seemed to be lost in the memories of some far distant time, perhaps of the boy he himself once had been. It jolted Freddie to realize how much in tune she was with his feelings, what he was thinking. She knew what he was going to do before Jack did, perhaps even before Max did himself.

When they were all once more settled into the carriage, Max thrust the reins at Jack, saying abruptly, "Here."

"Sir?" Jack stared at the leather looped in his hands, his breath caught between wild hope and bewilderment.

Max settled back, regarding him with a lazy lift of his brows. "You did request to drive, did you not?"

"A-aye, sir, but you said—"

"Are you going to argue or commence? You should not keep the horse standing about."

"No, sir!" His eyes huge in his round face, Jack turned earnestly to his task. But he was quivering with so much suppressed excitement, he slapped the reins too hard, nearly causing the chestnut to bolt.

Max's strong arms came around the boy immediately, his much larger hands covering Jack's smaller ones. Murmuring words of advice and encouragement, he guided Jack to a lighter touch.

Absurdly Freddie found herself obliged to look away, hide a sudden smarting of tears behind her eyes. If she lived to be a hundred, she thought she would never forget that moment. Long after this day was lost to her, she would remember the look on Jack's face when Max placed the reins in his hands.

But most especially she would remember Max, the deep rumble of laughter from his chest, the light that shone from his eyes as he shared in the boy's delight.

Max balanced Jack's sleeping form in his arms, carrying the boy up the stairs to the second floor landing of Freddie's town house. She preceded him up the darkened stair, the single taper in her hand lighting the way.

The soft glow of the candle spilled over Jack's cherubic features, his mouth still sticky from the lemon ice he had recently enjoyed, his lips curved with some secret dreamings, perhaps of taming the lions and tigers he had seen in the Royal Menagerie.

The boy had had a full day of it, treats from Gunther's famous pastry cook establishment, a drive down Pall Mall, where Jack was rewarded by a glimpse of the prince emerging from Carlton House, a leisurely tour of London's infamous Tower, whose most dangerous prisoners these days seemed to be the collection of wild animals in the yard. Certainly not the brief outing Max had intended upon first setting out that morning. But he had to admit he had only himself to blame. It had been he who had kept thinking up excuses to prolong the excursion, strangely loathe to allow this day to end. Only when Jack's weary head had dropped upon Freddie's shoulder had Max finally given up and headed his horses for home.

Even at the door he could have surrendered the care of the boy to Freddie's butler. But his excuse had been the boy's weight would be too heavy for the nearsighted old man. He had visions of Stubbins walking with Jack into the rail, both of them tumbling headlong down the steps.

But in truth Max liked the way the child nestled so trustingly in his arms, stirring tender sensations Max had never thought to possess. Recovering from his youthful infatuation with his brother's bride, Max had long ago resolved not to marry, burden himself with the care of a wife and babes. That at least was one advantage to being the younger son. He was under no obligation to produce an heir.

Yet, as he gazed down upon Jack, he was consumed by a sudden longing, a bleak feeling that there might be something in life he had missed.

A rather idiotic notion to be coming from one who considered himself a confirmed bachelor. Max gave himself a brisk mental shake. Likely he also had had too long a day and was suffering from a surfeit of lemon ices and tigers, a little boy with an engaging grin and a vagabond lady whose blue eyes could have melted a heart of stone.

Max followed Freddie to the small bedchamber at the end of the hall. He eased Jack down onto the bed, but quickly, and stepped back as though already seeking the distance he had found so comfortable. Freddie lit the oil lamp, the burning wick casting a rosy glow over the room.

She began to strip Jack out of his garments, the boy roused only enough to regard her muzzily through the entire process. Max had an impulse to help, but he quelled it. In any case, Freddie stood in no need of aid from him. Crooning soothing words low in her throat, she eased Jack into a nightshirt many sizes too large for him, smoothing the fabric over his small frame with those comforting gestures only women seemed to know how to make. Watching her with the boy stirred a curious ache in Max's chest.

Feeling very much in the way, he backed across the threshold, mumbling something about waiting for Freddie in the hall below. Absorbed in tucking up the child, Freddie nodded. She was on the verge of extinguishing the lamp when Jack's eyes fluttered open again. "Grandmama?"

Freddie rustled back to his side in an instant. "Yes, love?"

"I had a bang-up holiday," the child murmured sleepily.

"I am glad to hear it."

"You must tell Mr. Warfield that I said thank you and—and I am sorry I did not like him so much at first. You see, I thought you were going to have him replace my grandpapa."

Freddie smiled, caressing the boy's cheek. "No one would ever be able to replace your grandpapa, dearest."

Why were those soft words like a knife thrust to Max's heart? His presence just beyond the door undetected, Max felt like an intruder. Yet he did not seem able to tear himself away from the sight of Freddie bending over the child like some spritely guardian angel, her golden curls tumbling about a face that was as dreamy-eyed with innocence as the boy's own.

She snatched up the reticule she had been carrying earlier and began fishing within its silken depths. "I have something I have been saving to give you, Jack. Now seems as good a time as any."

At the prospect of a gift, like any eager child Jack came more fully awake, sitting up in bed. From where he stood,

Max could see Freddie press something into the child's hands, a small gilt-framed miniature.

Jack stared at it with wide-eyed wonder. "Why, 'tis a portrait of me. However did you manage to obtain my likeness so quickly?"

"Not you, my dear. 'Tis your grandpapa when he was about your age. It was one of the few portraits left to me after he—he went away and I had to leave Dunhaven." She ducked her head, continuing in muffled tones. "There is a more recent portrait of your grandfather, a quite magnificent one that used to hang in the front hall. I believe your papa has moved it to the gallery at the back at the house. If . . . when you ever go to visit Dunhaven, you might just want to have a look at it."

"So I shall." Jack clutched the miniature as though it were a treasure, his small chin stiffening with resolve. "And if I ever can manage it, I shall move that picture back to the main hall, where it belongs."

"That . . . that would be good. I am sure your grandpapa would have been very proud of you, very pleased."

Jack tipped his head to peer beneath the cascade of hair shielding Freddie's face. "Faith, lady, you are not going to cry on a fellow, are you?"

Freddie shook her head, trying to smile. "No, 'tis only I shall rather miss you, young Master Jack."

And she enveloped the boy in a fierce hug. Fearing that he had already witnessed more than he had any right, Max turned and beat a quiet retreat. As he neared the darkness at the top of the stairs, he paused.

He could hear Dora's voice below calling out something to the ancient Stubbins and the old man's cheerful reply. Then came the definite cooing sound of a babe and distant echoes of feminine laughter, both Dora's and that little housemaid's. It was odd how sound carried in Freddie's house. Perhaps it was the lack of furniture.

More likely it was the warmth that seemed to pervade this half-mad, topsy-turvy household so different from the precision and the quiet he insisted upon in his own.

Max rubbed his fingers against his eyelids, thinking perhaps it might be best not to wait for Freddie after all. He could as easily speak to her in the morning when he came to fetch the boy. He would be better rested then, better able to deal with that brand of delicious madness which ever seemed to follow in her wake.

But Max formed this resolve a trifle too late. Before he set one foot on the stair, Freddie slipped out of Jack's room, squinting toward the shadows where he stood.

"Max?" She breathed. "Is that you?" She stepped forward, holding the wax taper aloft with a soft laugh. "You should have taken the candle away with you or you will be bumping into the walls like my poor Stubbins."

She glided forward, bringing light to his darkness, candle-shine picking out the golden glints in her hair, the jewellike facets of her eyes. Max felt an almost irresistible tug of attraction and drew back stiffly.

"So did you manage to coax Master Jack to sleep?" he asked.

"No, but he soon will be. He is quite exhausted."

"The boy needs his rest. I fear I must come early to fetch him away. You look rather done in yourself, so I had best bid you good night."

Max stepped down the first two risers, but Freddie darted forward to intercept him, placing one smooth, cool hand over his on top of the post.

"I never got the chance to thank you," she said.

Being slightly below her brought her face closer to a level with his. There was no escaping the sweet, earnest expression in her eyes, the slightly shy smile. It was obvious Freddie's own defenses were down tonight which made this situation doubly dangerous.

Max eased his hand from beneath hers. "Thank me?" he said. "For what?"

"For your kindness to a small boy today. And also to another child many years ago."

"No thanks are necessary. It was a very careless sort of kindness, my dear. I never do anything that proves an inconvenience to me."

"Don't you? I suppose that is why you insist upon driving Jack yourself all the way back to school. You could send him on the stage with a servant to accompany him."

"It so happens I have an inclination myself to travel in that direction."

"Oh, I am sure. During the height of the London season, most gentlemen experience this urge to go haring off to the wilds of Yorkshire."

She was laughing at him, but Max found he did not mind that nearly as much as he pretended. "Minx," he growled.

Freddie blushed as prettily as though he had just paid her a compliment. But her saucy look faded, an anxious furrow appearing between her brows.

"Jack will be all right, won't he, Max? You don't think his tutors will—will beat him or anything?"

"Not if they place any value on their heads," Max said grimly.

"And what about Sir Wilfred?"

"Oh, I think I can handle him as well. I have a good many scores to settle with that gentleman." His resolve to keep his distance already forgotten, Max could not resist running his fingertips over the tiny creases of her brow.

"I know you don't have much cause to believe in my promises, Freddie. But I assure you that I will do all in my power for Jack, to see him bestowed safe and sound."

Her eyes shone with such gratitude, it took his breath away. A gratitude he felt far from deserving. Before he could stop her, she caught his hand and pressed a gentle kiss against the back of it. Max snatched his hand away as though he had been stung. Her lips had felt so soft, so delicate. For all her bravado, it was borne in upon him how vulnerable she really was. And how helpless he was to protect her.

"Damme!" he said. "If I could only tuck you safely back into the schoolroom as well."

She wagged her brows at him in teasing fashion. "Alas, sir, I fear I am a bit old to be sent back to stitching samplers."

He was worried nigh to distraction, and *she* was making jests about it. "I am quite aware of your age, madam. You are not so easily disposed of as young Jack."

"Disposed of?" she echoed. He thought a flash of hurt appeared in those speaking blue eyes, but she rallied behind a quick smile. "Yes, like Jack, I always have been something of a nuisance to my relatives."

"Curse it all, Freddie! You know I did not mean—"

"But," she said brightly, "I am no one's problem now."

No one's but her own, Max thought with a frown. The outing with Jack had distracted him from the immediate threat to his peace of mind, Freddie and her blasted list of eligible rakes, whatever outrageous plans she might be forming.

She attempted to brush past him, precede him down the stairs. But he caught her arm, detaining her on the landing. "When I get back from Yorkshire, Freddie, I want you ready to close up this house and move to Lady Bentley's. Then we will sit down and discuss what is to be done with you."

"That might not be convenient. I will likely be out with General Fortescue."

"Freddie! I want an end to this nonsense. You will never form any sort of connection with Fortescue. You are only trying to provoke me. I know you are not the sort of woman to engage in such a liaison."

"Alas, I fear you are quite mistaken. If you want a true notion of my character, you have only to ask Aunt Jameson or Sir Wilfred. Don't go about telling everyone, but . . ." She leaned forward and said in a conspiratorial whisper, "I am a very wicked woman, Max."

Max was not even tempted to smile. "Ever since you were a little girl, you have gotten up to your naughty tricks, thumbing your nose at the world's disapproval. But you are too old for these childish games of defiance now. This reckless way you have been living . . . gaming, flirting, talking about becoming someone's mistress—it is a little more dangerous than climbing trees or purposefully blotting your copybook. You are going to get hurt, Freddie. And what is more, you are going to hurt the people who care about you, believe in you."

"And who might that be?" she asked softly. She looked up at him, her eyes lit up with a wistfulness that rivaled the candle's glow.

"There is Miss Applegate for one."

"Dora completely understands and approves of everything I do."

"And then there is young Jack."

"He is going away."

"And—and your household. Stubbins and that little housemaid."

"And what about you, Max?"

He shot her a look of pure exasperation. "Damn it, of course I care what happens to you, you little fool. Why else would I be trying to make arrangements for you, place you somewhere safe, where I don't have to worry about you anymore?"

Her face fell. She said tautly. "Well, I *certainly* would not want to worry you. But I refuse to be dependent upon anyone's charity. Not even yours, Max."

"You would rather trade yourself to some old man for a few trinkets?"

She flinched a little at his bluntness, but replied steadily enough. "Yes, I fear that I would. Besides, it would not be as crude as you describe it."

"How would you know? How many times have you been anyone's mistress before?"

Freddie's face settled into that expression of mulelike stubbornness that Max had ever found so exasperating. "None," she admitted. "But I have learned and observed a great deal since coming to London."

"You have learned nothing. You are green as any chit out of the schoolroom. Someone ought to show you exactly what it would be like to satisfy the demands of a wealthy lover."

"Perhaps General Fortescue will oblige." The candle wavered in Freddie's hand. She kept her chin upraised in defiance, but she felt wearied, unequal to continuing this quarrel with Max. She wished he would simply go away, but he continued to block her path to the stairs.

He seemed calm enough, but a hard, dangerous light had sprung to his eyes, which she found very unsettling. He groped inside his waistcoat pocket, drawing forth several golden guineas which he counted out into his hand.

"Wh-what are you doing?" she asked.

"Nothing." His smile was grim with determination and not particularly pleasant. "I have merely come to the conclusion that if anyone shows you anything, it should be me. After all, you did ask me first."

"Ask you what?"

"If I wanted you as my mistress."

"B-but you said no and I was only teasing you when—" She retreated an involuntary step as Max stalked closer. "Oh, don't, Max. I am too tired for any more lectures or you trying to teach me a lesson."

"No lesson, my dear," he murmured, his voice both silk and steel. "Merely a simple business transaction."

He took her left hand, upended her palm, pressing the guineas into it, forcing her fingers to curl about the coin. "There. That should take care of a new bonnet or a gown. Now, what will you offer me in return?"

"A box on the ears!"

"Wrong." Max pressed closer. She was forced back another step. "That is not the correct response, Freddie. That is not at all what a lover who paid handsomely for your favors would expect."

He backed her all the way against the wall, so that she nearly stumbled over the hall table.

"Stop it, Max," she cried, her heart thudding with a strange mixture of fear and excitement. She tried to hand the money back to him. But he snatched the candle from her instead.

His eyes holding hers with an intensity and heat that left her breathless, he blew the candle out, leaving them in darkness. He set the taper down upon the hall table and reached for her. The coin tumbled from her fingers, jangling across the floor. Freddie attempted to bolt. But Max yanked her hard against him.

She struggled wildly, but he pinned her hands with ease. His mouth found hers, taking her lips in a hard, plundering kiss, sending a jolt through her entire frame. She stiffened. Unable to defy his strength, she sought to make herself icy, unyielding, until he should pull back in defeat.

But he surprised her by gentling the kiss, his mouth now whispering softly over hers. His bullying she could resist, but his tenderness proved her undoing.

Against her will she found herself relaxing against him. No! She knew why he was doing this. It was only Max trying to frighten her, to demonstrate what a naive fool she was. She would not give in to the delicious warmth that had begun to steal over her.

But his lips worked magic in the darkness, teasing the corners of her mouth, caressing her cheeks, tasting the curve of her jaw. A soft sigh escaped her as he released her wrists, his arms circling protectively around her.

He murmured her name as he kissed her once more, and suddenly Freddie no longer cared why he was doing this. She melted against him, returning his kiss, awkwardly at first, then with increasing eagerness.

He coaxed her lips apart. Slowly, seductively, his tongue invaded the moist recesses of her mouth. She gasped at the shock of such intimate contact, then found the sensation almost unbearably sweet. She was hazily conscious of how well she fit against Max's hard-muscled form, of how right it felt to be in his arms.

All thoughts of resistance gone, she buried her fingers in his hair, giving herself up completely to his embrace. She did not demur, even when Max's kiss became even more demanding, his hands moving over her feverishly, stroking an ache of longing within her, feelings of desire that should have terrified her but did not.

When his mouth moved down to caress the pulse pounding at her throat, she arched her neck back with a soft whimper of pleasure. Max drew back a little, breathing raggedly. He did not release her, but she sensed him fighting to regain control.

"Freddie, this is madness," Max groaned. "What am I doing?"

"Perhaps," she whispered, "perhaps you do want me after all."

Her words had a strange effect on him. He wrenched her arms from his neck and put her away from him. He took a step back. Even in the darkness Freddie could see how unsteady his hand was as he raked it back through his hair.

She longed to be able to clearly see his face. She longed to know if he was feeling the same powerful currents as she. More than anything, she longed to be back in his arms.

But then he spoke, saying the words she most dreaded to hear.

"Freddie, I am sorry." And the regret in his voice told her all she needed to know. She had taken a tentative step toward him, but she stopped, left suddenly chilled, bereft.

"I never meant to . . . that is, I had no right—" he stumbled on. "Damn! I have behaved like a perfect boor."

She wanted to beg him to stop. The last thing she desired was for him to apologize for what had been some of the most wondrous moments of her life. But she could not seem to speak past the thickness gathering in her throat.

He sighed. "I fear this lesson got a little out of hand."

A lesson . . . that was all the past few moments had been to him. How stupid she had been to lose sight of that fact.

"Don't fret, Max," she managed to say hoarsely. "It was not entirely your fault. I have always been entirely too precocious."

He gave a shaky laugh. "Kissing like that was not exactly what I was trying to teach you. I think I had best be going. Doubtless we are both just overtired."

Was that how he kissed when he was exhausted? She could not help wondering with a tiny shiver what Max was like when he was well rested. Not that it mattered. She had a sinking feeling she was never going to be permitted within a yard of Max Warfield again. He was already moving toward the stairs.

She felt as though she could not bear to let him go like this.

"Max!" she cried desperately.

He had descended the first riser, but she sensed him pause, shifting to glance back at her.

"Max, I . . ."

"Yes?" His tone was not encouraging.

Freddie was suddenly glad of the concealing shadows. She groped through the darkness, seeking her abandoned pride until she found it.

"Nothing," she said. "I wanted only to bid you good night."

"Good night. I will be back in the morning for the boy. See that Jack is ready." Max started quickly down the stairs. Shortly thereafter, she heard the front door close behind him.

Freddie touched one hand to her lips, still tender and tingling from the force of Max's embrace. Part of her wished she had made more of an effort to detain him, and part of her was glad he had left and so quickly, too.

That was all that had saved her from making a complete idiot of herself. One moment more and she might have been tempted to tell him just how much she wanted him.

Another moment longer and she might have confessed how much she needed him. And one more moment and she might have done something really foolhardy.

She might have told him that she had fallen in love with him.

Chapter 10

Freddie had not dreamed of Leon once since his death. But during the many days following Max's departure with Jack into Yorkshire, Freddie's slumberings were frequently disturbed by a vision of her late husband.

Leon appeared to her just as he had been on their wedding day, garbed in his elegant brocades and lace-trimmed cravat, his silvery hair tied back in a queue. He stood waiting outside the church, a stately presence beaming reassurance. And she was a nervous bride again, clad in that awful pea green silk Aunt Jameson had bestowed upon her most grudgingly for a wedding gift. Freddie stumbled on her own train and Leon caught her, easing her tensions with one of his dry jests, saying that while he hoped one day she might come to fall in love with him, he had never meant for her to do it so precipitously.

The scene was all so clear that Freddie was nigh driven to cry out in her sleep. Only when Leon escorted her into the interior of the church did the vision begin to seem more dreamlike. She could see naught of the pews, only shifting mists and glowing candles. She clung tighter to Leon simply to find her way down the aisle.

But to her dismay, he tugged his hand free. "Nay, my dear," he said. " 'Tis time to let go."

She looked up at him uncomprehendingly. He gave one of those gruff laughs that crinkled the lines around his eyes. Shoving her gently on her way, he urged, "Go on now, sweeting. Would you be late for your own wedding?"

Freddie took a few faltering steps forward, then glanced back toward Leon. But he had already faded into the mists. She had no choice but to creep forward, groping to find her way.

Suddenly the altar itself loomed up before her and another figure stood waiting. Tall, strong, and steady, the waves of night dark hair swept back from his brow. Familiar hooded eyes watched her, not with their usual brooding cynicism, but lit by a smile of great tenderness.

"M-Max?" Freddie murmured.

He held wide his arms. A sob of joy escaped her and she started running forward. Running, but no matter how she tried, she seemed unable to reach him. The church floor spun out from beneath her and she was falling, tumbling down into the relentless white mist.

It was at that point she awoke to discover the morning sun streaming through her bedchamber window. She was not fighting the mist but her own bedcovers. She sat up slowly, hugging her pillow to her chest.

"Damme!" she said, drawing in a shuddering breath. Three times! Three times since she had last seen Max she had had that nightmare or one very like it. If she believed in portents the way Dora did, she might be tempted to think that Leon was in some way attempting to communicate with her, to tell her something. Perhaps even . . . to give her his blessing?

Freddie murmured, "If this is the case, you are quite off the mark, old friend. There is nothing to bless."

How could one give a blessing to a wedding when the bridegroom was so unattainable, vanishing into the mist? She sighed, trying to shake off the feeling of hopelessness, telling herself it had been only a ridiculous dream after all. But like many dreams, it had a disturbing way of mirroring the waking world.

For Max was indeed out of her reach. He had not needed a fog to accomplish his disappearance, either. Yorkshire had done just as well. Freddie had the miserable feeling that Max could not flee from her far or fast enough.

If she had any doubts on that score, she had only to think back to that morning when Max had come to fetch Jack away. She had spent a dreadful night after that scene on the stairway landing, tossing and turning, hoping that when she awoke, this strange madness would have passed like a brief but virulent bout of influenza. But it hadn't. As soon as she had seen Max again, she had felt the longing to fling herself into his arms. The sight of him was at once familiar and strange, as though she had always known this man, known she would come to love him one day, as though she were seeing him for the very first time, the feelings coursing through her startling and new.

But Max had, as always, been Max, cool, with the customary briskness in his manner, her very distant cousin. In the hubbub of bidding Jack goodbye, soothing Dora's sobbing, trying not to cry herself, Freddie had not even found time for a private word with Max.

No mention was made of what had passed between them the night before. Max bundled Jack into his traveling carriage and Freddie thought he meant to depart without another word. But at the last second he had paused, regarding her with a frown.

"You will be all right while I am gone?" he murmured.

"Of course," she had said cheerfully. She could hardly tell him she did not think she was ever going to be all right again.

"I suppose it would be pointless to ask you to promise not to do anything rash in my absence."

Freddie had hesitated but an instant, then replied softly, "Yes, I promise."

But Max was already following Jack into the coach and Freddie was not sure that he had heard her. Blinking back her tears, she had stood waving until the carriage vanished down the street, watching Max go with a mixture of love and resentment.

Foolish man! She would have promised him anything he asked, and he had not even noticed.

If he gave her any thought at all during his sojourn in Yorkshire, Freddie knew what it would be. Stow Freddie someplace where she could no longer be a nuisance, where she would no longer cause Max a moment's worry. At one time, she had mightily resented that attitude.

Of late she was feeling dispirited enough to oblige him. True to her promise, she had done nothing more to forward her plan of finding herself a wealthy protector.

Max had been odiously correct. She was a naive little fool, quite incapable of carrying off such a clandestine arrangement with the aplomb of Lady Deidre McCauley. Especially not now, realizing how she felt about Max. Even if Max would never be aware of her love, never return it, to offer herself to any other man seemed to Freddie the worst sort of betrayal.

Which, she thought glumly, brought her right back to where she had started, trying to find some other way to survive. She had discovered during the past few days that Max had directed his man of business to pay off most of her debts. Loving him as she did, Freddie found the prospect of accepting his charity more intolerable than ever. Going begging back to Aunt Jameson was equally unthinkable.

Lady Bentley had once offered Freddie the use of that house in Bath. Max's pressure upon his sister notwithstanding, Caroline would still be quite eager to see the last of Freddie.

Freddie could not avoid the melancholy conclusion that Lady Bentley's suggestion offered Freddie her only real choice. She could live more cheaply in Bath. In order to salvage some of her pride, perhaps she could offer to act as caretaker of the place, obtain positions for Till, Stubbins, and Dora as well. Freddie had a shrewd notion Lady Bentley would agree to anything simply to get Freddie out of London.

The prospect of spending the rest of her life in Bath was not the most appealing one. But what did that matter? Far better to put distance between herself and the city, herself and Max. Confirmed bachelor he might be, but there was still the unfinished matter of that wager at White's. Someone would win it eventually. A man like Max was not meant to be celibate. He would be bound to take a new mistress, perhaps Lady Channing. Freddie wanted to be far away when that happened, where she would catch no hint of the rumors, no glimpse of Max driving the lively brunette through the park in his phaeton, waltzing with her at a ball, slipping off to some balcony, kissing her as he had Freddie, not to teach any lessons, but with wholehearted passion.

Even imagining Max with another woman in his arms was enough to drive Freddie half mad with jealousy. She doubled her pillow over her head in an effort to blot out the unwelcome images.

It was thus that Dora found her when the older woman whisked cheerily into Freddie's bedchamber, bringing her a steaming cup of chocolate.

"Are you awake, Freddie?" Dora cried in a jolly, booming voice. " 'Tis past ten. This is most unlike you to—"

She pulled up short, regarding Freddie's position with some perplexity. "Have you got a headache, my dear? I don't think using that pillow as a compress will serve the purpose. It would be far better to let me bathe your forehead with Hungary water."

Freddie shifted the pillow from her head, feeling singularly foolish. "You know I loathe Hungary water, Dora. Besides, there is nothing wrong with my head. I . . . I was just testing out a new remedy for—for straightening unruly curls."

"Indeed?" Dora asked with great interest, and Freddie winced with shame at her own falsehood, wondering how long it would be before she found Dora with a pillow strapped to her own head.

She sought to divert Dora's attention by accepting the saucer and cup, thanking her friend for her kindness although at the moment Freddie had no appetite for anything, let alone the sticky sweet chocolate.

She forced herself to sip it while Dora plunked down on the edge of her bed. It was often Dora's habit to visit upon rising, settling in for what she termed a comfortable prose. Freddie had never felt less like sharing confidences. She replied to Dora's nonstop chatter in monosyllables, trying to make her responses fall at the appropriate times.

Despite her own cloud of distraction, Freddie could not help observing that something was different about Dora this morning. She scrutinized her friend closely for a moment, then realized what it was.

"Dora!" She interrupted her friend in midsentence. "You cut your hair."

"What? Oh, that. Yes, I did." Dora patted her short bob of curls with a self-conscious gesture. "Or, rather, Till did. She is very skilled at such things."

"It is quite fashionable and most becoming," Freddie said, and that was not merely a kind lie. The style was more suitable to Dora, the cluster of ringlets softening the angles of her face.

Dora blushed at the compliment, the color enhancing an unexpected brightness in her soft brown eyes.

"Your complexion has improved, too," Freddie continued. "At least the air of London seems to agree with one of us. You make me feel positively haggard by comparison."

"You have been looking a little pale of late, my dear." Dora reached out to give Freddie's hand a motherly pat. "But I daresay you will be feeling much better when Mr. Warfield returns from Yorkshire."

"Why would you suppose that?" Freddie asked with some dismay. Were her feelings for Max that mortifyingly obvious?

Dora beamed at her. " 'Tis only that I have observed that you seem in much finer fettle when Mr. Warfield is about, even when you are quarreling with him." She paused to vent a sentimental sigh. "The two of you looked so charming that day you took Jack out for his holiday, just like a little family. Mr. Warfield was astonishingly attentive. I almost wondered . . ."

Dora shot Freddie a nervous sidelong glance. "Now, don't be angry with me, dear. But I almost wondered if Mr. Warfield might be thinking of marriage?"

Freddie pulled a wry face. "Far from it. In fact, the night before he left, he reconsidered my offer to be his mistress."

Dora looked a little crestfallen, then rallied. "Of course, that must have pleased you. That *was* what you wanted."

"No, I was only pretending when I made Max that offer."

"Oh, dear. How very awkward it must have been when he decided to take you up on it."

"No, he was only pretending as well."

Dora's brow puckered, then she shook her head. "Being a wicked woman can be very confusing sometimes."

"Yes, it can," Freddie agreed gloomily. She did not feel equal to broaching the subject of the future with Dora just then. But she owed it to her friend to tell Dora as soon as possible of the decision she had reached.

Freddie set the cup of barely tasted chocolate on the bedside commode and straightened. "Dora, I have been doing a great deal of thinking. Bath is really not such a dreadful place. It might even be amusing to go there and take the waters. Perhaps we ought to take Lady Bentley's advice and—"

"And leave London?" Dora cried.

Freddie had not been certain exactly what Dora's reaction would be, a little disappointment perhaps, but nothing like the stricken expression that crept into her friend's eyes.

"Oh, no, Freddie. You cannot mean it. You would not want to leave London now." Dora cast down her eyes, coloring deeply. "Not just when—when everything is becoming so interesting."

"A little too interesting for me," Freddie said dryly. She entertained a fleeting memory of Max's kiss and was hard pressed not to blush herself. "I could use a little quiet."

She forced herself to meet her friend's gaze frankly. "The truth is, Dora, I no longer know what else to do."

"But what of your plan to find an eligible rake?"

"I fear I am no more successful at that than I was at cards."

Dora bit down upon her lower lip, then said hesitantly. "There is always General Fortescue. He calls practically every day, stays for tea. Perhaps if you ever joined us . . ."

"The general is a kind man, but we are simply not well

suited. As I told you days ago, I have quite given up on my plan to attach him."

"So you said. But, oh, Freddie, are you quite certain?" Dora asked, staring at her with a peculiar intensity.

"Very certain," Freddie said firmly.

"But he has applied for tickets to the museum at Montagu House and is coming around later this morning to escort us there and to the circulating library."

Museums? Libraries? Neither of these sounded much like the rakish old general, but Freddie felt too wearied to give the proposed expedition much consideration.

"I am sure it would be most diverting, Dora," she said. "But I fear I must beg off."

"The general will be disappointed."

"Then you accompany him."

"Oh, dear, I am not sure that I should. I feel so wicked to always be taking your place."

"My dear Dora, I have no claim upon the man," Freddie said impatiently. "You have my full permission to go off with the general, flirt with him, and be as wicked as you like."

Freddie shifted lower on the bed, nestling her head back onto the pillow. She had not had a headache when Dora entered, but she felt the nigglings of one now.

Dora rose to her feet. She emitted a tremulous sigh. "If you truly mean that . . ."

"I do!" Freddie said, wishing Dora would stop hemming and hawing, simply leave her in peace. She rolled over to her side. "Now, pray, you must excuse me. I find I am still very tired. I have not been sleeping too well of late."

"And here I have been chattering away at you." Dora was instantly contrite. "I should let you get your rest. You have been worrying too much again about how we shall get on and with never any help from me."

"Nonsense," Freddie murmured. "You have always been a great support to me."

As Dora hovered, Freddie grimaced, fearing her friend would now stay, fussing over her. But Dora did no more than lay her hand upon Freddie's brow, her touch gentle and soothing.

"Go back to sleep, dear," she cooed. "And don't you fret about moving to Bath or any other such. I will take care of the general and . . . and everything."

Freddie had a hazy notion that perhaps she ought to ask

what *everything* was. But her headache was already escalating into a full throb. She closed her eyes, scarcely aware when Dora slipped out of the room.

Max approached the steps of Freddie's town house with some trepidation. The quickening in his veins was no doubt owing to the fact that he never knew what might be taking place behind Freddie's walls, what fresh disaster awaited, what latest chaos lurked, threatening to pull him in like a whirlpool.

In all honesty, Max had to admit it was not entirely such apprehensions that sent him scurrying to her doorstep only an hour after his return. Upon arriving back in the city, he had but paused long enough at his own house to change his traveling clothes.

As he strode up to her door, this eagerness, this peculiar unsettled feeling, was new to him. But he had finally arrived at some conclusions regarding his emotions and Freddie, hard-won conclusions after many distracted days during his sojourn in the north.

He had scarce been able to get Freddie off his mind for a moment, vexing, tantalizing sprite that she was. Never had there been any woman who could make him lose his temper so swiftly, who could so easily overset his self-control. He had always been a man to let his head rule even in his amorous relationships with women.

And then came Freddie.

He should have known something was different that night on the staircase landing when he pulled her into his arms to teach her a lesson. The lesson had been his to learn, one of passion and tenderness, desire and a deeper longing than he had ever experienced before.

He had wanted to spend eternity with her heart pounding against his. He had wanted to hold her protectively, fiercely, in his embrace forever. And he had wanted beyond all thought, all reason, to make love to her there and then. Her shy but eager response to his kiss had been nearly enough to overset any scruples he had. And also enough to rouse his suspicions regarding the exact nature of Freddie's relationship with her late husband. She was astonishingly innocent for the widow of as old and accomplished a rakehell as Raincliffe.

He did not know why that should relieve him so. It was ridiculous this continuing jealousy of his over the part that the viscount had played in Freddie's life. Perhaps it was owing to his fear that Freddie yet mourned too much for her beloved Leon. Max had devised a new plan for Freddie's future, and was more than a little afraid that she would reject it.

Unaccustomed to such nervous qualms, irritated by them, Max seized the door knocker and rapped it with more force than necessary. He rocked back on his heels, trying to curb his impatience, knowing that it took Stubbins forever to answer the door.

He was therefore almost thrown off balance when the door was flung open. It was not the half-blind butler who blinked up at him, but Freddie herself.

She looked quite breathless, her golden hair a wild tangle, as though she had just arisen from her bed. This conjured up a far too agreeable image for Max, and he fought to quell his quick arousal. Harder to quell was the desire to gather her into his arms. God, how he had missed her these past two weeks.

She stared almost blankly at him, then stumbled back, saying, "Oh, Max. It's only you."

Max winced. He never knew what sort of reception he was going to get from Freddie. Only one thing was certain. She never failed to disconcert him.

"Thank you," he said, crossing the threshold and closing the door behind him. "It's good to see you again, too."

"I didn't mean ... 'Tis only that I thought—I hoped you might be Dora."

Max removed his high-crowned beaver and began stripping off his gloves. He tossed them on the hall table. "Never tell me you have managed to mislay Miss Applegate."

He was astonished when his wry jest elicited no answering retort. He glanced up, for the first time noticing how pale Freddie was, the deep circles rimming her eyes.

He immediately crossed to her side, taking her hand. "Freddie? What is it, my dear?"

Freddie swallowed hard, too close to tears to be able to speak.

"Is it something to do with Miss Applegate? Good heavens, the woman cannot truly be lost?"

Freddie shook her head.

"Do you fear there has been some sort of accident?"

Another negative.

"Then what the deuce is amiss?"

Freddie drew in a deep breath, then blurted out, "Dora—sh—she has run off with General Fortescue."

With all the will in the world Max could not seem to help himself. A bark of incredulous laughter escaped him.

Freddie glared at him. "This is not amusing."

"No, I am sure it would not be," Max said soothingly. "If it were true. But Dora and Fortescue? I fear you have been letting your imagination get the better of you."

"*This* is not imagination." Freddie took an object she had been clutching in her other hand and thrust it at him.

Max accepted it, staring at the crumpled piece of vellum. He raised an inquiring brow.

"It's a letter from Dora," Freddie said. "Delivered just before you arrived. Stubbins accepted it, so I had no chance to question the messenger. You just read that and then see if you are inclined to laugh."

Frowning, Max obeyed, smoothing out the sheet of paper. Miss Applegate possessed a fine, neat hand. It was a pity, Max thought as he scanned the page, that she did not also possess a clarity of expression.

My dear Freddie,
I must write you in haste, for the general is all afire to be gone. He did not obtain tickets for the museum after all because his mother lives in Hampstead. Forgive me for my wickedness, but I will not be home for tea. The general has begged so ardently, what could I do but say yes and so I am off with him in a coach and four. Well, it is more of traveling brougham, actually, but don't worry, for I will send you my address directly. Do not serve up those raspberry tarts in the pantry for I fear they have gone bad.

Most affectionately yours,
Dora Margaret Applegate

As he reached the end of this missive, Max placed a hand to his brow, his head throbbing with the effort to make sense of Dora's letter. He supposed he could read it again, but he doubted that it would do much good.

He refolded the peculiar message while Freddie paced the length of the hall, fretting. "It is all my fault."

"What is? You mean about the raspberry tarts?"

"No! Dora and Fortescue. It all becomes so clear now."

"Then I wish you would explain it to me," Max said irritably. "I thought Fortescue was dangling after you."

145

"He was, but after I promised you that I would stay out of trouble, I stopped seeing him. But he still kept coming around to tea. If I had not been so selfish, lying about moping, I might have noticed what was going on. All this time he has been plotting to seduce my poor Dora."

"Forgive me, Freddie. Your friend Miss Applegate is a very fine woman, but she is scarcely the sort to invite seduction. She is a little too—er—*solid* for such a thing."

"She *was* before she came to live with me. But I told her it was all right. I told her to go off and be just as wicked as she chose, and now she has."

Max rubbed his neck and vented a weary sigh. He was exhausted from his recent journey, and this was not at all the sort of tête-à-tête he had hoped to enjoy with Freddie. Despite the jumbled letter, he still had trouble accepting the notion of Dora Applegate being wicked with anybody, even an old devil like Fortescue. But Freddie clearly believed her friend's virtue to be in imminent peril. Max sensed how distraught she was, only her fierce pride preventing her from dissolving into tears.

She turned to face Max, proclaiming dramatically. "If anything happens to Dora, I will never forgive myself. I have been the most deplorable influence on her. Go ahead and say it, Max. You warned me I was courting disaster and I would not listen."

"There will be time enough later for me to say I told you so. Right now I suppose we had best do something about recovering Miss Applegate."

Freddie bit down on her trembling lip. "When I answered the door just now, I hoped that it was her, that perhaps Dora had come to her senses and returned."

Max thought that anyone who could write such a muddle-headed letter very likely had no senses to come back to. But he wisely kept such a reflection to himself. Instead, he asked, "How long has Miss Applegate been missing?"

"She went off late this morning on an outing with the general." Freddie stomped her foot, her eyes glittering with sudden anger. "That old villain! I might have known he never had any tickets to the museum."

Max let this confusing statement pass. He consulted his pocket watch. " 'Tis nearly five o'clock. If she did go off somewhere with Fortescue, which, mind you, I still cannot quite believe, the most they could have is a few hours' start."

"I shall have to hire a carriage and try to follow them."

146

"Don't be ridiculous," Max said. He reached for his hat and gloves, already bowing to the inevitable. "I will go in search of her."

"That is very good of you, Max," Freddie said. "But Dora is my friend. I see no reason why you should be bothered."

"Don't you?" Max said. "Let us just say that I suppose I had better grow accustomed to dealing with these unusual situations."

Freddie looked confused by this cryptic comment, but Max was not about to go into any explanations just now.

"My first step," he said, "will be to make inquiries at the general's lodgings."

Freddie looked as though she might be inclined to give him an argument. But finally she said, "Fine. If you insist upon it, I suppose I would be grateful for your help. Just give me a moment to fetch my shawl and bonnet."

"Freddie, I think it would be better if you waited here."

"I'll do no such thing. It will be far too humiliating for Dora to have you come upon her alone. She will need me."

"And what about Fortescue? If he does have improper designs on Miss Applegate, he will be less than pleased by my interference. There could be a most unpleasant scene."

"All the more reason I should be there," Freddie retorted. "To keep you from doing anything rash. This is the sort of situation that frequently involves gentlemen in some ridiculous duel."

"Yes, by God, I suppose it is," Max said, a slight smile curving his lips.

"Now what the devil amuses you?" Freddie snapped.

"Nothing," Max said dryly. "Only that I have never fought a duel over a woman in my life. Yet this is the second time this month I may come close to trading blows. And all for the honor of Miss Dora Applegate!"

Chapter 11

Freddie clenched her hands in her lap, leaning forward on the seat of Max's curricle. She peered through the gathering darkness, willing the chestnut to go faster along the road leading out of London. Ominous-looking clouds had gathered on the horizon, threatening to steal away what remained of the daylight.

A rumble of thunder caused her to shrink instinctively closer to Max.

"Perfect," he muttered. "It's going to rain."

"Perhaps the storm will hold off until we reach Hampstead," Freddie said hopefully.

"If we reach Hampstead and don't end up in a ditch first." Max swore under his breath as he guided his curricle past a particularly nasty rut in the road. It was getting increasingly harder to see. He would need to stop and light the running lamps soon.

Freddie sensed the tension in him, the barely restrained impatience. She knew Max believed that they were off on some harebrained chase. Freddie feared much the same thing herself. When they had inquired at Fortescue's lodgings, they could get no answers from the general's tight-lipped valet. But the boot boy had told them he had heard the general planning to set our for Hampstead and with a lady in his company. Yet the shrewd-faced little rascal had demanded a half crown for this information and Freddie was not certain how reliable the lad might be.

She could not help voicing some of her own doubts aloud. "It makes no sense. Dora's letters said something about Fortescue's mother. Why would a man take a woman he had designs upon to Hampstead if his mama was living there?"

"Why would a man take anyone to Hampstead?" Max groused. He tightened his grip on the reins, concentrating on the road ahead. He looked less than pleased with the situation he found himself in, and Freddie could barely blame him. She knew he had just arrived back from Yorkshire and must be close to exhaustion.

She almost wished it had been anyone else but Max who had arrived on her doorstep, only to find her caught up in a fresh disaster. As if he did not already think her enough of a nuisance, a perpetual scapegrace!

Yet despite the scowl marring his handsome features, Freddie found herself glad of his steady presence at her side. No matter how gruff he pretended to be, no matter how he complained, Max always helped. If anyone could find her poor Dora, Freddie was confident it was he. Max had always fixed everything from her broken dolls to keeping her out of debtor's prison.

There was only one thing past his power to mend, her breaking heart. Having him so close, having to hide the fact she loved him was the most indescribable torment. She longed to press a kiss against the hard set of his lips and had to scoot a little farther away on the seat to suppress the temptation.

As the curricle rattled onward, Freddie thought anything might be better than this grim silence that had settled over them. She sought to break it by inquiring after Jack. That seemed a safe enough topic.

"Was all well with Jack when you left him? It has been so hard thinking of him back at that horrid school."

"But he isn't," Max said. "He's been moved to Eton, where I went as a lad. My old master, Dr. Douglass, is still there. If he survived dealing with me, he can do the same with Jack. He'll look after the boy, see that he gets sent home for holidays. Jack will even be permitted to receive any chance visitors that happen his way."

"Oh, Max. You don't mean that I could . . ."

At Max's nod, Freddie exclaimed, "However did you persuade Wilfred to agree to all of this? He is such an insufferable bully."

"Only where women and children are concerned. But I fear I am something of a bully myself, besides possessing the advantage of taking regular sparring exercises at Gentleman Jackson's."

"You never hit Wilfred?" Freddie asked, torn between horror and delight at the notion.

"How does one hit a man cowering behind a settee?"

For the first time since Max had gone away, Freddie felt an inclination to laugh.

Max continued. "My clinching argument with Sir Wilfred

was more in the nature of blackmail. He has great ambitions for the unprepossessing Cliveden, hopes he will cut quite a dash in the world. I informed my lord if he did not pay more heed to his younger son, Cliveden will not be cutting anything, anywhere. Especially not in the London clubs like Brook's, White's, anyplace where I hold influence."

"Max," Freddie said admiringly. "You are utterly ruthless."

"Yes, I am when it concerns getting my own way." He shot her a sidewise glance and looked about to say something more.

But at that instant a jagged streak of lightning cut the sky, illumining the distant shapes of the houses of Hampstead. Though often described as a village on the fringes of London, it was more the size of a small resort town these days, noted for its spring water.

As Max's chestnut labored, drawing the curricle up the hill, Freddie wondered with some despair how they would ever go about searching for Dora. The streets with their close-packed rows of cottages and lodgings was nigh as bad as London.

"What do we do now?" she murmured, trying to curb her mounting fear that it might already be too late to save Dora from being compromised. "We can hardly go about knocking at every door."

"Our best chance is to inquire at the inns," Max said. He risked a glance upward at the uncertain sky. "If nothing else, we will be near shelter when the storm breaks."

Freddie offered no disagreement as he sought out the nearest inn. It was a snug stone structure whose creaking sign proclaimed it to be the Good King Harry. It appeared to be neither an establishment of the first order, nor one entirely disreputable.

When Max drove into the yard, an ostler came forward promptly to help with the horse. As Max lifted Freddie down from the curricle, he commanded, "I want you to hurry inside. I already felt a drop. I will be in as soon as I make inquiries of this fellow. Even if Fortescue did not stop by here, it is possible the ostler may have noticed the carriage passing through."

Freddie was reluctant to obey, but the wind was picking up, tugging at her bonnet and shawl. When Max gave her a nudge in the direction of the inn, she went.

Entering the long, narrow taproom, she meant to make some inquiries of her own. But she saw no sign of anyone. Before she could locate the host, Max had joined her. The rain had

150

begun to tap against the windows, and he brushed beads of moisture off his hat and greatcoat.

"The luck appears to be with us," he said with grim satisfaction. "A couple answering very closely to the description of our truants arrived at this inn about an hour ago." He looked around him with distaste. "Though if Fortescue were planning a tryst, one would think he could do better than this."

"This is hardly the time to be criticizing another man's seduction methods," Freddie said. "That fiend may have Dora abovestairs even now."

Her heart pounding with dread, she started toward a rather rickety-looking banister, the creaking wooden steps that led upward to the next floor.

But she had not even mounted the first riser when a woman wearing a soiled apron came through the taproom door from the region of the kitchens. She had a heavy, drooping bosom, an even heavier scowl.

"And where do you think you are going, miss?" she demanded of Freddie. "We have no more accommodations available here."

"We are not seeking a room, my good woman," Max said. "What we desire is—"

"I have a fair idea of what the pair of you desire." The woman looked Max and Freddie up and down, her eyes dark with condemnation. "But you won't find it here. This is a respectable establishment."

Max's brows flew up in his haughtiest expression, but the effect did little good when his hair was so windblown. Freddie touched a hand to her own disordered curls crushed beneath her bonnet. She was suddenly conscious of what a disreputable pair she and Max made.

"Please, ma'am," Freddie said, trying to be placating. "My cousin and I are very tired. We are searching for—"

"Cousin indeed!" The landlady snorted. "Be off with you. I need no more trouble. I already regret letting my private parlor to that other pair. Said he was a general. What kind of general travels with no servants and his lady, not even a nightgown to her name!"

Freddie scarce heard the rest of this diatribe, the only words that registered with her being "private parlor." She glanced around anxiously for another door and saw one to the right of the bar counter. She rushed forward to open it, ignoring the landlady's furious expostulations.

Freddie burst into a small wood-paneled dining chamber. It was bare of furnishing but for an oak table and a few chairs. Fortescue was seated on one of them, Dora pulled down onto his lap, gasping and struggling to be free.

"Unhand her, you villain," Freddie cried, running forward. It was not until she began raining blows upon the startled general's arms and head that she realized that far from being in distress, Dora was breathless with laughter.

Her giggles stilled at the sight of Freddie. She leapt up from Fortescue's knee, her cheeks turning bright pink.

"Freddie!"

Fortescue had flung up one arm to defend himself. He peered cautiously around his sleeve. " 'Pon my word! Lady Raincliffe. What a surprise."

"Not as surprised as you are going to be, you—you miscreant rogue," Freddie spluttered. "I don't know what lies you told Dora to get her to come away with you, but you shall be sorry for it."

"Oh, Freddie, no!" Dora whisked herself in between Freddie and the general.

But Freddie thrust her aside, glowering menacingly at Fortescue. Quite forgetting her own resolve to prevent any dire confrontations, she blurted out, "Max Warfield is here, too. If you have offered Dora any insult, he—he will call you out for it."

"He mustn't," Dora wailed. " 'Tis too soon for me to become a widow. I just got married."

"Married!"

The stunned echo did not come from Freddie, but Max. He had finally managed to force his way past the irate landlady. As he crossed the threshold, Freddie was not sure if he looked more amused or ready to strangle someone.

Freddie had a fair idea who that someone might be. She put a hand to her throat and sort of quavered. "M-married?"

Fortescue snapped to his feet in his best military manner, looking both sheepish and proud. "That's right, b'gad. We meant to keep it secret awhile longer until I have had a chance to break the news to my mother." He took Dora's hand, beaming down at her. "But you must allow me to present you to the new Lady Mordant Fortescue."

Dora blushed deeply and lowered her eyes. Freddie was glad Fortescue had vacated his chair. Her own legs no longer seemed able to hold her. She sagged onto the wooden seat, her mind reeling. "Married?" she repeated. "Dora, what does this mean?"

"I explained it all in my letter," Dora said. "The general did not have tickets to the museum. He had a special license instead."

"I am afraid you forgot to mention that," Max drawled.

"Did I? Oh, dear."

"We were married in the little church at the head of the lane," Fortescue said. "M'parents wed there when they eloped. Family tradition, eh what?"

Freddie still felt too stunned to take it all in. Max appeared to have recovered faster. He shook the general's hand with surprising good humor for a man who had just been dragged off on a useless quest to save a lady's virtue.

He was even demanding his right to kiss the bride, when he was interrupted by the sounds of a fracas coming from the taproom.

He grimaced. "The landlady, no doubt. She threatened to return with reinforcements to cast us all out."

When Dora gave a small cry of alarm, he added, "Don't fret. I will deal with our gracious hostess." He moved briskly across the room, intercepting the red-faced landlady just as she was about to burst over the threshold. He forced her back out, closing the door behind him, muffling the sound of the ensuing argument.

Dora bustled over to Freddie. Bending down before her, she caught both of Freddie's hands. "Are you all right, my dear? I did not mean to cause you such distress. I am sorry I did not make my note more clear, but I was so distracted. Mordant's proposal took me so by surprise. But everything will be wonderful, Freddie. You will see. I am a married woman. I finally will be able to repay you for your kindness, rescuing me from a lifetime of only being Sir Wilfred's poor relation. Now I will be able to take care of you."

"Oh, Dora," Freddie said, eyeing her friend in horror. Regardless of the general's presence, she whispered, "Please do not say that you have sacrificed yourself for me."

"No." Dora gave a tinkling laugh. She cast a fond look up at the general which he returned. "I have been falling in love with this dear, foolish man ever since we met."

"Why didn't you tell me?" Freddie asked.

"You had enough to worry about, and for a long time I thought you were interested in the general." A wistful look came into Dora's brown eyes. "Even after you relinquished all claim, it still seemed so silly, the notion of me being in love, that anyone could love me in return. I never imagined that anything so romantic and daring as an elopement could ever happen to a plain, ordinary spinster."

The general tut-tutted and loudly objected to Dora's description of herself.

Dora gave Freddie's hand a squeeze. "I trust you are not so very angry with me, dear?"

"No, I was only worried. I thought—" But as she gazed down into Dora's honest, open countenance, Freddie broke off with a tremulous smile. "Well, never mind about that."

"I know my behavior has been most irregular," the general said. "But I do hope you will give us your approval, Lady Raincliffe."

"Dora does not need my approval."

"Indeed I do," Dora said. "You are my dearest friend. I should be truly miserable if I thought you could not be happy for me."

Freddie did not reply at once. She angled a fierce glance up at the general. "You truly love her, sir? You promise to take the best of care of her?"

"My word of honor upon it, my lady," Fortescue said gruffly, gradually softening into his rogue's smile. "She is the sort of woman I have always needed to keep me out of trouble, don't you know? Such a solidly sensible sort of gel!"

Freddie turned back to Dora. Her friend hunkered before her, regarding her with huge, pleading eyes.

"So what do you think?" Dora asked anxiously.

"I think," Freddie said, brushing back a stray tendril of Dora's hair, "that you make the most beautiful bride I have ever seen."

Dora emitted a half sob of relief, and she flung her arms around Freddie. They hugged, laughed, cried until the general cleared his throat, looking mighty uncomfortable with this feminine display of emotion.

"I hate to remind you, my dear," he said to Dora. "But we must be going soon."

"Oh! Oh, yes." Dora straightened hastily. When Freddie gave her a puzzled frown, she said, "We stopped here after the ceremony only to have a sort of wedding supper. This is not the sort of place Mordy approves of to spend the night."

"Bad sheets," the general explained. "Too many holes. We plan to travel on to m'mother's estate, just beyond Hampstead."

"And I am so nervous about meeting her," Dora moaned.

"Nonsense. She'll adore you just as I do." The general winked at Freddie. "Mama is also a most sensible sort of a gel."

"Afterward," Dora continued, "we are going to Rome. Imagine me, Dora Applegate traveling abroad."

"Dora Fortescue," Freddie reminded her with a tender laugh. While the general left to see about the carriage, she helped bundle Dora into her cloak.

Beset by a last-minute attack of nerves, Dora clutched at Freddie's sleeve, murmuring, "I wish you were going with me."

"Goose! On your bride trip?"

"But I feel so guilty. I have been so thoughtless, so inconsiderate. Who is to look after you?"

"I still have Till and Stubbins. Now, stop your fretting."

"When we get back, you are to come live with us. Even Mordy has said so."

Freddie made no reply. There was time enough to argue that point after Dora returned. She was a little anxious about her friend traveling during a storm, but when the general returned to fetch his bride, he assured Freddie the rain had already slackened off to a mere drizzle.

As the general linked his arm through Dora's, she looked so radiant, Freddie felt a lump form in her throat.

Dora sighed. "I am so very happy, Freddie. And I owe it all to you. None of this would have happened to me if we had not come to London to be wicked women."

Freddie laughed. She managed to keep smiling as Dora and Fortescue left the room.

"Good-bye, Freddie," Dora called. "I shall be sure to write. I am going to miss you very much."

It was only after Dora had gone that Freddie murmured, "And I shall miss you, too, my dear friend." She had not realized quite how much until that moment. A strange sensation of melancholy stole over her, and she felt left quite alone, abandoned.

She ought to be nothing but delighted for Dora and she was berating herself for her own selfishness when Max returned. He strode into the parlor, complaining. "Can you credit it? That infernal landlady had actually summoned the constable. I thought we were all going to spend the night in jail, like some wandering brigands. It is astonishing what an outlay of blunt it takes to convince people of one's respectability. But it all comes of hanging about with runaways like—"

Max paused, frowning as he gazed around the empty room. "And where the deuce is the happy couple?"

"Gone," Freddie said. "Fortescue really does have a mother near Hampstead. They are journeying on to her house."

"What!" Max's sharp tone caused her to jump. "You mean that shatterbrained woman has just gone off and left you?"

"This is Dora's wedding night," Freddie reminded him. "I think I would be infinitely de trop."

"Do not either of you possess a single wit? I have done my best to convince that harridan of a landlady of our respectability. And here you are, left alone with me, at night, at a public inn. If this ever gets abroad, your reputation will be in tatters."

"I have never worried overmuch about my reputation."

"I know."

Max shot her an impatient look. "Fortunately, there is a reasonable solution. You will have to marry me."

"What!" Freddie felt all the color drain out of her face.

"Perhaps I did not put that as well as I might." He raked his hand back through his hair with a rueful gesture. "Damn it, Freddie. I keep turning phrases over in my head, but none of them seem quite right. What I mean is . . . would you do me the honor of becoming my wife?"

"No!"

The vehemence of her reply appeared to take him aback, but he recovered, saying dryly, "If you are that uncertain of your answer, don't worry. I will give you more time to think about it."

Freddie faced him, trembling. Why did he not simply thrust a knife through her heart and be done with it? Because she had just witnessed Dora's glowing happiness, this grudging offer from Max was all the more painful by contrast.

"I don't need any more time," she said. "You don't have to do this, Max. I am going away—to Bath."

"What the devil does Bath have to do with my offer of marriage?"

"Because it is a place away from London and—and away from you. I don't know why you have this sense of obligation, this absurd notion that you are saddled with the responsibility of looking after me, even to the point of sacrificing yourself on the altar of matrimony."

"Freddie!" He started toward her, but she backed away, her eyes filling with proud tears.

"I have already had a lifetime of people doing their duty by

156

me, Max," she whispered. "I don't want any more of it, especially not from you."

Spinning on her heel, she rushed blindly out of the parlor. She brushed passed the landlady in the taproom, scarcely registering the woman's disapproving expression. Freddie bolted out the inn door, into the night, the rain misting against her cheeks to mingle with her tears.

She did not know where she was going, and she didn't care, only seeking to escape Max. But she did not get far when he overtook her.

Seizing her by the shoulders, he spun her around. "Freddie! What do you think you are doing? Come back inside before you get soaked and catch pneumonia."

"Leave me alone, Max," she cried, trying to twist away from him.

He swore. "I should have known better than to expect you would make this easy." He seized her shawl and dragged it up, arranging it like a scarf to shield her head from the rain. He did not seem to realize his own hair was already dripping with moisture, plastering to his head.

"You little fool," he murmured. Only Max could turn such words into an endearment. The light spilling through the inn windows illuminated his face. Freddie shrank from the tenderness she saw glowing in his eyes, not daring to place any faith in it.

He held her fast, saying, "Do you really believe I would ask a woman to marry me out of a sense of duty? You obviously have no comprehension of what a selfish man I am."

Freddie sniffed. "I suppose you are going to try to convince me you have been overcome with a sudden passion for me. Like some sort of a fit."

"More like a consumption. It comes over you so gradually, you don't realize you've caught it."

"And just when did this affliction strike you?" Freddie tried to lace her words with scorn, but her voice cracked.

Max stroked back a tendril of her hair which was by now very damp, as bedraggled as she felt. "Oh, the signs were always there if I had but had the wit to interpret them. That night I nearly lost control, kissing you on the stairs. The way I have been driving myself half mad, worrying what to do with you. The simplest solution has always been to find you a new husband. But I never seemed able to get around to considering any candidates. I finally said to myself, Max, you dolt. Why not marry the girl yourself? No, my nobler half argued. You want better for Frederica than that."

His lips quirked into a lopsided smile. "But as usual, my selfish side won out. You will never know all that you have brought back into my life, Freddie. You taught me to care again. So I am asking you most humbly, will you marry me?"

Her lips quivered. "You are being very stupid, Max. Offering marriage to someone as desperate as me, with no prospects. I might just accept you. And then where would we be?"

"Happy, I hope," he said solemnly. "But I don't want you thinking you have to accept me for that reason. You do have other choices. I did not spend all that time in Yorkshire solely on Jack's behalf. I did some investigating into the terms of your late husband's will."

"You wasted your time, Max."

"Regarding the will, perhaps I did. But I uncovered another interesting fact. There is a portion of the Raincliffe estate by tradition that has always been set aside to provide for the viscount's widow. A dower house. Living there would not make you wealthy, but you would remain independent."

"Wilfred would never permit such a thing."

"Oh, I think I could guarantee that he would. So you see, Freddie, you do have a choice. You can go on being Leon's widow, the dowager viscountess. Or you can settle for being plain Mrs. Warfield."

Freddie gazed up at him, stunned, heedless of the rain trickling down her face. "You—you did that for me? When you could easily bully me into marrying you, at the same time, you offer me an escape?"

"Quite magnanimous of me, isn't it?" He reached down to cup her chin, his fingers firm and warm. "I failed you once, Freddie. I never want to do that again. I—I may never be able to replace Leon—"

"I would not want you to try. Leon was my very dear friend. He will always have a place in my memory. But you, Max"—she swallowed thickly—"I have carried you in my heart for a very long time. I love you. That is why you must be really sure of your reasons for wanting to marry me. I could not bear it if I ever lost you again."

"You won't." He held out his arms to her.

She hesitated but a moment more, then with a mighty sob cast herself into his arms. He kissed her, straining her close, murmuring, "I love you, Freddie. Come in out of the rain."

THE LADY
WHO HATED
SHAKESPEARE

To Betsy,
for the hours of research,
for the years of friendship.

Chapter 1

Miss Cordelia Renwick kicked off her green kid boots, glaring through tear-filled blue eyes at the peaceful village of Stratford-upon-Avon, which nestled in the valley below her. "A pox on you, Will Shakespeare," she said with a sniff, shaking her tiny fist at the distant spire of Holy Trinity Church where the wretched man's bones lay buried.

She tucked a stray golden curl inside her large, gypsy-style bonnet, adjusting the saffron silk ribbon that tied beneath her chin. Stealing a furtive glance from under the straw brim, she checked to see if anyone had overheard her strange remark. She was alone on the violet-dotted hillside except for a flock of grazing piebald sheep. Good! She did not wish to be accounted an eccentric, and most people would deem it odd that she should passionately detest a gentleman who had moldered in his grave for nearly two centuries before she was born.

No one would credit how intimately acquainted she was with Mr. William Shakespeare, Cordelia thought bitterly as she undid her ribbon garters, and yanked off her stockings to dig her toes into the cool grass. She was aware that her behavior was extremely improper for a young lady of quality, especially when she considered that Peter, Lord Walsing, often rode this way in the morning, but she was too distressed by her latest quarrel with Papa to care.

Plopping herself down, she conceded to propriety enough to tuck her bare feet out of sight beneath the hem of her high-waisted, yellow jaconet gown. Then she snatched up her sketchbook and tried to immerse herself in her drawing, the only diversion that ever soothed her.

When her charcoal pencil snapped in two, she knew all efforts to suppress her emotions were of no avail. Fresh tears of frustration and hurt stung her eyes. Angry at herself for being such a watering pot, she wiped her eyes on the back of her sleeve. She supposed she must learn to follow the advice her father had flung at her across the breakfast table.

" 'What's gone and what's past help should be past grief.' "

Papa had an annoying habit of quoting Shakespeare at every opportunity so that often she had not the least notion what he was talking about. But this morning, his meaning had been plain enough. There was no way of avoiding the odious cousin who had invited himself to spend a month with them in Stratford. The unkindest cut of all was that Papa did not even wish to do so.

"I have not seen Miles Renwick for years. He is one of our few relations who has a proper appreciation of Shakespeare," Papa had said, nibbling at his toast. "Od's bodikins! What conversations we will have!"

Cordelia had frozen in the act of refilling her teacup. "But—but, Papa, we were going to Brighton this summer." She had planned the trip to the lively seaside resort for weeks. Seabathing, the Prince Regent's magnificent domed palace, scores of eligible gentlemen, dancing until dawn, and, best of all, she would get Papa away from Shakespeare. She had imagined sunny mornings walking along the shingle beach with her father, breathing in the brisk salt air, enjoying a peaceful tête-à-tête with him while the waves rolled up to shore. At Brighton, her father would not be able to shut himself up in the study as he had done ever since her young stepmother had died. Mayhap away from Rose Briar Cottage, he would even remember that he had a daughter very much alive.

But her father had quashed all such hopeful notions when he said, "Going to Brighton is of no consequence. I'd much rather have Miles here to visit. Of course, you will see to all the arrangements for his comfort." After uttering that assumption, Papa had ducked behind his folio so that all she could see were his bushy eyebrows.

Swallowing the lump in her throat, Cordelia had struggled to hide her wounded feelings. "But, Papa, Aunt Violet is already staying in the guest chamber," she had said. "Where is this man going to sleep? And you haven't even told me when he is to arrive."

He had replied with a brush of his hand, as if shooing away flies, Papa's usual indication that he was trying to read and found further conversation an annoyance.

Cordelia had clattered her teacup down into the saucer. "Well, if we go to Brighton, I am willing to forgo my other plans. But if we remain here, I will have all manner of social engagements forthcoming, not the least of which is the ball at Walsing Manor. I won't have time to entertain a guest."

She had sounded so petulant she could have slapped herself, but Papa's only response had been to peer over the top of his ponderous volume and remind her that her duties as mistress of the household came first, adding as a clincher: " 'If all the year were playing holidays, to sport would be as tedious as to work.' "

Scooping up his coffee cup, he had retreated to his study without even pausing to deposit a kiss on her brow when he passed by her chair. Cordelia had shoved aside her plate, the food left untouched as she stared down the length of the empty table. Fighting against the feelings of loneliness and abandonment that threatened to overwhelm her, she had focused upon her anger.

She knew full well whom she had to thank for the arrival of this unknown cousin, who was three or four times removed. That creature whose receding hairline and beady eyes stared at her from the hall portrait when she ascended the stairs to bed each evening! As if it wasn't enough that Will Shakespeare had robbed her of her father, now the Bard must torment her with another of his worshipers.

She could envision clearly what Miles Renwick would look like: a long spidershanks of a fellow with red-rimmed eyes from reading too late at night. She would be required to show him those local points of interest so fascinating to all these Shakespearean lunatics, so deadly dull to herself. And what little attention Papa spared from his studies would be given up to this stranger. Instead of drawing closer to her father, Cordelia visualized him drifting farther away from her than ever.

It was thoughts such as these that had driven her into grabbing up her sketchbook and fleeing the house unaccompanied by her maid. She did not pause for breath until she was well clear of the town, wanting no sight of anything that would remind her of Papa and his dearly beloved Will Shakespeare. Too exhausted to put as much distance between herself and Stratford as she would have liked, she had taken the footpath up to Welcombe Hills, her favorite refuge when troubled.

She would spend the entire afternoon sketching up here. Mayhap Papa would miss her, be worried by her absence. No, most likely he would not even notice she was gone. Winking away the last of her tears, Cordelia opened her pencil box and reached for a fresh stick of charcoal.

Forcing the unpleasant scene with Papa from her mind, she concentrated instead upon the half-finished portrait on the page before her. It was a veritable Adonis with tightly curling hair, aquiline nose, and dimpled chin. She had meant to depict one of the Greek gods—Apollo, perhaps—but that her drawing bore a striking resemblance to Lord Walsing was no small coincidence.

She had not quite caught the dreamy expression of his eyes, she thought as she began to highlight the classically sculpted cheekbones. Lord Walsing was so charming, but he did have a marked tendency to flirt with any lovely female who crossed his path. Even if she did attend the ball at his lordship's manor, was there any hope that such a paragon would distinguish her above the other hopeful young ladies?

"Pretty," she had heard herself described. "Pretty vapid" was Cordelia's disparaging self-description as she considered the boyish slimness of her too-short frame, her insipid golden curls and cornflower eyes, her heart-shaped face and small, upturned nose.

"About as alluring as a Dresden figurine," Cordelia muttered, bending over her sketch. No, Lord Walsing would never develop a tendre for such a china doll as herself. A pity since eligible males—at least those who did not come to offer burnt offerings at the grave of the Bard—were sadly lacking in Stratford. She had a strong fancy that Lord Walsing would make a perfect husband, so tenderly devoted and considerate. He would never neglect his wife for a set of musty books.

As her mind wandered, the pencil slipped between her fingers. Much to her dismay, she smudged Lord Walsing's—that is, Apollo's nose. With a cry of vexation, she rummaged through her pencil box for an eraser and set out to repair the damage. Deeply absorbed, she paid no heed when a twig snapped nearby until a shadow fell across the page.

Biting her lip in annoyance at having her lighting disturbed, she glanced behind her to request politely that the intruder move, only to stare straight at muscular legs molded by tight-fitting navy trousers and gleaming black leather military boots that were turned down at the knee. Cordelia stifled her exclamation of surprise as her eyes traveled upward to a brilliant scarlet coat shining with gold buttons. The braids of a colonel were set to advantage upon a pair of broad shoulders. One bronzed hand rested lightly on his hip while the other held a satin cockaded hat.

By the time she reached his face, Delia's head was tipped back as far as it would go. The colonel's lips parted into a smile. Never had Delia seen such a smile. Every muscle, every feature seemed bursting with good humor, from the indentation in his chin to the neatly trimmed ebony mustache, which was the same color as the hair waving back from his forehead. Two heavy black brows accented twinkling brown eyes, the half-lowered dark lashes doing little to conceal the stranger's bold, admiring appraisal. But for the very proper cut of his uniform, he was the image of a swarthy buccaneer home from the sea.

A long sigh escaped Delia. When he reached down one strong hand to her, she placed her own within it as if mesmerized. Propriety dictated she flee his presence at once. But she did not demur as he helped her to her feet; no, not even when he carried her hand to his lips, his mustache astonishingly soft as it brushed against her skin. Then he opened his mouth and ruined everything.

" 'Such war of white and red within her cheeks!' " he quoted in a deep-timbered voice. " 'What stars do spangle heaven with such beauty, as those two eyes become that heavenly face? Fair lovely maid, once more good day to thee.' "

"Shakespeare!" Cordelia hissed, snatching her hand away.

"Well, yes, it was," the man said, clearly bewildered by her sudden change in mood. "I meant it as a compliment."

Cordelia pursed her lips together as she bent down to gather up her sketching materials and her boots. Then she nodded her head in the direction of the town.

"The church lies that way, sir, where you may go and drool over the poet's bones like the rest of the fools who flock to our town."

"I shall certainly want to see Shakespeare's grave, but that is not to say I have no interest in the other beauties of Stratford as well."

Cordelia's glare quickly withered the hopeful smile on his face. "You are not numbered among my acquaintances, sir. I desire that you do not speak to me."

"That's rich, upon my word! You did not appear at all adverse to having me address you only a few moments ago." He frowned and replaced the hat upon his head.

165

"That was before . . ." Cordelia faltered as she realized the truth of his accusation. She had been shamelessly offering him every encouragement. What had come over her?

"You are entirely mistaken, sir," she said. Tucking her pencil box and sketch pad under one arm while carrying her boots in the opposite hand, she flounced off down the hill without a backward glance. She had only gotten as far as the narrow brook when she realized the impertinent creature was following her.

Rounding on him, she snapped, "Go your way, sir. If you continue to plague me, I shall have you taken up by the constable."

"I beg your pardon, but I believe you are forgetting these." He grinned, holding out her stockings.

Heat suffused Cordelia's cheeks. She dropped her sketching materials and snatched the intimate apparel out of his hands.

"You're very welcome," the colonel said.

She stuffed the stockings inside the boots, once more storming away from him.

"Aren't you going to put them on? I'll wager the water will be cold."

Cordelia froze, fighting an unladylike urge to swear at her tormentor. She replied in haughty accents, "You, sir, are no gentleman. Desist from following me this instant."

She steeled herself to wade across the narrow brook. It was no more than a few yards wide and only inches deep, but the water would be like ice. Besides, when she hiked up her skirts, she would afford the colonel an excellent view of her ankles, which was doubtless what he was waiting for.

To turn and go back was equally unthinkable as she would be obliged to pass by that infuriating man once more. While she hesitated, fretting over her most dignified course of action, the colonel reached her in a few quick strides.

"I cannot allow such a slur upon my character to go unanswered. I will show you how much of a gentleman I can be."

Before she could guess his intent, he had swept her off her feet as easily as if she were a child. He held her tight against his chest and started to wade across the stream.

"Put me down!" Delia swung one of her boots, delivering a resounding smack against the side of his head and knocking his hat off into the water. "Put me down!"

"Damme!" Nearly losing his balance, he grimaced. "Anything to oblige a lady."

He bent over and dropped Cordelia into the stream. She gasped as she landed on her bottom with a jarring thud. The chilly water seeped through the sheer fabric of her dress, penetrating as high as the small, sausage-shaped bustle she had tied about her waist to give the gown more of a fashionable Grecian flow.

"You miserable wretch," she shrieked, struggling to stand but weighed down by her sopping skirts. He was already on the opposite bank, scowling as he examined his waterlogged hat. The brute did not even have the decency to help her out of the brook. Cordelia doubled up her fists. Floundering out of the water, she swung wildly at him. He sidestepped all of her blows, a slow smile crossing his face.

"Ohhh, I hate you," she said. "There is only one other person I hate more than you."

"Dear me." The colonel laughed. "Well, I have never been one to accept coming in second."

With that, he pinioned her arms behind her back and crushed her against him, his mouth ruthlessly possessing her own. Cordelia's mind reeled with shock at the first touch of his warm lips. She trembled, but not from the clinging coldness of her wet gown. A strange heat tingled through her veins. She had just begun to return the embrace with equal fervor when she caught herself and jerked her head away from the disturbing contact.

Breathing hard, the colonel released her, looking fully as confused as she felt. Tears of impotent fury and indignation stung her eyes.

"If I were only a man," she said through clenched teeth, "I would—would . . ."

"Eat my heart in the marketplace?" he suggested helpfully.

"Yes!" Occasionally, even Shakespeare had a good notion. She retrieved the only one of her boots she could find.

"If I ever see you again, I shall kill you." With a final stomp of her foot, she raced off, dripping, down the hill, her hat ribbons dancing with the force of her indignation.

With great forbearance, the colonel held his tongue. He watched her until she was out of sight, then rubbed a finger across his lips, remembering the sweetness of his stolen kiss.

He supposed he had spent too much time in the rough company of soldiers. His manners of address with the ladies wanted polishing. Still, what a virago! Her hot temper was completely at variance with her gentle golden beauty. So frag-

ile she had looked as she sat and sketched, so fresh and un-
spoiled, a delicate English flower. Exactly as he had always
imagined Miranda in *The Tempest* to be. Then she had glanced
up at him with eyes bluer than any sea he'd ever sailed, her
lips parting in that shy, sweet smile. By God, she made all
those smirking ton beauties his sister-in-law had been shoving
at him in London seem like positive anecdotes by comparison.
He'd completely forgotten that he had only approached the
lady to ask directions. For a moment, he'd thought he was un-
done at last. Then for no reason at all, she'd begun to rip up
at him.

He still did not comprehend it. It would be best to forget the
little fire-eater. He did not even know her name. But perchance
it was marked somewhere in the sketching materials she had
left behind.

He recrossed the stream to pick up the pencil box. It was in-
scribed with the initials *CMR*. The sketchbook might prove
more useful. He opened it to study the man's portrait she had
been working on when he had interrupted her. Her betrothed,
perhaps? That would be a great pity. The fop looked far too
bland to master the affections of such a tempestuous lady. She
had not signed her name to that sketch, but he met with better
luck on the next page. There in the corner, he could just make
out the words *Cordelia Renwick*.

"Oh, Lord," groaned Colonel Sir Miles Renwick, closing the
book again with a sharp snap.

Chapter 2

Rose Briar Cottage nestled on the outskirts of Stratford beneath the shade of two great mulberry trees. Vines of red roses and jasmine clung to the half-timber frame walls of the two-story house. The thatched roof and latticed windows lent the cottage a quaint air of fairy-tale enchantment, but Delia was in no humor to appreciate the picturesque qualities of her home as she strode up the walkway to the front door.

"May a thousand demons seize that blackguard," she muttered under her breath. She derived a great deal of satisfaction imagining a myriad tiny devils thrusting their pitchforks into various parts of the colonel's muscular anatomy.

Flinging open the massive creaking door, she bounded inside the dark interior of the entrance hall, the uneven stone floor chilling her bare feet. Inevitably, the first object that met her gaze was Shakespeare's portrait, which hung at the foot of the narrow oak staircase leading to the first floor. Delia glowered at the flat, imperturbable face.

In a whirl of sodden skirts, she turned toward the door leading to the tiny sitting room, seeking a more sympathetic soul to hear the tale of her wrongs. Bursting into the chamber, she paused on the threshold in dismay. It had never occurred to her that Aunt Violet might be entertaining company at this hour of the day.

Two young ladies were seated upon the pink-striped beechwood settee, its gilt elegance quite at variance with the cottage's plain whitewashed walls. Miss Rosamund Leighton's dark head snapped up, her striking beauty in no way diminished by the unbecoming puce frock that adorned her tall frame. The shorter blonde at Rosamund's side bounced to her feet. Miss Frances Pryce set up a squeal of astonishment that grated along Delia's already raw nerves.

Before either girl could question Delia, her aunt exclaimed, "Cordelia, what on earth, child!" Aunt Violet leaped up from her armchair, her lace cap nearly flying backward off her snowy white hair. She bustled over to Delia. "Why, you look like you've been nearly drowned."

"Did you fall in the river?" Miss Pryce asked, her round blue eyes opening wide.

"No, Fanny, I most certainly did not!" Delia's cheeks flamed once more at the memory of how the odious colonel had dropped her.

"Why, 'tis a wonder you have not caught your death of a chill." Rosamund crossed the gold- and rose-hued Aubusson carpet to Delia's side, Fanny gliding after her like a shadow. "My poor Delia, the back of your gown is quite soaked through. Do come closer to the fire." She drew Delia nearer to the flame crackling in the grate of the imposing brick hearth.

Fanny paraded around behind Delia to gawk. "So it is. Why, Miss Renwick, never say you have been sitting, actually sitting, in a pool of water."

"No, I haven't," Delia choked. She read a world of sympathy in Rosamund's eyes. Dying to tell her friend everything that horrid man had done to her, Delia's pride revolted at reciting such a tale before the loose-tongued Fanny. The story of her humiliation would be broadcast all over Stratford before a cat could lick its whiskers.

"I—I had best go change my dress. I am dripping on the carpet." Delia gave Rosamund a speaking glance. "I will tell you all about it later when I am dry."

Fanny's lower lip jutted out in disappointment, but Rosamund nodded in understanding.

"Do go along at once, child," Aunt Violet urged, although she looked about to bust her stays with curiosity. "I would not have you take a chill now. Not with the ball at Walsing Manor less than a fortnight away."

"Yes, Auntie. I do beg your pardon for barging in upon you in this fashion."

As Delia quit the room, she could hear the ladies still exclaiming over her bedraggled appearance. Fanny's childish, treble voice floated after her. "Why, Mrs. Nicolson, your niece is such an—an *unusual* girl. Some of the most peculiar things

170

happen to her. Whatever do you suppose she has been about this time?"

Delia ground her teeth as she strode down the hall. Unusual girl, indeed! A pleasing image of dropping Fanny Pryce down the garden well drifted into her mind. What was she doing here at Rose Briar, anyway? Trailing along after Rosamund most likely. Although Miss Pryce had only been in Stratford a week, she contrived to attach herself to Miss Leighton whenever possible. There were few other people besides Roz who would tolerate Fanny's affectations.

"Only imagine what it must be like for Fanny," Rosamund would plead. "An orphan, shunted from one relation to another, to whomever happens to need the convenience of an unpaid companion. Now poor Fanny is bound to stay with Mrs. Forbes-Smythe, and you know how tiresome she can be, with all her imaginary ailments."

Delia tried to sympathize with the girl's plight, but she could not help feeling that there was a most unattractive slyness about Fanny. No one could be as artless as she appeared to be. It had to be a sham, and Cordelia detested people who shammed.

But Fanny's most unforgivable offense in Delia's eyes was that by some perverse trick of nature, Fanny came close to being her mirror image. The same height, weight, and coloring— both of them pretty little pieces of porcelain, Delia thought scornfully. Bad enough to have such uninteresting blond and pink features without having to see a near-perfect copy of yourself in one who was such a fool!

It was a great pity that that ruffian who had assaulted her on the hillside had not come upon Fanny instead. She probably would have swooned dead away. At least, Delia thought with grim satisfaction, she had dealt him a good clout on the ear, to say nothing of ruining his hat.

But it was not enough to pay for the insufferable insults he had heaped upon her. Not enough by half. She could still feel the warmth of his kiss upon her lips—not because she had enjoyed the embrace in the slightest, but out of horror that such a shocking liberty had been taken with her person.

Cordelia had reached the foot of the steps when the closed door to her father's study caught her eye. Papa. He was the one who should hear her complaint, not Aunt Violet. This wanted a man's hand. Perhaps Papa could have the colonel court-martialed. Delia was cheered greatly by the prospect.

171

There might be more than one way to rouse Papa from his fusty old manuscripts, to force him to prove that he had some affection for his only child.

She rapped briskly at the study door, then entered before her father could lodge a protest. Her eyes adjusted themselves to the room's somber interior of linenfold oak paneling as she breathed in the familiar scents of leather and musty parchment, scents she had associated with her father since the days of her childhood.

Papa leaned forward in his dark leather chair, squinting down at several volumes spread out before him on the octagonal library table. He didn't look up; his fingers groped for his quill pen and the scrap of paper on which he took notes.

"Delia," he said in hushed tones. "I veritably believe this edition of Shakespeare by Edward Capell is the most accurate yet. Far superior to Alexander Pope's. Only see here where he—"

"Oh, Papa, as if there are not already enough versions of those boring plays. I have something very *important* to tell you."

"I wonder how Dr. Johnson would interpret these particular lines of Lady Macbeth." Walter Renwick reached for the small circular rosewood bookcase, slowly revolving the shelf as he examined the volumes on it. "Now where did I put that? Delia, would you please take the steps there and check up on top of—"

"Papa!"

"My dear, to finally possess such a scholarly, researched version of Shakespeare! You do not know what it means."

"It means that you are not paying the least attention to me."

She bent over the bookcase, placing her hand on one side to stop her father from turning it. If Papa could but see himself: so spare from not eating properly; his peppery hair parted in the center, hanging frazzled down both sides, and swept back from his balding forehead; a hint of a mustache on his upper lip. Merciful heavens! She realized with a jolt, *He's even starting to look like Shakespeare.*

"Papa, you must let Farley cut your hair. And—and get some new clothes. I declare that coat looks like something that might have been worn by Great-Grandpapa."

Her father donned his wire-rimmed spectacles and regarded her sternly. "This is what is so important that you interrupt my studies?"

"What? No, of course not." She straightened, proclaiming dramatically, "Papa, I was accosted by a strange man on Welcombe Hill."

She waited for her father to blanch with distress. Instead, his brow knotted into a frown. "Ah, Cordelia, I expect you have been traipsing over the countryside again without your maid. And flirting, too! How oft must I warn you against such unmaidenly behavior?"

"I was not flirting," she cried, although she did wince as she recollected that she had encouraged the colonel to kiss her hand. " 'Twas all *his* doing. He followed me. He picked me up and dropped me in the stream."

"Mmmm. And what did you do to provoke a total stranger into doing such a thing?"

"Papa! What a question!"

It was the selfsame question he had asked the time when she was twelve and had hit Squire Newbold's nasty little son, Bernard, over the head with a cricket bat, then came in tearfully to report how her curls had been pulled. Papa was not taking this seriously.

She placed her finger to trembling lips. "This man made me kiss him, Papa. 'Twas the most vile, odious, dreadful . . ." Cordelia struggled for words strong enough to express her disgust.

" 'The lady doth protest too much, methinks,' " her father murmured, bending back over his books.

Cordelia blinked back a tear, appalled by her parent's heartlessness. "Just look at my gown. 'Tis ruined."

Papa glanced up briefly, then sighed. "And what is the name of this thrice-damned villain?"

"I—I don't know. But he is a colonel in the army."

"Scarcely much to go on, my dear. I can hardly call him out if I do not know his name."

"Very amusing, Papa." Cordelia bit her lip. "As if you would in any case. You would only get angry if he said Shakespeare was all a hum. After he ravished and murdered me, I suppose the two of you could trade quotes over my grave."

Her father finally showed a gleam of interest. "Od's bodikins! He was familiar with Shakespeare, then?"

"Yes, he . . . Never mind! I see I am obliged to look out for myself." Delia turned on her heel, then stalked toward the door. She paused long enough to glance resentfully over her shoulder. "I am so sorry to have troubled you, Papa, with this very trivial incident."

He shook his head, thumbing a page before his lips curved into an odd smile. "Ah, Delia, Delia, 'It is a wise father that knows his own child.' "

On this completely mystifying comment, Delia left him. As she raced up the stairs to her room, she dashed aside the salty drops with the back of her hand. She might have known how futile it would be to bring her troubles to Papa. He had shown beyond a doubt that he did not care a fig about her.

She closed her bedchamber door, then leaned against it as she strove to swallow the lump in her throat. "Oh, Papa, how have things ever come to such a pass between us?"

He had loved her once. She could remember that. After Mama had died, he had been with her every minute. She had felt so lost, scared, swallowed up by the large nursery. Even though she had been all of nine years old, Papa had come every night to rock her to sleep as if she had been only a babe. Instead of lullabies, he had recited Shakespeare in his low, monotone voice. But it had been pleasant as the playwright had not yet become an obsession with Papa.

Delia could not say for certain when Papa had begun to change. Perhaps sometime after he had brought her stepmother home to the handsome Georgian manor that Papa had owned in Warwickshire. Yes, that was when.

Delia moved away from the door, her gaze traveling restlessly around the room. The war she waged with Papa against Shakespeare and his world had carried over even here in the privacy of her own bedchamber. She'd lost the battle to replace the Jacobean four-poster and its heavy damask bedhangings with a French sofa-bed. But at least the elegant satinwood dressing table with its miniature cheval glass, and the mahogany wardrobe with the ivory handles were of her choosing. What truly annoyed her was that the massive bed appeared at home to a peg in her timber-paneled bedchamber while her own delicate furnishings did not.

She sank down into a cushioned cross-framed stool in front of the dressing table, studying her unhappy reflection in the mirror. Jerking at the ribbons beneath her chin, she swept the straw hat from her head. One blond curl drooped down over her brow. Somehow she had contrived to smudge dirt across her nose. Reaching into the center drawer for a lace handkerchief, she pulled a face at herself. She looked even more lackluster than usual. What a sad contrast she presented to the woman whose miniature was displayed to the right of the mirror. A beautiful woman with masses of dusky hair, her elegance was revealed in every line of her lovely profile. Amaryllis, her dearest stepmama. This small portrait did not do her justice as had the full-length one that had hung belowstairs, revealing her willowy figure, the round, dimpled arms. But Papa had gotten rid of that picture and hung Will in her place.

Delia reverently lifted the miniature, staring into those dark eyes that so long ago had been closed by death. She would never understand it. Why should Papa have become such a reclusive scholar just when Amaryllis had come into their lives, bringing them so much excitement and laughter? It made no sense at all.

Why, Amaryllis had filled Renwick Manor with a brilliant company of people, music, dancing, card parties. . . . How fond dear Amaryllis had been of cards! How magnificent she had looked in her rainbow array of gowns designed especially for her by a London modiste. And her jewels. Amaryllis had always glittered.

Most of all, Delia recalled how Amaryllis had doted upon her, "her darling little Cordelia." Most women would have shown little affection for a child from a husband's previous marriage. But Amaryllis had adored Delia from the first.

"What a perfect little doll you are," Amaryllis would coo, but Delia hadn't minded when *she* said that. "You must promise me never to grow up," her stepmama had said. "I don't ever want any other child but you."

Amaryllis had dressed her in the most enchanting frocks, all frothy with lace. Often she had helped Delia escape from her studies, bringing her into the parlor to sing for all the handsome gentlemen and teaching her to lisp all manner of clever sayings that had set their guests to roaring with laughter.

But Papa had spoiled everything. Inexplicably, he had sold their beautiful Renwick Manor and moved them to the miserable converted farm house that was Rose Briar Cottage. To be closer to his beloved Shakespeare, Delia supposed. How unhappy Amaryllis had been. All the lively parties had ended. Very few people had come to call, and her youthful stepmama had grown more listless each day.

Amaryllis had spent most of her time pacing the confines of the small garden in the back of the cottage. Delia had tried desperately to think of something, anything, to bring the bright smiles back to her face. She had thought that on the occasion of her thirteenth birthday they might have a party. That surely would delight Amaryllis.

When the day dawned, bright and sparkling, Delia had scrambled out of bed. It was strange. There was no Bessy to help her wash and dress. Nothing daunted, she had readied herself, even remembering to drag a comb through her tangled curls. Then she had fairly skipped down the hall to Amaryllis's room.

No. Delia gripped the edge of the dressing table, squeezing her eyes shut and attempting to blot out the painful memory. But it was futile. As clearly as if it had just happened, she could still see her young stepmother writhing in agony as Papa attempted to restrain her thrashing. Horrible rasping sounds tore from her throat. And the blood . . . The bed was soaked with it. Delia had stared in terrified fascination until Bessy had come to drag her away.

In the intervening five years, Delia had never gone near Amaryllis's room. No one would ever tell her what had happened, especially not Papa. She could only guess that Amaryllis had harbored some mortal wasting illness that she had valiantly kept a secret. If Papa had paid less attention to his books and more to his wife, he might have noticed in time to have saved her.

Delia gave a heavy sigh, replacing the miniature on the table. She picked up the handkerchief to blow her nose, but a large black spider jumped out of the folds of linen. As the creature skittered across her hand, Delia lowered it gently to her dressing table. She had long ago accustomed herself to such unexpected company. Rose Briar Cottage hosted any number of eight-legged guests such as the one that now dangled by Amaryllis's portrait. It was only one more of the charms to be found living under a thatched roof.

A sharp rap at her bedchamber door startled Delia in a way that the spider's appearance had not. Before she could speak, a plump maid dressed in a starched white apron and mobcap whisked into the room.

"Do come in, Bessy," Delia said in a voice laden with sarcasm, which was lost on Bessy. She had been with the Renwick family for too many years to be intimidated. Too presumptuous by half, Delia thought, but the woman's way with dressing hair was nothing short of magic. And who but Bessy could get coffee stains out of one's best morning gown?

The buxom woman paused behind Delia, placing her hands

176

upon her ample hips. Her double chin quivered with indignation. "Your aunt bade me to see how you are going on, Miss Delia, and a good thing she did. Sitting there all glassy-eyed in that damp gown as if you were properly dicked in the nob! Whatever has come over you?"

"I was thinking," Delia said, rising slowly to her feet.

"Well, 'tis no suitable occupation for a young lady." Bessy glared down at the dressing table, but whether it was at Amaryllis's portrait or the spider, Delia was not quite sure. The maid picked up a brush, then took a wild swipe at the intruder. The spider escaped by a hair's breadth, but Bessy did succeed in flattening Amaryllis.

"Don't be so clumsy, Bessy," Delia lovingly righted the portrait.

"Humph! Not another word out of you, miss, until I have you nice and dry." She whirled Delia around, then tugged at the buttons on the back of her gown. Delia suppressed a retort. If only Bessy would remember she was no longer just out of the nursery. She submitted to the maid's ministrations, allowing her to slip off the soiled gown and chemise but steadfastly ignoring all of Bessy's clucking.

"This dress is not more than a month old, Miss Delia. How shall I clean that muck from the hem, I'm sure I don't know. When will you ever stop behaving like such a hoyden?"

Delia gave a small shrug. She owed no explanation to Bessy. Wouldn't the woman scold if she knew Delia had been kissing a strange soldier! No, Delia corrected herself. He had been kissing her.

Holding the gown away from her as if it were a dead rat, Bessy moved toward Delia's wardrobe to select a fresh garment. As the door opened and closed, Delia obtained a glimpse of lilac-pink satin.

"What?" She gasped.

Bessy blocked her way, shaking out a simple white muslin sprigged with mint-green flowers, but Delia dodged around her and flung open the wardrobe door. "Bessy, you wretch! Why did you not tell me Miss Tandy had finished my gown for Lord Walsing's ball?"

"You were not at home." Bessy tapped her foot impatiently while Delia removed the gown from the wardrobe and laid it across the bed. When Aunt Violet had brought her the shimmering length of satin back from London, Delia had almost feared to trust it to the skill of the local seamstress. But Miss Tandy had surpassed herself.

The design was simple: high-waisted with short puff sleeves, the neckline cut daringly low. Miss Tandy had employed the lilac-pink as an underdress over which she had layered a transparent tunic of ecru net edged with lace. The satin hem was embroidered in a delicate design of green acanthus leaves. Delia had never possessed such a beautiful gown in all her life.

"Oh, Bessy, with my white fur stole and crystal beads, won't it be just perfect?" She held the gown in front of her, admiring the way the crisp folds swished around her ankles. With such a gown as this, it was possible that even Lord Walsing might be charmed.

"Have done, Miss Delia," Bessy growled, "before you fill the skirt with so many creases I'll never get them all out."

Reluctantly, Delia permitted Bessy to return the gown to the wardrobe. But as she held her arms aloft for Bessy to lower the white dress over her head, it was not plain muslin but the feel of cool satin Delia imagined next to her skin. As she hummed the strains of a waltz, Bessy dragged her back to the dressing table and thrust her onto the stool. The maid grabbed up a comb, then ruthlessly attacked the mass of snarls in Delia's fine hair.

"Hold still, miss, or I will never have you ready in time. Your aunt is entertaining a very important gentleman belowstairs."

Delia twisted her head around, wincing as Bessy stretched one of her curls out to the roots. "Bessy! Why do you never tell me these things?"

"Thought I just did. Sit!" The maid clamped one large hand on Delia's shoulder as she attempted to rise. "Unless you want to rush into the sitting room looking as woolly as a newly washed sheep."

Delia bit her lip but did as Bessy commanded. An important gentleman. There was only one man of any importance hereabouts. Aunt Violet's caller must be Lord Walsing. Delia squirmed in her chair, her head snapping back as Bessy waxed more vigorous against the knots. Surely Lord Walsing would not come to Rose Briar simply to seek out the company of her aunt. Delia's heart began to pound a little faster.

What if Lord Walsing had somehow heard about the beastly way the colonel had treated her? Of course Delia would die before she ever told his lordship, but just suppose he had found out some other way. A delicious image rose in her mind of Lord Walsing's normally placid face twisted with fury as he rode to avenge her honor. He would be so beside himself with wrath, he would not wait for the formality of a duel but set out to thrash the wicked colonel with his bare fists.

Practicality, however, intruded upon Delia's flight of fancy. She was forced to admit she had never seen any man with such a huge muscular frame as the colonel's. If Lord Walsing was ever so rash as to come to fisticuffs with the tall soldier, Delia greatly feared his lordship's perfectly aquiline nose might end up bent to a very odd angle, indeed.

"There." Bessy threw down the comb. " 'Tis the best I can do with you a-twisting this way and that."

Delia took one last anxious peek in the mirror, pinching some color into her cheeks. She leaped to her feet and rushed toward the door. "It's about time. You have kept me here forever with your poking. Lord Walsing may be on the verge of leaving."

She was out in the hall and halfway down the steps before Bessy got around to calling after her, " 'Tis not Lord Walsing. 'Tis your cousin what's come for a visit."

Delia paused in midstep, turning around to glare at the maid. Bessy grinned before wisely retreating to the room she shared with Cook and closing the door.

Her cousin!

"Hell-kite!" Delia muttered, her eyes meeting the heavy-lidded ones of the Bard's in the portrait on the wall. Even Will seemed to be mocking her. She stood for a moment, fuming over her disappointment. To be expecting Lord Walsing and then to find out it was no one but her bookish cousin who had arrived to plague her. She was of half a mind to flounce back up to her room. But it would be rude beyond forgiveness to leave poor Aunt Vi alone to act as hostess to the boring fellow.

Besides, Delia was intrigued by some of the noises issuing from the direction of the sitting room. When she reached the foot of the stairs, she could hear high-pitched giggling. Her aunt alone could not produce such a volume of feminine laughter. Miss Pryce and Rosamund must have lingered to meet Delia's cousin. It sounded as if they were all being mightily entertained.

When Delia reached the sitting-room door, she opened it a crack, cautiously peering inside. All she could see was Aunt

179

Violet mincing in front of the fireplace. The elderly woman fluttered a small fan before her eyes like a coy young girl.

"Fie upon you, Cousin Miles. You have a naughty, flattering tongue in that handsome head of yours."

Handsome? Delia could contain her curiosity no longer. She slowly opened the door, making her presence known, her eyes searching the tiny room for this new cousin of hers. She found him perched on a gilt armchair whose tapering scrolled legs looked far too fragile to bear the weight of his large frame. He balanced one of the Wedgwood teacups and saucers on his knee, appearing to have made himself very much at home.

An odd cry escaped from Delia's throat, something between a shriek and a croak. Only the fact she clutched the door handle saved her from sinking into an undignified heap. Her cousin looked up, quirking one dark eyebrow in her direction.

A wave of fury took possession of Delia, infusing new strength into her limbs. "You!" she cried. Heedless of her aunt's startled gasp, Delia tromped into the room, her hands doubling into fists.

The toe of her soft leather slipper caught on the edge of the Aubusson carpet. Before she could prevent it, she was tumbling forward. Teacup and saucer flew through the air as she sprawled across a pair of masculine legs. Strong arms closed around her waist, rolling her over so that she stared directly into the laughing brown eyes of the roguish colonel.

Chapter 3

Stunned into speechlessness, it took Delia a few moments to realize that she was all but sitting on the colonel's knee. His hands at her waist tightened, an expression of wicked pleasure at having her thus positioned crossing his strong, chiseled features. With great difficulty, she restrained herself from boxing his ears right in front of Aunt Violet, whose mouth already gaped open in horror.

"Oh, Delia! My dear Colonel!" The old woman fluttered.

Delia wrenched herself from the colonel's grasp and staggered to her feet. "Auntie! This man—he—he . . ."

"He is your cousin, Sir Miles Renwick, my dear," Aunt Violet said. "Ah, such an unfortunate way for you to introduce yourself to him."

The colonel rose to his feet, regarding them both with keen amusement. "But not at all, Cousin Violet. Cousin Cordelia and I already met earlier this morning." He arched one thick black brow teasingly in Delia's direction.

She closed her mouth, caught completely unawares. She had thought the man would hang his head in shame, try to hide his ungentlemanly behavior toward her. The thought that he was prepared to proclaim boldly the tale of what had happened between them filled her with dismay.

Before another word could be spoken, Fanny startled them all with one of her earsplitting shrieks. "Oh, do look. You poor man." She rustled over to the colonel's side. "Delia has spattered hot tea all over his—his . . ." She blushed when she could not pronounce the unmentionable word, contenting herself to point at the wet stain spreading just above the knee of his navy trousers.

"Why, you must be scalded!" Aunt Violet exclaimed. "Do

181

go upstairs to one of the bedchambers at once and take them off."

Fanny permitted her wide blue eyes to fill with tears. "Indeed, we must send for a doctor."

"Ladies, ladies, please. 'Tis nothing." Miles held up a hand in protest, all the while contriving to appear heroically oblivious of his injury.

Rosamund rushed forward, shoving Cordelia to one side. "Here, hold this against it. 'Tis a napkin I have dipped in cold water."

Miles took it from her, smiling into her gentle hazel eyes. "How kind of you, Miss Rosamund."

Delia thought she was going to choke. That man could not have been in the house above half an hour. Was he already on a first-name basis with all of them?

"No one seems to mind in the least about the stain on our carpet," she ground out. Elbowing her way through the fussing women, Delia snatched up another napkin, then vented some of her spleen by rubbing the Aubusson nigh threadbare. She could not help noticing that she was eye-level with Miles's huge, bronzed hand holding the damp cloth against his muscled thigh.

He leaned forward, murmuring in a low voice, "You are dreadful hard on a gentleman's wardrobe, Cousin. First my hat, now my trousers . . ."

She jerked away, glaring at him.

Aunt Violet sighed. "I have never known you to be so clumsy, child. So many accidents in the space of one morning."

"Yes," Fanny piped up. "How strange. Colonel, did you not mention something about having already met Delia today?" Her tiny, heart-shaped face greedy with curiosity, she breathlessly awaited his answer like a cat about to pounce upon a canary.

Delia paused in the act of gathering the pieces of the shattered teacup, making no effort to conceal her apprehension. Once she had thought she desired nothing more than to shout her wrongs to the world, but the knowledge of Miles's identity altered the situation greatly. How dare the villain be her cousin? How dare he! There was no hope that Papa or Aunt Violet would take her part now. At best, they would simply shake their heads at Miles. At worst, Fanny's gossiping tongue would spread the embarrassing tale all over Stratford. With considerable trepidation, Delia listened for Miles's reply.

After studying her face for a moment in a way that left Delia blushing, he shrugged. " 'Twas such a fine day. I dismounted from the mail coach too soon, lost my way. I asked directions into Stratford of Cordelia." He could no longer restrain his wicked smile. "Of course, at the time, neither of us dreamed there was any connection."

Instead of being grateful for Miles's adept handling of Fanny's question, Cordelia seethed with indignation at the hidden gibe in his words. What a smooth liar the scoundrel was. Biting her lip, she returned to her task of picking up the broken china. Unfortunately, at the same moment, Miles stooped to help her and banged his head into hers.

Delia saw stars as she rocked back on her heels, her eyes watering. Miles straightened, rubbing his brow. "Faith, Cousin, for so soft and fair a lady, you have a remarkably hard head."

"Good heavens, Delia." Her aunt clucked. "I shall ring for Elise to clean that mess. Do leave that be and get up before you kill poor Cousin Miles."

"What a splendid idea," Delia mumbled under her breath, although she did as she was told. Holding her forehead, she felt as if her skull had been cracked in twain. But the other women ignored her, closing in around Miles, urging him to take up a more comfortable seat upon the settee. Fanny fetched a stool to prop his injured leg up on, while Rosamund sat beside him, stuffing a plump pillow behind his back.

"Don't stand there gawking, child." Aunt Violet nodded briskly at Delia. "Fetch Cousin Miles another cup of tea and a plate of those cakes."

Delia put her hands on her hips, her jaw tightening. Good God! This man had assaulted her, nigh ruined one of her best gowns. Was she now expected to wait on him? 'Twas too much to be borne.

But at that moment Fanny purred, "Dear me. Then if you were with Delia this morning, Colonel Renwick, you must have seen how her first accident came about. She came home with her dress positively sopping."

Miss Pryce directed a sweet smirk at Delia, who glowered back at her. If Fanny possessed a tail, Delia thought, it would surely be swishing at this moment. Spinning on her heel, she stomped over to the tripod tea table and busied herself with the tea service laid out upon its lacquered, pie-crust-shaped top, trying to appear indifferent to the conversation taking place. Her hands shook as she lifted the Sèvres teapot. As she poured out a cup, Miles's jovial voice carried over to her.

"Alas, no, I did not witness Cousin Delia's accident. However, you may be sure if I had, I would have been only too delighted to hasten to her rescue."

As Fanny sighed with disappointment, Delia bit back an oath. She flung several of the tea cakes onto a delicate china dish enameled with pink rosebuds. Before she had stormed halfway across the room, with cup and saucer clenched in one fist, the plate in the other, Miles halted her with an upraised hand. "If you please, dear Cousin," he said in a voice of deceptive meekness, "I really do not care for tea cake. Mayhap I could try one of those delicious-looking muffins . . ."

Delia's breath issued between her teeth in an angry hiss. It was bad enough that he sat there on the striped satin divan with one foot propped up, his swarthy complexion and dark mustache making him appear like some Turkish sultan surrounded by his adoring harem. But if he thought she was going to act like another of his slaves, the man was much mistaken.

"This has gone far enough," she started to sputter when Aunt Violet deftly removed the cup and saucer from her grasp.

"Let me have that before you spill another cup of tea onto the carpet." Aunt Violet's mouth puckered in disapproval. "Whatever is amiss with your manners today, Delia? Give your cousin whatever he wants."

Behind Aunt Violet, Miles grinned wolfishly, allowing those bold dark eyes of his to wander up the length of her figure, pausing to linger on her lips. Despite her anger, Delia felt a strange tingling sensation course through her veins. Flushing, she fled back to the tea table, scooping up a muffin to butter it with savage energy.

"And some jam, too, please," Miles called after her.

By the time she marched back to his side and thrust the plate at him, her momentary discomfiture was forgotten, her temper once more in full steam. Miles accepted the muffin, rolling his eyes in exaggerated fear.

"Is that a dagger I see before me?" he muttered.

She thought he had taken leave of his senses when she realized she still clutched the butter knife in her hand. His low chuckle rumbling in her ears, she returned the piece of silverplate to the tea table, regretting that the knife had not been a trifle sharper.

Then there seemed naught to do but settle herself in the gilt armchair Miles had vacated and listen in sulky silence to the other three women chattering away to that perfidious man as if he were numbered amongst their oldest and dearest acquaintances. Cordelia seethed. How would she ever endure these next weeks with that tormenting man constantly underfoot? Never had fate played so dastardly a trick upon her. She still could not credit that the ruffianly soldier she had looked forward to seeing drawn and quartered now proved to be her own cousin, the scholarly relation whose arrival Papa had anticipated with such delight. Now she would be obliged to curb her temper, to show at least a semblance of courtesy to the man. And she suffered few illusions on that score. Miles was going to make it damnably difficult for her.

With a heavy sigh, she slumped back in her seat. The colonel bit back a smile at the way her small nose crinkled in frustration. He had no difficulty imagining what murderous thoughts were chasing behind Delia's lovely brow. Her vivid blue eyes shot sparks every time they chanced to gaze in his direction.

Anger brought a becoming flush to her cheeks, as becoming as the way the sunlight filtering in through the window gilded her soft curls with a touch of gold. All the same, Miles wished she would smile at him as she had the first time their eyes had met upon the hillside.

Delia Renwick had changed quite a bit since he had last seen her at Renwick Manor seven years ago. She'd been naught but a precocious child, paying scant heed to Miles, her Papa's quiet, boring visitor. Far too preoccupied in entertaining her stepmama's guests, Delia had seemed like a little blond marionette, animated only when Amaryllis pulled the strings. But now . . . Miles's gaze roved appreciatively over his cousin's slender curves. It was obvious Delia was quite grown-up, a lady who possessed a very decided mind of her own.

He sank his teeth into the muffin, flashing Delia his most engaging grin. But his first overture at peacemaking was met with a sniff and a toss of the head as she rigidly fixed her eyes on the fire.

With a start, Miles realized that Aunt Violet was addressing him. "I daresay Stratford will not be as exciting to you, newly returned from Paris, Cousin Miles. But now that Lord Walsing has come into his estate and returned from America, we do not go on so quietly here as we were wont to do. He is a very dashing young man."

185

Miles laughed. "The only Walsings I ever met had noses so long my horses would have envied them."

"There is nothing wrong with Lord Walsing's nose, I assure you," Delia bristled. "He is by far the handsomest man I have ever seen."

Miles raised his eyebrows at the defensive note in her voice. So Lord Walsing must be the fellow drawn with such loving care in her sketchbook. Handsome, perhaps, but if Delia's portraiture was true to life, the man looked as if he had all the fire and spirit of a sheep.

Miss Pryce giggled. "Oh, fie, Miss Renwick. I am sure Lord Walsing is not near as handsome as Colonel Renwick." She batted her lashes at Miles in such a way as to nearly cause him to gag on the muffin. "I have been in such close attendance upon my aunt since my own return to Stratford that I have not yet seen his lordship. But I was intimately acquainted with Lord Walsing during his sojourn in America. While I was companion to my cousin, Lady Margaret Huntley, her husband was one of the ambassadors to Washington after the war. Well, Lord Walsing . . ."

Cordelia squirmed with annoyance. Oh, Lord, she thought, here we go again. More of Fanny's endless boasting about her journey to America, her intimate acquaintance with everyone from Lord Walsing to President Madison. She hailed with relief Rosamund's gentle interruption of Fanny's stream of chatter.

"You have indeed chosen an excellent time to visit Stratford, Colonel Renwick," she said. "In July, we will be holding celebrations in honor of the bicentenary of the poet's death."

Miles frowned. "Shakespeare's death? That strikes me as an odd excuse for festivities."

"In my opinion, that is the only event in Stratford worth celebrating," Delia remarked acidly.

"Indeed?" Miles twisted the thick, satiny ends of his mustache. "Then I suppose I must get rigged out for these jollifications, order some new suits of clothes. Have you a good tailor hereabouts?"

"Oh, Colonel Renwick," Fanny trilled. "You would not wish to employ a Stratford tailor. Not fashionable enough by half!"

"I value comfort above fashion, Miss Pryce. I also have the need to engage a valet since I lost my orderly when I resigned my commission. At the moment, I am afraid I look a little too uncivilized to be standing up at a ball with a lady."

While the other women cried out, assuring him that no, indeed, he looked quite handsome, so elegant in his uniform, Delia cut in, "It would not hurt you to shave. I do so detest mustaches."

"Delia!" Aunt Violet reproved. When even Rosamund looked shocked by her rudeness, Delia realized she might have gone too far and floundered, trying to make amends.

"That is to say, Colonel Renwick, mustaches are so—so scratchy against one's face. At least so I would imagine. I—I . . ." She stopped, the color suffusing her face as she realized what she was saying.

Miles's dark eyes sparkled with mischief as he feigned a look of serious consideration. "My dear Cousin, I had never considered that possibility. I do beg your pardon."

The three ladies stared from her to Miles in bewilderment at the turn the conversation had taken. Feeling ready to sink through the floor, Delia's hand fluttered to her cheek, imagining that the spot where the rough velvet of Miles's mustache had abraded her skin must show as blatantly as if she had rouged her face. Damn the man! Could he never train those bold, staring eyes of his someplace else other than on her?

Once more it was Rosamund who came to her rescue by interjecting a question. "Colonel Renwick," she began diffidently. "I was wondering . . . of course, it is absurd, there are so many men in an army. But I was wondering if you knew a Captain Michael Devon."

"Captain Devon of the Forty-fifth? Never tell me you are Dev's Rosamund."

Rosamund blushed all the way to the roots of her dusky curls. "Well, we are very good *friends*, but he . . . has never spoken yet of . . . But I believe he is expected home within the month and then . . ." Her voice trailed off in pretty confusion.

Miles flashed her a wide smile. "I did not mean to embarrass you, Miss Rosamund, or to steal any of Dev's thunder. But he has talked of little else but his beautiful Rosamund ever since I first met the man. I have been quite green with envy that he should have such bliss awaiting him, while I . . ." Miles fetched a huge sigh, rolling great, sorrowful eyes in Cordelia's direction. "I return to no one."

Delia yawned, conveying what she was hoped was an expression of complete and utter indifference. Miles turned back to Rosamund, proceeding to quite win that young woman over by descriptions of Michael Devon's heroism in battle. Delia

187

watched in dismay as her dearest friend listened to Miles with rapt attention, drinking in his every word. She had hoped later to have some speech with Rosamund alone. At least Roz would sympathize with Delia against the colonel. She wanted to make her friend understand that the gallant-looking soldier so boyishly licking muffin crumbs from his fingers was truly a fiend in disguise. But by the time Rosamund and Fanny rose to take their leave, it was obvious that Miles had charmed away Delia's last hope of an ally.

As Miles bowed over her head, Rosamund actually invited the rogue to tea, doubtless so that she could hear more praise of her beloved Michael. She left the cottage, looking so starry-eyed she scarcely remembered to bid farewell to Delia. If that was what being in love did to one, Delia was quite sure she wanted no part of it.

Aunt Violet walked out with the two young women, and Delia suddenly found herself alone with Miles. Before she could hasten after the other ladies, he covered the space between them in two quick strides. She had not even time to protest before he seized her by the hand, her own seeming lost in the rugged strength of his grasp. She tried to draw away but felt her heart melting at the warmth of his smile.

"We got off to a very bad start, Cousin," he said softly. "I admit my behavior this morning was abominable. Do you never mean to forgive me?"

"I—I . . ." she stammered, wondering at how heated the room had become. She tried to tell herself that she was still furious with him, but it was so hard to remain steadfast against the coaxing plea in those twinkling eyes. All might have been well if Miles had ended there, but some evil demon prompted him to quote, " 'For by this light whereby I see thy beauty, thy beauty that doth make me like thee well.' "

"Oh!" Delia wrenched her hand away. "Do you take me for a fool, sir? I know perfectly well that is what Petruchio says to Katherina in *The Taming of the Shrew*, and I do not find the comparison amusing."

Miles groaned. "Damme, it just slipped out. I was not even thinking of the context. Believe me, I in no way intended to imply you are like Shakespeare's Kate."

But Delia was already marching toward the parlor door.

"Delia!" he called desperately after her. "I was only trying to cry truce."

"Truce!" Delia hissed over her shoulder. "Sir, this war has just begun!"

When the door slammed behind her, Miles wondered if perhaps he had been too hasty in accepting Walter Renwick's invitation to come to Stratford. The fire smoldering in his cousin's blue eyes promised to make Waterloo seem like a mere skirmish.

All the same, the invitation had proved most timely. It had provided Miles with a good excuse to escape from his older brother's household in London before he had been driven to murder Stephen. As Miles's senior by ten years, Stephen exhibited the same marked tendency to arrange Miles's life that had driven the colonel to join the army in the first place.

"Walter Renwick," Stephen had harumphed when the letter from Stratford had arrived. "Haven't heard anything about him in ages. You know his old estate in Warwickshire is up for auction again."

"What has that to say to anything?" The reed-thin voice of Miles's sister-in-law had broken in. "Miles has more important things to occupy his time now than old Walter Renwick. He could not possibly be thinking of leaving us to bury himself in Stratford."

Miles had fixed a smile on his face to conceal that that was exactly what he was thinking. Despite not having seen Walter Renwick for years, Miles felt much more akin with his old friend and distant relation than he did his only living brother.

"Of course, of course, my dear." Stephen had agreed with Caroline as he always did, then had launched into the familiar lecture Miles could almost recite by heart.

Now that the war was finished, Stephen had argued, Miles must discard his uniform. 'Twas high time Miles put the fortune he had inherited from their father to good use, purchased an estate of his own, made a suitable marriage. Caroline would be only too delighted to introduce Miles to any number of proper, wealthy young women. . . . Then there were the more important tasks of finding Miles a good tailor, horses, a carriage, a valet.

"And do be sure to select for me a good brand of tooth powder," Miles had interrupted. "Seven years as colonel of a regiment has left me ill-prepared to make any sort of decisions."

Stephen had scowled. The chief thing his brother lacked, Miles had thought, was any sort of a sense of humor. Thereafter he had merely given a noncommittal smile to everything Stephen and Caroline had said, then had gone out to do exactly as he pleased.

He had not taken time to hire a rig but had caught the next mail coach to Stratford. A choice he still could not bring himself to regret, Delia's reception of him notwithstanding. Miles grinned at the closed parlor door through which Delia had made her angry exit. Faith, mayhap the lady had reason for remaining so furious. Miles's apology had lacked a certain amount of sincerity. He was still not sorry for that stolen kiss.

Before Miles had the opportunity for any further contemplation on what his future conduct toward Cordelia should be, the door burst open to admit Walter Renwick.

"Miles, m'boy! Why did no one tell me you had arrived?"

Miles returned the old man's embrace with much enthusiasm and hearty backslapping. Covertly, he studied Walter Renwick to see what changes the years had wrought. The hair was a shade grayer, thinner perhaps; a few more wrinkles about the eyes. In spite of that, Miles thought the man looked younger, more fit than when he had seen him last. Not nearly so harassed as when he had been burdened by his marriage to . . .

Miles cleared his throat, wondering if he ought to express his regrets at having been in Spain when Amaryllis died. Nay, he had written then. Far better to let the subject rest along with the lady herself.

Renwick stepped back, beaming as he inspected Miles. "Od's bodikins, but I believe you have grown taller still. Or is it I who am shrinking?"

"I trust not, sir." Miles laughed.

"And so you have already seen Cordelia?"

"Er, yes. We—we took tea together just now."

Renwick cocked one bushy gray eyebrow. "And earlier this morning on Squire Newbold's hillside?"

Miles felt a small twinge of embarrassment creep into his cheeks. "Oh, she told you about that?"

"Well, she did not know the name of the ruffian she wanted to see boiled in oil." Renwick chuckled. "But a dashing colonel who could quote Shakespeare—moreover one bold enough to wrest a kiss from a spitfire like Delia . . . Well, I must admit I had strong suspicions."

Miles flushed more fully now. The old man was as acute as he had ever been. "Sir, I assure you I don't generally go about accosting young females—"

"Tush, tush, no harm done." Renwick waved aside the apology Miles tried to make. "I know my Cordelia well enough to assume the fault was not entirely yours. The girl runs completely wild, forever slipping off without her maid. When my sister was widowed a year ago, I thought Violet might be able to take the child in hand, but . . ." Renwick's voice faded into a heavy sigh. Then he straightened, clapping Miles on the back once more. "Ah, well. I am so glad *you* are here now."

Miles tried to return the cheery smile Renwick gave him but was assailed by an inexplicable sense of misgiving. Why, Cousin Walter looked like a beleaguered army captain who sights the cavalry riding to the rescue or like . . .

Miles tugged at his collar. Or like the father of Katherina when he first clapped eyes on Petruchio swaggering into Padua to take a wife.

Cordelia's stomach churned as she attempted to swallow her temper enough to eat her dinner. Her lips pursed, she pushed her portion of salmagundi aside with her fork, the mixture of chicken, anchovies, lettuce, and eggs doing little to tempt her appetite. She had graciously deferred to her aunt, permitting Mrs. Nicolson to take her place at the foot of the table, but this forced Delia to sit directly opposite Miles. While maintaining the most innocent demeanor, the man constantly found opportunities to brush his foot against her ankle beneath the long, narrow Elizabethan table of heavy oak.

Although she glared at him repeatedly, it had no effect. Miles met her dark looks with the blandest of smiles. As for Papa, he noticed nothing. Sitting at the head of the table, Walter Renwick carved the haunch of mutton while engaging Miles in lively conversation. She had not seen Papa so jovial for many a day, Delia thought resentfully. He had even neglected to bring a book to the table, as was his wont.

Spearing a piece of lettuce with such energy that her fork rang against the china, Delia felt Miles's foot caress the toe of her slipper once more. With indrawn breath, she leaned back into her heavily carved chair until the Tudor rose grated against her shoulder blade. With all the strength she could muster, she administered a sharp kick to Miles's shinbone. But instead of bearing his punishment in stoic silence, he yelped, turning reproachful brown eyes upon her. With her aunt's and Papa's stares now drawn in her direction, Delia flushed, then mumbled an apology.

Although she had scarcely tasted a bite, she sighed with relief when Aunt Violet rose, signaling that they should leave the gentlemen to enjoy their port. As was their custom, she and her aunt retired to the parlor. The housemaid, Elise, flitted about the room lighting candles.

While Aunt Violet drew forth some of her needlework, Delia ensconced herself behind the pianoforte, her fingers traveling listlessly over the ivory keys. Atop the glossy mahogany surface, the marble eyes of Shakespeare's bust seemed to follow her every movement, the stone lips half-tipped in an inscrutable smile as if he enjoyed some secret jest at her expense. Delia banged down on the keys, hitting a discordant note, before turning the bust so that it faced the wall, then restlessly beginning another tune. She usually enjoyed this quiet part of the day when she and Aunt Violet were alone, but tonight her eyes kept traveling toward the door, dreading the moment, she told herself, when Miles would descend upon her once more.

She smoothed out the soft folds of her sky-blue silk with the petal puffed sleeves. The pearl buttons that closed the bodice matched the strand of pearls Bessy had woven through Delia's braided topknot of curls. Delia was glad that she had decided to humor herself by wearing one of her favorite gowns. It was a dress she saved for only very special dinner guests, but tonight she had needed something to give her spirits a boost if she was to endure Miles's exasperating presence a moment longer. Forcing aside the memory of the gleam that had come into Miles's eyes at the sight of her garbed thusly, her hands stumbled over the keys. The parlor door inched open, but it was only Elise bringing in the heavily laden coffee tray.

Fretfully, Delia drummed her fingers down a scale. What was taking Papa so long? Usually he was most eager to join them since he spent the evenings reading Shakespeare aloud. She wished he and Miles would come and get the torment over with.

Besides, Aunt Violet's conversation was excessively tedious this evening. She could do naught but sing the praises of Miles Renwick.

"So handsome, my dear Delia, and such a military bearing. Very charming, do you not find him so?"

Delia mumbled a disgruntled reply, but her lack of enthusiasm did little to daunt Aunt Violet. "I declare," the old woman said with a sigh, paying little heed to her stitching, "he makes me feel quite young again. I never thought much about those fusty old plays your papa is forever reading, but Miles strikes me as being very like one of the heroes, a Romeo . . . or a Lysander or a Benedick."

"More like Caliban," Delia said, breaking into the strains of a waltz.

Aunt Violet paused in the act of untangling a thread long enough to frown at Delia. "How can you say such a thing, Delia? There was nothing in the least witchlike about Miles's mother. Lucy Dysan was an enchanting creature, quite a belle in her day."

"Mayhap so," Delia murmured, "but I would wager odds upon his having had the devil for a father."

"My dear!" Aunt Violet looked much shocked. "Morgan Renwick was a gentleman, as much so as Miles."

The ormolu clock upon the mantel chimed out the hour. Aunt Violet began to stuff her tambour frame inside the drawer of her worktable, so she did not see the face Delia pulled.

"Well, it is my turn to be ill tonight," Aunt Violet said cheerfully.

Delia halted her playing in dismay. She and Aunt Violet had devised a system whereby they took turns having megrims, thus each enjoyed an opportunity to escape Walter Renwick's evening recitals of Shakespeare without arousing his suspicions. But Cordelia had thought Aunt Violet would forsake her privilege this once.

"Surely you will not abandon me tonight, Aunt Vi?" Delia pleaded.

"You will have Cousin Miles for company."

"Him! He is as bad about Shakespeare as Papa! He has the same habit of tossing off quotes and—"

Aunt Violet firmly compressed her thin lips. "I am sorry, my dear. An agreement is an agreement, and it is definitely my turn to be ill. I would not insist upon it except that I know Walter means to read from *Antony and Cleopatra* and I cannot abide hearing about that Egyptian creature. Shameless hussy! Do make my excuses to the gentlemen."

All further appeals were to no avail. Delia watched forlornly as Aunt Violet made good her escape. It was shortly afterward that the gentlemen entered, Papa bearing the heavy tome that Delia knew far too well. When she conveyed Aunt Violet's message, he shook his head in perplexity. "Dear me! I believe I shall have a physician in to look at both you and your aunt.

It cannot be natural for anyone to suffer from so many head-aches. Mayhap 'tis something in the air here at Rose Briar Cottage."

Before Delia could protest, she was disconcerted to find Miles leaning against the pianoforte and smiling down at her. She could not help noticing how tall the man was. His unde-niably masculine presence seemed to quite overwhelm her and the delicate, spindly legged instrument. He had discarded his uniform in favor of a simple black evening jacket of fustian, the cut not quite in the latest style but well-set across the broad plane of his chest. Miles would never have to resort to the use of buckram wadding to pad out his shoulders. But neither would Lord Walsing, she reminded herself with a start, feeling she had somehow allowed her thoughts to become disloyal.

The silver candelabrum lent a soft glow to Miles's dark eyes as he said, "It has been a long time since I have had the plea-sure of a beautiful young lady playing music for me."

Although her heart thudded strangely, Delia closed the pianoforte with a loud bang. " 'Twill be longer still, Colonel Renwick."

"You must call me Miles. After all—"

" 'Tis Papa's custom to read to us each evening, *Colonel Renwick*," she continued as if she had not heard. "Shake-speare! That no doubt should thrill you to the marrow of your bones."

"Well, to tell you the truth—" Miles began, but Delia reached for the candelabrum and whisked it over to where her father had settled himself comfortably in the wing-backed chair. Positioning the candles upon a cherrywood tripod table near Papa's elbow, she soon saw that her zeal in avoiding Miles had been a strategic error.

The colonel seated himself on the striped settee, the only other comfortable place in the room. Delia eyed the straight-back cane chairs with loathing while Miles shot her a challeng-ing look, almost daring her to sit beside him. Well, this interloper was not going to get the best of her in her own home. Chin thrust high, Delia marched to the settee and settled herself primly next to the colonel. There, that would show him she was not to be intimidated. But from the smile that twitched at the corner of his lips, Delia was not altogether sure that she had won the victory.

Papa beamed at both of them, opening the massive volume

on his knee. He cleared his throat. "*Antony and Cleopatra.* Act Three, Scene Four."

Delia sighed. She loved her Papa dearly, but his reading voice lacked all expression. He recited the lines in such a dreary monotone that even the impassioned love scenes between the Queen of the Nile and her Roman swain sounded like the grimmest of Sunday sermons.

Although she avoided meeting his eye, Delia could sense Miles growing more relaxed. He slumped down farther and farther upon the settee until, much to her outrage, his crisp black locks rested against her shoulder.

How dare he! In front of her own papa! She was about to give him a sharp poke in the ribs when she realized the colonel had fallen sound asleep. She could not help noticing how appealing his face was in repose, one ebony curl drooping boyishly over his brow, the heavy lids fanning dark lashes across his strong cheekbones, the full, sensual lips slightly parted, issuing warm sleep-blurred breaths. . . .

Her own mouth curved in an expression of unholy joy. Papa had once tweaked her ear for drifting off during one of his readings, calling her an ignorant, soulless chit with no appreciation for the immortal Bard. What would he think of his brilliant, scholarly Miles Renwick now?

"Papa," she called softly so as not to disturb the gentleman blissfully slumbering upon her shoulder. When her father glanced up, his bushy brows knit together in annoyance at having been interrupted, she continued, " 'Twould seem that Cousin Miles no longer has any interest in young Octavius's advancing legions."

Papa removed his spectacles. Her own face set in an expression of virtuous attention, Cordelia waited gleefully for the explosion to come. But Papa merely regarded Miles with an expression of avuncular fondness.

"Poor lad. He is exhausted from his journey. How inconsiderate I have been."

Delia's jaw dropped open. "B-but, Papa. He fell asleep while you were reading Shakespeare to him."

"Yes, imagine how worn to the bone he must be for that to have happened! Wake him gently, Delia, and we shall send him up to his bed."

Her lips parted, but no words would come. Spluttering with indignation, Delia felt Miles's weight snuggle more heavily against her. Wake him gently! Grinding her teeth, she wrenched her body forward, staggering to her feet. Deprived of his support, Miles tumbled over, falling off the settee. He sat up, blinking at his surroundings in bewilderment. Mindful of her father's disapproving stare, Delia bent over the colonel, saying in accents of honey-sweetness, "Do wake up, dear Cousin. 'Tis time to retire."

As realization dawned on Miles, a flush of mortification spread across his cheeks. He rose slowly to his feet. "I do beg your pardon, sir, Cousin Delia. I do not know what happened. I—"

"Think nothing of it, my boy. Happens to the best of us. What you need is a good night's sleep. Delia, I trust you have made all the arrangements for Miles's comfort."

She shrugged. "He is your guest, Papa. I thought that you would have done so."

Her father eyed her sternly, and Delia knew that later she would be treated to a well-deserved lecture, but at the moment she did not care. Papa behaved as if . . . as if Miles were his son and she the intruder at Rose Briar Cottage.

Looking embarrassed by Delia's surliness, Papa turned back to the colonel. "Well, come along, Miles. We shall contrive something for you."

Miles stifled a yawn. "Even a sack of hay sounds good. Good night, Cousin Delia."

She nodded curtly. Settling into Papa's vacated chair, she drew forth a book, affecting to read, having deliberately chosen one of those sentimental Minerva Press romances she knew would annoy her father most. It was not until the two men had quit the room that she realized she was holding the text upside down.

Although she tried to concentrate on *The Enchantress*, the print blurred before her eyes as her conscience pricked her. Papa would have no choice but to put Miles in Amaryllis's room. Delia had not even instructed Elise to air it out or change the sheets. It would be odiously damp and stuffy in there.

"Well, serves him right foisting himself upon us in this fashion," she muttered. "Mayhap if he is uncomfortable enough, 'twill shorten his stay."

A few minutes later, Bessy thrust her head in the doorway to adjure Delia not to ruin her eyes by reading too late. Delia could sense that the woman was longing to scold her for being negligent about the preparations for Miles's arrival. Mr.

Renwick had had to rouse Bessy to come to his aid. She started on a long explanation of what arrangements had been settled upon, but Delia refused to listen. It was one thing for her father to lecture her, but she refused to tolerate any more of Bessy's impertinence. The maid shortly gave up her attempts to bring Delia to a sense of her own inadequacies as hostess and ducked out again, leaving Delia to the comforts of a very dull book and a dying fire.

Abovestairs, Miles nestled deeper beneath the counterpane. Despite the softness of the feather-tick mattress beneath him, his fatigued brain carried him back to the sterner bedding of a hard cot, the heavy damask curtains drawn all around transforming into the canvas lines of a tent.

Miles tried to rouse himself. Wasn't he due at the Duke of Wellington's ball? Nay, 'twas time to buckle on his saber. The French were advancing. Soon they would overrun the rolling farmland in Waterloo.

The next instant something launched itself at him out of the darkness, landing with a startled *ommph* upon his chest. Sneaking French! How had they slipped past the sentinels? With a cry of rage, Miles grappled for his life, flinging the enemy off him, pinning the man beneath his weight. It was not until his fingers closed around a soft, whimpering throat that the thought that something was terribly wrong penetrated his consciousness. The body writhing beneath his was the most strangely contoured Frenchman he had ever encountered. Shaking his head to clear his sleep-fogged brain, he opened his eyes, struggling to focus in the darkness. Slowly, he released his captive's throat, his fingers moving up to explore a mass of silken curls, a small, pointed chin, velvety cheeks . . .

"Who the—Delia?" he breathed.

"Get off of me, you great oaf!" her familiar voice sobbed.

He rolled to one side, his mind reeling with confusion. Dear God, he had heard of men who sleepwalked, but he had never done so before. His vision gradually cleared enough for him to recognize the heavy damask bed curtains. Nay, unless there were two identical beds at Rose Briar, he had not stirred a step from the room to which Walter Renwick had guided him hours before.

Keenly aware of his own thundering pulses, Miles turned back to the quivering young woman at his side. "What on earth do you think you are doing, Cordelia?" he said sternly. "You scared all hell out of me."

"I scared you!" she squeaked, the tear-edged quality in her voice turning to fury. He could just make out the silhouette of her form jerking into a sitting position. "You nearly killed me. What—what are you doing in my bed, you brigand? I shall summon my father."

But even as she drew breath, Miles clamped his hand over her jaw. "Your bed? What do you mean, your bed? This is the guest chamber where your father bade me sleep and *ouch*! Damme!" He yanked his hand away as Delia's teeth sank into the fleshy curve below his thumb.

"This is my room," she said, "and if you don't get out of here at once, I shall scream to bring the house down around your ears."

"Now, Cousin," he said, nursing his injured hand. "I am sure there has been some mistake. . . ."

"And you made it." She launched two small fists against his chest, attempting to shove him backward off the bed. At that moment, a sharp rap sounded upon the bedchamber door. Aunt Violet's sleepy voice drifted from the hall outside.

"Cousin Miles. Cousin Miles? What is amiss in there?"

Delia froze, suddenly conscious of her knuckles pressing against the warm, hair-roughened skin along the V of Miles's nightshirt. She shrank away, fighting down the urge to break into frightened sobs again. When she slipped into the welcoming darkness of her own room, she had never dreamed anything was wrong other than the fact that Bessy had forgotten all about her. Scorning to summon the maid, Delia had struggled out of her own clothes, then groped in the wardrobe for a nightgown. Scrambling into the lawn garment, she had dived between the bed curtains, seeking the comforting warmth of her blankets. Instead of soft mattress, she had landed upon hard, sinewy muscle. Two great, rough hands had nearly squeezed the life out of her, and now she was about to be caught in a most compromising position by her prim and proper aunt.

"What are we going to do?" she wailed to Miles. "No one will ever believe . . ."

"Be quiet and stay behind the bed curtains," he hissed. Before she could say another word, he had leaped off the bed. She could hear him striking the flint to light a candle. Despite his command, she peered fearfully past the damask hangings.

The candle's glow illuminated Miles garbed only in his night-shirt, so Delia was afforded an excellent view of bare calves and firm, molded buttocks beneath the thin cambric. With a little gasp, she quickly closed the curtains.

"Cousin Miles!" Aunt Violet's rapping became more insistent.

"One moment," he called, "I am looking for my robe." After a few seconds more, Delia heard Miles's bare feet padding across the floor. The door creaked open.

"Cousin Miles, are you hurt? I heard the most frightful cry."

At her aunt's quavering tones, Delia cringed. Merciful heavens! What if Aunt Vi should come into the room? She burrowed beneath the covers until only the top of her head stuck out.

She heard Miles affecting a yawn. "So sorry to have awakened you, Cousin Violet. I was having a nightmare. Alas, ever since the war . . ."

"Poor boy. I shall rouse Cook to make you a glass of warm milk."

"Oh, no, that will not be necessary. I shall be fine. Never have more than one nightmare a night. Now you hasten back to your bed and don't fret over me."

"Well," Aunt Violet said reluctantly, "if you are certain there is naught I can do."

"Nothing, nothing at all, thank you." Despite Miles's non-chalance, Delia could detect the nervous desperation just below the surface. "Hurry along before you catch your death in that drafty corridor, Cousin Violet. If you are not looking lovely and fresh-faced in the morning, I shall never forgive myself for having disturbed your rest."

Delia heard her aunt titter, then bid Miles good night. The door closed, but Delia did not move until she heard her aunt skittering down the corridor. Then Miles was back, flinging open the bed curtains, drawing down the coverlet until his devilishly glinting eyes stared into her own.

"You can come out now."

Yanking the bedclothes from his hand, she jerked upright, holding the downy quilt protectively across her breasts. Although Miles was now attired in his dressing gown, the red satin, open at the neck, gave him a most rakishly improper appearance. She could see the tip of a jagged pink scar slashing across the bronzed expanse of chest just visible beneath the sashed garment. Averting her gaze, she said, "You mean you can get out now. Out of my room."

"I shall be only too happy to oblige you, my dear. That is, if you have some alternative suggestion as to where I should sleep."

"You can go down the hall to my stepmother's—I mean, the guest chamber. I do not know what Papa was thinking of, showing you in here." She could scarcely keep the hint of wounded feelings from her voice. That must have been what Bessy had come down to tell her, that she was expected to sleep in the room where Amaryllis had died. How could Papa be so insensitive! Aware that Miles was studying her face, Delia stiffened her spine. She would not permit him or anyone else to know that she was afraid to sleep in that bedchamber.

"I cannot believe you expected me to give up my room," she said to Miles. "Why, the guest room is musty, full of cobwebs, and—and the chimney smokes."

Miles's hands came to rest upon his hips. "But you have no compunction in consigning me to such a place. Thank you so much for your hospitality, Cousin, but I prefer to remain where I am."

To her outrage, he flung himself back down upon the bed. As quickly as he settled beneath the covers, she scampered out the other side.

"Why, you—you blackguard!" she stammered furiously.

"Please, Cousin, 'tis very late." Miles plumped up her pillow, burrowing his head into it with a lusty sigh. "We can talk in the morning. I recommend you either retire to the guest chamber or climb back into bed."

At her gasp, he raised his head long enough to favor her with his devil's grin. "Of course, there will be the greatest uproar in the morning when we are found. I expect I will be obliged to marry you to save your tarnished reputation."

"Marry me!" Delia stomped her bare foot upon the cold wooden floor. "I'd as soon lead apes into hell than have you for a husband."

"A not unlikely possibility, considering your disposition." Miles drew the warm, thick quilt more snugly about his neck. "Would you be so good as to snuff the candle, Cousin? I should not like to have to venture back out into the cold."

Delia shivered, suddenly realizing how chilly the room was when clad only in one's nightgown. Tears of helpless anger stung her eyes. "If you were a gentleman, you would never deprive a lady of her own bed."

"If it were a lady's bed, I daresay I would not."

Her hands clenched into tight fists. How she longed to fling herself upon him, to cast him bodily out into the hall—nay, out of the house. She had a pleasant vision of Miles locked outside, shivering in the snow, his only protection that scandalously thin nightshirt, while she peered out of the window at him, toasty warm by the fire.

Delia sighed. It wasn't snowing, and there was no way she could physically eject that great mountain of a man from her bed. Indeed, if she lingered here much longer, it was she who would freeze, to say nothing of the risk of being caught in these improper circumstances.

Miles peeked sleepily at her from beneath the covers. "Was there something else you wanted, Cordelia? Perchance a cousinly kiss good night?"

"Oh, plague take you!" Snatching up her own robe from the wardrobe along with the candle Miles had lit, she stormed out of the room, retaining only enough discretion to remember not to slam the door behind her. Her fury carried her the length of the hall, fueling her courage that only began to desert her when she had actually crossed the threshold into Amaryllis's room.

Easing her robe onto a chair, she held the candle aloft, examining the chamber where no one had slept since Amaryllis had died five years ago. Obviously, the housemaid still entered to clean, but most of her stepmother's personal effects had been cleared away. Only the bare articles of French gilt furniture remained, casting tall, wavering shadows against the decaying bamboo-tree wallpaper, spectral reflections of the room's former occupant.

The candle trembled in Delia's grasp as she forced herself to step nearer to the elegant sofa-bed that occupied the center of the chamber. Winged cherubs held back the gauzy draperies, their chubby faces wreathed in sly smiles as if they invited her to the embrace of a silken shroud. Delia wrenched her eyes away, sternly telling herself not to be nonsensical. 'Twas but another room, another bed. Yet as she reached out to turn back the satiny white counterpane, she half expected to see the red stains spreading across the sheets.

She snatched her hand away. "No, I cannot do it. Cannot sleep in the very bed where Amaryllis . . ." Pulling one of the blankets free of the mattress, Cordelia shrank away from the bedside. Her eyes roved fearfully over the gloom-filled corners until she spotted two armchairs made of beechwood but painted to simulate bamboo. Arranging them to face each other, she huddled on the stiff cushions, trying not to fall through the gap between the chairs. The blanket smelled of must, but at least it afforded her some warmth and a feeling of protection.

But protection from what? Although Delia's tired eyes long to drift closed, they fluttered open at every creak of the old house. She did not believe in ghosts, but if ever an unhappy spirit had the right to haunt its earthbound dwelling, then surely Amaryllis . . .

Delia shuddered. It was going to be a long night. "Damn you, Miles Renwick," she fumed, adjusting her head against the hard chair back, futilely seeking a more comfortable position. "I shall pay you out for this. Just see if I don't!"

Chapter 4

Bleary-eyed, Cordelia stumbled out of the breakfast-parlor door into the garden, carrying her cup of chocolate. She was awake even before Papa this morning. Far too exhausted to breakfast in solitary splendor, she decided to slip outside into the brisk air lest Bessy find her slumped over the oak table using her toast for a pillow.

The Elizabethan Knott garden spread out before her, each bed of flowers and herbs ringed with precision by the tiny yew hedges. Roses, oxlips, crown imperials, lavender, daisies, rosemary, savory, marjoram . . . All bloomed snugly in their own special places as they had done for decades. Cordelia drew in a deep breath, savoring the blend of sweet and spicy essences. She had long ago given up sighing for the fashionable wilderness-style gardens such as the ones many of her friends had. Papa was adamant that the Knott garden remain undisturbed. In truth, she had grown accustomed to it, begun to find something pleasing about the symmetry, the sense of order in the neatly arranged sections. The clusters of bright-colored flowers all fit together like parts of a well-wrought puzzle, the only piece missing being the one bed of herbs, dug shortly after Amaryllis died and now choked with weeds.

Amaryllis . . . Delia sighed, sinking down upon the wooden settle nestled under the spreading branches of a large mulberry tree. She set her cup beside her, the steaming chocolate left untasted. What dreams she had had last night. Rubbing the nape of her stiff neck, she shuddered. Even in the morning sunshine, the shadowy phantoms from Amaryllis's bedchamber seemed to close around her.

She had dreamed that Amaryllis still lay in the silk-draped bed crying out for help, but the bed was ringed by a group of laughing strangers who would not let Delia by. All of a sudden, she realized Amaryllis was one of those laughing, her violet eyes mocking Delia's struggles to reach her. Then her stepmama was floating away, her hands stretched out like claws, pulling Papa after her ... and Miles. He followed Amaryllis, too, despite how Cordelia begged not to be left all alone.

All alone. Shivering, Delia pulled her cashmere shawl with its gaily embroidered blue peacocks more tightly around her shoulders. The morning quiet of the garden began to seem oppressive. She was grateful when some sparrows set up a shrill racket even though she knew what the tiny birds were about. Her eyes roved up the cottage's ivy-covered walls to the sloping roof. Those dratted birds were attacking the thatch again up by the chimney in order to build more nests. Delia would have to summon the thatcher to check for damage, and wheat straw was so wretchedly expensive since the war shortage. But Papa would never think to have repairs done until the roof was caving in about their ears.

As if the very thought was enough to summon up disaster, the tree branches above her head began to shake with an alarming ferocity, sending a shower of green mulberries tumbling into her hair. Startled, Delia leaped from the bench, backing away a few steps before venturing to look up. The tree continued to shake for several more moments before a pair of chubby legs encased in knee breeches appeared. With a final swing, a small boy of about ten years dropped to the ground, landing on his feet with the agility of a cat.

A smile curved Delia's lips as she looked down at a round face whose chief features were freckles and missing teeth.

"Tom! How long have you been up there?"

Young Master Thomas Leighton smoothed out the sleeves of his biscuit-colored jacket with the air of a London beau. "Why, I just now scaled the garden wall and climbed into the tree. Didn't you hear me?"

Delia shook her head. "You might have knocked at the gate."

"Pooh! There's no sport in that."

"I don't know how much sport you will find when your mama sees the mulberry stains on your jacket."

"Oh, 'tis nothing," Master Thomas replied cheerfully. "I tore a hole in the seat of my breeches, too. I shall get such a thundering scold for that, I daresay Mama won't even notice my coat."

Delia favored him with a curtsy of mock dignity. "In that case, pray be seated, sir. 'Tis prodigiously early to be receiving gentleman callers, but you are always welcome at Rose Briar."

With the ease of long acquaintance, Master Thomas adjured her not to talk like a perfect widgeon. Plopping down upon the wooden bench, he spotted the chocolate. His snub nose sniffed the cup in appreciation. "I say, aren't you going to drink this, Delia?"

"No. I do not care for my chocolate with mulberries floating in it."

"That wouldn't put me off."

"Then, please, feel free."

The boy thrust stubby fingers into the chocolate, fishing out the berries before diving his face into the cup. He emerged several moments later with a deep sigh, a brown mustache now gracing his upper lip. Delia groped for her handkerchief, but Tom had already wiped his mouth on his light-colored sleeve.

"This visit is quite a surprise, Master Leighton. Rosamund did not mention a word yesterday about you being home from school."

Tom's mouth curled into an expressive grimace that said all too clearly, *Sisters*! "Roz goes about like a regular mooncalf these days. I wish I were your brother. At least a fellow can talk to you about 'portant matters. Just look what I've brought to show you."

Delia watched in some apprehension as Tom shoved his coat flap aside, pulling free a rope knotted around his waist. At the end of the rope was a small, wriggling brown sack.

"You know I am not at all partial to snakes, Thomas," she began.

" 'Tisn't a snake. Look." Tom stuffed his plump fingers into the sack, then fished out a large bullfrog. The boy's chest swelled with pride. "Isn't he a particklery fine spec'men, Delia?"

Carefully, he transferred the frog to Delia, who struggled to keep a firm grip on the slippery creature wriggling to escape. The frog's bulging eyes seemed to regard her with reproachful dignity. Feigning to examine the creature with keen interest, Delia at last pronounced, "I do believe this is the most handsome bullfrog I have ever been acquainted with."

But her praise, instead of pleasing Tom, appeared to fill him

205

with gloom. His round shoulders slumped forward. "I want to keep him up in my room, but Papa will not let me. And when I showed the frog to Miffin just now . . ." Tom jerked his thumb toward the small stableyard on the other side of the gardens where the Renwicks' sole coachman and groom was exercising Delia's mare. "Miffin says the frog won't be happy away from the pond."

"I expect Miffin is right," Delia said gently.

Tom scuffed his toe in the dirt. "I don't care. I will be glad when I get to be very old like you are. Then I can do as I please."

Delia suppressed a smile. "I am afraid even someone as ancient as myself is not permitted to keep bullfrogs in my bedchamber."

She attempted to transfer the frog back to Tom, but with a powerful spring of its back legs, the creature vaulted out of her hands, landing in the primrose bed.

"Oh, no! Catch him," Tom wailed.

They both leaped toward the frog, but it escaped in a series of graceful hops, then proceeded to lead them a merry chase through the garden.

"Over there, under the hedge," Tom yelled.

Heedless of her gown, Delia scrambled after the frog on all fours, calling over her shoulder, "Come on, head him off on the other side. And don't step on the hollyhocks!"

The warning came too late. Tom made a mad dive for the frog, completely flattening the unfortunate flowers. The frog bounded away down the gravel path. Hiking up her skirts, Delia jumped over the small hedge, racing after the green amphibian. She cornered the creature by the stone wall beneath the mulberry tree. By the time the frog was returned to Tom's sack, she was breathless with laughter, her gown spattered with grass and dirt, her curls tumbling into her eyes. But she felt better, the wild romp after the frog dispelling her earlier feeling of exhaustion and depression of spirits.

She sank down upon the wooden bench to catch her breath. "I really think . . . you should take . . . the poor fellow back to the pond. Only think how you would like to be held prisoner in a sack."

"Papa makes me go off to school," Tom grumbled. " 'Tis the same thing." Although he tried valiantly to suppress it, his small chin quivered. "Papa quizzed me yesterday on what I have been learning and says I am a great dunderhead. No one even wanted to hear how well I did in the cricket match."

Delia tousled his unruly curls, longing to give him a great hug, but she knew Tom would never tolerate that. Poor lad. How well she knew what it was like to have a scholarly parent who had no time for one. She swallowed the lump in her throat. "Well, a cricket match! One of my very favorite pastimes and you did not breath a word of it to me!"

Tom's face brightened. "Do you really wish to hear about it, Delia?" At her nod, he backed up a step to allow himself room for the hand gestures necessary to convey the full glory of the match.

Peering at the boy and Delia, Miles pressed his face against one of the small panes in the breakfast-parlor window. Intrigued by what was happening in the garden, his meal of beefsteak and broiled kidney lay forgotten upon the table. On coming downstairs to find the parlor deserted, he had believed himself to be the first one awake. But when he ventured to the sideboard to help himself to the marmalade, he had detected strange movements in the garden.

Delia! Already up and about. What on earth was she doing crawling through the garden as if she had lost something, accompanied by a chubby young lad who bounced up and down with excitement? The next instant she bounded to her feet, leaping the low hedge with an athletic grace, permitting Miles a glimpse of a shapely pair of legs.

Miles ran to the next window in an effort to follow her antics. Delia swooped down by the garden wall and then whirled around, her face alight with triumph. Evidently she had found whatever it was they were looking for.

As she and the boy walked back toward the mulberry tree, Miles craned his neck to see what she had clasped in her hands. He bit back an oath at the sight of an exceedingly ugly green frog cradled in her grasp as tenderly as if she held a fluffy little kitten.

An astonishing woman, this cousin of his! Miles threw back his head and laughed, stopping abruptly at the strange stare he received from the housemaid who had entered to refill the coffee urn. Giving the girl an affable nod, which she returned with a nervous curtsy, Miles directed his attention back to the pair outside. What were they doing now? The lad was obviously regaling Delia with some exciting tale from the way his arms churned through the air. She leaned forward on the wooden settle, hanging upon the child's every word.

Even from this distance, Miles noted the becoming flush in her cheeks, the way the morning breeze tangled the golden silk of her curls, how her rose-tinted lips parted in an encouraging smile.

Bracing one arm against the window jamb, Miles fetched a deep sigh. "Is this the shrew who all but scratched your eyes out last night, Miles Renwick?" he muttered. "Faith, I think you must have had a nightmare or else you are dreaming now."

He caught the housemaid staring again and offered her a rueful smile. The girl backed away, skittering out of the room as if he were some sort of dangerous lunatic escaped from Bedlam.

"The wench is right," Miles remarked to himself. "I think I am going mad. Unless there are two Delias and I keep having the misfortune to encounter only the bad-tempered one."

Miles grinned at his own folly, being honest enough to admit he'd had a hand in arousing that bad temper. Glancing out the window, he admired the way the sunlight glinted off Delia's hair, forming an aureole around her face. She looked almost angelic, and Miles felt a twinge of conscience for his ungentlemanly behavior in driving her from her own room the night before. How had she fared? She looked blooming enough from this far away. He wondered if he dared to venture closer.

Stepping toward the door leading to the garden, Miles paused a moment to straighten his cravat and to run his fingers self-consciously over his naked face. Wincing as he touched a deep cut just above his lip, he remembered how painful it had been scraping off his mustache that morning. Damme, he'd all but slit his own nose. But 'twas time the mustache went, he told himself. He'd never liked it, anyway. All the same, he felt peculiarly exposed as he stepped out into the garden.

What was he going to say to her by way of apology for last night? As his eyes fastened themselves on her lovely profile, all he could think of was "If I profane with my unworthiest hand this holy shrine, the gentle sin is this. My lips two blushing pilgrims ready stand to smooth that rough touch with a tender kiss."

Miles promptly banished the thought from his head, an inner wisdom warning him that such an utterance would be a grave tactical error. Although he made no attempt to conceal his presence, Delia appeared too caught up in the boy's words to note his approach.

". . . and then the batsman was bowled out for a duck," the boy said, demonstrating a wild swing that sent him tumbling to the grass. "When the other team saw we had them thirteen for five wickets, why, the match was abandoned at once."

Delia laughed, clapping her hands as the boy bounded to his feet with a grin.

"Good morrow, Cousin."

Delia started at the sound of Miles's voice so near. Refraining from turning immediately, she steeled her features into a haughty, frozen expression. But the effort was all for naught because when she did swivel around, her mouth dropped open in the most foolish manner possible.

The man smiling at her so hopefully was almost a stranger. What had happened to her raffish officer? Miles looked very much the country gentleman, his powerful thighs encased in buckskin breeches, his single-breasted nut-brown frock coat straining across the broad set of his shoulders. And the mustache was gone. Miles, she was forced to admit grudgingly, had possessed a certain attractiveness before, but who would ever have guessed such a devastatingly handsome face had been hidden beneath those black bristles?

She could better remark the shape of his mouth, well formed, generous. Now what would it feel like if he were to . . . Delia moistened her lips, her cheeks flaming scarlet at the direction her thoughts were taking. She became aware that Miles was requesting to be introduced to her gentleman caller.

"Oh," she stammered. "This is Master Thomas Leighton, Miss Rosamund's brother and a very special friend of mine. Thomas, this is my cousin, Colonel Sir Miles Renwick."

Tom shook hands with Miles, staring up at her cousin's towering height. The widening of the boy's eyes showed that he was suitably impressed.

"Any cousin of Miss Renwick's will be numbered amongst my friends, sir." Tom adopted an air of youthful dignity that he destroyed a moment later by blurting out, "Delia is such a first-rate fellow. Don't you think so, sir?"

"Indeed," Miles said. "And she has the advantage of being one of the prettiest fellows I've ever seen."

He smiled, his warm brown eyes assessing her from head to toe. Delia had not thought it possible to blush any deeper but felt herself doing so. Her hands fluttered, trying to hide the green stains on her sprigged muslin, to fluff some order into her disheveled curls. Damn the man! She had meant to give Miles such chilling treatment this morning, he would have thought a blizzard torrid by comparison. Once more the infamous colonel had managed to disconcert all her well-laid plans.

Miles crowded himself beside her on the bench, draping one muscular arm lightly behind her back. "Did I hear somebody mentioning a cricket match?" he asked.

It was all the encouragement Tom needed to launch off into his tale again. While appearing deeply absorbed, Miles casually let his fingertips brush against her shoulder. Delia stiffened. She ought to ask in her most frigid accents if he had passed a comfortable night ensconced in her bed. He certainly looked well rested. But the thought of bed brought to mind Miles's powerful frame veiled only by that indecent nightshirt.

Delia pressed her hand to her cheek. At this rate, her face was never going to cool. Better that she keep silent, try to turn her thoughts elsewhere than to the disturbingly masculine figure at her side.

She averted her head, turning her eyes to the low stone wall that faced the road side of the house. The sound of iron-rimmed wheels and horse's hooves clattering down the road could be heard drawing nearer. Presently, a smart-looking curricle drawn by two flashy-looking bays trundled slowly into sight. Perched in the driver's seat was a slender gentleman garbed in a brown merino coat with at least fifteen capes, a spotted Belcher neckcloth knotted round his throat, and a high-crowned beaver hat perched upon his curling blond locks.

Lord Walsing! Quite forgetting her disheveled appearance, Delia leaped up, calling good morrow, her face dimpling into a dazzling smile. She expected him to acknowledge the greeting and sweep on past. To her intense delight, his lordship pulled back on the reins, drawing the curricle to a halt just outside the garden gate. Moving with what she hoped was a stately grace, she hastened to the gate.

To Miles, it seemed that Delia had sprung up from the bench and raced across the garden as if she were being bitten by gadflies. He had just begun to relax, congratulating himself that things were going rather well. True, Delia had not said much to him yet this morning, but she had not attempted to take his head off either. A frown creased his brow as he studied the man in the curricle. He had no difficulty recognizing the golden-haired Apollo from Delia's sketchbook.

"Who the devil's that?" he growled.

Thomas's reply confirmed Miles's suspicions. "Oh, that's Lord Walsing. New owner of Walsing Manor." The boy's nose crinkled in disgust. "Makes all the girls hereabouts act as if a brick had hit 'em on the head. Even Delia."

Tom took a running leap and began clambering up the mulberry tree. "I'm off," he announced to Miles before disappearing into the branches. "No use staying. You won't get another sensible word out of Delia the rest of the day."

Miles raised his hand in an abstracted gesture of farewell, his eyes returning to Lord Walsing. The colonel considered himself a most congenial man and was surprised to discover that he had taken a pointed dislike to his lordship.

Striding in Delia's direction, he decided it was time to remind her that he was still alive. Miles had thought some decidedly uncomplimentary things about his cousin, but he had never imagined she could act such a fool, gushing and fluttering her eyes like that.

Walsing had not alighted from the curricle, but he was leaning so far out, 'twas a wonder he didn't tumble over the gate onto his perfectly formed nose. Miles noted with great satisfaction that Delia's portrait had been true to life. Walsing's countenance did possess all the passion of a well-fed sheep.

Clearing his throat, he brushed close to Delia's side. She paid him no more heed than if he were a gatepost. Damme, if she simpered like that again, Miles would be sorely tempted to shake her.

"I never thought to find you awake so early, Miss Renwick," Walsing was saying in dulcet tones. "Is it not a fine day? I . . ." He paused, blinking at Miles. "Excuse me, Miss Renwick, but I believe that large fellow there wants something of you. Your gardener, is it?"

Miles stiffened, self-consciously adjusting the military collar of his frock coat that he suddenly felt must be showing its age.

"Heavens, your lordship." Delia giggled. "That is only my cousin, Colonel Sir Miles Renwick, who has come to visit my papa. Colonel Renwick, do permit me to present you to Lord Walsing."

"Oh, pray forgive me, sir." Walsing smirked. "Such a foolish error on my part. What can I say? Miss Renwick's loveliness entirely dazzled my eyes."

211

Delia's blush annoyed Miles as much as Walsing's affected manner of speaking did. How could she become flustered by such a ridiculously fulsome compliment? Reluctantly, Miles took the hand Lord Walsing extended and shook it briefly. He resisted the temptation to wipe his fingers on his handkerchief immediately after. Faugh! In accordance with the latest fashion amongst the dandy set, the man had painted his hands, tingeing the palms with vermilion, whitening the backs with enamel.

"So you are a military man, sir?" Walsing asked in jovial tones.

"No longer," Miles said. "In future, Delia, I should prefer if you dropped the 'colonel' when introducing me."

Delia thrust her pert nose into the air. "Of course. I shall always bear your wishes in mind, Cousin."

" 'Twould be more proper," Lord Walsing said. "If your cousin has indeed retired from the army and is now wishing to be thought a gentleman."

Miles's eyes snapped up to glare at him. Was this man asking to find his perfumed carcass sprawled all over the dust of the road? But Walsing was already falling over himself to apologize.

"Meaning no offense to the military, sir. Fine thing, the army. I was privileged to see ours in action during the last war in America. Such a stirring sight! The cannons blasting, sabers rattling, and all that."

"I am sure all the men who were killed that day died happy knowing your lordship was suitably entertained," Miles ground out. He doubted Walsing had ever come within twenty miles of any actual fighting. In fact, he doubted his lordship ever traveled anywhere he could not take his crimping iron.

It was clear from the way Lord Walsing continued to smile that Miles's sarcasm was lost on him. But Miles heard Delia suck in her breath. She thrust herself in front of him, deliberately treading upon his toes as she fumbled with the latch on the garden gate.

"Enough of all this *military* chatter. Won't you please alight and stop in for some breakfast, Lord Walsing?"

"I regret that I have some business to conduct this morning, but may I call for you later? Should you care to go driving with me?"

"Oh," Delia breathed. "I should love—"

"How unfortunate, sir," Miles interrupted. "My cousin is al-

212

ready engaged to show me the sights of Stratford this afternoon."

Miles had once seen a look like the one Delia shot him—on the face of a French hussar attempting to split his skull open with a saber. Glad that his cousin had no weapon, Miles crossed his arms over his chest, stubbornly holding his ground.

"Alas, fair lady, the loss is mine." Walsing sighed. He leaned back in the curricle, gathering up the reins. "Another time, perhaps. Good day to you, Sir—Sir Martin. I trust you will have a pleasant visit in Stratford." With a tip of his hat, he turned his dreamy, unfocused blue eyes upon the road and gave his horse the office to start.

As the curricle rumbled away at Lord Walsing's customary leisurely pace, Delia whirled upon Miles, her eyes spitting such fury he retreated a step.

She advanced on him, her hands clenched. "You—you unprincipled rogue . . . you villainous liar!"

"I told no lie." Miles retreated another step, keeping a wary eye on those two small fists. "Your father did promise last night you would show me Stratford."

"It needn't have been today," she shrieked.

"Why not? Let me tell you, Cousin, your manners are sadly lacking. Like it or not, I am a guest in your house. You will learn to treat me with courtesy or . . ."

"Or what?" Delia glared, stepping closer until her tiny nose was only inches from the middle of his chest.

Miles tried to maintain a stern front, but she looked so ferociously adorable that the laughter bubbled up inside him. "Or I may have to kiss you again!"

Two spots of color glowed in her cheeks. She shook her fist under his nose. "You—you try that again and I swear you will end up missing some of those wonderfully white teeth." She backed off, trying to recover her lost dignity. "I suppose you are piqued because Lord Walsing mistook you for the gardener and evinced not the slightest desire of furthering your acquaintance."

Miles snorted. "Please spare me! I am already acquainted with enough conceited popinjays without adding another to the list. Now if you will excuse me, fair Cousin, I believe I saw your aunt at the parlor window. I should pay my respects."

He turned on his heel and strode toward the house. At the door, he paused long enough to call back, "We shall set out for the town at one o'clock. Please be prompt. I should not like to have to come looking for you."

Delia drew in her breath with an angry hiss as the door closed behind him. When she thought of how close she had come to riding out with Lord Walsing, parading through town so that all might see her in his company . . . "Damn!" Delia vented her wrath against Miles upon the wooden settle, her slippered foot kicking out with all the force she could muster. A shooting pain traveled up the length of her leg, causing tears to well in her eyes. She hobbled to the bench and sank down, nursing her injured toes.

"Visit Stratford," she mumbled between little moans of pain. Shakespeare and Miles instead of Lord Walsing! "Very well, Cousin," she ground out. "If 'tis sights you want, then sights you shall have until you are as nigh sick of the Bard of Stratford-upon-Avon as I am!"

Miles trudged up High Street alongside Delia, heartily cursing the vanity that had inspired him to cast aside his comfortable army boots in favor of the gleaming new Hessians he had purchased in London. The golden tassels swinging so jauntily from side to side only served to remind him that every step increased the blister on his heel to the size of a half-crown piece.

It was just his luck that this afternoon should prove to be one of the first on which summer would make itself felt. Heat seemed to radiate off the plum-colored brick of the houses, the very pavement of the streets themselves. Closely packed, timber-frame buildings leaned up against each other, appearing as if they, too, were wilting under the sun's merciless glare.

Swiping his handkerchief across his perspiring cheeks, Miles wondered how Delia contrived to look so cool. Attired in a crisp green spencer worn over a rose-checked muslin gown, her face shaded beneath a beehive bonnet of plaited straw, she appeared completely unruffled by the sun beating down on them. But then, of course, she had that blasted parasol. The golden fringes of it slapped him in the eye as she turned to simper at him.

"Don't dawdle, Cousin," she said in honey-sweet accents. "I shall never forgive myself if I permit you to miss anything. There is a great deal left to see."

Miles wanted to assure her that there could not possibly be. She'd already dragged him all over the town hall to admire the portrait of the famous actor David Garrick contemplating the bust of Shakespeare. Then there had been the statue of Will himself. Comfortably shaded in his niche, the Bard could well afford to look down at Miles sweltering on Sheep Street and smirk like that.

After that, they had visited the Birthplace, unfortunately situated right next to the Swan and Maidenhead. Miles had been forced to watch while other men more fortunate than himself slipped into the dark interior for a cold mug of ale. Delia had heartlessly turned him over to the care of Mrs. Hornsby, the garrulous lady who lived at the Birthplace. Miles had thought he'd never escape that woman's clutches. Her artificial flaxen locks had bounced up and down beneath a dirty mobcap as she exhibited all her relics to Miles: the *very* broken matchlock with which Shakespeare had poached deer, the *very* sword the Bard had used to play Hamlet, the *very* lanthorn Friar Lawrence had lighted in the tomb of Romeo and Juliet. Miles left the Birthplace, his coat damp with sweat, his heel a great deal sorer.

He'd experienced a moment of hope when Delia had steered him toward the inn yard of the White Swan. He saw a coachman swilling from a frothy mug, the sight of which made Miles's mouth water. But Delia directed his attention to a bust of Shakespeare mounted in the yard. His tongue feeling as dry as a clump of wool, Miles tried to voice some suitable comment about the dull-eyed stone figure, something fit for the ears of a young lady.

All attempts to suggest refreshment were rebuffed by Cordelia. She seemed to have no more sense of the heat than the marble Shakespeare did. As they charged down Chapel Street, Miles wondered where in the name of God she was taking him now. He only hoped it wasn't to see another bust.

She pulled up short, waving her hand in a cheerful gesture. "Well, here we are."

Miles mopped at his brow, glancing about him. "Delia, this is a nothing but a stone wall."

She directed a glance of lofty scorn at him. "Behind this stone wall, Shakespeare's house once stood."

"Once stood? Once stood! You marched me nearly a quarter mile to stare at the place where a house *once stood*." Miles felt his patience beginning to give. Shifting from foot to foot, he would have given up a year's income to divest himself of those damned boots.

"This was also the sight of the famous mulberry tree," Delia continued, unperturbed. "Of course, it's gone, too." She sighed, looking at the high stone wall with an expression akin to ecstasy. "The most intelligent man to ever live in Stratford-upon-Avon once walked this land."

Miles tugged at his neckcloth. Damn, his shirt points felt as if they were melting. "I did not realize you had such a high opinion of Shakespeare."

"Not Shakespeare! I was speaking of Reverend Francis Gastrell."

"I haven't the slightest notion whom he might be," Miles said testily. He had no desire to know either, but he could see Cordelia was determined to enlighten him.

"Reverend Gastrell bought Shakespeare's home in 1756. Poor man. He had no idea what misery would follow. You see, crowds of Shakespeare fanatics"—she fixed Miles with an accusing stare— "tormented the reverend night and day trying to get into his garden where the mulberry tree grew. The tree was rumored to have been planted by Shakespeare himself. Well, one dark night"—Cordelia paused for dramatic emphasis— "the reverend could bear it no more. He had the tree chopped down.

"When the townspeople found their precious relic gone, they broke all of the poor clergyman's windows. Soon after that, the town council went through their records looking for all manner of property taxes to assess against Mr. Gastrell. But he showed them!"

Delia's face lit up with unholy glee. "He razed Mr. Shakespeare's home to the ground, left not a brick standing."

"What! A perfectly good house? The man should have been locked up and the key conveniently lost," Miles grumbled. He found that by scrunching his toes forward, he could relieve the pressure on his heel.

"Pray, don't be so downcast," Delia cooed. "At least 'twas not the end of the precious mulberry tree, as I shall show you now."

"Delia, I really think I have seen enough."

She scorched him with a withering stare. "First you deprive me of a lovely afternoon that I might have spent in a far more agreeable fashion, and now you have the effrontery to tell me you have seen enough. It passes all bounds. I—"

"Please." Miles raised one weary hand to stem the tide of angry words. "Forget that I spoke. 'Lay on, Macduff, and damn'd be him that first cries, "Hold, enough!" ' "

"So I should think," she said huffily. Shoulders thrust back, parasol gripped in her hands, she started back up the street, reminding Miles most forcibly of a drill sergeant he'd once known.

They backtracked over many streets they'd already crossed, and Miles nearly asked if this tour could not have been conducted with a little more efficiency, but the mulish set of her chin advised him to hold his tongue. They paused outside the bow window of a small shop. A sign creaked on its hinges above the doorway.

" 'Ye Olde Woodcarver's,' " Miles read, frowning.

Delia closed up her parasol with a snap. "You see, Mr. Gastrell sold the mulberry wood to an enterprising woodcarver who made all manner of clever trinkets from it for souvenirs. Of course, these days such trinkets are very rare, but I am well acquainted with the shopkeeper and we may contrive to find you one."

"I don't think . . ." Miles began, attempting to study Delia's expression beneath her demurely lowered lashes. He had a bad feeling about this, the same he'd once had before being thoroughly fleeced by a cardsharp. But Delia was tugging insistently upon his sleeve, and it did look by far cooler inside than out on the street.

The shop bell tinkled as they crossed the threshold. Miles's nostrils were assailed by scents of fresh-cut wood and lemon polish. Gazing about him at articles of furniture in various states of construction, Miles almost failed to note the rosy-cheeked elf of a man who sat behind the counter until he leaped off his stool. Waddling forward, the proprietor wiped his hands on his leather apron, beaming and bowing in Delia's direction.

"Miss Renwick, so pleased to see you again. Your father is wanting another bookcase, perchance?"

"No, Mr. Quincey, though at the rate Papa buys books, I am sure he soon will. Today my cousin, Sir Miles, is your customer."

Miles tried to disclaim, but the elf was already upon him, wringing his hand with delight.

"And how may I serve you, sir? A toothpick case, perhaps? A writing standish? A new snuffbox?"

"No, no, I—" Miles said, but he was cut off by Delia.

"My cousin is looking for a very special remembrance of Stratford, something carved from The Mulberry Tree."

Mr. Quincey spread his hands over his round belly, rocking back on his heels. "The Mulberry Tree? Dear, dear. I don't know, Miss Renwick. Such articles are exceedingly rare."

"Alas, what a disappointment," Miles drawled. Rather than cool, he was finding the shop horrendously stuffy. "Delia, we may as well be on our way."

With a quickness that astonished Miles, Mr. Quincey blocked the door. "But for a cousin of Miss Renwick, I have just the thing."

With lightning speed, the cherubic little man whipped open the door of a cabinet, drawing forth a small wooden casket.

"Oh, how delightful," Delia trilled.

Miles wondered if, in the dim light of the shop, Delia's eyesight was failing her. In his humble opinion, the box clutched between Mr. Quincey's plump fingers was the most hideous creation he had ever seen. Carved across the top were three wonderfully buxom nude women cavorting around a lank-haired man whose brow was crowned with laurel leaves.

"Shakespeare and the Three Graces," Mr. Quincey explained.

Miles refrained from commenting that the Graces looked more like three London doxies. Delia blushed, averting her eyes. But that did not stop her from exclaiming, "Charming, utterly charming. Miles, you must have it."

Mr. Quincey thrust the abomination into Miles's hands. He could feel the dust from the bottom coating his fingers. "How much?" he asked in long-suffering tones.

The price Mr. Quincey modestly named was so outrageous that even Delia gasped. But Miles turned out his pockets, emptying them down to his last shilling without attempting to barter. No amount was too great to buy his freedom from this wooden oven. Eagerly, he accepted Mr. Quincey's offer to deliver the box to Rose Briar Cottage. With luck, the little shopkeeper might forget to do so.

Outside, Miles slicked back the ends of his damp hair, his shoulders slumping in defeat. He no longer manfully attempted to conceal his discomfort but limped along, hoping that Delia was now quite satisfied.

"How fortunate you are, Cousin Miles," she chattered. "A genuine mulberry trinket. Papa will be green with envy. You must be certain to show it to him."

Out of the corner of her eye, she observed the way he hobbled, and compressed her lips. What ploy wouldn't the man think of to gain her sympathy! And even if he had injured his foot, it served him right.

All the same, she drew her face deeper into the shadow of her parasol, the first pangs of guilt besetting her over the affair of the mulberry casket. She wished she hadn't suggested that Miles show the box to Papa. Instead of making Miles appear a perfect fool, it might incense Papa against her for gulling her cousin. And the shocking price Miles had paid, every last penny he had, believing in the genuineness of the piece. Delia had no knowledge of his financial circumstances. What if he truly could not afford to waste his money in such a fashion?

Her fingers played nervously with the parasol handle, fearing that she had carried her vengeance much too far. When they rounded the next corner and Delia saw what shops lay ahead, she emitted a small squeak.

"Ah, no, Cousin. We—we don't want to go down that way. Let us turn back."

She seized Miles by the elbow, but it was too late. He had already seen the sign. Shaking her off, he hopped over to a large shop front. Delia frowned, watching with a sinking heart as he perused the notice in the window.

For Purchase: Many fine articles of furniture and trinkets all carved from the genuine mulberry tree planted by Shakespeare's own hand.

Inside the shop was piled a hodgepodge of mulberry articles: occasional tables, writing desks, tea caddies, toys, caskets . . .

Miles pursed his lips and Delia waited for the explosion. She glanced anxiously at the other pedestrians. Well, he could not murder her on a main street in full view of spectators—or could he? When he turned to face her, she held the parasol between them as if it were a shield.

"I have to thank you, Cousin," he said. "I am now doubly glad you persuaded me to buy that mulberry casket."

"You—you are?" she croaked.

"Indeed." Miles thrust his hands in his pockets, assuming a thoughtful air. "Imagine still producing so many goods sixty years later. That tree had to have been the eighth wonder of the world."

"Miles, I—I am sorry."

He raised one eyebrow. Refusing to listen to her apology, he

219

went on at great length with his speculations about how large the tree must have been, with such absurd descriptions of how many houses were flattened when the tree fell that Delia was reduced to a state of helpless laughter. The more she giggled, the more outrageous the exaggerations Miles spun until they both were leaning against the window of the shop, laughing until their sides ached.

A stout dowager passing by, followed by a skeleton of a man and a brood of children, eyed Delia and Miles with extreme disfavor. "Shocking," she snorted. "Staggering drunk down the center of the street in midafternoon." She turned to glower at the thin man trotting at her heels. "I told you we should not have taken a holiday in Stratford, Arthur. Too many vulgar people by half!"

Still laughing, Miles swept the woman a deep bow, feigning that he was about to fall flat on his face. The outraged dame gathered her gaping children about her like a flock of chickens and hustled off down the street.

"M-Miles, do behave yourself," Delia said, gasping, but she choked so on her laughter that the scolding was all but inaudible. "We—we are attracting . . . no little degree of attention here. 'Tis—'tis time we went to visit the—"

Clutching his side with one hand, he flung up the other in a dramatic gesture. "Hold! Enough!" he cried.

The expression of comic dismay on his face set Delia off again. "Oh, stop it," she begged, wiping her streaming eyes. "I—I shall look a p-perfect fright."

Miles drew in a shuddering breath. "Never. You—you look so . . . enchanting when you . . ." The laughter ended abruptly as Miles's velvet-brown eyes locked with hers. "You have no idea how enchanting . . ." he murmured, his voice dropping to a deep, intimate timbre.

The busy thoroughfare seemed to grow strangely quiet. Her heart skipped a beat. How odd that she should feel her blood race so through her veins. As Miles's dark head bent toward her, he appeared on the brink of forgetting where they were. Equally disconcerting was her own wish that he would. She tipped her face up to meet his, her lips quivering with anticipation.

A cart clattered past on the cobblestones, the drayman handling the team shouting out a crude remark. The moment was shattered. Miles abruptly straightened.

As if giving himself a shake, he flexed his shoulders and

then spoke, striving to resume the lighter tone of moments before. "Cousin, I am all eagerness for the next Shakespearen delight you have in store for me, but I beg a brief respite. 'The quality of mercy is not strain'd, It droppeth—' "

"If you will spare me the quote, I shall willingly accede to your wishes." Delia retied the ribbon on her bonnet, which had worked itself loose, allowing herself time to recover from her earlier confusion. It was difficult when her pulses still fluttered so. Biting her lip, she said, "I was about to suggest that you might like to rest your feet for a bit. We could go sit on the riverbank and watch the barges."

"What clever notions you do get in that charmingly beautiful head of yours, Cousin. By all means, let us do so."

She stepped forward, preparing to lead the way, but Miles gently restrained her. He linked his arm through hers, guiding her gloved fingers until they rested against his sleeve. His warm, strong hand covered hers until she relaxed, accepting the arrangement. They covered the distance to the riverbank in silence, Delia suddenly feeling quite shy and tongue-tied.

Despite her protests, Miles insisted on divesting himself of his frock coat, spreading the silk-lined garment out for her to sit on. Then he settled beside her, leaning back on his elbow, stretching out his long legs with a heartfelt sigh.

For the first time, Delia realized what a lovely afternoon it was. Lazy wisps of white clouds drifted across an azure sky, casting shadows upon the neat, red-shingled roofs of the cottages nestled by the riverside. Sunlight sparkled in the green depths of the Avon while sails billowed on barges bearing their corn-laden decks upriver to Shropshire. On the opposite bank, sheltered amidst the rustling branches of ancient elms, stood Holy Trinity Church, its gleaming spire straining toward the heavens.

Yet Delia's gaze kept wandering from the bucolic panorama before her to the silent man at her side. Most gentlemen of her acquaintance would have been yawning with boredom over such a way of passing the time. But Miles seemed to possess such a keen enjoyment of simply being alive. His dark eyes were half-hooded beneath langorous eyelids, a soft smile half-tipping his lips as he regarded her through thick black lashes.

She could feel the pink stealing into her cheeks and searched desperately for a topic of conversation, lest Miles manage to disconcert her again.

"Papa informs me you were acclaimed quite the hero after

Waterloo. Is that where you sustained that wound across your chest? I—I mean . . ." She faltered when Miles grinned. Bad enough to have seen the man half-naked without admitting she had taken a good long look. She thrust her chin forward in defiance. "I could scarcely help noticing the scar last night."

"Oh, no, of course, you could not. I am only flattered that my person was of enough interest to you that—"

"Are you going to tell me about your wound or not?" she snapped, her cheeks flaming.

Miles shrugged. "There is nothing very clever about being cut by another fellow's saber. In fact, it is an incredibly stupid thing to do."

"A saber?" Delia whispered. "Dear heavens, you might have been killed."

But Miles tossed off another jest, refusing to discuss the matter further. What a puzzling man he was, Delia thought. From the moment when she had first seen the colonel, he appeared the perfect image of a bluff soldier, likely inclined to boast of his exploits like most of the other young officers she knew. But Miles showed little desire to reminisce about his wartime experiences.

"I'm sure you must have been quite brave," she prodded. "If you can make such jests about nearly being cut in two."

Miles laughed softly. "Brave! I was quaking in my boots before the battle even began." He plucked a blade of grass to run it abstractedly between his fingers. "I kept thinking that I might never come back, never see my home again. I knew so many others, men that I had trained myself, good friends that never . . ."

His voice trailed off as he sat up, resting his hands upon his knees. His eyes were softened with an expression of wistfulness, melancholy, as he studied the bright blue sky, the sparkling river. How shallow Lord Walsing's descriptions of the glory of battle seemed now. Delia suppressed a strong urge to caress the hair back from Miles's brow, sorry that she had stirred such unhappy memories. He spoke low, as if more to himself. "Imagine never to see England again. 'This other Eden, demi-paradise . . . This blessed plot, this—' "

He broke off with a sheepish grin, seeming to recollect himself. "Sorry, coz. I do tend to get a little swept away."

"I shall contrive to forgive you this once." She smiled gently.

"Normally, I do not bore young ladies by reciting poetry.

'Tis Shakespeare's spirit. I veritably believe his inspiration lingers on here in Stratford."

Delia's nose crinkled with distaste. "Haunts it, you mean!"

"Tell me, Delia, why do you hate him so much?"

"Who?"

"You know full well whom. Shakespeare. You bristle like a kitten with its fur rubbed the wrong way every time you so much as hear the name."

She poked the tip of her parasol into the ground, dislodging clumps of brown earth, before replying. "I have good cause. Those plays monopolize all of my father's time so that—well, he no longer cares what becomes of me." She felt her eyes water and ducked her head.

Miles placed his fingers under her chin, forcing her to look up. "That simply isn't so," he said softly. "Your father has your interests more to heart than you could possibly imagine."

Delia swallowed, easing Miles's hand away from her face. But she made no objection when his large fingers closed around her own, cradling them against the warmth of his palm. "I'm afraid your judgment is faulty in this matter, Cousin. Shakespeare is my father's entire life." She gave a nervous laugh. "Even if it weren't for that, I find the poet's work greatly overrated. Such tedious, dull stuff. 'Tis all I can do to stay awake when Papa reads to me."

"Ah, but surely when you attend a performance—"

"I have never been to a performance of Shakespeare."

"What! Never?"

"No, Papa says that stage performances of Shakespeare are an abomination. The theater profanes the purity of his work."

Miles suppressed a smile. "Well, I have seen some productions that justify your father's complaint. But with all due respect to Cousin Walter, Shakespeare was not meant to be read. The words, the poetry cry out to be acted upon the stage. If you ever had a chance to experience the passion, the grandeur, the wit, the—the . . . Please. Allow me to take you to the theater some evening. Come, Delia, say that you will."

"Well, I—I . . ." Her gaze flitted from her own hand enfolded in Miles's grasp to the firm curve of his coaxing lips, the dark eyes that sparkled with such earnest enthusiasm. The excitement in his voice found an answering chord within her own heart. She bit back an impulse to tell him he might take her anywhere he liked.

What on earth was happening to her? Within the space of

two days, Miles had confused her thoroughly. Considering his nefarious behavior in dumping her in the stream and appropriating her bed, she was supposed to be avenging herself. She should be vexed, missing Lord Walsing, not sitting here on the riverbank, blushing like a schoolroom miss and clasping Miles by the hand. In another minute, the persuasive rogue would even have her convinced that she liked Shakespeare.

Snatching her hand away, Delia staggered to her feet. "I—I shall consider your invitation to the theater, Colonel Renwick," she said primly. "But I much fear Papa would not approve. The hour grows late. We really should be going if we wish to see the church."

Miles emitted a gusty sigh, but he stood, brushing off his trouser legs and retrieving his jacket. This time, when they set off, Delia rigidly avoided his taking her arm. The close proximity of Miles was by far too unnerving. She wished to conclude the tour and escape his company as soon as possible. She needed time alone to compose herself, to sort out her tangled emotions about this exasperating cousin of hers.

She avoided so much as glancing in his direction until they were in the light, airy interior of Holy Trinity Church. Guiding him toward the chancel, she pointed out the plain stone slab set behind the railing and stepped back to give Miles the chance to regard Shakespeare's tomb in worshipful silence. But he scarcely glanced at the gravesite. His gaze traveled to the arched recess above. Two fat cherubs were poised over a statue of Shakespeare, who was depicted as a puffy-faced burgher with half-moon eyebrows and a nose far too small for his broad, coarse face.

Delia suppressed a smile when she heard Miles groan, "Not another bust!"

"This one is my favorite," she said. "Exactly what I think Shakespeare must have—" She broke off at the sound of footsteps clattering behind them in the nave of the church. A stentorian female voice echoed off the rafters.

"Yes, Vicar, if you incorporate my suggestions for the adornment of the tomb, I will send you the flowers from my own hothouse. And if you follow my other advice, you will find your sermons improved immensely."

Delia turned in time to see the harried vicar nod, his reply inaudible. But whatever he said, his companion—an extremely tall woman with silver-gray locks, straight, square shoulders, and a large, sloping bosom—appeared satisfied, her severe features relaxing into a condescending smile.

"By God," Miles whispered in Delia's ear. "What a commanding female. I wonder if she ever posed for a figurehead on the prow of a ship."

Delia scowled at him. "Do hush. That is Lady Herkingstone, a very important woman in this district. She is Lord Walsing's aunt and quite dominates our local society."

"I would imagine she dominates anything she can lay her hands upon, including her poor husband."

"The lady is a widow."

"Thank you for the warning. I shall be sure to stay clear of her."

"Very prudent," Delia said. "For of a certainty, Lady Herkingstone would wish to marry you, with all your devastating charm . . ."

"I know, I know." Miles threw up a deprecating hand. "I try to control it, but the ladies will—"

An unwilling giggle erupted from Delia. She gave Miles a sharp nudge with her parasol. "Will you finish admiring your precious Shakespeare's tomb so we can go home?"

"I finished admiring it two seconds after our arrival. When you have seen one poet's tomb, you have—" But whatever words of wisdom Miles was about to impart on the subject of memorials were lost to Delia. Her attention was claimed by the imperiously beckoning finger of Lady Herkingstone.

She winced. "Her ladyship wishes to speak to me. I hope to heaven she did not overhear any of your remarks. You wait here."

To Delia's considerable relief, Miles meekly obeyed. She would have had no objections to presenting her cousin, but who knew what outrageous comment he might deliver next? And Lady Herkingstone was far too formidable a dame to risk offending her.

As Delia scurried forward to make her curtsy, her ladyship condescended enough to offer a regal nod.

"Miss Renwick," she pronounced in her customary clipped tones. "Such a fortuitous circumstance encountering you here. It spares me the trouble of writing you a note."

Delia's eyes widened. "I am honored that your ladyship should even think of such a thing. If I had known you wished some speech with me, I should have walked over at once."

"I was already occupied with the vicar . . ." Lady Herkingstone glanced around, but upon Delia's approach the vicar had escaped. "No matter," she continued. "That does not really concern you. I need your help with a far different matter."

"M-my help? I cannot imagine what I could possibly . . ."

Her ladyship fixed Delia with a sapient eye. "If you cease interrupting, I shall explain."

"I—yes, your ladyship, I am sorry."

"As you well know, I am considered in these parts the ultimate authority on Shakespeare."

This was surprising news to Delia, but she politely murmured assent.

"As such, I feel it my civic, nay, my cultural duty to play a large part in organizing some genteel celebrations in honor of Shakespeare's death."

"I had thought the town corporation was planning the bicentenary festivities."

Lady Herkingstone looked down the considerable length of her nose at Delia. "I said genteel celebrations, Miss Renwick. Not a display of fireworks for the vulgar herd."

"Oh, of course," Delia said. "I am sure anything your ladyship turned your hand to—"

"Then I may count on your support." It was not a question, and any attempts on Delia's part to answer were firmly dismissed.

"Good, I shall do you the honor of coming to tea very soon. All details can be settled then." With a nod of dismissal that informed Delia the audience was at an end, Lady Herkingstone turned and swept majestically out of the church. Delia was left in midcurtsy, feeling stunned. She had the strong notion that she had just pledged her help to something, but she had not the least notion what it was.

Footsteps sounded behind her. Miles's hand gripped her by the elbow, steadying her as she rose out of the curtsy. "Well, shall we be going, Cousin? 'Tis almost time for tea and I am famished." An expression of annoyance crossed his features as he added, "Though I expect all that toadeating may have dulled your appetite somewhat."

Delia jerked her elbow away. "I explained to you how important Lady Herkingstone is."

"Ah, yes, the pillar of Stratford society. She certainly makes an excellent one."

"I think it is excessively rude of you to make such remarks

about a woman you do not even know. Her ladyship is a most amiable, gracious . . ."

Delia hesitated when Miles placed his hands on his hips, his mouth quirked in disbelief. "In any case, it matters not a jot what you think," she said. "My father does not make the least effort to ingratiate himself in this community. It is entirely left to me to do so."

"That's right." Miles sneered. "You do have your future to think of. I suppose it would scarcely matter if her ladyship were a gorgon with two heads. She is the aunt of the yellow-haired fop you are so enamored of and thus you will bend over double being charming to her."

"I hardly see that this is any of your concern, *Cousin*," Delia grated. She stalked out of the church, her face burning with anger. What had come over Miles? Why should he have a fit of pique simply because she had been civil to Lady Herkingstone? Well, mayhap, she had been a trifle more than civil, even a trifle unctuous, but—but Miles refused to understand. With Papa living the life of a recluse and no mama to present her, Delia was obliged to promote her own interests, no matter how distasteful the task. It was only natural she should wish to take her place in society and make a good match, which was her only hope of ever escaping Papa's obsession with Shakespeare.

As she stormed through the churchyard, Delia heard Miles calling for her to wait, but she only increased her pace until she was brought up short by yet more evidence of her father's neglect.

The grave marker was partially obscured with weeds. With a small cry of indignation, Delia bounded over several other memorial stones, then dropped to her knees by the solitary gravesite. Her eyes stinging with tears, she began uprooting the weeds herself. It was bad enough that Amaryllis had been buried in this obscure corner of the churchyard, her grave marked by a pitifully small stone bearing only her name and her birth and death dates. But for it to be treated with no more respect than if she had been a pauper or some sort of felon was more than Delia could bear.

A crunch of pebbles beneath booted feet alerted Delia to Miles's presence. He squatted down, his previous annoyance dissolving into an expression of concern. Gently, he touched her shoulder. "Delia?"

She turned around, shoving a fistful of weeds into his startled face. "Just look at this. My stepmother's grave nigh overrun. But another proof that all my father thinks of is his accursed Shakespeare."

"Surely you cannot blame your father for this. 'Tis the sexton's duty to make certain the churchyard is properly kept."

"But the fact that he would dare to neglect my stepmama's grave is a reflection of my father's attitude of indifference."

" 'Tis a miracle they even permitted her burial in the churchyard," Miles muttered.

"What?" Delia leaped to her feet, unsure whether she had heard him correctly.

"Nothing." Miles sighed, rising to stand beside her. "Delia, there is so much that you do not know. . . ."

"I know my father killed Amaryllis with his neglect. 'Tis no wonder he scorns her memory as well."

Miles gripped her by the shoulders, his fingers tightening until she winced. "Now you listen to me, Cordelia Renwick. Your father is a fine man. He has ever been my friend, and if any man criticized him as you have just done, I would thrash him senseless." He relaxed his grasp as if suddenly becoming aware that he was hurting her.

"I make allowances for you because you were far too young to understand the situation between Amaryllis and your father."

Delia twisted violently until she broke free from him. "And, pray, how do you come to be such an authority? You, a virtual stranger to our family?"

Miles compressed his lips into a grim line. "I was not always so. I visited Renwick Manor upon many occasions although I daresay you never noticed me. Your stepmama had too many other gentlemen dangling about."

Delia let out an outraged gasp. Exactly what was Miles trying to imply?

"I spent most of my time with Cousin Walter, who was very kind to a young man who had recently lost his own father and had no notion of what he wanted to do with his life. But your stepmother . . . I never knew anyone more vain, selfish, emptyheaded—"

"Oh, be quiet!" Delia's fingers curled with the longing to rake her nails across Miles's hateful, lying face. Tears of rage flowed freely down her face. "You ignorant, boorish ruffian. How could you ever appreciate a lady like Amaryllis? I suppose simply because she did not know Shakespeare—"

"She knew nothing except how to waste—" Miles broke off,

228

running his hand distractedly through his hair. He gave her a look composed of regret and exasperation. "Don't cry, Delia. I am sorry. If your father does not choose to tell you, then it is not my place to say anything."

"No, it isn't." She sniffed. "I wish you knew where your place was and—and that you would go back there and leave me alone."

"I regret to disoblige you, madam," he said stiffly. "But I came to Stratford at your father's invitation, not yours. I am quite comfortable at Rose Briar Cottage and intend to remain as long as it suits me."

Delia's eyes blazed with angry tears. "Quite comfortable! Are you indeed, *Cousin*? We shall see how long you continue to remain so!" With this parting threat, she whirled in a rustle of skirts and stomped out of the churchyard.

Chapter 5

Assembled within the bandbox was the finest collection of crickets, caterpillars, beetles, and sundry other multilegged crawling creatures that the garden at Rose Briar could afford. It had taken Delia, with the enthusiastic assistance of Tom Leighton, the better part of an hour to gather the insect menagerie.

Clutching the bandbox in her hand, she tiptoed through the upper hall. Not a sign of Bessy or Aunt Violet. Most important of all, Delia could hear Miles's laughter rumbling from Papa's study. Trading witty quotes, no doubt. She felt a stab of betrayal when she recalled what Miles had let slip in the churchyard. He said he had come to Stratford at Papa's invitation. Papa, who had pretended that it had been Miles's own decision!

Papa had never had any intention of taking her to Brighton this summer. He had plotted all along to foist this beastly cousin upon her. Her lip quivering with hurt indignation, Delia stole another glance around before slipping inside her bedchamber.

The invasion of Miles Renwick was never more evident than within her own room. His shaving gear deposited amongst the perfume bottles on *her* dressing table, his jacket slung across *her* chair, and his boots deposited by *her* bedside were all disturbing reminders of his presence in the house. These encroachments plus recollection of all the cruel things he had said about Amaryllis saved Delia from having any regrets over what she was about to do. Insolent man! He knew nothing about her dear stepmama. Nothing at all.

She stepped to the bed and drew back the counterpane, feeling indebted to Tom for this scheme. He had described with great relish how he and his friends at school had rid themselves of a stuffy classmate, an odious tale-bearer. Hiding snakes in the boy's bed and clothes had driven the cowardly youth to write home to his mama, begging to be taken away from the nasty place.

While Delia could not tolerate the notion of snakes roaming abroad through her room, she could well stomach a few insects for the sake of sending Miles packing. Carefully, she began secreting the wriggling creatures amongst the sheets, beneath the pillow. She did not wish for Miles to detect his bedfellows until he was snugly tucked beneath the covers. Delia suppressed a chuckle of anticipation. The crickets were a particularly nice touch. Even if they did not make themselves felt, they were certain to make themselves heard.

Her task complete, she smoothed back the counterpane, fairly hugging herself with satisfaction. Now she would see how much comfort Miles found at Rose Briar Cottage. Even someone as thick-skinned as her cousin would have to regard this as a strong hint that his presence was most unwelcome. Besides, it would pay him back for the wretched nights she was forced to spend in Amaryllis's bedchamber. She would be glad to see the last of Miles. What an annoying trick he had played upon her, charming her into believing she actually liked him. Seated on the riverbank, she had been conscious of a most dangerous tug of attraction. How fortunate that the quarrel at the church had restored her to her senses. She heartily pitied the foolish woman who ever fancied herself in love with him.

Opening the wardrobe to whisk the bandbox out of sight, Delia's gaze fell upon the lilac-pink gown. She could not resist taking it out to admire the gossamer folds just one more time. To think that in less than a fortnight she would be waltzing at the ball in Walsing Manor. With this lovely gown, she might manage to turn a few heads. Holding the shimmering length against herself, she imagined Lord Walsing overcome with admiration. Quite forgetting all notions of propriety, he would lead her out to dance for the third time, setting the room ahum with speculation as to when their betrothal would be announced. Lord Walsing . . . such a gentleman. What a remarkable husband he would make.

Delia closed her eyes, sinking into a deep curtsy and then executing a few quick steps. But it proved truly frustrating. She had difficulty keeping Lord Walsing's golden, blue-eyed image fixed in her mind. His features kept blurring into crisp ebony locks, roguish brown eyes.

Caught up in her daydream, Delia did not hear the click of the door as it opened. Miles paused on the threshold, a smile curving his lips at the way her glossy curls bobbed up and down, the dreamy expression crossing her delicate features, her thoroughly feminine delight in the rustling silk. He wondered what partner danced across her imagination. Of a certainty, he thought ruefully, it was not himself. How could he have behaved so boorishly? 'Twas painful to hear one's idols criticized. Even if Delia's youthful adoration of her stepmother was greatly misplaced, Miles had had no right to disillusion her.

When Delia's cavortings brought her close to where he stood, Miles could not resist the temptation. He linked his arm around her trim waist, falling into step.

Her eyes immediately flew open. With a startled gasp, she stumbled back, clutching the dress in front of her as if he had caught her in her chemise. Color flooded into her cheeks.

"Upon my word, you might have made your presence known, Colonel Renwick. This is most—most improper."

"I did not realize you were in here. I have left the door open."

She glared. "You were supposed to be belowstairs. I only took a moment to recover a few things from *my* room."

Replacing the gown with great care into the wardrobe, Delia prepared to sweep past Miles, mustering all the hauteur of which she was capable into her short frame.

But Miles caught her by the arm, gently detaining her. "Delia. Cousin, must we be forever quarreling? I want to tell you how sorry I am for the things I said in the churchyard. I have no wish to distress you, ever. Will you not forgive me?"

" 'Tis of no consequence. Pray, do not give it another thought. I assure you I will not."

She tried to slip past him again, but Miles persisted. "Then there is the matter of your room. I did not understand about the other bedchamber having belonged to Amaryllis. Your aunt told me. I only wish you had explained. I would not have teased you by forcing you into a room that must hold unhappy associations for you. Starting tonight, I will sleep there."

"Oh, no!" Delia cried out. To Miles's astonishment, she turned quite pale. "I—I mean, I am quite satisfied with things as they are. Must you be forever disrupting my—our household arrangements?"

"I only thought to please you, Cousin."

"I am quite pleased with my present situation, thank you. Now if you will excuse me, I must dress for dinner."

She looked quite flustered as she shoved him aside to quit the chamber. Miles reluctantly stepped back, his shoulders sagging in defeat. Never had he met any female so—so prickly as Delia. One never knew what was going to set her off. He made a last attempt to restore himself to her good graces.

"Will you not wear that dress you held a moment ago? You would look enchanting—"

"That dress is for Lord Walsing," she snapped.

That fop again! Did she never think of anyone else? Miles felt himself flushing with annoyance. "I am sure he will look quite charming in it. Exactly the sort of apparel to best suit his manly figure."

"I meant the dress was for the ball at—Oh!" She clenched her fists. "You know full well what I meant."

She stomped down the hall to Amaryllis's bedchamber. The sound of her door slamming was echoed loudly by the bang Miles made slamming his own.

Midnight was a perfectly dreadful hour to have regrets over something it was too late to change. As the hall clock chimed twelve, Delia tossed on her makeshift bed, listening to the rain drumming against the leaded windowpanes. She was beset by a fear that she had behaved with incredible childishness. What on earth had possessed her to hide all those insects in Miles's bed? A brilliant suggestion from Tom Leighton, but Tom was all of ten years old. True, Miles had greatly vexed her, but she should have found some more dignified way of retaliating. What if he were to make her infantile behavior public knowledge? She would die of shame if Lord Walsing ever heard of it. Indeed, she did not know how she was going to face her own family in the morning, especially Miles. Curse the man! He had a positive talent for bringing out the worst in her.

Such thoughts as these kept Amaryllis's ghost at bay but were not much more conducive to sleep. For the second morning in a row, Delia dragged herself down to the breakfast table, wondering how she would stay awake long enough to drink her chocolate. The task was made easier by the presence of her father and aunt. As usual, Papa was absorbed in his folio, but Aunt Violet kept up a constant stream of chatter, most of which Delia found very disconcerting.

"How strange that Cousin Miles has not come down yet," Aunt Violet said. "He is such an early riser."

"M-more tea, Aunt?" Delia asked.

"No, my dear. You've already offered it to me three times. I suppose Miles must be finding a real bed such a comfort after those hard army cots. Delia, take care. You are spilling chocolate all over the tablecloth."

Delia sponged up the mess with her napkin, her eyes straying nervously to the place set across from her. Miles's empty chair glared at her with silent reproach. She wondered if he would be angry. She had seen Miles look mildly vexed but never truly angry. He was such a large man. If he decided to fling her over his knee and administer a few sound swats, she feared neither her aunt nor Papa would lift one finger to stop him.

"You seem uncommonly fidgety this morning, child," Aunt Violet said. "Are you feeling quite the thing?"

"I? Nonsense, Aunt. I am fine." Delia caught herself shaking a large quantity of salt upon her toast and set the silver shaker down with a sharp rap.

"Oho. We know what is amiss with you, don't we, Walter?" Her aunt chuckled.

"You do?" Delia gasped. How could Aunt Violet and Papa possibly know? Had one of the servants seen her filling the bandbox?

"Yes, I daresay it has something to do with the presence of a very handsome young man in this house." Aunt Violet sipped her tea, looking infuriatingly smug. "You have been most reticent about what took place on your outing with Miles yesterday."

"I told you, Auntie. Only the customary boring tour of Stratford." Delia hoped Aunt Violet was not going to begin to quiz her about that again. She was spared any further questions by the event she most dreaded, the entrance of Miles himself. Delia stole one look, saw the dark rings under his eyes, and quickly averted her gaze to her plate. She gripped her hands in her lap, steeling herself for the furious accusations.

"Good morning, Cousin Walter," he said in hearty accents. "Cousin Violet. You look ravishing as always. Quite take my breath away."

Aunt Violet tittered. "Flattering young rogue!"

"And Cousin Delia." As Miles paused, Delia tensed, waiting for the blow to fall. "Ah, but what words has a mere mortal

234

suitable to describe you? I defy even the genius of Shakespeare to paint an accurate portrait."

As he strode over to help himself from the sideboard, Delia's clenched hands went limp as though she had received a stunning buffet about the head. Miles settled himself opposite her, tucking into a well-laden plate.

"Did you sleep well last night, Miles?" Papa asked.

"Like a rock," came the cheerful reply.

Delia dared to look up at last. Miles smiled sweetly at her across the table. Why, what a dreadful liar the man was. She could see the lines deepened around his eyes, which were positively bloodshot from lack of sleep. So he meant to torment her by pretending nothing had happened. All her earlier misgivings and regrets fled as she watched Miles complacently chewing his beefsteak. Her own breakfast was quite cold because her trepidation had left her incapable of tasting a bite. Plague take him! She wished now that she had not been so squeamish about using snakes.

Nothing seemed capable of disturbing her cousin's infuriating equanimity until Elise entered bearing a note that had been delivered for Delia. She ripped it open, scarcely noting the heavy red seal. It was from Lord Walsing, but the pleasure she normally would have felt was quite dissipated by her growing anger at Miles. She had gone to considerable trouble to enrage the man, then worried half the night that she had done so. How dare he sit there buttering a muffin, looking so unruffled!

"Who is it from, dear?" Aunt Violet called.

"Oh, 'tis nothing. Only a special reminder from Lord Walsing not to forget the ball at his manor on any account."

Miles's brows snapped together. Now he was looking out of sorts, much more like a man who had passed a thoroughly wretched night.

"Dear me." He sneered. "You mean the fellow actually knows how to write?"

"Having heard you were staying with us," Delia said, "he has very civilly included you in the invitation—that is, if you will still be in Stratford at the time."

"Rest assured, Cousin. I would not dream of parting with your enchanting company so soon."

Their eyes locked across the table like two duelists gauging each other before crossing foils. Papa surfaced from his folio, beaming from Miles to Delia.

"Well, well, and how are things getting on? Miles, I am sure you will enjoy it when Delia takes you to visit Stratford."

"We did that yesterday, Papa," Delia said.

"What? Oh, so you did. How did you enjoy the outing?"

"Extremely interesting," Miles grated.

"Vastly diverting," Delia snapped.

Papa studied them both for a moment before plunging back into his book. "Ah, well, 'The course of true love never did run smooth.' "

Delia rolled her eyes. Papa's quotes were becoming more disjointed, more irrelevant every day. Aunt Violet's behavior was nigh as bad, the way she simpered so dotingly over Miles.

"I am glad Delia is making your stay with us so pleasant," she gushed.

"Indeed." Miles regarded Delia with a strange glint in his eye, his teeth baring in a feral grin. "I only hope I will be able to return the favor one day."

Delia choked on a large bite of salted toast. She hailed with relief Bessy's announcement that Miss Rosamund had come to call. Muttering her excuses, she escaped from the dining parlor, fretting over Mile's last remark. She had a disquieting premonition that her cousin was not going to overlook his insect-ridden bed as she had first believed. No, the villain was only biding his time.

Bursting into the parlor, she looked forward to pouring out her apprehensions into Rosamund's sympathetic ears. But one look at Miss Leighton was enough to assure Delia that her friend was beset by troubles of her own. Rosamund paced before the fireplace, her despondent gaze resting from time to time on a large parcel deposited upon the settee. It was obvious from her reddened eyes that she had recently indulged in a bout of weeping.

When Delia entered, Rosamund halted, offering her a wavering smile. "Delia, I trust you will forgive me for disturbing you at such an early hour. I badly need your help and could not wait a moment more."

Delia's own problems were swept aside by concern for her friend. Taking Rosamund by the hand, she persuaded her to sit down by the parcel. "My dear Roz, you know you may call upon me at any time. Whatever is amiss?"

Rosamund swallowed, then affected a tiny shrug. "No great matter. 'Tis only that my dress for the ball has come back from the seamstress. You—you have such a sense of fashion. I should like to hear your opinion of it."

With trembling fingers, Rosamund tugged at the strings, unwrapped the gown, and shook it out for Delia's inspection. She stared at the low-waisted dress of apple-green silk adorned with balloon sleeves, purple bows, and layers of furbelows.

" 'Tis hideous!" she blurted out, then flushed, trying to cover her tactlessness. "I mean—I am sure . . ."

"No, Delia. Do not retract your first honest reaction. I quite agree with you. Now tell me what may be done to improve it."

The suggestion of stuffing it into the fire popped into Delia's head, but this time she managed to refrain from being quite so blunt. "Well, mayhap Miss Tandy could . . ." Delia sighed, shaking her head. "Good Lord, I simply cannot believe Miss Tandy would even make such a thing."

"She didn't." Rosamund's dusky curls drooped as she began gathering up the misshapen length of silk. "Mama engaged Mrs. Robbins. She—she is not quite so expensive as Miss Tandy."

Delia bit down on her thumbnail in vexation. Mrs. Leighton's lack of taste was only equaled by her parsimony. "I am sorry, Roz. You'd best order a new gown at once. There is still time before the ball."

"I am afraid I cannot do that," she said in a small voice. "You see, with the bills for Tom's school and Mama's new carriage, 'twas already shockingly extravagant of me to even have this gown."

"But, Rosamund, you cannot seriously mean to wear that! I—I mean, not that it would be so terrible, but—but . . ."

Rosamund gave a shaky laugh. "But I will look a dreadful quiz."

"No, never! Not someone as beautiful as you. You know I have always been quite envious of your lovely dark hair, such—such remarkable green eyes . . ."

"You are too kind, Delia." To Delia's distress, the tears began to flow quite freely down Rosamund's pale cheeks. She groped for her handkerchief to offer her friend, feeling quite at a loss. Rosamund was so serious-minded. She had always worn the dreadful clothes her mama selected for her without complaining. It was most unlike her to become agitated over something as frivolous as a ball gown. Sensing there was more behind her unhappiness, Delia shoved the ugly dress to the floor and seated herself beside Rosamund to coax the truth from her.

After much prodding, Rosamund admitted, "Ordinarily, I would not mind about the gown, but I learned yesterday that Captain Devon will return on the evening of the ball. 'Twill be the first time Michael—I mean, Captain Devon—has seen me in over a year."

She sniffed, blowing her nose into the handkerchief. "Despite Colonel Renwick's kind assurances, I worry that perhaps Captain Devon's interest is not quite so fixed as—as your cousin supposes."

"Oh, Rosamund, you dear goose." Delia gave her friend a quick hug. As if Rosamund needed an elegant gown to attract the admiration of Captain Devon or any other man. But she would never convince her modest friend that her beauty could shine through the dreariest rags.

If only she had the resources to lend Rosamund enough money for a new gown. Or even . . . The thought popped unbidden into Delia's head. She felt the color drain from her cheeks.

Oh, no, I couldn't, she thought. But Rosamund's unhappy features swam before her eyes. Rosamund, her dearest friend, the one who had commiserated when Delia's face had shown a dreadful tendency to throw out spots, saved her from having to stand up with the squire's clumsy son by dancing with him herself. Rosamund, who had comforted her when Amaryllis died . . .

Delia emitted a deep sigh. "Wait here, please," she said briskly. She raced out of the room, returning a few moments later with the lilac-pink gown clutched in her hands. Never had the rustle of the silk sounded so beguiling, the material felt so soft in her hands.

"Here," she said, resolutely thrusting the garment into Rosamund's hands.

"Delia, what—what . . ."

Delia fixed what she hoped was a bright smile upon her lips. "The most absurd coincidence. I am thoroughly disgusted with my new gown as well. 'Twould look dreadful on me, but perhaps you might find it tolerable."

"Delia, you are mad. 'Tis lovely." Rosamund reverently spread the gown over the back of the settee. " 'Twould look charming on you, I am sure."

"Nay, I abhor lilac-pink, and that sheer overdress! So . . ."

Delia averted her gaze from the enticing, shimmering fabric. "So frilly. I cannot abide it. You must take it away and prevent Papa from discovering I made such a costly error."

Rosamund continued to demur, but after much argument Delia managed to convince her. Her own pangs of regret were suppressed when she noted with pleasure that the sparkle had returned to Rosamund's eyes.

"How shall I ever thank you, Delia?" she asked, giving her a hug as they prepared to part at the garden gate. "When you have found your particular gentleman, I hope that I can do something to help you."

"Pooh! You are such a romantic. I will never reduce myself to such a nervous state over any man."

Rosamund only laughed and bent forward to plant a kiss on Delia's cheek. Delia watched her friend wander, dreamy-eyed, down the lane and clucked her tongue. Rosamund had once been such a sensible young woman. To think of her being ready to throw her cap over the windmill merely for a young officer when there was someone like Lord Walsing available.

Lord Walsing: a man of position, breeding, perfect, handsome features ... It was much more practical to wed such a man who would be charming, attentive, instead of forever teasing, tormenting her with Shakespearean quotes like—like her odious cousin. Of course, with the loss of the ball dress, it would be exceedingly difficult to dazzle his lordship. But at least Miles would never have the pleasure of seeing her wear the gown he had so admired, either. Her grim satisfaction at this thought was reflected in a deep, melancholy sigh.

Mistrusting what her roguish cousin might plot by way of revenge, Delia spent the rest of the morning in Amaryllis's bedchamber, guarding the place where she slept. Her couch was uncomfortable enough without finding it infested with crawling things. She caught only a glimpse of Miles when she forced open one of the mullioned windows to allow some air into the stuffy chamber. She breathed in the aroma of freshly baked pastry emanating from the kitchen directly below. Her cousin was inspecting the vegetable garden while calling out some teasing remark to Cook. Whatever the plump woman replied, Miles threw back his head, the quiet morning filling with his rich baritone laughter. Delia's lips tilted in a smile of involuntary response. At that moment, Miles chanced to look up. He leaped over the rows of carrots, then dropped dramatically to one knee.

" 'What light through yonder window breaks? It is the east, and Juliet is—' "

Delia quickly ducked back from the window. She could hear Miles roaring with laughter as she stalked away from the casement. His attempt to aggravate her had met with wonderful success. Still, the sound of Miles's laughter was so—so infectious. Like smallpox, she told herself, determined not to be charmed.

Flouncing over to Amaryllis's French gilt writing desk, Delia set herself to the task of answering letters. She had already made a point of informing her family that she was too busy this morning to be disturbed. That should put an end to any expectations on Miles's part that she would waste another day entertaining such a mannerless ruffian.

But with the sun sparkling so brightly on the rain-washed flowers, it was hard to remain cooped up within doors. Delia fidgeted over her self-imposed imprisonment, managing to produce half of a letter by midafternoon. Perchance she was being rude, she decided. How could she accuse Miles of a lack of manners when she behaved no better herself? She had certain duties as the daughter of the house. Feeling quite virtuous, Delia set her quill pen and the violet-scented parchment aside. Heading briskly toward the steps, she determined to make one more attempt to treat her cousin with dignified civility.

But the rooms below were strangely quiet. "Bessy," Delia asked as she passed her maid midstairs, Bessy's arms full of mending, "do you know where my aunt and cousin have gone?"

"Miss Violet has taken Sir Miles out with her a-calling. I think they were going to the vicar's, then to the Leightons'."

"What! And they never invited me to accompany them!"

Bessy gave her a sly grin. "Why, miss, what with you being so frightfully preoccupied, they were a-feared to disturb you."

Delia glared at her maid's retreating back before flouncing down the rest of the steps. Well, so much for any attempt to be gracious. There was simply no way of being polite to a man so unpredictable as Miles Renwick. Now the prospect of a lonely afternoon stretched before her, more dull than the morning had been.

She toyed with the notion of setting aside her pride. She could walk to the Leightons herself—oh, simply for the exercise—and feign astonishment at finding Miles and her aunt also present. But before she had time to put such a course into action, she heard the rumble of wheels and the stamping of horses reining to a halt before the cottage. Peeking out the parlor window, she saw a ponderous barouche-landau pulled by a team of four stout roan horses. The coachman sounded a trumpet and two elegantly liveried footmen leaped to pull down the coach steps, then flung open the coach door.

The commotion brought Papa storming from his study. "What the deuce is all that racket? I cannot hear myself think." Frowning, he crowded forward to peer over Delia's shoulder. She felt her heart flutter in anticipation as Lady Herkingstone was handed from the carriage, the plumed feathers on her black taffeta bonnet wafting in the breeze. Delia waited hopefully for the sight of a slender, golden-haired young man. Lord Walsing had been known to accompany his aunt on other occasions. But instead of her handsome nephew, Lady Herkingstone was closely followed by another woman, a thin shadow of herself. Despite the warmth of the day, the anemic-looking Mrs. Forbes-Smythe was muffled in an Indian shawl of blue worsted. She glanced in the direction of the cottage with distaste, applying a handkerchief to her nose. Cringing, Delia half expected to see the woman's niece, Fanny Pryce, emerge from the coach. After all, the girl boasted that she was indispensable to Mrs. Forbes-Smythe. To Delia's relief, the only other person to appear was a small woman whose diminutive features were nearly obscured by a large, poke-front bonnet. The spry Miss Pym jumped to the ground without waiting for assistance from the footmen.

Papa scowled. "Delia! Why is this—this gaggle of elderly females descending upon us?"

"Really, Papa! I believe Miss Pym is not as old as you are. They have only come to call on me. I believe it has something to do with the Shakespeare bicentenary."

"I forbid you to have anything to do with that disgusting folly. Celebrating Shakespeare's death! Bah! And for this I am expected to endure a clatter of shrill female tongues wagging in the parlor. Tittering, clucking. How shall I ever concentrate on my work?"

"I am sure they shan't stay long." She drew back from the window as the ladies marched up the walk. "Please, Papa. Do not say anything uncivil."

"I intend to say nothing at all!" He hastened toward the parlor door, but Elise blocked his way by announcing the arrivals. Papa thrust the maid aside and made a desperate bolt to regain the safety of his study. But Lady Herkingstone outflanked him and, in another moment, Papa was completely surrounded. Cordelia scuttled forward, dreading what might follow.

"You—your ladyship," she stammered. "What an honor."

But Lady Herkingstone barely acknowledged the greeting, her attention fixed on Papa. "Sir, how fortunate we find you at home."

"Madam." Mr. Renwick dipped into a curt bow. "The parlor and my daughter are at your disposal. However—"

"Certainly we have come to solicit the aid of your daughter in our enterprise, but it would be most advantageous if you would participate as well. I think that you and I know Shakespeare better than anyone living in Stratford."

Mr. Renwick snorted. " 'He that is giddy thinks the world turns round.' "

"Papa." Delia gasped. But fortunately, before Lady Herkingstone could puzzle out the meaning behind Papa's quote, Miss Pym edged her tiny frame forward.

Her birdlike blue eyes twinkled as she made her curtsy to Papa. "My dear Mr. Renwick. I have been wanting to ask you something forever."

"Indeed, madam? I cannot imagine what that might be." His manner was so far from encouraging that Delia hoped that Miss Pym would desist. She regarded the elderly spinster as rather a sweet creature and had no desire to see Papa hurt the woman's feelings.

"Please, won't you come into the sitting room?" Delia began, but Miss Pym was not to be so easily diverted.

"Is it true," she trilled, "that you read Shakespeare to your daughter every night?

"Yes, it is. What of it?" Papa asked gruffly.

Miss Pym seized Papa by the hand, giving it a hearty shake. "I want to congratulate you, sir. So few gentlemen would take such pains over improving their daughters' minds. Such an excellent father you must be."

"Well, one does one's best."

Although Delia seethed with indignation over Miss Pym's remark, she was relieved to see her father relax his defensive posture, looking a trifle mollified.

Lady Herkingstone pursed her lips, elbowing past Mrs. Forbes-Smythe who thus far had done nothing but hug her skirts close about her as if she feared they might touch something. "That will do, Letitia." Her ladyship scowled at Miss

Pym. "We are not here to turn Mr. Renwick's head with compliments but to—"

"To take tea," Papa interrupted. "Delia, see to the ladies. I must be about my work." Placing his hand upon Delia's arm, he drew her closer to his side.

"Keep these infernal creatures away from me," he hissed in her ear, his eyes softening somewhat when they rested on Miss Pym. "Although at least I have the consolation of knowing you will be in the company of one sensible female."

Despite Lady Herkingstone's efforts to detain him further, Papa made good his escape. As the study door slammed shut with obvious finality, Delia offered the ladies an apologetic smile, then ushered them into the tiny parlor.

Lady Herkingstone immediately took possession of the wing-backed chair, leaving the settee to the other two women. Before seating herself, Mrs. Forbes-Smythe coughed, giving the cottage's stone walls a dour stare. "So excessively damp," she murmured, drawing the shawl she had refused to relinquish more tightly around her thin shoulders.

"But so charming. I do love these older homes," Miss Pym said. "Rose Briar is enchanting, my dear Miss Renwick."

Delia flashed her a grateful smile, but before she could express her thanks, Lady Herkingstone rapped her silver-tipped cane against the carpet. "We are not here to discuss architecture."

"Certainly not, your ladyship." Delia rubbed her damp palms together. Lady Herkingstone possessed the remarkable capability of making one feel on trial for one's life. "May I not offer you some refreshment? Our cook has been baking today. Mrs. Jergens makes the most exquisite tarts."

"How kind. I should adore some," Miss Pym said. The only response Delia received from Mrs. Forbes-Smythe was another cough.

"Oh, very well. Ring for tea." Her ladyship waved her hand with an air of resigned impatience. Delia summoned Elise and conveyed her instructions, all the while wishing Aunt Violet were here to see her through this ordeal. Miles was to blame, monopolizing her aunt's time when Delia was in great need of support.

Perching on the edge of the straight-backed armchair, Delia fidgeted with her skirts and attempted to appear at ease. She so desperately wanted to make a good impression on Lord Walsing's aunt. Would it seem too foolish if she inquired after his lordship's health, having seen him, herself, only yesterday morning?

But before Delia could say a word, Lady Herkingstone took command of the visit. "As you well know, Miss Renwick, I and my two companions represent the Ladies for Shakespeare Committee, an organization founded by myself to ensure that lasting tribute be paid to Stratford's most famous son."

"A—a most noble objective." Delia swallowed, the effort of telling such a gracious lie almost proving too much for her. Her eyes strayed involuntarily to the bust of Shakespeare atop the pianoforte. To her embarrassment, she realized the marble head was still turned ignominiously to face the wall.

But Lady Herkingstone was too absorbed in her speech to pay the least attention to any of the details in the room. "Our latest project is a supper-ball to celebrate the bicentenary of Shakespeare's death."

"If our health permits," Mrs. Forbes-Smythe sniffed into her handkerchief.

"Stuff and nonsense. I have never been ill a day in my life." Her ladyship shot Mrs. Forbes-Smythe such a quelling look that it caused the woman to shrink back in her seat. "We also intend to organize a private theatrical performance of *Othello*, the roles to be played by our local gentry, not crude, so-called professional actors."

Lady Herkingstone went on at great length to explain how the committee had settled on *Othello* as the choice for production, but Delia found she was having difficulty concentrating. Her ladyship's mention of the theatre had triggered a memory of Miles yesterday on the riverbank. Delia so clearly recalled the manner of his smile, how his dark eyes had glowed while coaxing her to attend a performance of Shakespeare with him. She was surprised to feel a pang of regret at her refusal. Of course Papa would never have approved. Imagine sitting close beside Miles in a dimly lit theater, feeling the occasional brush of his hand against her own, his deep voice murmuring in her ear.

"Well, have you nothing to say, Miss Renwick?"

The question, phrased in Lady Herkingstone's sharpest accents, snapped Delia back to the present. She became aware that all three of her guests were staring at her with varying degrees of expectancy.

"I—I . . ." Delia floundered.

Lady Herkingstone rapped her cane. "We came here today

for the express purpose of having an answer, Miss Renwick. You are designated for the part of Desdemona. Will you undertake it?"

Desdemona. Good heavens! They expected her to take the lead part in their theatrical production. Delia felt the heat of dismayed embarrassment creeping into her cheeks. Whatever would Papa say? Indeed, the thought was most repugnant to her. Memorizing all those beastly lines of Shakespeare! Not even to accommodate Lady Herkingstone could she agree to such a thing. But her ladyship looked as if she would brook no refusal. Delia felt a wave of gratitude when Miss Pym kindly intervened.

"Well, my dear, take your time and think it over. If you feel too shy or that it would not be within your capabilities—"

"Certainly it is within her capabilities," her ladyship said. "I should not have selected her otherwise. She looks the part of Desdemona, just as my own nephew will make a perfect Othello."

"Your ladyship, I regret—" Delia's timid refusal died upon her lips as comprehension of Lady Herkingstone's last remark penetrated her consciousness. "Lord Walsing is to play Othello?"

"Did I not just say so?"

Delia sank back in her chair, a whole vista of new possibilities opening before her. Lord Walsing playing Othello to her Desdemona. She would be obliged to spend hours in his company rehearsing under the most romantic circumstances. Why, he would even be obliged to touch her during the strangling scene. Would she ever have a better opportunity to win his heart?

"I—I would be delighted to have the part," she heard herself whisper. Her acceptance was all but swallowed up by the clatter of Elise entering to set down the tea tray.

"Ah, tea at last," Mrs. Forbes-Smythe said. "My poor head. So glad this tedious business is settled."

Miss Pym and Lady Herkingstone also expressed their satisfaction at Delia's acceptance, but their words were lost on her. She poured out tea, handing forth the cups and saucers in a semidaze. Visions of herself on such intimate terms with Lord Walsing were already being disrupted by unpleasant speculations. Papa! Never would he permit Delia to take part in what he would term a desecration of Shakespeare. She would have to find some way of wheedling her father into a more reasonable frame of mind.

Delia wracked her brain for a way of doing so as she pressed a china plate into Miss Pym's hand.

"Gracious, what large tarts your cook makes," the tiny woman exclaimed. "I fear I shall never be able to eat all of this."

Lady Herkingstone sipped her tea. "Very wasteful. I shall have to have my chef send over a recipe containing his method of doing pastries."

Delia agreed, scarcely knowing what was being said as a more disturbing thought popped into her head. Miles. What would he think of her spending so much time in Lord Walsing's company? He had already expressed his contempt for Delia's pursuit of his lordship on several occasions. Delia shrugged, trying to dispell the discomfiting worry as she offered more sugar to Mrs. Forbes-Smythe. Let Miles be scornful if he chose. What did she care for her cousin's good opinion?

"How very odd," Miss Pym said. "My dear Miss Renwick, what does your cook put in these pastries?"

Delia broke off her reverie enough to note Miss Pym gingerly poking at the top of her tart with a silver fork.

"Why, raspberries, sugar mostly. Does it not taste quite the thing?" Delia asked.

"I don't know, but—but I distinctly thought I saw the crust move!"

"Stuff!" her ladyship boomed. "Do eat and stop making such a fuss, Letitia. I hate to see anyone pick at her food."

Mrs. Forbes-Smythe sighed. "I daresay Letty's eyesight is failing. My own has gone off sadly in the last year."

Although Delia could see nothing amiss with the tart, she offered to fetch Miss Pym another, but the woman clung stubbornly to the plate, her chin quivering with indignation. "No, I tell you there is nothing wrong with my eyes. I—Oh! Look!"

Delia felt her heart lurch in horror. This time she had seen it, too. The crust of the tart moved up and down. Uncertain as to what was amiss, Delia moved instinctively to conceal it. "Please, Miss Pym." She struggled for possession of the dish. "No, don't do that," Delia begged.

But Miss Pym paid no heed. Her eyes bright with fascination, her head cocked to one side, the elderly woman slid her fork under the edge of the crust. The entire top of the tart lifted off, exposing a shell devoid of all filling except for three plump toads, their bulging eyes winking furiously back at Miss Pym.

"My word!" she exclaimed. Delia made a frantic effort to contain the toads by flinging a napkin over the tart, but it was too late. The creatures made their bid for freedom by leaping from the dish into Mrs. Forbes-Smythe's lap. That lady did not regard the toads' introduction into the parlor with the same equanimity as Miss Pym. With a bloodcurdling shriek, Mrs. Forbes-Smythe flung her cup and saucer into the air, clawing and swatting at her skirts.

"Oh, don't, Margaret," Miss Pym said. "You'll frighten the poor little things."

Delia attempted to catch the frantically leaping creatures, but Lady Herkingstone thwarted her efforts. Her ladyship swung out her walking stick, completely missing the toads but catching Delia in the shins with bone-jarring accuracy. Her eyes watering with pain, Delia suppressed an urge to wrench the cane away from her ladyship and rap her over the head with it.

"This is an outrage. An outrage," her ladyship huffed. With baleful looks, she dared the scampering creatures to venture any closer to her exalted person.

Properly awed, the toads bounded off to a place of safety beneath the pianoforte. After rubbing her bruised flesh, Delia turned her attention back to the unfortunate Mrs. Forbes-Smythe. The woman slid down onto the carpet, fluttering her eyes and moaning. "Oh, my heart. Such spasms. Such palpitations."

Mercy, Delia thought, tearing at her curls in distraction. What should she do now? Burn feathers? Where did Aunt Violet keep her smelling salts? Before she could race around in a frantic search for them, Miss Pym pushed forward, calmly reaching for Mrs. Forbes-Smythe's reticule. She fished out a small bottle but was assailed by such a fit of the giggles that she could not uncork the vinaigrette. It was left to Delia to remove the bottle from her grasp and try to revive the half-swooning Mrs. Forbes-Smythe.

"Oh—oh, Miss Renwick." Miss Pym gasped. "Such—such a jest. And to think I—I always thought you such a p-poor, spiritless little thing like Fanny P-Pryce." The small woman doubled over, holding her sides.

But Delia felt no inclination to join in the laughter as Mrs. Forbes-Smythe collapsed against her lap. Above them, Lady Herkingstone loomed like a wrathful goddess about to let loose a thunderbolt. For several moments, her ladyship's jaw worked, incapable of expressing her fury.

"Miss Renwick! Never—never have I been subjected to such an indignity."

"You, subjected!" Mrs. Forbes-Smythe squeaked, relieving Delia's apprehension that the woman was dying. She managed to struggle to a sitting position, still moaning pitifully.

"Your ladyship, I—I am so sorry," Delia faltered. "But you cannot think that I—"

"Do not add falsehood to your other crimes," Lady Herkingstone said. "Pressing us to take tea! You plotted this hoydenish trick from the beginning."

"Now, Amelie . . ." Miss Pym tried to come to Delia's defense but was too overcome with laughter.

"No, no, I plotted nothing," Delia said. "I was as astonished as you. I assure you—"

"Mannerless chit! Be silent! You may forget all proposals that were made to you this afternoon. Indeed, from this time hence, you are quite beneath my notice." Pointing her nose in the air, her ladyship swept past Delia. Torn between humiliation and the dread that Lady Herkingstone meant to leave Mrs. Forbes-Smythe swooning in her arms, Delia cried out one final appeal. Then the parlor door swung open with some violence. Papa burst into the room, waving his quill pen about with the vigor of a Hotspur laying into his enemies.

"Delia, you try my patience! Such a caterwauling! What, by God's teeth, are you women doing in here?"

Lady Herkingstone poked the end of her cane against Papa's chest, his plume a woefully inadequate defense. "We are on the point of leaving, sir, never to cross this threshold again. Your daughter is most disgustingly ill-bred. Rest assured, she shall not play Desdemona in our production."

"Madam, how dare you presume to criticize my daughter's manners when your own are so sadly wanting? I . . . What did you say? Delia p-play Desdemona?" The mere suggestion of such a thing rendered Papa momentarily speechless.

Her ladyship cast a last disdainful glance to where Mrs. Forbes-Smythe sagged against Delia. "Margaret, if you wish to expire on the floor of this hovel, I am sure that is your own concern. But if you are not on your feet within five seconds, you will find yourself walking home."

Her ladyship stalked out of the room. To Delia's amazement, Mrs. Forbes-Smythe made a startling recovery. Issuing another small squeak, she staggered to her feet, only to lean heavily against Miss Pym. The two women made to follow Lady Herkingstone, but Miss Pym paused long enough to whisper assurances to Delia that she should not fret, that she, Miss Pym, would make everything right with her ladyship.

But as the ladies disappeared into the hall, hot tears of embarrassment and disappointment cascaded down Delia's cheeks.

Papa gave over staring at the departing guests in affronted astonishment. He hurried over to Delia's side, drawing her head against his shoulder. "My dear child!"

The unexpected expression of sympathy from her father completely overset Cordelia. She muffled huge, gulping sobs against his waistcoat.

"That odious woman," Papa crooned. "No wonder that you are so distressed. Imagine her trying to bully you into taking part in such a defamation of Shakespeare."

"Oh, Papa!" Delia wrenched herself free. As usual, Papa understood nothing about what was taking place. With a loud sniff, Delia rubbed her tear-misted eyes, for the first time noticing the large masculine frame filling the doorway.

Miles's dark eyes regarded her with concern. "Delia, my— What has happened? I just returned and saw Lady Herkingstone leaving. Was someone taken ill?" His words trailed off at the sound of a loud croak. He looked down to see a toad hopping past his boot. From there his eyes flicked guiltily to the empty pastry shell Miss Pym had dropped onto the settee. "Oh, Lord." Miles groaned, his cheeks flushing a deep red.

Realization flooded Delia. "You!" she shrieked. "It was you!" Rushing across the room, she flung herself upon Miles, venting all her anger and mortification by pummeling his chest. "You—you r-ruffian. You bl-blackguard."

He made no effort to stop her, manfully taking his punishment. It was Papa who brought her to reason, seizing her by the wrist and hauling her back.

"Cordelia! Stop it at once. Have you taken leave of your senses?" He did not release Delia until she lowered her arms to her sides, her fingers still clenched into fists.

"N-not I!" She glared at Miles through her tears. "B-but your p-precious Miles has run mad. Just ask him what he has done!"

"Delia." Miles attempted to touch her shoulder, but she pulled away.

"D-don't you touch me!"

He sighed. "Delia, I am sorry." Miles's lips twisted in a rueful, coaxing smile. " 'Twas only meant as a jest. I never imagined you would have company for tea. I thought I would be here and—"

"Will one of you have the goodness to explain to me what is going on?" Papa interrupted.

Miles ran his hand through his hair in a discomfited gesture. "I fear a prank of mine has misfired. I put toads in an empty pastry shell. 'Twas a jest often played in the officers' mess."

"This is not an officers' mess!" Delia shouted. "This is a gentleman's house."

Papa eyed her sternly. "So it is. Kindly lower your voice, miss, and behave toward your cousin in a manner more befitting a lady."

"Of course you would take his side," Delia said with bitterness. A part of her knew that she was behaving dreadfully, that Miles had some justification for the prank he had played. He was looking extremely abject and sorry for what he had done. But the keenness of her disappointment overrode her more reasonable self. Not only had she lost the part in the play, but Delia knew that Lady Herkingstone had the power to see that she was cut by most of Stratford society.

Mopping her eyes, she raised her chin and leveled what she hoped was a chilling stare at Miles. "I trust you are now quite satisfied, Cousin. My misery appears to have been your objective ever since your arrival in Stratford. Now you can leave knowing you have achieved your goal. You have at last managed to—to ruin m-me."

The effect of her dignified speech was shattered as she once more burst into tears. Despite her father's presence, Miles tried to draw her into his arms, but she evaded him, fleeing to her room to weep out her sorrows into an unfeeling pillow.

Chapter 6

Miles's fingers trailed over the empty trunk stored in the corner of Delia's room as he considered the possibility that he should pack and leave. Over a week had passed since the incident of the toads, but Delia showed no sign of relenting. If only she would shout reproaches at him or snap out brisk rejoinders as she had been wont to do. Her studied politeness was driving him to distraction. He longed to see those vivid blue eyes sparkle again, even in anger, but too often they were awash with sadness, their brightness dulled by gloom-filled reflection.

Plague take that Herkingstone woman! His hands smacked against the trunk's hard leather covering. It was her fault that his ill-conceived jest had been blown all out of proportion. Miles had made several efforts to see her ladyship, to clear Delia of all blame for the prank, but the stubborn old harridan refused to admit him to her presence, returned all his notes unopened. And Delia was already feeling the effects of her ladyship's displeasure.

Only last Sunday his cousin had been virtually ignored by most of the women as Miles had escorted her and Aunt Violet from the church after services. Even Rosamund Leighton's anxious chatter could not disguise the cool nods of dismissal from the other ladies. Aunt Violet had wrung her hands.

"Dear me," she had said, glancing nervously at the grim-faced Mrs. Forbes-Smythe and Lady Herkingstone as they huddled in the churchyard whispering with a group that included Fanny Pryce in their midst. "Cousin Miles, do tell Miffin to hurry with our carriage. I feel ready to sink into the ground. My dear Delia, if only I could take you away from Stratford until this nonsense is forgotten."

251

Delia had thrust her chin into the air, a wooden smile upon her face. "Don't be foolish, Aunt. I shan't be driven from my own home by such silliness. As if it matters a jot what Lady Herkingstone thinks of me."

"If only Miss Pym had not been taken ill." Rosamund had sighed. "I am sure she would not be so unkind." She had given Delia's hand a squeeze, but before she could offer further consolation, she had been called away by an imperious summons from her mama, which she had reluctantly obeyed.

With Rosamund's departure, Delia had appeared even smaller and more forlorn, despite how she had set her fragile countenance into a mask of overbright defiance. Miles had both longed to gather her into the protection of his arms and to charge into that line of prim-faced females to ... To do what? That was the damned exasperating thing about women. If Lady Herkingstone had been an affronted man, she would have delivered Delia an honest clout on the jaw. They would have met with pistols at dawn, thereby making a clean end to the business. But no, ladies must indulge in sly glances, cruel whispers, and well-bred maliciousness that seared and bled one more slowly than any ball and powder ever devised.

Miles chafed at his own helplessness to shield Delia, his guilt at being the cause of her unhappiness. He grimaced at the memory of how she had ridden home from church in rigid silence, her pale lips trembling from time to time. And there was nothing he could do to mend matters. Not a blasted thing.

His eyes rested again on the trunk. Well, mayhap there was one thing. He could rid her of his unwanted presence. Then, at least, she might find some comfort within the walls of her own home.

He seized the trunk's handle and was hauling it to the center of the room when he was interrupted by a knock at the bedchamber door. Calling out a curt bid to enter, Miles flung the trunk lid open.

Walter Renwick paused in the doorway, his gray strands of hair looking longer and wispier, the ever-present folio of Shakespeare grasped in one hand.

"Miles, I want to show you—" He stopped, his age-lined eyes widening with dismay. "Why, what are you doing? Never say you are thinking of leaving us so soon."

Miles straightened, then spread his hands in a rueful gesture. "I fear my departure is long overdue, sir."

Renwick's bushy eyebrows beetled together in scorn as he

stepped into the chamber, closing the door behind him. "Leave simply because Delia is a trifle vexed? Od's bodikins! You, who have heard 'great ordnance in the field, and heaven's artillery thunder in the skies'? Will you be routed by a mere slip of a girl?"

Miles's lips upturned into a reluctant smile. " 'Tis not a question of being routed but more of the unhappiness I bring Delia by staying. I have already unintentionally caused her a great deal of mischief."

"Bosh. Delia sets too much store by these society fribbles." Mr. Renwick paced up and down the room, coming to an abrupt halt by Cordelia's dressing table. He frowned at the miniature of the lovely, dark-haired woman. In a voice gruff with emotion, he added, "All these years and Delia has still not outgrown the deplorable influence of my late wife."

" 'Tis only natural that Delia should long for society."

"Society!" The elderly man waved his Shakespearean folio about in agitation. "What she longs for is to present me with some cabbage-head for a son-in-law like that simpering Walsing fellow."

Miles sighed, turning back to his trunk to thunk a pair of boots into it. "Walsing is what I suppose would be referred to as an eligible *parti*. If Delia has a tendre for the man, then—" He broke off, leaving the disagreeable thought unfinished.

Mr. Renwick positioned himself in front of the trunk to prevent Miles from packing anything more. "Why, Delia is no more in love with that ass than—than Titania was with Bottom. She is dazzled by his looks, his wealth, his position, that is all. Mistaken notions she inherited from Amaryllis." An expression of deep-rooted pain suffered for a moment in Renwick's clear gray eyes. "But I'll not stand by and watch my daughter repeat my wretched error—rush into marriage for all the wrong reasons."

Miles clapped one hand lightly on Renwick's shoulder, his throat tightening at this sign that his old friend was yet troubled by pained remembrance of Amaryllis. "I am sure you need not fear for Delia, sir," he said gently. "But if I thought there was anything I could do to ease your mind, I would gladly stay."

"When I invited you to Stratford, I had hoped that you—" Seeming to recall himself, Renwick stopped, the wistful expression on his face quickly replaced with a guilty smile. "I had hoped you would at least remain long enough to escort my ladies to that accursed ball tomorrow night. How I despise such affairs, but Delia will give me no peace if she does not attend."

The ball at Walsing Manor. Miles was tormented by a vivid recollection of Delia waltzing around the bedchamber, her slender hands caressing the lilac silk, her face alight with girlish dreams, dreams Lady Herkingstone would make a shambles of. She might even persuade that sheep-faced nephew of hers to ignore Delia completely whereby the other gentlemen might follow their host's lead. Miles had an awful vision of his cousin, garbed in that lovely, rustling gown, spending the evening trying to shrink into the wall, her eyes proudly blinking back her tears. Damme. Even if Delia would as soon dispense with Miles's escort, how could he leave her to face such an ordeal alone?

"Well, I suppose I could remain until Sunday," Miles conceded aloud. Walter Renwick beamed at this pronouncement. Wringing Miles's hand, he quit the chamber looking as if a huge weight had been lifted from his shoulders. But Miles could not share the older man's relief. If his continued presence in Stratford were to make any kind of a difference, he would have to do more than foist himself on Delia as an escort. He must make one more effort to right the wrong he had done her, prevent Lady Herkingstone from ruining the ball Delia had awaited with pleasure for so long.

His mouth setting in a grim line, Miles unpacked the boots and dragged the trunk back to the corner. It was high time to stop being such a gentleman. Lady Herkingstone had best have a stout-hearted butler, Miles vowed. He would kick in the front door, if necessary, to trap the old dragon in her lair. Aye, even if she roasted him alive.

The ancient Renwick carriage lumbered through the high iron gates leading into Walsing Park. Outside the coach windows a pretty wilderness of trees rolled by, poplars, oaks, beech, their shadowy branches rustling in the night breeze. Above them, the moon glinted off the eerie battlements of a crumbling stone wall.

Aunt Violet leaned forward. "Oh, look. There are the ruins of the old monastery. 'Twas dissolved by King Henry the Eighth after his falling out with the pope. For a time, the Walsings converted it into a manor house. But of course it has been ages since anyone has actually lived there."

Miles obliging peered out the window in the direction Aunt Violet indicated, but Delia huddled deeper into her sarcenet-lined Wellington mantle although the night was quite warm. She was more concerned with her own social ruin than the tumbledown remains of a centuries-old dwelling. After Papa had canceled their journey to Brighton, Lord Walsing's ball had been the only remaining bright spot in Delia's summer. To think she had so looked forward to this evening, but now the coach journey between Rose Briar Cottage and Walsing Park seemed all too short. In a matter of moments, the carriage left the wooded parkland behind, sweeping up the curving drive that led to the main house. Lord Walsing's elegant mansion towered over the carriage like a great Palladian block of stone, an austere court of judgment. Even the lights blazing through the tall glass windows, the lanterns casting a pink glow over the lichen-covered ashlar walls conveyed no sense of welcome to Delia. True, Lord Walsing had not sent a note hinting that her presence would be unwelcome now that she had offended his aunt. But he had made no effort to speak with her during the past week, either.

"Well, here we are," Miles said cheerfully as the coach lurched to a halt. Delia thought he moved with unnecessary alacrity to leap to the graveled drive. Swirling his cape in a dashing style, he offered his arm. She stood, pulling her hood forward and retreating farther into its sheltering folds. Miles could well afford to appear so jaunty, so pleased with himself. It was not he the ladies would regard with icy glances, barely vouchsafed acknowledgments. Not that Miles would mind in the least if they did. The man was utterly impervious to snubs, as Delia could well attest.

Although it almost cost her a sprained ankle, Delia pointedly avoided touching Miles as she jumped to the graveled drive. He looked rather downcast for a moment before turning to help Aunt Violet. As soon as her aunt's feet met the ground, she hissed into Delia's ear.

"Delia! When will you cease to treat Miles so shabbily!"

When Birnam Wood comes to Dunsinane, Delia thought resentfully. Her only satisfaction during the past week had derived from attempting to bring Miles to a sense of his own iniquity. But it had proved a most peculiar form of satisfaction. When her arctic manner had driven Miles repeatedly into the seclusion of Papa's study, Delia had felt an unaccountable urge to burst into tears.

As Miles closed the coach door and sent the carriage on its way, Aunt Violet continued to scold. "How can you be so hard and unforgiving, child? Miles has gone out of his way to make amends. He shows you great kindness even when you are abominably rude."

Delia compressed her lips. "Yes, I daresay Henry the Eighth was equally as kind to Anne Boleyn before he sent her to the tower to have her head lopped off."

Indeed, Delia had never thought of it before, but Lord Walsing's manor did look rather like a tower, a large stone fortress. She swallowed. She should have feigned an illness, remained at home. Why go through such an ordeal? "Because," she told herself sternly, "you have never been hen-hearted before. You are not going to commence now."

All the same, Delia felt a twinge of gratitude when Miles forced her to accept the strong support of his arm going up one side of the exterior double staircase that led to the portico formed by six columns. Two bewigged footmen wearing gold and scarlet livery sprang forward to swing open the massive double doors leading into the imposing entrance hall. Inside, others hustled forward to take their cloaks and those of Mrs. Gunthrope and her two red-haired daughters, who had arrived just before the Renwick party. Reluctantly, Delia surrendered her mantle, giving a self-conscious tug to the neckline of her ivory satin. Besides having seen far too many balls, the gown lacked sophistication. The bodice *à l'enfant*, whose rounded décolletage was drawn up high on her shoulders, and the pink sash tied into a bow at her waist seemed more suited to a schoolgirl. She noticed Miles studying the frock, a puzzled frown creasing his brow. But whatever uncomplimentary thoughts he harbored, he kept them to himself. Defiantly, Delia stared back at him while inwardly sighing for her new gown of lilac-pink. She hoped the dress would do Rosamund some good this evening. At least her friend might enjoy the ball.

The Misses Gunthrope tittered behind their fans, ogling Miles as he swept off his cape. Silly creatures, Delia thought, bristling. She had to admit that her cousin cut quite a figure, his muscular frame enhanced by the simple lines of the black evening jacket designed by Stratford's best tailor. His double-breasted waistcoat of silk serge exposed the frills of his shirt-front, accenting his handsome, bronzed countenance in marked contrast to the snowy-white folds of his cravat. Indeed, Miles looked quite elegant, but it was still no excuse for those shameless chits to stare so boldly. Delia longed to slap both their simpering freckled faces.

Miles might pretend to be unaware of their admiring regard, but he was tipping his head in such a manner as to present his profile, the candlelight gleaming off his waving sable hair and bringing a soft glow to his dark eyes. When he stifled a muttered exclamation, Delia realized her cousin was staring at the wall space above the hall's paneled frieze of winged cherubs dancing amidst flower garlands.

High above them, ringing the entrance hall, were portrait after portrait framed by heavy-guilt-trimmed oak. The people portrayed were garbed in doublets, armor, plumed cavalier hats, or neck ruffs. Still others wore the white-powdered wigs of the last century. Whatever the differences in costume, the subjects in the paintings all bore the same coal-black hair, dour countenances, and exceedingly long noses.

"Delia, Miles," Aunt Violet whispered. "What are you gawking at? Oh, the Walsing family portraits. They are a frightful lot, are they not?"

"Lord Walsing favors his ancestors not at all," Delia said in a low voice. "I expect his mother must have been quite lovely."

Miles snorted. "Lovely? She must have been a diamond of the first water to counteract that many generations of pudding faces."

His loud comment sent the Misses Gunthrope into another fit of the giggles.

"Oh, do hush!" Delia said. When the young women directed more coy glances at Miles, Delia made haste to link her arm back through his. Although his dark eyebrows jutted upward in surprise, Miles patted her hand, smiling at Delia in such a way as to cause her heart to do a peculiar flip.

She put the sensation down to nervousness as they began to ascend the curving, red-carpeted marble stairs, leading up to the ballroom. Miles leaned over, his warm breath tickling her neck as he murmured into her ear, "Dare I hope you will save the first waltz for me, fair Cousin?"

"You may hope, sir, but there is little chance your wish will be realized."

"Then perhaps I will drop to one knee before you and refuse to budge off these stairs until my request is granted."

"You would not dare to create such a scene!"

But Miles had already begun to bend. Delia tightened her

grip on his arm. "No, stop! I—I will dance with you." She added in forlorn accents, "I daresay no one else will be bold enough to incur her ladyship's disapproval by asking me."

"Ah, the gracious manner of your acceptance quite overwhelms me, Cousin."

When they arrived at the landing where Lord Walsing stood greeting his guests, Delia froze in dismay at the sight of a tall woman resplendent in a gold silk turban embellished with ostrich feathers. Lady Herkingstone! What a simpleton Delia had been not to realize that she would act as her nephew's hostess. Braced to fall under her ladyship's frigid notice at some time during the evening, Delia quailed at the prospect of facing the formidable dame right off. But there Lady Herkingstone loomed, guarding the entry to the glittering ballroom beyond like some steely-eyed Medusa prepared to turn unwelcome guests into stone. Why, what if her ladyship should refuse Delia admission?

All too quickly the Misses Gunthrope and their mama paid their respects to her ladyship, then it was Delia's turn. She shrank against Miles as their presence was announced. Lady Herkingstone's thin lips split into the most pleasant smile Delia had ever beheld on that rigid countenance. Delia glanced behind her to see who else had come in, but she, Miles, and Aunt Violet stood alone upon the landing.

"Ah, Peter," her ladyship said. "Here is Mrs. Nicholson, her pretty little niece, and their most charming cousin, Sir Miles."

"Enchanted that you all could attend." Lord Walsing's misty blue eyes encompassed them each in turn. But Delia scarcely noticed him as she continued to gape at Lady Herkingstone. Her legs wobbled as she sank into her curtsy, Aunt Violet's tug on her elbow all that saved Delia from collapsing to the floor. In astonishment, she watched Miles bow and actually dare to kiss her ladyship's outstretched hand. Lady Herkingstone rapped Delia's knuckles with her fan. "Miss Renwick, why did you never tell me about this naughty man?"

"Well, I—I . . ." Delia stammered.

"The rogue! Putting toads into the tart! Margaret Forbes-Smythe took to her bed for days after. Such a droll jest."

Delia sensed that her mouth was hanging open and snapped it shut. A droll jest? Why had the same incident been termed vulgar and ill-bred when her ladyship thought Cordelia responsible?

"How—how did you learn that it was Miles who placed the toads?" Delia summoned up enough courage to ask.

"Why, he rode over yesterday afternoon to explain to me."

Delia directed a reproachful glance at her cousin. Miles arched his eyebrows, looking exasperatingly smug at having kept his secret so long. The villain had known all along that Cordelia would not be snubbed by her ladyship tonight, but he had not breathed a word, allowing her to go on quaking and fretting and—and, oh! Plague take him!

Lady Herkingstone permitted herself a well-bred chuckle, then turned to her nephew. "Peter, when I denied this rogue entrance, Sir Miles climbed up my rose trellis to the balcony. Made me the prettiest speech, straight out of *Romeo and Juliet*."

"How vastly athletic," Lord Walsing drawled. He found Delia's hand and carried it to his lips. "You do look so lovely tonight, Miss Renwick."

But Delia snatched her fingers away, her indignation mounting as she stared accusingly at Miles. To think her cousin had once had the effrontery to accuse her of toad-eating Lady Herkingstone. Only fancy! Climbing her balcony! Reciting poetry! And he did not even have the grace to blush.

Aunt Violet sighed. "I trust Cordelia is now restored to your ladyship's good graces."

"And may she have the part of Desdemona?" Miles added.

Her ladyship shrugged. "I neglected to tell you yesterday, Sir Miles, the part has already been offered to Mrs. Forbes-Smythe's niece, Fanny. The two girls look so much alike, you know." Lady Herkingstone nodded at Delia with affable condescension. "However, I am sure we can find some other small bit for Miss Renwick to do."

"Too kind of you, I am sure." Completely forgetting that she should be feeling relieved, Delia struggled to control her rising anger. Bad enough to learn that Miles had discussed her, rearranged her life behind her back, but the thought that she had been so easily replaced in the production by Fanny Pryce, of all people, was nigh insupportable.

"Now, the part of Othello is still not cast," her ladyship continued, glowering at her nephew. "Peter absolutely refuses to undertake it."

"Alas." His lordship sighed. "My modesty forbids it. I should not wish to make a great cake of myself."

"Why such scruples at this late date?" Miles mumbled under

his breath. He became uncomfortably aware that Lady Herkingstone was regarding him with a speculative gleam.

"Now you, Sir Miles, do not seem to be shy about displaying your abilities."

"Oh, no, not at all," Delia said. "My cousin never permits such trifles as the fear of appearing ridiculous to weigh with him."

Miles winced at the waspish tone in Delia's voice. What was amiss with the woman now? She might show some spark of gratitude for all that he had done for her.

"I am sure Sir Miles could play Othello to perfection. What say you, sir?" her ladyship demanded.

Miles felt himself pale at the prospect. "I—I believe we take too much of your time. You have many more guests arriving." Restraining the urge to scoop up Delia and Aunt Violet, one under each arm, Miles managed to escape into the ballroom, propelling his ladies in front of him.

Despite the vast length of the chamber, the ballroom already showed signs of becoming uncomfortably crowded with gentlemen in varying shapes and sizes, their dark jackets like stems amidst a pastel flower garden of silk-gowned ladies, whose jewels glinted in the blazing light provided by three massive crystal chandeliers. Walsing Park was by far too ostentatious for his taste, Miles thought as he looked askance at the gilt entablatures adorning the alabaster columns and the pastoral tapestries, representing classical ruins and grottos, lining the walls. A heavily ornate mirror hung above the fireplace. Within its depths, Miles could see reflected the dainty face of his cousin, her hair drawn up into a cluster of curls adorned with pink roses. How could someone who looked that angelic appear so savage? Not even Lady Macbeth could have waxed more murderous when she was nagging her poor husband to do away with King Duncan.

While Aunt Violet busied herself greeting Squire Newbold and his lady, Miles drew Delia off to one side, finding her a place to sit in one the Louis XV armchairs scattered about the room. But Delia showed no inclination to be seated. She stood before him, fists clenched, biting her lip as if she could not find words hot enough to express what she was thinking.

"I trust you do not mean to embarrass me in public, Cousin," Miles said tartly, "by flinging your arms about my neck in a fit of gratitude."

"Gratitude!" Her blue eyes smoldered. "What reason have I to be in your debt?"

"Oh, no reason. Only the small matter of how I made things right for you with Lady Herkingstone, getting you out of the devil's own scrape."

"A scrape that you thrust me into in the first place!" Delia paused long enough in her angry tirade to direct a polite smile to the vicar when he passed by. "What do you mean by shabbing off to Lady Herkingstone behind my back? The least you could have done was to have told me, not let me worry myself sick about how she would receive me this evening."

"I thought it would be an agreeable surprise."

"I have had quite enough of your surprises!"

Miles felt his own temper begin to rise. Delia was enough to try the most saintly man's patience. Ungrateful little witch! When he thought of what he had gone through to placate Lady Herkingstone . . . ! The woman had nigh cudgeled his brains out with that blasted cane of hers when Miles had first appeared unannounced on her balcony. Perhaps Walter Renwick was right about his daughter's legacy from Amaryllis. Spoiled, unreasonable, selfish . . .

"Mayhap I should have told you," he said. "But I saw little sign earlier today that you stood in dread of anything. In fact, your chief concern appeared to be convincing me that I should go hang myself."

Delia whipped open her fan with an angry snap, waving it before flushed cheeks. "You will never be obliged to hang *yourself*, Cousin."

Not trusting himself to say anything more, Miles stalked away leaving Cordelia to her own devices. He had set out for the ball in such good spirits, congratulating himself that he had at last done something right, something to win Delia's good opinion. But there was no pleasing that woman. Renwick had made a great error when searching through Shakespeare to name his daughter. She should have been called Kate . . . Kate the curst!

Crossing his arms over his chest, Miles withdrew, fuming, into the shadows of one of the archways. He spotted his old friend, Michael Devon, but did not feel in good enough humor to greet him. Besides, Dev was quite preoccupied with the lovely Rosamund. The dark-haired girl was a vision tonight gowned in that silken—Miles straightened abruptly.

Delia's lilac-pink gown. There was no mistaking it. Miles

had wondered earlier what had become of the dress, had even nurtured a shameful suspicion that Delia opted not to wear it out of spite knowing that Miles admired the gown. He could not know for certain why Delia had given her cherished garment to Rosamund, but it was not difficult to guess. He had seen some of the other, more tasteless samples of the fair Rosamund's wardrobe.

Miles noted the wistful expression on Delia's face when she regarded the lilac-silk gown, an expression she quickly disguised, chattering brightly to her friend and Devon. Delia—spoiled, selfish? Miles's lips curved into a rueful smile. Ducking past the simpering Gunthrope sisters, Miles recrossed the room to Delia's side, muttering an oath when he saw that Lord Walsing was going to reach her first.

Delia scarcely noted his lordship's approach, her attention riveted on Michael Devon and Rosamund as they glided away from her. The veiled satin shimmered in the candlelight just as Delia had always imagined it would, but it held no comparison to the radiant glow on Rosamund's face. Sighing, Delia vowed that her sacrifice had been worth it. She had no doubt what the outcome of this evening would be. When Michael Devon's eyes roved about the room, Delia could swear that the man saw naught but Rosamund wherever he looked, making no effort to conceal his devotion. She wondered what it would be like to inspire such love in someone. Mayhap Roz was not such a great fool after all. Inexplicably, Delia thought of Miles and her angry dismissal of him. She had offended him. That had been obvious from the way he had stalked away, but upon calmer reflection she could no longer convince herself that he deserved such cavalier treatment. He had performed a noble deed on her behalf. She knew no other gentleman brave enough to confront Lady Herkingstone, capable of charming the woman into forgetting her overweening sense of consequence. And all to spare Delia further distress.

Her cheeks burned as she began to feel positively ashamed of her outburst of temper. Would she never learn to think first before speaking?

"Miss . . ." Delia started when a soft voice spoke close to her ear. Lord Walsing's perfect features bent alarmingly close to her own. She drew back.

"Miss Renwick," his lordship pronounced. "How fortunate I am to find you alone."

Alone? Delia eyed him quizzically. Scarcely that in this

crush of people. Lieutenant Turner was at this moment crowding close to her elbow to claim the first dance, while on the other side of her stood . . . Delia's heart skipped a beat. Miles. He had come back to her. But he appeared to be still vexed as he glowered at Lord Walsing.

His lordship could scarcely fail to take note of Miles's tall, forbidding presence. He extended a white-gloved hand. "Ah, Bernard. I am so pleased you came after all."

"My lord!" Delia exclaimed. " 'Tis my cousin you address, Sir Miles Renwick."

"Forgive me, sir. So awkward at remembering names. I trust I have not given offense."

Miles sneered. "None whatsoever. I certainly would not have you suffer any great mental strain on my account."

His lordship clumsily withdrew the hand that Miles declined to take. Delia fidgeted with her fan, striving for some remark with which to break the tension. Miles was always so civil to everyone. Why had her cousin taken such a dislike to Lord Walsing, the most perfect of gentlemen?

She breathed a sigh of relief when the musicians in the gallery above the ballroom struck up the notes of the opening dance.

"Miss Renwick, could I persuade you to . . ." His lordship paused, squinting at Delia. "My word! I had no idea you had a twin sister."

Delia thought his lordship had taken leave of his senses when, with a gasp of indignation, she realized his meaning. Fanny Pryce had minced forward to stand beside Delia, adopting an almost identical pose with her outspread fan. Her ruffled white gown was all girlish femininity, clusters of golden ringlets framed her cherubic face, soft pink lips upturned in a delicate simper. Her twin sister? That fluffy little ninny? Delia winced. Was that how she appeared to Miles— and Lord Walsing?

"Pray do excuse me for being so forward," Fanny cooed, "but I arrived late and have not had a chance to greet anyone. Colonel Renwick, still here in Stratford? Such good fortune for us ladies."

Miles bowed perfunctorily over Fanny's hand.

"And dear Miss Renwick. I see you wore your ivory satin. How becoming! I did so admire it at the assembly last month."

Delia flushed with annoyance, but before she could reply to

Fanny's seemingly artless chatter, the girl had turned breathlessly to face his lordship.

"And Lord Walsing. I have been dying to be presented ever since I saw you driving down Church Street last Sunday."

"Charmed, I'm sure. Miss—Miss . . ."

As his lordship floundered for the name, Delia could not forbear shooting a triumphant glance at Miles. So much for all of Fanny's shameless boasting to the colonel about her intimate acquaintance with Lord Walsing in America. But it was his lordship that Miles regarded with contempt, not Fanny.

"Miss Frances Pryce," Fanny filled in when Lord Walsing showed no sign of recollection. "Surely, sir, you must recall all the times I visited your family in New York."

Lord Walsing froze, his fair countenance waxing paler. "Well, I—I . . ."

"You cannot imagine how *interested* I have been in renewing our acquaintance," Fanny purred.

Delia tapped her foot with impatience. Did that foolish girl have no sense of decorum? Anyone but Fanny would realize that his lordship found her attentions excessively embarrassing. He tried to retreat, but Fanny stepped after him, saying, "Oh, listen. They are about to begin the cotillion."

She waited with such a suggestive expression on her face that there was naught poor Lord Walsing could do but excuse himself to Cordelia and lead Fanny out to dance.

"What daylight robbery," Delia fumed, completely forgetting the fact that the sun had set long ago. "He was on the verge of asking me!"

She glanced up to see Miles's reaction, but her cousin had lapsed into thoughtful silence, stroking his fingers across his chin, a deep wrinkle in his brow as he studied Lord Walsing arranging himself across from Fanny in the set of dancers.

"Miles! Do you not think Fanny behaved shockingly forward? I do not know how Lord Walsing can contrive to smile at her in that charming manner. But there! His lordship always appears so amiable."

" 'There's no art to find the mind's construction in the face,' " Miles murmured.

Delia started to ask him what he meant by that, but she had no desire to encourage him to recite Shakespeare in the middle of the ballroom. Her shoulders slumped with dejection. "I daresay it made no difference to his lordship which of us he danced with. After all, Fanny and I look so much alike."

Miles's voice rumbled with amusement. "My dear Cousin, you do not resemble Miss Pryce in the least."

"Oh, Miles. You truly believe not?"

"You have much more fire in your countenance. Sometimes I swear your eyes remind me of blue flames, setting your whole face aglow."

Delia guiltily hung her head, unable to meet his eyes. "I suspect you refer to my dreadful temper." She swallowed. "Miles, I want to tell you how sorry I am that—"

But her apology was cut off as Lieutenant Turner elbowed his way forward. "Forgive my impatience, Miss Renwick, but you did promise me this dance."

Miles stepped back. "My fault entirely, Lieutenant, for keeping my cousin here talking."

There was naught for Delia to do but allow the officer to lead her away. As they took their place in the set, she fretted, convinced that she would know no peace until she had made up her latest quarrel with Miles. It helped not a jot to see him standing up with one of those giggling Gunthrope wenches. Delia's only consolation was that Miles was pledged to claim her for the first waltz.

But Lord Walsing's musicians proved excessively perverse, striking up a reel as the next number, followed by a minuet. Delia began to despair, fearing that mayhap Lady Herkingstone with her old-fashioned notions had forbade the waltz to be played. In the next dance, Delia found herself standing up with Michael Devon. Propriety dictated that the young man could not spend the entire evening in Rosamund's pocket. There was no rule, however, to prevent him from boring on forever about Miss Leighton's many virtues.

As they glided together, Delia desperately sought a change of subject, throwing out a question about Devon's service in the military. Much to Delia's delight, the man showed more inclination to talk about Miles than himself.

"Sir Miles, I mean," Devon remarked with a laugh, taking care not to trod upon Delia's slippered foot. " 'Tis still difficult for me to become accustomed to the title, having been his friend before he was knighted."

Delia was ashamed to reveal that she knew so little about her own relation, but she could not refrain from asking, "Oh, the title is a recent acquisition?"

"Since Waterloo. For years of distinguished military service."

It took little prodding to induce Devon to recount how Miles had organized his own cavalry regiment at a time when Wellington's army stood badly in need of mounted soldiers. His troop had served all through the rigors of the Peninsular campaign, gaining fame as one of the most disciplined and daring units in the army.

"I should not be here now if it weren't for Miles." Devon shuddered. "At the battle of Ciudad Rodrigo, our cavalry unit plunged too far into the enemy line. We were quickly surrounded, but Miles slashed his way forward, forcing the French to give us an opening. When I lost my sword, he placed his shoulder between a French saber and my head."

Delia sighed, remembering how Miles had jokingly passed off all references to his wound. It occurred to her that she had not taken enough pains to really get to know her cousin. She looked wistfully to where Miles was putting a beaming Lady Herkingstone through her paces.

"Your account of my cousin's heroism comes as no surprise to me," Delia said. "After all, did he not save me from the clutches of a horrible dragon?"

"I—I beg your pardon?"

Delia spent the rest of the dance trying to explain away her odd remark. When the music stopped, Devon drifted irresistibly back toward Rosamund. Delia's own attention was claimed by Miss Pym.

"I am glad to see you are recovered from your illness," she said to the elderly woman. "I trust it had nothing—nothing to do with that day. I mean, the toads . . ."

Miss Pym gave a tinkling laugh. "Good gracious, no! After all, I didn't eat them. 'Twas nothing but an annoying bout of influenza." She ducked behind her fan so that only her large, bright eyes peered over the rim. Delia was beset by a strong suspicion that the silk screen concealed a blush spreading over the little woman's cheeks.

"I—I was wondering if your papa suffered from the same complaint. He is not present this evening."

"Miss Pym! You know Papa never attends these affairs if he can avoid them."

"I thought that mayhap this once . . ."

"No, he is at home, likely reading his Shakespeare."

"How delightful. He is wise to avoid these tiresome crushes. I daresay I shan't stay long tonight, either. At my age . . ." Her voice trailed away, her eyes growing misty as if her thoughts wandered far from the ballroom. Then she started, seeming to snap to an awareness of her surroundings.

"Well, I won't keep you, my dear. Doubtless you are eager to get back to your handsome gentleman. I know what it is like to be young and in love."

Delia's eyes widened as Miss Pym bustled off to collect her wrap. Why, who on earth did the little spinster fancy Delia was in love with? True, she had a decided partiality for Lord Walsing, but she had never indulged in any vulgar display of emotion for the man. Puzzling over Miss Pym's words, Delia unconsciously began to hum when the orchestra struck up the next piece of music, her foot tapping out the three-quarter time.

Three-quarter time. The waltz! Delia felt a strong arm encircle her waist. She spun around, brushing up against the hard plane of Miles's chest.

"Cousin," he said softly. "Our dance."

Oddly breathless, she placed her hand within his warm grasp, her heart pounding out a rhythm of its own. Miles had a positive talent for taking her completely unawares. As they glided into the midst of the swirling dancers, she struggled to find her voice.

"I—I did not have the opportunity to finish my apology." She forced herself to meet his gaze, summoning up an expression of earnest repentance. "I want you t-to know how sorry I am for being such a shrew earlier. I hope you—you are able to f-forgive me."

Miles's dark eyes glinted. "My dear Cordelia, when you look at me like that, I could forgive you anything."

Delia promptly stared down at his waistcoat, feeling the warmth steal into her cheeks. Normally a graceful dancer, she missed a step, causing Miles to blunder into Devon and Rosamund.

"Take care, Cousin." Miles chuckled. "You nearly caused me to tred upon the hem of your lilac-pink dress."

"Oh, Miles, pray do not say such things. I should not like to embarrass Rosamund by letting anyone know that."

"Never fear. The secret is safe with me."

He whirled her around in a graceful circle before adding, "I am glad you gave the gown to Rosamund. 'Twould have been wasted on you."

"What?" Delia croaked.

"You in that dress would be 'to gild refined gold, to paint

the lily, to throw a perfume on the violet' and—I beg your pardon, Delia. 'Twould seem I am at it again. Please do not be angry. I could not help it."

She laughed shakily. How could one possibly be angry with such sentiments, no matter how they were expressed?

Miles continued, "If I do not take refuge in jests or hide behind Master Shakespeare, I fear I am too bashful a fellow to express my deeper emotions."

His cheeks were tinged with pink, the teasing light in his eye softened to a warm glow, and she realized there was much truth in his lightly spoken words. His hand tightened upon her waist, drawing her closer. She wondered if her feet continued to touch the marbled floor or if Miles was not raising her off the ground, lifting her into a world spun of bright music and dizzying color.

Her hand remained nestled within his after the waltz came to an end. She pulled back as reluctantly as he released her. His lips twisted into a strange half-smile. "I thank you for the dance, Miss Renwick."

She made a prim curtsy. "You're very welcome, Sir Miles."

Delia thought they might have remained in the midst of the dance floor all night staring into each other's eyes. But Fanny insinuated herself between them, reminding Miles that he was pledged to her for the next dance. As Miles left her with a rueful backward glance, Delia vigorously fanned her flushed cheeks, trying to regain possession of her faculties. A dozen confusing sensations assaulted her until she felt peculiarly light-headed. She did not even retain enough presence of mind to avoid the squire's obnoxious son when he staggered up to ask her to dance.

Delia had never liked Bernard Newbold, with his sly, piglike eyes, thickset neck, and spotted complexion. Nor had he ever shown much preference for her since the childhood episode in which she had cracked his skull with a cricket bat for attempting to tie her braids into knots. The years had not done much to improve Bernard, who was still a clumsy bully, Delia decided as he leered, making her an awkward bow.

But it was not until they began moving through the figures of the next cotillion that Delia realized the man was shockingly well to live. He weaved on his feet as he spun her about, breathing the fumes of strong spirits into her face.

" 'Pon my word, Mish Renwick," he slurred. "You've grown into a . . ." He paused to hiccup. "A handshume piece.

How come I ne'er thought to dishtinguish you with—with my notish before?"

Delia did not know. She only wished to escape his notice now. The other couples giggled when Bernard circled completely out of their set, becoming quite befuddled as he stumbled through the dancers trying to find his way back to Delia.

She seized her opportunity, slipping out of the line herself and through a set of double French doors leading out onto a terrace that ran the whole length of the ballroom. Leaning against the wrought-iron balustrade, Delia issued a sigh of relief, the night breeze cooling her heated cheeks.

Below her stretched a charming vista of clipped green hedges and rosebushes circling a pond. The full moon painted transparent shimmers upon the rippling water. Swans arched their long white necks, gliding with stately grace amongst the floating lily pads. Delia drank in the beauty of the scene, drawing in a deep breath. The air was redolent with the heady perfume of . . . of gin!

She whirled around to find Bernard lurching toward her, swilling from a tiny flask that he secreted back inside his coat pocket. He rocked precariously on his heels, squinting, his mouth splitting into a porcine grin.

"Sho there you are. Bad mann'rs, Mish Renwick. Bad mann'rs indeed. Running 'way from y'r partner. But shall forgive you for shake of one lil' kish."

Delia stiffened in outrage, wishing she had a cricket bat now. "Oh, go douse your head in cold water, Bernard, and stop making such a cake of yourself."

"Show you whosh a cake." He lunged at her, attempting to squeeze her tight against him. He was so drunk, so clumsy, that Delia braced her hands against his paunchy stomach, having no difficulty keeping him at bay. But she could not shake the varlet loose, either. It was truly revolting the way his thick, wet lips strained toward her, making disgusting smacking noises. If he did manage to kiss her, she was certain she would be ill for a week.

Doubling up her fist, she cracked her knuckles into Bernard's pug-shaped nose. She winced as her tender flesh came up against the hard cartilage. Astonished at her own strength, she watched Bernard fly backward. But she soon realized it was not of her doing. The stocky man was being yanked from behind by Miles.

Delia scarcely recognized Miles's features, which were distorted with rage, his dark eyes narrowed to steely slits. Miles grabbed the stocky man by his coattails and the seat of his pants, lifting him off his feet. Bernard's arms flapped wildly through the air; he emitted one terrified yelp as Miles swung him forward, pitching him off the balcony.

Stunned, Delia watched Bernard plop into the pond, sinking like a rock amidst the frightened swans. "Miles! I do not believe he can swim."

Miles dusted off his hands as if he had just touched something vile. "Oh? Was there a pond down there?" Compressing his lips, he placed a possessive arm about Delia's shoulders, regarding with indifference Bernard's efforts to surface.

Choking and spluttering, Newbold finally recovered his footing, the water reaching only shoulder-level. Pursued by the furious, hissing swans that were beating their wings at him, he at last reached the safety of the pond's edge.

Shaking water from his hair like a soaked mongrel, Bernard glared back up toward the balcony. "Doxy," he roared at Delia. "Amazon! You'll pay for this."

Delia giggled. "Miles, he's so drunk he thinks I threw him off the balcony."

But when she glanced at her cousin, Miles showed no sign of sharing her amusement. "I'll drown that bastard yet," he ground out between clenched teeth.

To Delia's alarm, he strode to the balcony rail, preparing to climb down after Bernard. Delia flung herself at Miles, wrapping her arms about his waist in a woefully inadequate attempt to hold him back. She could feel the tension coiled in his powerful body. Never had she seen Miles so furious. She verily believed him ready to kill Newbold. A tremor passed through her.

"No, please, Miles. He is not worth the effort."

"Let me go, Delia. I'll suffer no man to speak that way to the woman I—"

Miles broke off, shaken by the sudden revelation. It was as though a flash of lightning had illuminated a darkened sky. The woman I love, he completed the thought. His fury against Newbold fled in the face of this astonishing revelation. But when had he fallen in love with Cordelia? When he had danced the waltz with her? Or had it been the day they had sat on the bank of the Avon and talked? Or when he had seen her with young Tom Leighton chasing the frog in the garden? Nay, it must have been even before that, on the hillside when he had stolen the first kiss. Damme, what did it matter when? He loved her.

Lost in wonderment over this discovery, he gazed down at the outline of her delicate profile bathed in moonlight. Her slender arms were still hugging him tightly.

"Nay, Miles," she pleaded. "You will cause the most dreadful scandal. And—and look. Bernard has already passed out beneath the bushes.

"Please," she added in a small voice. "Please stay here with me."

Delia thought that her words exercised a soothing effect on Miles. She felt him relax, his eyes fixing on her face with an unreadable expression. She flushed as it dawned on her that she was clutching him hard against her. But when she attempted to draw away, he slipped one arm around her waist, using his free hand to caress a stray ringlet back from her cheek. "My—my poor darling. Did he hurt you?"

Delia started to disclaim, but she could not resist the warm sympathy in Miles's voice, the temptation to play the wounded heroine proving too great to withstand. "Well," she said with a sniff, holding up her hand, "I—I bruised my knuckles when I punched his nose."

Miles reverently carried the injured fingers to his lips, kissing them one by one, but when he reached her thumb, his gravity forsook him. He threw back his head, his rich, booming laughter ringing in Delia's ears.

"Oh Delia, Delia," he murmured when he had regained control. "My sweet little firebrand. Mayhap 'tis fortunate for Bernard that I arrived when I did."

Delia feigned a pout at his teasing. 'Twas most improper to be standing here like this within the circle of Miles's embrace, an inner voice scolded her. She responded to this stricture of her conscience by nestling closer to his chest, fanning her lashes demurely over her eyes.

"Jest if you will, sir, but I am excessively grateful to you for rescuing me again. I do not know how I will ever repay you."

The cords in Miles's arms tensed, crushing her against him. "Perhaps with a cousinly kiss," he said huskily.

Delia's lips trembled. Miles was regarding her with that same singular expression she had seen on Michael Devon's face when he looked at Rosamund.

Tilting her head, she quivered as she offered Miles her cheek. But he twisted her around and captured her lips instead.

The kiss he bestowed on her was far from cousinly. The sweet, warm exploration of his mouth sent rushes of fire snapping along her veins. Delia's senses spun until she melted against him, clinging to him for support.

When at last he raised his head, she took a great shuddering breath to steady herself.

"Delia," he whispered. But the spell that seemed woven around them was shattered when a group of rowdy young people burst onto the balcony to enjoy the fresh air, followed by several clucking dowagers to chaperon.

Miles thrust Delia a decorous distance away. "I had best escort you back in to your aunt," he said in calm accents, as though nothing remarkable had occurred.

Perhaps to him it had not, Delia thought dejectedly. Her roguish cousin was the sort to have kissed a good many willing females. When he led her back inside, the bright glitter of the ballroom seemed oddly depressing after the secluded magic of the balcony.

Miles settled Delia into a chair, telling her he would fetch a glass of lemonade. She was looking decidedly overheated. Resentfully, she watched him head for the refreshment table, appearing quite cool, not a hair out of place. Delia self-consciously tried to smooth her own disheveled curls.

Nearby, she heard Squire Newbold's loud voice and winced. Whatever would the man say when he found his son, sopping wet, asleep under the rosebushes? At the moment, the bluff-faced squire was more concerned with harrying poor Lord Walsing to go shooting.

"I have been asking you forever," the squire growled.

"So—so many duties," his lordship stammered.

"Nonsense. Always time for shooting. I have the best coveys on my land. You don't want to make your aunt out a liar, do you, sir?"

"N-no, of course not, but—"

"But nothing. Lady Herkingstone has often boasted about the letters your father wrote. All about his son, the best marksman in America. The eye of an eagle."

"My father tended to exaggerate." Lord Walsing flushed, backing away until he bumped into Delia's chair. Looking down, he seized her with eagerness. "Miss Renwick! You have not honored me with a dance yet this evening."

Delia was astonished to hear herself reply, "Pray excuse me, my lord. I am very tired."

Frantic to escape the squire's tedious conversation, Lord Walsing paid no heed to her words, all but dragging Delia onto the dance floor. To her dismay, the orchestra launched into another waltz. She had so counted on having that dance with Miles.

The thought startled her. Only a fortnight ago, she would have given all she possessed to be in Lord Walsing's arms. Now she found his conversation tiresome compared with Miles's teasing, his sparkling humor. Must his lordship agree with everything she had to say? His attentiveness, his civility, began to seem carried to cloying excess.

For the first time, Delia took a critical study of his features. Why, the man's blue eyes were positively insipid. And there was something most displeasing about the way Lord Walsing smiled all the time.

Although she tried to suppress it, one of her father's readings from Shakespeare popped into her head. "That one may smile, and smile, and be a . . ." Be a what? Try as she might, Delia could not recall the rest of the line.

But it scarcely mattered. She had no desire to contemplate Shakespeare, even less Lord Walsing. In fact, Delia discovered with wonderment, there was only one person in the world she desired to think about: Miles.

Chapter 7

Delia had no notion that summer could be so beautiful in Stratford. In the days following the ball, she ceased repining over the canceled visit to Brighton. How could she have ever been so silly as to wish to go there? The notion seemed perfectly absurd, especially on one fine morning when she returned from a ride with Miles.

Changing from her riding habit, she bounded down the steps to the first floor, her cheeks aglow more from the way she had caught Miles looking at her than from the exercise. Even Will appeared to nod his approval from the hall portrait. Delia giggled, pausing long enough to give the solemn-faced Elizabethan poet a mock curtsy.

Nothing could ruffle her good humor this morning. What a glorious ride she and Miles had had over the countryside. Since he had been a cavalry officer, it did not astonish her at all to discover that her cousin had a very good seat. He looked so dashing on horseback, and he had not quoted Shakespeare one time. No, not even when they had galloped past the quaint cottage where Anne Hathaway had lived before her marriage to the Bard.

With a skip in her step, Delia waltzed toward the parlor to see if Miles had finished changing and come downstairs yet. To her astonishment, she found Miss Pym on the point of rising from the settee and taking leave of Aunt Violet. Not that it was surprising that Miss Pym should call on Delia's aunt, but the true source of wonderment was scrambling to his feet from the wing-back chair. Papa!

Delia's jaw dropped open as she took in the scene. An empty cup and saucer on the little table by her father's elbow bore mute testimony to the fact that Mr. Renwick had emerged from his study to drink tea with the ladies. Papa, who on more than one occasion had assured Delia he would rather *"be a kitten and cry mew"* than waste his time in such dull-witted fashion.

Miss Pym fluttered over to Delia. "My dear, a most timely arrival, indeed."

"Good morning, Miss Pym. I am sorry to have come just as you are on the point of leaving."

" 'Tis I who should apologize for calling at such an early hour, but I have been so busy." The little woman clasped her hands together. "All these preparations for the production of *Othello.*"

Delia stole an anxious glance at her father. Mere mention of that project was enough to send Walter Renwick up into the boughs. He had expressly forbidden Delia to have anything to do with it, nay, even to speak of the production.

Miss Pym smiled demurely. "I have persuaded your papa to permit you to assist us, Miss Renwick."

Delia cringed, waiting for her father's angry contradiction. When Papa nodded in affable agreement with Miss Pym's statement, Delia felt a strong need to be seated. She sank into the chair her father had vacated, staring at him as if he had suddenly sprouted wings.

Mr. Renwick cleared his throat. "Of course, I have not given you permission to do any acting, Delia."

"Oh, no, I quite understand your scruples upon that head, sir," Miss Pym cooed. "Though, I assure you, our performance will be conducted with the utmost decorum and respectability."

"Then what—what am I to do?" Delia faltered.

"The ladies desire you to design the scenery," Aunt Violet said. "I fear I have been doing a little vulgar boasting, showing your sketchbook to Miss Pym."

"Not at all. Your niece is most talented with pen and ink. I do hope she will be persuaded to put her remarkable abilities to our use." Miss Pym cocked her head to one side like an eager bird, awaiting Delia's reply.

Although Delia found she had little interest in the *Othello* production these days, she could do naught but state her willingness to help with the sets, especially in view of Papa's startling change of heart.

After expressing her pleasure at Delia's acceptance, Miss Pym gathered up her reticule and prepared to depart. Still feeling unnerved by the shock she had received, Delia remained where she was while her father and Aunt Violet walked with Miss Pym out to her gig.

Delia slumped back against the cushions, marveling. She would have given a monkey to know what persuasions Miss Pym had employed to convince Papa. Mayhap her parent was mellowing with age.

Picking up her father's empty cup and saucer, she started to return them to the tea tray when Delia noticed a sheet of paper settled beneath the delicate china. A quick perusal told her that it was a letter addressed to Papa. Evidently he had been reading it upon Miss Pym's arrival and had absentmindedly set it aside. Delia rose to her feet with the intention of returning it to him. She did not mean to pry into her father's personal mail but could not refrain from doing so when one of the phrases caught her eye. The letter was from one of Papa's old acquaintances in Warwickshire who wrote to say, "You may be interested to know that your former home, Renwick Manor, is up for auction again."

Her heart thudding with excitement, Delia rushed out into the entrance hall. Her father was just heading to his study when Miles came striding down the steps looking very dapper in a square-cut forest-green jacket and cream-colored breeches. He grinned at Delia.

"My dear Cousin, you never cease to amaze me. That any woman could change her clothes with such swiftness—"

But Delia interrupted him, waving the letter about. "Oh, Miles! Papa! Renwick Manor is up for sale."

Papa paused at his study door, frowning. She continued on in a rush. "That horrid man who bought our house died and his widow says the place is too much for her. Papa, we could have the manor back again."

She glanced eagerly from Miles to her father. Miles froze on the last step. Looking exceedingly uncomfortable, he fixed his gaze on the portrait of Shakespeare. Mr. Renwick's shoulders sagged, the age lines about his eyes appearing to deepen. Then he stalked over and snatched the letter from Delia's hand.

"You have no business reading my private correspondence, miss."

"I—I didn't mean to, Papa. You left it lying in the parlor. Oh, but to move back to our old home!"

"We are better off situated here in Stratford." Her father turned on his heel, then strode away without another word. The study door slammed behind him.

276

Delia's excitement faded, to be replaced by a hollow sense of disappointment. To think that there was a chance to have their beloved old home back again, and her father flung it away without a second thought. Her eyes drifted toward the portrait of Shakespeare. "Better off for whom, Papa?" she said bitterly. "Living in this wretched cottage certainly never did my stepmother any good."

When she encountered the look of stern reproof in Miles's eyes, mingled with a certain amount of sympathy, Delia lowered her head. Walking slowly back into the parlor, she dropped down upon the settee. Miles followed her and stood leaning against the mantel of the fireplace. A constrained silence descended upon them.

Despite the new feeling of intimacy that had sprung up between them, there were still two subjects they avoided.

Neither Amaryllis nor Delia's unhappy relationship with her father were ever discussed by herself or Miles, for fear of disturbing their newly found harmony.

After staring thoughtfully at the fire irons for many long moments, Miles straightened his shoulders as though arriving at some decision.

"Delia, I fear I shall have to be leaving Stratford for a while."

Her head snapped up, her heart turning over in dismay. After her disappointment about the manor, this was not the sort of tidings she cared to hear.

"How sudden," she said. "You mentioned nothing about going away during our ride this morning."

Miles scowled, thrusting his hands deep into his jacket pockets. "I expect it slipped my mind. Tedious matters of business. I cannot remain such an idle fellow forever."

"I suppose not," she whispered. Nor could he be expected to remain at Rose Briar Cottage forever, she thought sadly. At one time, all she had desired was to see Miles riding away. Now the prospect filled her with sensations of deepest melancholy. She forced a brittle smile to her lips.

"I—I trust you do not mean to abandon us completely, Cousin, but will return soon for another visit."

"I shall, so have all your worms, crickets, and spiders in readiness." He crossed the room, then took both her hands within his strong grasp, drawing her gently to her feet. "For I don't mean to stay away from you for long."

Delia attempted a chuckle at Miles's teasing references to

her prank, but the laughter constricted in her throat when she saw the intent look in his dark brown eyes. Currents raced through her pulses and her lips tingled, certain that Miles was about to bestow upon her one of his "cousinly embraces."

But at that moment Aunt Violet bustled into the parlor and Delia was forced to be content with a handshake.

Delia stood amidst a rainbow array of paint pots, ruefully staring at what seemed like miles of canvas flats propped against the walls of the ballroom at Walsing Park. Design scenery, indeed! How had she ever let herself be cozened into this mess? Her notion of submitting sketches with her plans for the sets, then slipping back to Rose Briar Cottage, had quickly been put to rout by Lady Herkingstone. The next Delia knew she was supervising the actual construction of the flats, the workers her ladyship had engaged being quite adept at painting barns but rather clumsy at transforming plain canvas into the canals of Venice, the streets of Cyprus.

Sighing, Delia lifted her brush, glad that she had worn one of her oldest gowns and tied her hair back with a scarf. Mayhap it was just as well that Lady Herkingstone kept her so busy. It left her little time to sit in her room moping over Miles's continued absence. Gone over a fortnight, and not a word from the villain. She had thought that a very lasting friendship had developed between them.

The hand wielding the brush faltered. Nay, she lied. Friendship was by far too paltry a word to describe her relationship with Miles. No other *friend* had ever had the ability to make her feel as breathless as if she stood teetering on the brink of an extremely high precipice. And yet no one but Miles had ever given her such a sense of security, of belonging. But it would seem that the time they had spent together meant nothing to him.

Pursing her lips, Delia dipped her brush into the pale blue pot, then splashed it onto the Venetian sky with a vigor that sent drops spraying everywhere. Well, no matter how strangely Miles made her feel, she was not about to make the mistake of fancying herself in love. Whenever the great Sir Miles deigned to return, he would have a very cool reception awaiting him.

She tried to block him from her mind, but oh, how empty, how dull Rose Briar seemed without him. What if . . . What if he never meant to return? The sudden tears that misted her eyes were entirely owing to the paint fumes, she told herself.

Although she attempted to suppress her imagination, she began to wonder if some other young lady was enjoying his "cousinly" attentions. After all, the man was a dreadful flirt, never appeared to harbor a single serious thought where the ladies were concerned. Delia blinked fiercely, forcing herself to concentrate on the canvas flats. Fretting about Miles's perfidy could only bring on a headache. The din in the ballroom was enough to do that without worrying what or who might be keeping him from her side.

Around Delia and her crew of painters chaos reigned as all available servants were pressed into the service of transforming the ballroom into a temporary theater. Hammers banged constructing rows of benches in a semicircle in front of the newly erected stage below the musicians' gallery. Lord Walsing might come to regret heartily turning over his ballroom to Lady Herkingstone for her production. Not that the poor man had much choice in the matter.

Miss Pym skittered about directing the housemaids in their task of covering the classical tapestry scenes with plain gold brocade. A pale, distracted Mrs. Forbes-Smythe met with still another group to inspect materials for costumes, slipping off to a corner for a pull at her smelling salts whenever Lady Herkingstone was not looking.

In the center of all this pandemonium, her ladyship rehearsed her principal actors in their scenes. With many shrill cries and the wringing of hands, Fanny Pryce as Desdemona protested her innocence to her lord and master. Delia paused in her brush strokes to watch Bernard Newbold rail his accusations of infidelity. The squire's stocky son showed surprising histrionic talent, Delia was obliged to admit. He might make a creditable Othello if her ladyship could keep him sober the night of the performance. At least he shouted his lines loudly enough, which was more than could be said for Fanny. "Now the strangling scene," Lady Herkingstone commanded. Delia nearly kicked over a paint bucket when Bernard leaped at poor Fanny, his thick hands closing around her neck, a look of vicious pleasure upon his face.

"Stop calling Fanny *Cordelia*, Bernard," her ladyship snapped. "you have the wrong play. That's *King Lear*."

Delia shuddered, glad that she was not playing Desdemona. She could not help thinking that it was her own face Bernard imagined when he pretended to throttle Fanny. The man had made it clear by his surly looks that he had not forgiven Delia his ducking in the pond.

Just when Delia thought Fanny would turn blue, her ladyship threw up her hands, exclaiming. "No, stop! Stop! This will not do at all."

Bernard reluctantly released the girl. Fanny sank down on one of the benches, rubbing the red fingermarks upon her neck.

"No, the strangling scene must go," Lady Herkingstone said.

Miss Pym paused in measuring out the gold brocade long enough to exclaim, " 'Must go,' Amelie? Why, the entire tragedy turns upon that one event."

Lady Herkingstone shook her head. " 'Tis immoral. The very notion of a man choking his own wife . . . No, I don't like it. 'Twill have to be changed."

Delia turned back to her painting to hide her smile. A brisk argument ensued between her ladyship and Miss Pym, but Delia did not hear the result of it. Her attention was distracted by one of Walsing's stable boys, who pointed to the canvas with pride. "What do you think of the Venetian galley, Miss Renwick?"

Somehow the majestic ship of Delia's sketch had failed to materialize. But she did not have the heart to tell the lad that his painting reminded her most forcibly of a boat she'd seen last week punting down the Avon.

Rubbing one shoulder grown stiff from wielding her brush, Delia gasped when she saw Lord Walsing enter the ballroom. He brandished the most evil-looking curved sword she had ever set eyes upon.

"Look here, Aunt," he called. "Will this do for your Moorish guard? I found it mounted on the library wall."

Her ladyship ceased bickering with Miss Pym long enough to inspect the weapon. "Ah! The very thing." She seized the sword from Lord Walsing, and took a few wild swings with it, causing Fanny and Bernard to duck behind one of the benches.

"This sword has been in the family for years. One of our ancestors brought it back from the Crusades."

"Dear me," Lord Walsing said. "Perhaps it is too valuable to be employed as a prop."

"Nonsense." Her ladyship pointed the sword in Cordelia's direction. "Miss Renwick's coachman has undertaken to play the guard. She will see that he takes proper care of such a cherished relic."

Delia shrank back. What other tiresome responsibilities

would her ladyship thrust upon her before this affair was done? Her eyes traveled to where poor Miffin was being fitted into a Hungarian busby by Mrs. Forbes-Smythe. He looked at Delia with an expression of most pathetic appeal. His only crime had been driving Cordelia to Walsing Park, but no one of any rank or station was safe from Lady Herkingstone's quest for actors.

Delia set her brush aside, stopping long enough to mix some colors to get just the shade of sea green she imagined Venetian canals to be. While she did so, she noticed Lord Walsing seated close to Fanny on the bench, engaged in intimate conversation. Strange, Delia thought as she watched them covertly, not wishing to be caught staring. She would never have thought the simpering little Miss Pryce fascinating enough to so absorb his attention. But she was seen quite often in Lord Walsing's company of late. Stranger still, Delia found she did not mind in the least.

Dipping her brush in to test the new shade on the canvas, Delia failed to notice the tall, broad-shouldered man who slipped into the ballroom behind Fanny and Lord Walsing.

With such a scene of confusion spread out before him, it took Miles several minutes before he recognized Delia as the lady bundled into the gypsy-red scarf and painting-spattered gown. Grinning, he strode in her direction.

Although he knew he was taking his life into his hands, he could not resist sneaking up behind Delia and saying, " 'Good morrow, Kate, for that's your name, I hear.' "

She spun around, smearing a streak of green water across a white, puffy cloud. "Miles!" she squeaked.

The rouge! How like him it was to steal upon her in this fashion, when she was looking so positively dreadful. She tugged off the scarf, trying to remember all the cutting things she had meant to say to him about being gone so long without so much as writing a line. Instead it took all of her restraint not to fling herself against his chest.

Those dark eyes twinkling with mischief, that teasing smile—how she had missed them! "When did you . . . I—I am so glad . . . I mean . . . Oh, you did come back!"

His wicked eyebrows jutted up. "Why Cousin? Can it be that you have missed me?"

She smoothed out her ringlets, striving for as much dignity as she could under the circumstances. "Well, even when one recovers from the toothache, it takes a while to become accustomed to the fact that the nuisance is gone."

When Miles laughed, Delia reveled in the sound. He extended his hand but jerked back when she nearly placed her dripping brush against his palm. Carefully guarding his immaculate buff-colored jacket, he dabbed his lined handkerchief on her nose.

"This shade of green definitely becomes you, my dear."

Delia blushed, wondering how Miles could regard her with such a look of warm admiration when she knew she must appear a perfect fright.

"As much as I would like to chat with you," she said, attempting to sound severe, "you can see I am fully occupied."

Miles settled on a nearby bench, stretching out his long legs, and yawning like a lazy great cat. "Do not stop on my account. I am only too happy to sit and watch you work. You may catch me up on all that has happened while I was gone."

Delia resisted the temptation to dab green specks all over his gleaming Hessians. "Well, Rosamund and Michael Devon have announced their engagement."

"That is not news. I could have guessed as much." The indolent smile on his face suddenly disappeared. "I saw that Newbold ruffian here. He has not been bothering you again, I trust? I swear I should have thrashed the blackguard, forced him to apologize."

Delia shrugged, then snatched a rag in an attempt to repair the damage to the cloud. "Bernard was so drunk, I daresay he would not even remember why he was apologizing."

Miles did not look satisfied, but he was startled by Lady Herkingstone bearing down upon him.

"Sir Miles!"

He snapped to attention with such alacrity, that Delia half feared her cousin would forget himself and salute her ladyship.

"So!" her ladyship said in frosty accents. "Now you return when all parts are cast, when the work is nigh completed."

He bowed, then spread his hands in a deprecating gesture. "Your ladyship, my regrets. The most pressing business—"

"Never mind." She slapped a quill pen into Miles's outstretched hand. "You may still make yourself of use."

Miles rolled his eyes desperately in Delia's direction, but she summoned up her sweetest smile and said, "Thank you, your ladyship. You have no idea how disappointed my cousin has been, thinking that he would be left out of the proceedings."

Miles arched one brow, the look in his eye telling Delia she would pay dearly for her remark at some future date. He attempted to return the quill pen to Lady Herkingstone.

"I cannot imagine how I might be of service. To the best of my knowledge, Shakespeare did finish that particular play and—"

"I need someone to copy out the changes I am making."

"Changes?" Miles looked at Delia in bewilderment. She broke into a sudden fit of coughing to hide her amusement.

"Yes, changes," her ladyship repeated, as if talking to an idiot. "You do not think we can play *Othello* as it is written?"

"Well, if 'twas good enough for Shakespeare—"

Her ladyship's voice was laced with patient condescension. "Sir Miles, you cannot believe that all of that play was written by Shakespeare. Alas, we have no pure copies of his works, only versions that have been amended by crude, vulgar actors.

"For example, the part of Bianca." Lady Herkingstone gestured to where the youngest Miss Gunthrope sat struggling to memorize her lines. "Shakespeare surely did not mean for her to be one of . . . one of those *sort of females*."

"He didn't?" Miles asked. "How very disappointing."

Her ladyship's glare quickly subdued his levity. "So we shall make her into a virtuous young lady whom Cassio may marry. And Othello shall not kill Desdemona or himself. 'Twill save the whole piece from ending on such an excessively morbid note."

Miles appeared too confounded to say anything. Apparently taking his silence for consent, her ladyship turned to Delia, who was yet struggling to contain her mirth.

"Miss Renwick, you shall not be obliged to do up those other flats of scenery. I have decided we will have no time to follow up *Othello* with a farce."

"You won't need one," Miles groused.

But his comment was lost on her ladyship, who was summoned away by the printer who had arrived to submit the engraved tickets of invitation for her approval. When she was out of earshot, Delia could no longer contain herself. "Oh, M-Miles. If you c-could but s-see your face."

She doubled over with peals of laughter at Miles's indignant expression. He regarded her, hands placed upon his lean hips. "Aye, you may well laugh, Cousin. But have you given any thought to what your papa will say if he gets wind of Lady Herkingstone's *trifling* changes?"

Delia's laughter abruptly ceased. Oh, dear. Papa. She had

been encouraged by the fact that her father was being so much more social of late. He had even invited Miss Pym to dine with them one evening. What if he decided to attend the play? The wrath of God destroying Sodom and Gomorrah would be nothing compared to Papa's reaction. She could imagine her outraged parent pulling all those painted flats down around Bernard's and Fanny's ears if they spoke the wrong lines. Delia closed her eyes, begging forgiveness for her blasphemy, and at the same time devoutly praying that Lady Herkingstone's play would be one social event her Papa would forgo.

Chapter 8

When Walter Renwick's ticket of invitation arrived, he paused long enough in his reading to wad up the red-and-gilt engraving and to fling it into the empty grate, much to the relief of his daughter. It was Delia's only source of relief the night of the performance.

All those days of preparation seemed like a well-ordered drill compared to the chaos backstage a bare half-hour before the play was to begin. Delia could scarcely hear the hum of the audience taking their seats over the din of frantically scurrying actors and workers behind the scenes. She shrank back to avoid being trampled by burly grooms bearing table, chairs, and other props into position. Taking one last examination of her painted scenery, Delia sighed in vexation. She had worked to the last possible moment. Indeed, Lady Herkingstone had kept both her and Miles so busy they had barely found two minutes to be alone together this past week. It was truly frustrating, for Delia had often thought Miles on the verge of telling her something important, but the time never seemed to be right. And now, after all Delia's valiant efforts, the paint on the white columns for the palace scenes was still not dry.

To make matters worse, Miles was not in his customary good humor this evening. Charging up to Delia, he waved sheets of bound parchment under her nose.

"Where does her ladyship want these blasted prompt sheets?"

"I haven't the least notion," Delia said. "Ask her yourself." Thank God, after tonight they would be done with this tiresome play. Wild horses would not persuade her ever to participate in another. She tried to flag down Bernard, Fanny, and the other actors to warn them about the wet paint, but no one paid the slightest heed to her.

Miles thumbed through the pages copied out in his own bold, sprawling hand and grumbled, "I cannot believe I took part in these abominable rewrites. I feel as if . . . as if I pried open Shakespeare's tomb and scattered his bones."

"Then why on earth did you so? With your vast charm, surely you could have dissuaded Lady Herkingstone from the changes."

"That woman is as stubborn as you are. The reason I helped was to keep the damage to the play at a minimum."

"How vastly noble of you!"

Miles's lips drew down into a rueful scowl. "I only hope your father never learns of my participation in this mess. 'Twould be enough to make him refuse me permission to——" Miles broke off, looking suddenly self-conscious.

"Yes?" Delia prompted breathlessly. "Permission to what?"

But before Miles could reply, they were interrupted by Mrs. Forbes-Smythe. Muffled in her shawl, the sharp-faced woman rubbed her thin arms, moaning. " 'Tis a disaster! A disaster! Certain death for all of us."

"My dear Mrs. Forbes-Smythe, calm yourself," Miles drawled. "No matter how bad the production, I do not think the audience will resort to violence."

Sniffing, she turned her back upon him, and clung to Delia for sympathy. "That boorish Squire Newbold is out there bellowing that all the French doors should be opened. Such a draft will be created. The actors will freeze. Influenza will spread amongst us."

Delia patted Mrs. Forbes-Smythe's trembling hand, trying to calm her, while hoping she would go away so that Miles would finish his statement. "The squire may be right, ma'am. With so many people crowded together, the ballroom will become odiously stuffy."

But Mrs. Forbes-Smythe refused to be convinced. "The squire is a selfish beast. He has layers of fat to keep him warm!" She glared from Delia to the unsympathetic, chuckling Miles. "I see I shall be obliged to stop him myself."

The woman stormed over to the canvas frontispiece strung across the width of the stage to serve as a curtain. Pawing at it, she groped for the slit that would allow her access to the audience.

Delia felt Miles close his hand over hers. He raised his eyebrows quizzically, jerking his head toward a door that would enable them to slip outside. Her heart racing, Delia nodded her willingness to follow him, only to find their hands rent apart by Lady Herkingstone striding onto the stage area.

"Margaret! What are you doing there?" her ladyship bellowed at Mrs. Forbes-Smythe. "Why are so many of the actors flitting about unprepared? 'Tis your task to see that they all get into their costumes."

For once Lady Herkingstone did not intimidate Mrs. Forbes-Smythe. She thrust the flap of the frontispiece aside as though fighting for her life. She started to step forward, shrieking the squire's name, when she froze, her hand upon the canvas. Delia saw the woman's face go white, apparently overset by the unexpected shock of so many eyes trained in her direction.

"Oh—oh, dear." She wobbled backward, allowing the canvas to fall back into place.

"Catch her, Miles," Delia cried out. "She's going to faint."

Miles reacted in time to fling himself behind the woman, who flopped into his arms, a dead weight, no partial swoon this time. She was completely insensible from her bout of stage fright. Miles rolled his eyes, looking about the cluttered stage for someplace to put her down.

"What am I supposed to do with her?" he roared to Delia, but she was scurrying about hunting for Mrs. Forbes-Smythe's smelling salts. Miles sank to one knee, supporting the sprawled woman against his chest. Delia knelt beside him, uncorking the *sel volatil*. Even as she waved the small bottle under the woman's thin nose, Delia was ashamed to discover that her thoughts were not on poor Mrs. Forbes-Smythe but Miles. He had said something about asking permission. Could he possibly mean asking Papa's permission to . . . to marry her? Even as her pulses fluttered at the notion, Delia told herself she was being absurd. It was unthinkable that any man would attempt a proposal of marriage in the midst of all this madness. Oh, but wouldn't it be just like Miles to do such a thing!

Yet when their eyes locked above Mrs. Forbes-Smythe's inert body, Delia found she did not care where they were. "Miles," she began softly, but jumped when she heard Lady Herkingstone bellow, "Useless creature!" Scornfully stepping over Mrs. Forbes-Smythe's legs, she seized Delia by the elbow. "Come with me, Miss Renwick. You shall supervise the costuming."

"B-but, your ladyship—" Delia's protests were ignored as

her ladyship yanked her to her feet. "Miles!" she cried, but there was little he could do to rescue her with Mrs. Forbes-Smythe draped over his lap. As Lady Herkingstone propelled Delia from the stage area, her last glimpse was of an extremely disgruntled Miles fanning Mrs. Forbes-Smythe with the script.

At the rear of the ballroom, a door discreetly painted to resemble the chamber's classical panels led to the backstairs employed by the servants at Walsing Park. Delia flattened herself against the wall as Lady Herkingstone dragged her up the steps. In addition to those concerned with the production, harried maidservants and footmen rushed along, preparing the sumptuous collation that would be served to the guests after the performance.

On the next floor, a long corridor ran the length of the manor's elegant bedchambers, many of which had been commandeered by Lady Herkingstone for use as dressing rooms. Lord Walsing strolled past the bustling actors in various stages of costuming. Completely oblivious to the general state of panic, he smirked to himself, whistling a merry little tune.

"Your ladyship," Delia tried to protest. "Please. I must go help Miles with . . ."

Her words fell on deaf ears. Never loosening her grip, Lady Herkingstone paused to scold her nephew. "Peter! What are you doing here?"

"I live here," he said in aggrieved tones. He leaned forward to smile at Cordelia. "Ah, Miss Renwick. Good evening. How pleasant—"

"Never mind that." Lady Herkingstone blocked his lordship's attempt to reach for Delia's hand. "Be off with you. You are very much in the way!"

"But, Aunt, I only came up to suggest to the players that they use the old set of servants' stairs when going down. There would be much less confusion."

Her ladyship snorted in scorn. "Those rickety old things. So poorly lighted, besides which one must then walk all the way through the kitchen."

Delia squirmed, trying to pry loose her ladyship's pinching fingers while the woman launched into an argument with her nephew. Delia's head began to throb. She began to see that much might be said for her father's method of enjoying Shakespeare, those quiet, dull readings in the peace of one's own home. She glanced back toward the stairs, hoping to see Miles come charging after her.

Lord Walsing at last conceded defeat. "Perhaps you are right, Aunt. 'Twould not do to have your actors tromping through the kitchen. My chef is such a temperamental fellow. French, you know, Miss Renwick." Walsing smiled at Delia. He attempted to take her hand one more time, but her ladyship struck his fingers aside.

"No more nonsense. You should be out front seeing to your guests, sir."

After his lordship bowed, departing in sulky silence, Lady Herkingstone complained to Delia, "That is what comes of attempting to raise a gentleman in the wilds of America. Peter has not the least notion of what is required of the lord of the manor. What shall I ever do with him!"

Her ladyship sighed, then snapped, "Why are you standing about, Miss Renwick? Go check on Fanny and those other silly girls. I want them belowstairs within five minutes."

Glad to procure a release for her bruised arm, Delia scurried to do her ladyship's bidding. If she made haste, she might yet find time to steal a few moments alone with Miles before the play began. Entering the chamber her ladyship indicated, Delia found Miss Pryce seated before an elegant French gilt mirror rubbing rouge into her cheeks. The maid had just finished dressing Fanny's pale curls.

"Is there aught else that you need, Fanny?" Delia asked.

"No, everything is quite perfect." Fanny stood up, preening in the charming gold-shot silk Venetian gown that comprised her costume. She settled a small hat trimmed with ermine on her head before turning to simper at Delia.

"So kind of you to come and inquire after me. And so generous. Alas, if I had been in your shoes, I fear I would have been quite green with envy."

Fanny placed her fingers to her lips, indulging in a titter. "But how silly of me. Your shoes would be much too large to fit me, would they not?"

Delia smiled sweetly. "Mayhap so, but I am glad to see they have made the hat big enough to fit your head."

As Fanny's smirk faded, Delia made her exit, adjuring the girl to hasten below by her ladyship's express command. Then Delia went to check on Miss Gunthrope. Although the girl was fully costumed, nerves were getting the better of her. She huddled in one corner retching into a chamber pot. Fortunately for Delia, Miss Pym arrived on the scene. Between the two women, they managed to get Miss Gunthrope on her feet.

289

Murmuring reassurances, they guided the pale-faced girl down the quiet hallway. Most of the other actors had already gone. Lady Herkingstone appeared herding the musicians toward the door that led to the orchestra gallery. Rosamund, who was to play the pianoforte, led the way looking like an angel in white. She pressed Delia's hand in passing, her face aglow with excitement.

"Do look, Delia," she whispered. "Michael has volunteered to play the tambourine so that we might be together this evening."

Delia followed Rosamund's gaze to where Michael Devon mingled with the other ladies and gentlemen carrying their violins. The fond way Rosamund stared at him no longer struck Delia as being so foolish as she had once thought.

Involuntarily, her own thoughts flew to Miles. Surely he could not be still below, holding the unconscious Mrs. Forbes-Smythe in his strong arms, arms that might be put to much better purpose. Delia blushed at her own imagination. If Miles did propose to her, what would she say to him? They seemed so ill-suited; Miles forever teasing; she losing her temper. Yet it was not their quarrels Delia found herself remembering but the way Miles had looked at her that night on the balcony, the warmth of his lips stealing over hers. . . .

She was startled from these reflections by a chilling scream. Even the redoubtable Lady Herkingstone blanched.

"What—what . . . ?" she stammered.

"I—I think it came from down below," Delia said. Everyone crowded forward, but her ladyship said. "You musicians take up your positions in the gallery. Miss Renwick, you come with me."

Her heart still racing with reaction to the terrifying sound, Delia ran after Lady Herkingstone, astonished that the elderly woman could set such a pace. When they reached the foot of the stairs, Miles leaped forward.

"Delia! Thank God! I heard that dreadful screech, then I could not find you anywhere."

He swept Delia into his arms, crushing her so tight that she could scarcely breathe a reply, but Lady Herkingstone shoved them apart.

"None of that, Sir Miles. A little propriety, if you please! Your cousin is all right, but who the dickens made that noise?"

The other cast members crowded around, but everyone was present, everyone except for Frances Pryce.

"Oh, Fanny! Fanny!" Miss Gunthrope wailed.

"Hush that noise! I have heard enough screeching," her ladyship barked. Before she could say anything more, a tall figure garbed in an apron emerged from the direction of the kitchen. His mustache bristling with rage, the chef carried a pink bundle in his arms. Fanny moaned, tears streaking down her cheeks.

"Par Dieu," the man exclaimed to Lady Herkingstone. "How am I to practice my art with young women tumbling into my kitchen? The sauce is quite ruined."

Ignoring the chef's indignant description of how Fanny had fallen down the backstairs, Miles hastened forward to take Fanny from him. Delia bristled at the way the girl's arms entwined themselves about his neck. He started to lay the whimpering Miss Pryce down on one of the props, a four-poster bed, when Delia rushed forward to intervene.

"No, not there, Miles. 'Tis not sturdy. Lady Herkingstone thought it immoral to have a real bed on stage, so we constructed a fake one of spare lumber parts."

His brow furring in exasperation, Miles pushed through the crowd of ladies squealing their concern and settled Fanny onto a chair. Delia was quick to help him unwind Fanny's arms.

Lady Herkingstone stomped her foot to gain attention. "Miss Pryce! What do you mean being so clumsy this close to performance time?"

"Clumsy!" Fanny sobbed, bending down to rub her ankle. "Someone flung me down those stairs. Quite on purpose." She glanced around, her eyes resting on Cordelia with angry accusation.

Delia gasped. Why that—that silly little chit! Did she dare imply that Cordelia had had anything to do with her accident? But it scarcely mattered what Fanny thought, for Lady Herkingstone dismissed the entire notion that anyone had assaulted Fanny as utter rubbish.

Miles frowned. "Did you actually see anyone behind you, Miss Pryce?"

"No, but I felt two great hands upon my— Oh, owwww!" Fanny lapsed into another howl as Miss Pym examined her ankle.

" 'Tis swelling," she pronounced in grim accents. "The child had definitely sprained it."

"Oh, no, I haven't!" Fanny made several efforts to rise, each of which sent her collapsing into sobs back on the chair. A solemn silence descended over the company. For a moment, Lady Herkingstone appeared daunted, her shoulders slumping in defeat. She gazed at the stage, the sets, the actors with despair until her eyes came to rest on Cordelia. Suddenly her ladyship straightened.

"Miss Renwick," she said in a soft, speculative manner.

"Y-your ladyship?"

Lady Herkingstone snapped her fingers to Miss Pym. "Convey Miss Pryce upstairs and remove her costume. Miss Renwick shall take her place."

Delia and Fanny chorused their objections at the same moment.

"No! No! I shan't give up my part to her!"

"Please, your ladyship. 'Tis impossible. I do not know the lines."

"Never fear. I shall prompt you from offstage. Now hurry, there is no time to lose."

Delia tried to dodge when her ladyship bore down upon her, remembering well the strength of the woman's grip. She winced when Lady Herkingstone seized her in the exact same spot as before.

"I don't want Miss Renwick for my Desdemona," Bernard Newbold was heard to say, but his protest produced no more effect than Delia's own.

"Miles, please!" Delia appealed to her cousin as her ladyship prepared to drag her away. "Your ladyship, my—my cousin had something important he wished to discuss with me."

But the perfidious man merely quirked one eyebrow, folding his arms across his chest. "Oh, no, nothing that wouldn't be better kept until after the performance."

Delia shot him a reproachful glance. Despairingly, she pleaded with her captor. "Please, my lady. I will never be able to act with a proper spirit. I have no feeling for Shakespeare. Ask Sir Miles. He will tell you. Miles?"

His dark eyes dancing with mischief, Miles grinned at her. "Pray, don't let my cousin's bashful modesty carry any weight with you, Lady Herkingstone. I am sure she will be splendid as Desdemona."

Delia's free hand curled into a fist, but to her intense frustration, Miles was not within striking range. "A pox on you!" she shrieked.

"Excellent, my dear," Lady Herkingstone said. "But save yourself for the performance.

Delia felt her palms grow damp with sweat as she stood offstage listening to Lieutenant Turner, who played the part of Iago, recite the opening prologue her ladyship had written. A thousand curses upon Miles. She blinked back her angry tears. He was likely sitting out there in the audience at this moment, waiting to see her make a complete fool of herself. And to think she had been so foolish as to imagine the man dying to declare himself! Why had she ever had anything to do with this wretched production or that roguish cousin of hers?

The least he could have done was to remain backstage and see her through this ordeal. Instead it was Bernard Newbold who hovered by her side, glaring at her, his thick lips fixed into a pout. Oh, but he did look ridiculous garbed in those striped Turkish trousers, and yellow satin sash, his head wrapped in a small silk turban, his face blackened with charcoal. What if she burst into a fit of nervous giggles onstage whenever Bernard addressed her?

Miss Pym, who stood on Delia's opposite side, afforded no more consolation than Bernard. Stepping forward to peer around the set at the audience, she wrung her small hands. "Oh, dear, oh, dear, Miss Renwick, and after I promised your papa that you would not act. Whatever will he say to me? I should never have called upon him this afternoon to persuade— Oh, dear! Oh, dear!"

Delia was far too much caught up in her own attack of nerves to pay any heed to Miss Pym's lamentations. The opening scenes in which Delia played no part sped by far too quickly for her peace of mind. It afforded her no comfort at all when she saw how badly the others were doing. In their nervousness, the men completely forgot Lady Herkingstone's strictures and crossed in front of each other. Delia's worst fear was realized when Lieutenant Turner in his black velvet doublet backed into the pillar she had painted. The villainous Iago came away with a white streak straight up his back, which sent ripples of mirth through the audience.

Delia placed a trembling hand over the region of her stomach, which was doing flip-flops. Onstage, Bernard said, " 'Here comes the lady; let her witness it.' "

An awkward pause descended. Bernard repeated in a louder voice, "I said 'Here comes the lady.' "

"Go on," Lady Herkingstone hissed. She placed her hand in the small of Delia's back and shoved. Delia stumbled out into the glare of the blazing lamps set below the stage. Her knees trembled, her throat constricted as she blinked at hundreds of staring eyes. She now understood what had caused poor Mrs. Forbes-Smythe to swoon.

The scenery began to sway before her eyes, when she gave herself a mental shake. She said to herself, "No, Cordelia Renwick. You will not so disgrace yourself."

Desperately, she sought for some way to get command of her feelings. When she caught sight of her aunt seated in the front row gaping at her in astonishment, an idea came to her. She would tell herself that she was not standing here in Lord Walsing's ballroom exposed to the ridicule of a tittering crowd. She and Aunt Violet were safely back in Papa's study. It was not Bernard who spoke the lines, but her father, droning over and over again the words she had so often absorbed without half realizing she did so.

Although she spoke too softly at first, to her amazement, Delia was able to repeat the lines her ladyship whispered. Soon, she went beyond that, discovering how much of Papa's reading she remembered without any prompting.

Delia could scarcely say when the magic began to take over, when the words took on a life and sense of their own. Suddenly the sky and the pillars she had painted became the streets of Cyprus. When she put Miles's face beneath Bernard's turban, she was able to pour out her affection for Othello with genuine feeling. Quite forgetting Miles had betrayed her to Lady Herkingstone, Delia's imagination soared, adding several inches to Bernard's height, darkening his hair, putting that particular sparkling light that was Miles's alone into Newbold's dull eyes.

In the last row of cushioned benches, Miles craned his neck forward, drinking in every word. Any compunction he had felt in abandoning his cousin to the clutches of Lady Herkingstone quite vanished. Why, Cordelia was magnificent. She even made Newbold and the others sound halfway intelligent.

Miles's eyes followed her progress across the stage, his senses aroused by the sight of her small, graceful figure outlined by the revealing pink gown. The stage lamps accented the pearly hue of her skin, the bright animation of her eyes, the golden glint of her curls. The musical flow of her voice so enchanted him that he nearly leaned against the plump dame who sat in front of him. When he finally realized the woman was giving him a haughty stare, Miles drew back, murmuring an embarrassed apology.

He fidgeted on the cushion, now heartily regretting his own refusal to play Othello as he watched the motion of Delia's soft pink lips set in the midst of her delicate, heart-shaped face. He would have ignored her ladyship's strictures that nothing so indelicate as kissing would take place upon her stage. He would have played out some scenes with Delia as would have rendered her ladyship speechless. Miles's lips curved into a smile of anticipation. Ah, but after the performance tonight . . . He had waited long enough. Despite the fact that Delia would be furious at him for not having rescued her, Miles had every confidence he could charm away her temper. He had received enough hints from Delia's earlier eagerness for him to speak that he dared to hope his proposal would not be unwelcome.

Miles turned to glare at those who sat near him on the benches, their whispers growing louder. What was the matter with these boors that they must speak whenever Delia was delivering her lines?

Mrs. Newbold, the squire's wife, said, "Who would have ever thought Fanny Pryce could display such talent?"

"Oh, Miss Pryce is a young lady with many surprising facets to her character," Walsing drawled.

Miles compressed his lips. Why, the damned fools! They had not realized the substitution. He became aware that many of the others around him labored under the same delusion. How could any of them mistake his spirited Delia, all fire and sparkle, for that bland little mouse, Fanny?

Miles suppressed his irritation, realizing that Delia would be given full credit when the performance reached its end. The play was well into the fifth act when Miles was further annoyed by a latecomer squeezing past him. Lord Walsing leaped to his feet, graciously offering his own seat before disappearing to stand at the back of the ballroom. When the other man finally settled himself on the bench, he went off into a sneezing fit. Miles directed a sidelong glance of reproach at Walter Renwick.

Walter Renwick! "Sir!" Miles croaked, which resulted in him being shushed from all sides. He watched in dumbfounded dismay as Mr. Renwick smoothed out the tails of a dark navy jacket cut in the latest fashion, his newly trimmed hair combed in such a way as to disguise his bald spot.

"I did not mean to startle you," the old man whispered, "but I thought I may as well come along and see this infamous production that has so absorbed Delia of late."

Miles flicked a nervous glance to the stage. Othello had just burst into his wife's bedchamber and Desdemona hastened forward to protest her innocence.

"You—you will not care for it, sir," Miles said, attempting to take Mr. Renwick by the arm, and leaning forward to block his view of the stage. "The most dreadful amateurish stuff."

Renwick pulled away, craning to see past Miles. " 'Twas pointed out to me that I have been neglecting my fatherly duties. Delia has worked so hard on the scenery. She would be disappointed if I did not at least—"

Even in the dim light at the back of the ballroom Miles could see his cousin Walter turn pale, his lips draw together into a tight, hard line.

Now we're for it, Miles thought with an audible groan. There was no possibility that Walter Renwick would not recognize his own daughter in the young lady who now dropped so dramatically to her knees, her golden curls falling back from her upturned, pleading countenance.

"Od's bodikins," Renwick muttered, heaving to his feet.

"Now, sir, I can explain," Miles began, but he saw that Renwick did not hear him. The man froze where he stood, his lips parting into an O of wonder. Delia had indeed risen to the height of her performance. Hands clasped before her, she begged Othello to believe she had wronged him not, to spare her life.

Completely forgetting that Lady Herkingstone had changed the script, she cried, " 'O, banish me, my lord, but kill me not!' "

Bernard, thrown off balance by lines to which he had no response, hissed, "What are you saying, Miss Renwick? That part is changed."

Still convinced that she was Desdemona, and fearing for her life, Delia caught hold of his hand. " 'Kill me tomorrow, let me live to-night!' "

"Stop it!"

" 'But while I say one prayer!' " Delia begged.

"I said, stop it!" roared the frustrated Bernard, wrenching his hand away. "I'm not going to strangle you, you silly chit. At least not yet."

The roar of laughter from the audience penetrated Delia's

haze. That, along with a small pillow shied at her head by an indignant Lady Herkingstone offstage. Overcome with confusion, she realized what she had done. Retreating to stand in the shelter of the fake canopy bed, she tried to gather her wits while Bernard moved center-stage to recite his speech that explained how he knew of his wife's innocence, that the true villain Iago was already on his way to the gallows.

Delia recovered enough to repeat the lines Lady Herkingstone whispered to her, magnanimously forgiving Othello for his mistaken accusations.

She said, "Now, my lord, may we all go forth merrily to the noble Cassio's wedding to his fair and virtuous Bianca."

"Sacrilege! Abomination!" a voice howled from the back of the audience. She and Bernard froze in startled silence, then Newbold stammered, trying to continue with his next speech. But heads in the audience were turning away, following the progress of a spare-framed man hurtling himself toward the stage.

"P-Papa!" Delia's heart sank into the toes of her satin slippers. With an agility that she never knew her parent possessed, Papa vaulted over the foot lamps, landing near Bernard with a loud *thunk*.

Delia shrank before the thick gray brows bristling over an enraged pair of pale blue eyes. Papa seized her by the wrist, his face mottled with anger. "My own daughter!" he choked. "OH! 'How sharper than a serpent's tooth it is to have a thankless child'!"

Bernard snatched off his turban and flung it down, so overset was he. The stocky young man made a pathetic attempt to absorb Walter Renwick into the performance.

"Villain!" he shrieked. "Unhand my wife."

"Your wife, sirrah!" Delia's mouth gaped open as Papa gave Bernard a mighty shove, toppling him onto the fake bed, which promptly cracked, the four posters bringing the canopy down to entangle Newbold hopelessly in the wreckage.

The audience clapped, howling their delight, with no one louder than the squire, who slapped his thigh, calling out, "Demned if I ever knew Shakespeare could be so entertaining."

Delia felt her cheeks burn as Papa began hauling her offstage, but Lady Herkingstone stormed into his path, her ample bosom quivering with outrage.

"How dare you, Mr. Renwick! How dare you make such a mockery of our performance!"

Nothing daunted by the quivering bosom, Papa pressed forward. "This performance is a mockery! Desecration! How dare you, madam, so trifle with my daughter's mind!"

"Please, Papa," Delia said quaveringly. But her plea was lost as Lady Herkingstone shouted out commands for the bed to be restored.

"Do not stir from your seats," her ladyship adjured the audience. A totally unnecessary command, for no one was going anywhere, their eyes glued to the stage with more breathless attention than they had shown for the entire performance.

"We shall finish!" Lady Herkingstone glared a challenge at Mr. Renwick.

"Not with my daughter you won't." Delia was released as her father squared off with her ladyship, both of them with their hands on their hips, glowering. What began as a dispute over the play ended with a personal diatribe by each against the scholarly pretensions of the other.

The audience obviously found it more diverting than any farce ever performed, but Delia's eyes stung with tears of humiliation. Two strong hands rested on her shoulders. Through a haze of tears she realized that Miles had come up to stand behind her.

"I tried to stop him, Delia. But he was already upon the stage before I realized what he meant to do."

But Delia rejected the sympathetic concern she saw mirrored in his warm brown eyes.

"Oh, leave me alone," she said with a sniff, striking his hands away. Somehow she found her way offstage, stumbling past the benches of chuckling guests. She did not stop running until she had fled from the ballroom, the manor house itself.

Her breasts heaving with sobs, she staggered through the landscaped grounds, heedless of where she was going, only wanting to get as far away as possible. How could Papa humiliate her so? And how could Miles let him? She would never be able to face anyone again as long as she lived.

Delia finally collapsed on a stone bench by the pond. Burying her face in her hands, she gave herself up to all the pent-up tensions of the entire evening. After her tears were spent, she felt somewhat better, able to sit up and dry her eyes, although she still burned with resentment against Papa.

Nonetheless, when she heard a twig snap behind her, she

hiccuped, whirling around gratefully. At least Miles had cared enough to come after her. But the dark-cloaked figure masked in a hood was definitely not her cousin.

"W-who . . ." she faltered, the question turning into a frightened scream as two black-gloved hands reached for her throat. Her cry was choked off, and her assailant's grip tightened, strangling all sound.

Nearly suffocating with terror, Delia flailed aimlessly at the dark cloak, then caught hold of the man's wrists and tried to pry those merciless fingers away from her neck. The blood drummed in her head, her lungs felt about to burst for want of air, and her throat was raw from the pain she was unable to express.

Dear God! This could not be happening. She was not going to die this way! But her hands weakened, slackening their desperate struggle. The black-masked phantom blurred before her eyes, his cape flapping in the breeze, spreading darkness until her entire senses were engulfed by his midnight world.

Chapter 9

It was painful to breathe, but Delia's lungs were starved for air. She heaved a great shuddering sigh, then whimpered. Something hot and wet splashed along her cheek. She licked her lips, tasting salt. The wind brushed through her hair. Above the roaring in her ears, she heard a voice calling to her as if through a storm.

"Delia! Delia, my love."

She was drawn close into a shelter that was warm, strong. With a grateful sob, she tried to cling to the arms that held her, but she felt a pair of thin hands tugging her away. Another quavering voice moaned, the words finally becoming distinguishable.

" '. . . That heaven's vault should crack. She's gone for ever.' "

Delia stirred, trying to shake aside the web of darkness that clouded her vision. Vague memory returned. The play! She had to get up. They were in the midst of the performance.

Yet she felt too weak to move. In any case, the strong bonds that cradled her refused to let her go.

"No, no, be still, my darling. Walter, we must get her back to the house."

But the other weaker voice continued to wail, " 'I might have sav'd her, now she's gone for ever! Cordelia, Cordelia, stay a little.' "

Delia focused on the dim shadow of the man who would wrest her from her warm fortress of security. Nay, this old fool spoke the wrong lines. They were performing *Othello*, and he was reciting King Lear's lament for his dead daughter, Cordelia.

But she *was* Cordelia! Her breath escaped in a ragged sob of fright. Was she dead, then?

"Walter, she's alive!" Miles's deep voice rumbled. "Let go! We must take her inside."

Miles! Delia could barely make out the outline of his strong, sculpted features. A glad cry tore past her raw, burning throat. She clutched the stiff linen folds of his cravat with her hand, hanging on like a drowning woman clinging to a lifeline.

Miles's arms trembled as he carried Cordelia back to Lord Walsing's manor house, Walter Renwick anxiously trodding upon his heels. When Miles had found her lying sprawled by the pond, her golden curls tumbled over a face so pale, so still, he had frozen with shock, a shock akin to the numbing sensation he had felt after Waterloo when he had stared at rows and rows of fallen comrades. But even then he had not been so paralyzed with dread as when he knelt beside Delia, half afraid to touch her lest his worst imaginings prove true.

When she gasped, moving against him, tears of relief had sprung to his eyes. He had pressed his lips against the silken curls, scarcely restraining himself from smothering her with kisses until he knew what the extent of her injuries were.

When he bore Delia back inside the house, for once Miles appreciated Lady Herkingstone's imperious manner of command. She drove back the other gawking, exclaiming guests, directing Miles to the privacy of one of the bedchambers. Carefully, he eased Delia onto a sofa-bed that was overhung by a domed chintz canopy. Her misty blue eyes fluttered open. Miles attempted to loosen the neckline of her gown, his fingers stilling at the sight of the purple bruises marring the ivory column of her throat. The muscles tensed along his jawline as he muttered a curse. Whoever had done this to Delia would not live long enough to regret the hour of his birth!

"You won't revive the girl by swearing at her, Sir Miles!" Lady Herkingstone pressed forward, carrying a tray that bore some hartshorn and a glass of water. "You have done your part. Now you may go. 'Tis improper for you to remain longer."

Miles bit back an urge to tell her ladyship what she could do with her notions of propriety. Delia struggled to a half-sitting position, propping herself against the bed's velvet bolster. She clung to Miles's hands, her voice coming out in a pathetic croak.

"Miles, don't leave me."

"Hush, sweetheart." He settled her back into a reclining position. "You are safe now. Can you tell me what happened?"

Her lips trembled; her grip on him tightened. "Down by . . . by the pond. A man . . . masked, black gloves. Tried to . . . to choke me."

She burst into sobs. But when he attempted to put his arms around her, he was thrust back forcibly by the muscular arm of Lady Herkingstone.

"Sir Miles! Your questions can wait."

Although Delia cried out his name, she was effectively cut off from him by her ladyship, who now had reinforcements in the form of Delia's aunt and Miss Pym. Reluctantly, Miles retreated to where Walter Renwick sat in a corner on a chair of painted rosewood. He watched his daughter in silent agony, his lined face so ashen that Miles began to fear for the old man's health as well.

Under her ladyship's brisk ministrations, Delia was now sitting up. Although she spluttered over the water, the color began to return to her cheeks. His mind relieved of any apprehension for Delia's recovery, Miles's thoughts bent in a grimmer direction.

"Come, sir. Leave Delia to the ladies. There is no more we can do here." Walter Renwick permitted Miles to lead him from the room, as dazed as a sleepwalking child.

Her initial shock subsiding, Delia rubbed her aching neck, tears starting in her eyes when Miles and her father closed the door behind them. How could Miles leave her? She had nearly been killed. It was his comfort that she wanted, not that of these fussing women. And Papa. He had not said a word except . . . except Shakespeare! She thumped one fist angrily against the bolster.

"There, there, dear." Aunt Violet patted her arm. "We quite understand how you feel."

"But I am sure your papa will apprehend the villain," Miss Pym added with a gusty sigh. "Such a brave man, Walter Renwick."

Lady Herkingstone nodded in stern agreement. "I shall have a few words to say to the rogue when he is apprehended. Such impertinence. No one indulges in murder at Walsing Park. Not in my presence."

Delia reached for the handkerchief Miss Pry offered, blowing her nose into it with a loud, outraged sniff. She could summon no interest in speculating with the other women as to why she should have been attacked. She was too hurt by the conduct of Papa and Miles. Their first interest should have been her recovery, not in chasing down her assailant. How could she ever have imagined that Miles had learned to care for her, even to the point of offering marriage? Hadn't he taken particular delight in vexing her ever since they met, teasing her with the thought that perhaps his attentions denoted some warmer emotion? And Papa! She had known for some time that he bore no affection for her, his only child. Delia sniffed into the handkerchief, completely giving over any attempt to think rationally.

Outside in the corridor she could hear trampling feet, excited male voices. "One of the grooms saw a hooded figure heading for the stables."

"Tallyho!" the squire's voice boomed. "Have Walsing bring up his hounds. We'll soon pick up the rogue's scent."

Delia flopped back against the bolster, her chin quivering with indignation. Why, they talked as if it were a fox hunt! She was glad that her having been nigh killed was affording all the gentlemen such diversion. Papa should be pleased. He had said she was to see to Miles's entertainment while he was in Stratford.

Lady Herkingstone's maid entered carrying a nightgown, but when the women tried to divest Delia of her clothing, she resisted.

"But, my dear," Miss Pym said. "You cannot think of traveling home in such a state."

Lady Herkingstone added, "No, you must spend the night here. Your aunt will remain with you. Gracious, with Mrs. Forbes-Smythe laid up in another chamber, and Fanny Pryce in the next, we are quite becoming a hospital."

It was the comparison between herself, Mrs. Forbes-Smythe, and Fanny that sent Delia over the brink. Resisting Aunt Violet's efforts to detain her, Delia pushed herself up onto legs that were yet a little wobbly. After much argument with the three older women, she managed to escape from the bedchamber.

When Miles returned with the men from a fruitless search of the grounds, he found Delia in the entrance hall demanding her cloak and carriage. One look at his cousin was enough to tell him that Delia was extremely overwrought. The night's events had played havoc with her normally high spirits, reducing her to a state of near hysteria.

"I will go home!" She stomped her foot at Lady Herkingstone. "I want my own bed!"

303

The sympathy being lavished upon her by Aunt Violet and Miss Pym was not producing any calming effect. What Delia needed was a more bracing, matter-of-fact approach. Miles strode forward, fetching Delia's cloak himself.

"My cousin is right," he said. "Home is the best place for her. Delia is not dying and she is by far too stouthearted to lie swooning over such a trivial incident."

Although he grimaced at the glare he received from Delia, Miles thought her anger better than seeing her dissolve into tears again. She snatched her cloak from his hands, then donned it herself.

"Oh, my dearest, reflect," Aunt Violet wailed, showing signs of the evening's strain herself.

"Send for my carriage," Delia shrieked. "And—and where is my papa?"

"He will be along directly," Miles said. He refrained from telling her that, on his advice, Walter Renwick was taking a few moments alone to collect himself. Renwick had nearly come to blows with Squire Newbold, taking much amiss the squire's hint that perhaps Delia had been slipping off to rendezvous with some fellow.

"And where is that precious son of yours?" Mr. Renwick had snarled. "Didn't everyone hear him threaten to strangle my daughter this very night?"

Miles, however, was not quite satisfied with placing the blame upon Bernard. Newbold had been in full view of the audience most of the time during which Delia had been attacked. No, Miles wanted more opportunity for further investigation before he reached any hasty conclusions. His hands knotted into hard fists. But when he was certain who the attacker was . . .

Delia stalked down the steps of the manor house with the wounded dignity of a queen who had suffered an assassination attempt by one of her subjects. How easily Miles had given over his efforts to bring her assailant to justice! But then, far be it for her to put her cousin to any bother over such a *trivial incident*.

She was fortified by her anger; it kept all tears and feelings of exhaustion at bay during the coach ride back to Rose Briar Cottage. Seeing that Delia no longer required her support, Aunt Violet felt free to collapse, and Delia was obliged to see her aunt to bed.

With such a turmoil of emotions churning inside her—

outrage, resentment, lingering traces of shock—Delia could not try to sleep. Ordering Bessy to attend Aunt Violet, Delia stormed back downstairs. When she passed Shakespeare's portrait in the hall, she gave it a petulant shove, knocking it askew.

She found Papa and Miles closeted in her father's study. They were fortifying themselves with brandy when she entered. Miles was perched on the edge of the library table, her father was seated in his leather armchair, and they were commenting on what a fatiguing night it had been. Delia slammed the door behind her.

Papa started, the golden liquid in his snifter sloshing over onto his sleeve. He set his glass down. "Delia, my child. I was just on my way up to check on you."

Miles slid to his feet. "You should be in bed."

"Pray, gentlemen. Don't disturb yourselves upon my account." She tromped across the room. Seizing the glass her papa had abandoned, she drained what brandy was left, wincing as the liquid burned her throat.

"Cordelia." Papa gasped. "You will make yourself drunk."

Delia smacked the glass back against the table. Good! She wanted to be foxed. She had heard that large quantities of drink numbed one, blotted out all painful sensations.

"I am glad to see you appearing more yourself, Cousin," Miles said, but his voice was tinged with doubt.

Delia flounced over to an armchair by the fire, jarring herself as she plunked down onto the cane seat. The brandy did little to numb or soothe her. In fact, she felt the beginnings of what promised to be a raging headache commence behind her eyes. Her hands rested on the small revolving bookcase; the titles were blurring, but she knew them all too well. *"Lear, Hamlet, Macbeth . . ."* She gave the shelf a vicious spin.

Her father exchanged a dubious glance with Miles, then cleared his throat. "Such a—a distressing evening. But thank God, you are unharmed."

Unharmed? Was her papa so blind he could not see the ugly bruises upon her neck? Apparently he was, for he sighed, saying, " 'All's well that ends well.' "

Delia clenched her teeth. Her hand clamped down onto one of the volumes, her gaze straying toward the fire. Miles abruptly crossed over to her side, prying the book from her grasp.

"Cousin," he said, a firm smile on his lips. "I see your

nerves are more unsettled than I believed. Mayhap some laudanum—"

Delia jerked away, then shot to her feet. She paced the room, her agitation growing by the minute, one thought only pounding through her throbbing temples. She had nearly been killed and neither Miles nor her father cared.

"Mayhap we should all retire," Papa suggested. "I am feeling quite overset, myself. When I first saw Delia lying there, not moving . . ."

"I know," Miles said softly. "Those lines from *Lear*. I have never been so moved by them before in my life."

His comment added the final fuel to Delia's smoldering fury. She whirled on both men. "Yes, indeed," she spat out. "Didn't I always say the two of you could trade quotes over my grave? How unfortunate I recovered, Papa. What recitations you and Miles could have done at my funeral!"

Her father blanched.

"Delia!" Miles frowned.

She regarded her tall cousin bitterly. "I knew from the first you were as bad as Papa. Neither of you care who dies as long as a single word of your precious Shakespeare not be lost."

"That's enough, Cordelia! I realize you are upset, and I care naught what you say to me, but I insist you show more respect for your father."

Papa made a deprecating gesture, hanging his head. The fact that he would not reassure her, that he would make no defense against her charges caused Delia all the more anguish. She leaned over him, fairly shouting into his ear, "Do you desire me to show you more respect, Papa? The same respect you showed Amaryllis when you drove her to her death." She broke into a wild laugh. "Aye, what a pity I didn't die tonight. With both me and Amaryllis gone, you have only to be rid of Aunt Violet, then you could be left in peace with your precious Shakespeare."

Appalled herself by what she was saying, Delia wished her father would upbraid her, strike her, show some sign that he felt something, that her words were wrong. Instead his shoulders sagged.

"I—I am more fatigued than I knew. I must bid you good night." Without looking up, he stumbled from the room, leaving the door ajar behind him.

Delia's whole body began to shake. She gripped the chair her father had vacated with white-knuckled hands to support herself. But Miles fell upon her, his face suffused crimson with fury. His fingers bit into her shoulders.

"You cursed little fool. How could you talk that way to him? Can you not see what he has been through?"

Although Delia trembled at Miles's fury, she thrust up her chin. "I see all too clearly. He does not care a groat—"

Her words were choked off as Miles gave her a shake, causing her head to snap back.

"Doesn't care! I'd like to beat some sense into you. Use your head for a moment. Think of how your father reads Shakespeare, so expressionless. Yet the way he spoke those lines from *Lear* tonight! Good God, Delia, he showed his love for you in the only way he knew how."

She twisted, trying to break his painful grasp. "Aye, the same way he showed his love for my stepmother."

Miles expelled his breath in an angry hiss. "Your stepmother! 'Tis high time you heard the truth about your beloved stepmother!"

"Not your version of it. Don't you dare say one word against Amaryllis." Delia continued to squirm to gain her freedom, but Miles thrust her into the chair, forcing her to listen.

"Amaryllis was a vain, spoiled, selfish woman whose first concern was her own pleasure. She married your father for his wealth, then drove him nigh to ruin with her extravagance, her love of gaming."

"That's a lie. Let me go, you beast." Delia attempted to blot out the sound of his hateful words, but Miles continued. "That is why your father moved you to Stratford. He sold off Renwick Manor in a last desperate effort to retain some of his fortune, enough to leave you a respectable portion when he died."

"No, 'tis untrue," Delia choked. "He did it because Shakespeare once lived here, and—and Amaryllis was h-heartbroken, already s-stricken with some strange illness."

Miles's lip curled in scorn. "Strange illness! She died by her own hand."

"Wh-what are you saying?" Delia felt the color draining from her face.

"She killed herself, Delia, in an effort to be rid of the child she carried."

"N-no!"

"She dug up some tansy root from the garden. It induces

307

abortion, but her plan backfired, destroying not only your father's babe but herself as well."

"No, stop it. Stop it. 'Tisn't true . . . 'tisn't . . ." As she doubled over, collapsing into sobs, she felt the tension go out of Miles's hands. His grip on her shoulders relaxed, his fingers tracing gentle circles where he had bruised her.

"Delia, I am sorry," he murmured. "But you had to be told the truth before your bitter delusions destroy all your affection for your father."

Delia pushed Miles's hands away, raising her head to regard him through tear-glazed eyes. "Leave me alone. I hate you!"

"So you told me when we first met." Brown eyes that had softened suddenly became hard, remote.

"And—and my f-feelings haven't changed," Delia cried. "I—I wish you'd n-never come to Stratford. I—I wish I would never s-see you again."

Miles's lips set into a bitter line. "Madam, that can easily be arranged." He made her a stiff bow, then strode out of the room.

Delia stared at the closed door for a few stunned moments before lowering her head onto her arms, indulging in a stormy bout of weeping. As she gained some measure of control, her mind sought to deny all the dreadful things Miles had said about Amaryllis. He didn't know, no matter how sure of himself he had sounded. He couldn't possibly have known the truth about her stepmother.

Delia summoned up remembrances in her mind to refute Miles's words, but somehow the only images of Amaryllis that swam into her mind were of that dark-haired beauty glittering with expensive jewels, her violet eyes sparkling as she sat down to a game of cards.

Delia rubbed her aching temples, trying to recall how much Amaryllis had loved her. Why, hadn't her stepmother said on more than one occasion to Delia: "What a perfect little doll you are. I don't ever want any child but you."

Delia's hand froze as Amaryllis's words took on a new, almost sinister meaning. No, no, she would not even let herself think such a thing. But once more she was seeing Amaryllis writhing upon the bed . . . the blood.

A chill coursed through Delia's body. As if led by some unseen pull, she rose from her chair and drifted toward the study window. Her hand trembled as she pushed aside the heavy damask curtains. Beyond the mullioned windowpane, the

Knott garden rustled in eerie shadows cast by the pale, slivered moon. By some perverse trick of nature, the blighted bed of herbs appeared to be the only part bathed in light.

"She dug up some tansy root from the garden. It induces abortion . . ." Delia's tears splattered down the cool window-pane. Her hand dropped limply to her side, the draperies falling closed.

Behind her, the study door slid open. Delia did not look around until she heard her father call her name softly. Then she turned, scarcely able to face him.

"Delia, Miles told me that he—" Papa's voice broke at the sight of her face. "Oh, he shouldn't have," he whispered vehemently. "He shouldn't have."

"Papa, I—I . . ." Her voice failed her. For the first time, she noted all those lines grief had carved upon his brow, the deep sorrow that lurked in his eyes. Why had she never seen them before?

"Oh, my child, don't look at me thusly. I should never have permitted you to find out this way. Forgive me."

He was asking *her* to forgive him? "Oh, Papa!" she choked, burying herself in his arms. He pressed her head against his thin shoulder, stroking her hair. She felt him swallow.

"I only wanted to protect you," he said. "You were already so grieved by Amaryllis's death. I could not burden you with the additional shock of how she died."

"B-but I don't understand, Papa. How could I—I have loved her so when she—she was so evil?"

Papa tipped her face up so that she was obliged to look at him. She marveled at the gentle love and patience she saw reflected in his eyes.

"Evil, my dear? No, scarcely that. Only an overindulged child. The cherished youngest daughter in a family who had fallen upon hard times. If there was any fault, 'twas mine for marrying her in haste, without knowing her character. She was such a lovely young thing, so gay. I thought she would restore some of the happiness to our home that had vanished when your mother died."

He fetched a deep sigh. "I never saw enough of her before the marriage to realize how ill-suited we were. Then after, I did nothing to check her childish whims, pouring out money where I could not give love. That is the burden of my guilt. Poor Amaryllis. Poor, pampered little girl who never quite grew to be a woman."

"Like me," Delia whispered.

"No, not like you, my dearest one." Papa's eyes gleamed. He smoothed the curls back from her forehead, planting a tender kiss there. "Not like you at all."

Delia flung her arms around his neck. "P-Papa! I am s-sorry for all those horrid things I said, for—for everything. Being such a d-disobedient daughter, acting in the play when—when I knew you would dislike it. I—I deserved to be strangled."

"Hush, my dear! I was quite proud of your part in the play." Her father's voice grew stern. "Until you spoke the lines that ridiculous woman wrote."

Delia emitted a watery chuckle but immediately succumbed again to her feelings of guilt. "I have behaved like such a brat, resenting your studies, treating your guest with such scorn. Miles—" She broke off, unable to bear thinking about what she had said to Miles.

Papa sighed, patting her shoulder. "Well, I can see 'twas my error about Miles. It has not worked out. I invited him here hoping that—that he and you . . . that you would . . ."

Delia stared at her father, sudden realization flooding through her. "Papa! You invited Miles here, hoping he would marry me!"

Her father flushed. "I—I am afraid that I did. Pray do not be angry with me. It seemed such an ideal match," he added wistfully.

An ideal match! To wed her to a man who loved his Shakespeare, an incorrigible flirt, a rascal who would be forever teasing . . . Well, she need not worry. She was quite certain she had given Miles such a disgust of her this evening there was no danger of his proposing now. Not ever!

Delia made a feeble attempt to smile. "You—you needn't concern yourself apologizing, Papa. Miles will be leaving soon. I—I told him I hated him." Her voice cracked as she buried her face against her father's chest, overcome by a realization she could no longer deny. "When I—I should have told him how v-very much I love him."

Chapter 10

The morning was nearly spent when Delia seated herself on
the garden settle, smoothing out the skirts of a simple cambric
gown, that was high-ruffled at the neck to conceal her bruises.
Her hair was parted in the center with curls flowing down her
cheeks *á la* Madonna. For once she felt quite content to appear
sweet, demure. Mayhap if she contrived to look angelic
enough, Miles might forget what a devil she had been last
night. She knew the effect must be entirely spoiled by her
eyes, yet puffy from crying herself to sleep. Mayhap if she
shrank back from the glare of the sun, more into the shade of
the mulberry tree . . .

Her stomach tensed into knots. She rehearsed different versions of an apology in her mind. Would there be anything she
could say to erase the dreadful words she had flung at him?
Mayhap he would not care to listen this time. So often in the
brief span of their acquaintance had she railed at him like an
archwife. What if she had finally gone too far?

Wistfully, she gazed at the silent, ivy-covered cottage, slumbering in the late-morning sun. No sign of Miles, and it must
be close to noon. Delia had breakfasted alone with Papa while
Aunt Violet, overcome by the past evening's excitement, lingered in her bed. It had been a pleasant meal, the first time she
and Papa had truly talked to each other in years. And yet Delia's eyes had strayed continually toward the door looking for
Miles, even as they did now.

What a fool she was! Rising in agitation, Delia paced along
the narrow paths bordering the bright rows of flower beds.
How could she expect Miles to want to see her, let alone to
forgive her? She had destroyed any chance that Miles might

ever return her love, uprooted all tender emotions, cast it to the winds.

Yet her heart bounded with hope when she saw a tall, wavering shadow stretching before her across the grass. She whirled around.

"Oh, Miles, I . . ." Her words trailed off as she realized it was not her cousin who had come up behind her but Miffin.

The coachman's eyes widened in surprise. "Beg pardon, miss. I didn't mean to startle you."

She shrugged. "Oh, 'tis of no consequence. I only thought—that is, I was expecting my cousin to—"

"Why, Miss Delia, your cousin is gone."

"Gone?" she repeated in a whisper. The world could not have appeared more black to her than if the clouds had blotted out the sun.

"Aye, Sir Miles saddled the chestnut gelding and rode out early. Didn't say where he was going, 'cept that he would be back by late afternoon."

"Oh." Caught up in her mingled feelings of disappointment over Miles's absence, and relief that he meant to return, it took Delia several moments before she realized that Miffin's placid face was screwed up into an expression of dread.

"Is—is something wrong, Miffin?"

"Oh, Miss Delia," the man burst out, raking huge hands back through his wheat-straw hair. "Her ladyship will have me taken up for a thief, and that's certain. Whatever am I to do?"

Delia adjured the coachman to calm himself and explain more clearly the source of his distress.

"It's that damn—begging your pardon, miss—that wicked sword Lord Walsing give me for part of my guard costume. I was so fatched, what with you nigh being choked and all, that I forgot and brought that sword away with me when I drove the coach home."

Miffin sighed, staring at the ground in abject misery. "I'll be hung for a thief, sure as rain."

Delia patted the huge man on the shoulder. "Don't distress yourself. I shall return the sword to Lord Walsing myself and make all right with him."

Her reply had a magical effect on the groom. Miffin beamed with relief. "Oh, thank you, miss."

Delia nodded graciously, wishing that her own problem with Miles was capable of such easy solution. Not expected back until late afternoon! Was he avoiding her then? She bit her lip, a new scheme forming in her mind. There was scarcely any point in lingering in the garden, fretting for his return. It might do her good to escape from the confines of the cottage for a while. She could convey the sword to Lord Walsing and easily be back before Miles.

Impulsively ordering Miffin to bring round the gig, Delia hastened into the house to don a bonnet. She hesitated, realizing she ought to summon her maid to accompany her. But Bessy would scold so, besides leveling her sharp-eyed stare at Delia and speculating on the cause of her mistress's long face. The drive would scarcely afford her the solitude she desired.

But Papa would never approve of her tearing about the countryside alone. On the other hand, she would not be gone long, and she did not actually mean to call upon Lord Walsing, merely to leave the sword and a message with one of his servants. Having swept aside all qualms, Delia raced out to the waiting gig before anyone could discover her purpose and stay her. Miffin was by far too grateful to express his customary disapproval of Delia going out alone, and so she rattled down the rough, dirt lane unhindered.

She had not gone far when she encountered Thomas Leighton. That the boy had been fishing was obvious from his dusty bare feet, damp-hemmed trousers, and the small pike he carried on a string.

Delia pulled up to greet him.

"Halloo, Delia! Do look what I caught. Shan't I have a fine supper? Though mayhap I will try to preserve it and keep it in a box 'neath my bed."

Delia advanced the strong opinion that the fish had much better be eaten.

After some consideration, Tom agreed, then asked eagerly, "Where are you going? May I come, too?"

Despite her wish to be alone, Delia was not proof against those pleading eyes so large in the round, little face.

"I suppose you might," she said reluctantly. "If you put on your shoes and manage to look more presentable. I am driving over to Lord Walsing's."

Tom's initial whoop of joy died on his lips, turning to an expression of ineffable scorn. "That ridiculous gudgeon? No, thank you."

Although Delia attempted to be stern with him for his disrespect to Lord Walsing, she could not help laughing at the face Tom pulled. When he bid her farewell, stepping out of her horse's path, Delia started off again, feeling better for the brief encounter.

The journey to Walsing Park was uneventful, but the sight of the huge stone mansion brought forcibly to mind the events of the previous evening. She shuddered as she guided the gig into the stableyard, one hand fluttering nervously to her neck. She even regarded with nervous suspicion the groom who hustled forward to take charge of her horse. Helping her to alight, he leered, raising an eyebrow at the sight of a young lady so bold as to arrive at a gentleman's house unaccompanied. But Delia decided the man was not sinister so much as impertinent.

Who could have attacked her? Delia wondered as she made her way to the house. It was a question she had not given much thought to, owing to her preoccupation with Miles. She did not assume that she was universally loved, but that anyone should despise her enough for murder . . . ! Surely not even Bernard Newbold would . . . Yet the marks lingering on her flesh told her that someone definitely had. Mayhap some lunatic was at large in the neighborhood. Shakespeare's tomb attracted enough of those to Stratford. That was a far more comforting supposition than the fear that her assailant might actually be an acquaintance of hers.

Lord Walsing's solemn-faced butler opened the front door in answer to Delia's brisk knock. His imperturbable features relaxed enough to express surprise and speculation. Delia supposed the tale of her attempted murder must have spread through most of the servants' quarters in Stratford by this time.

Before she could explain the reason for her visit, the butler informed her that Lord Walsing had departed only an hour before. His lordship meant to be gone indefinitely. The grim-visaged manservant unbent enough to add that the entire household was at sixes and sevens owing to the suddenness of Lord Walsing's departure.

Murmuring her regrets, Delia took her leave. When she clambered back into the gig, she reflected that the entire world seemed to have been turned upside down since the unfortunate performance of *Othello*. What had called Lord Walsing away? The question did not interest Delia enough to occupy her mind for long.

She had tooled the gig most of the way down the long drive, nearly past the ruins where the old Walsing monastery had once stood, when she realized in vexation that she had completely forgotten why she had driven to the park in the first place. The curving sword gleamed on the seat beside her.

Muttering exclamations at her stupidity, Delia started to turn the gig around when her attention was caught by the soft nicker of a horse. Drawing her own animal to a halt, Delia peered through the trees at the crumbling stone turrets. She could see a flashy bay, still in harness, cropping the grass.

Why, that was Lord Walsing's horse. How very odd. She had assumed that he must have left in his carriage, but she had not asked. What if Lord Walsing had ridden out and met with an accident? The poor man might be lying senseless even while she sat and stared at his horse.

Delia eased the gig off the roadside. Leaping down, she hitched the reins to one of the oaks near the drive, then rushed into the line of trees, shoving back branches in her impatience to reach the ruins. The horse grazed near the building that had once been the monk's chapel.

Delia's footsteps did not falter until a disturbing thought occurred to her. What if he had not met with any accident? What if the same fate had befallen him that had overtaken Delia last night? Perhaps the murderous lunatic with the black-gloved hands was lying in wait amidst the ancient walls of Cotswold stone, lurking, ready to claim his next victim.

Delia gulped; her knees grew weak. The trees about her loomed like threatening giants guarding the vine-covered stonework; the rustling leaves seemed to hiss a warning for her to leave this place. Delia was quite willing to comply. Best she run back to the house, seek help . . .

At that moment, a muffled groan caught her attention, the piteous sound echoing hollowly from inside the towering walls. Delia needed no further encouragement to depart at once. She picked up her skirts and did not stop running until she reached the safety of the drive. Leaning against the gig, she paused to catch her breath, her conscience catching up with her at the same moment. That awful groan had obviously been the cry of someone in distress. All of Delia's saner instincts urged to flee, but a small voice inside her cried shame. How could she be such a coward? In the time it took her to summon aid, poor Lord Walsing might be quite dead.

With trembling fingers, Delia withdrew the heavy sword from the carriage seat, the sunlight glinting off the sharp edge of the blade. Thus armed, she plunged back into the trees. Advancing cautiously to the side of the chapel, Delia flattened

315

herself against the wall. Walsing's horse stopped biting at the grass long enough to eye her with curiosity.

Delia began inching forward, seeking an opening. All was quiet within; the eerie moan was not repeated. Was she already too late? She could not decide what she feared most, finding a murderer within or a corpse. The high, arched windows had been denuded long ago of their magnificent stained glass by a vengeful King Henry. The ivy had crept forward, covering the openings as if to conceal the chapel's shame. Delia stood on tiptoe, her hands scraping on the vines as she carefully parted the greenery enough to peer inside.

Although the barrel-vaulted roof had long since collapsed, leaving the chapel open to the sky, the overhang of the great oaks cast the interior into gloom-filled shadow. Delia took a cursory glance around, feeling a wave of relief when she presumed the abandoned building to be empty. Perhaps that dreadful sound had been made by the wind whistling through the cracks in the mortar.

But not a breath of air was stirring, although something huddled in the corner was. A blue bundle topped with golden curls. Delia gasped. It was the last person in the world she expected to find. Frances Pryce.

Delia found a scarred oak door hanging off its hinges and inched her way inside, the sword poised protectively in front of her. Her eyes darted around the chapel, as hollow and cheerless as an abandoned well. Pews, screens, altar, floorboards—all had been ripped out and burned ages ago, but the musty smell of incense still seemed to linger in the air.

"Fanny?" Delia called softly. Her feet padded across the soft turf as she made her way toward the girl. On closer inspection, Delia saw that Fanny was bound and gagged. Her wide, frightened blue eyes stared up at Delia, begging for release. Delia sank to her knees. Setting the sword down, she reached for the scrap of linen tied around the girl's mouth. But before Delia could undo the knot, she heard a loose stone crunch. It did not take the look of alarm that flashed into Fanny's eyes to send Delia whirling around. Heart thumping, her fingers sought the hilt of the sword. She relaxed at the familiar sight of a slender figure, waving blond locks, and harmless blue eyes squinting at her.

With a tremulous sigh of relief, Delia let the steely weapon drop to the ground. "Oh, Lord Walsing! Thank God, 'tis you.

316

I feared you had been murdered. But only look how I have found poor Fanny."

"Yes, Miss Renwick," he murmured. "Most unfortunate that you have." His perfect white teeth flashed in an amiable, almost apologetic smile.

A shiver worked its way up Delia's spine. At this most absurd and inconvenient moment, she suddenly remembered the rest of the Shakespearean quote she had tried to recall the night she danced with him.

"That one may smile, and smile, and be a villain!"

With a frightened gasp, Delia tried to bolt past him. He grabbed her about the waist, ruthlessly yanking her backward. Astonished by the quickness and strength that his foppish appearance belied, Delia opened her mouth to scream, only to have the sound choked off by Lord Walsing's hand clamping down upon her throat.

In a matter of seconds, she was thrust into the ground beside Fanny and gaged with his silk handkerchief. Her frantic struggles were to no avail. Walsing pulled snug the rope binding Delia's hands behind her back, then employed another length to secure her ankles. She winced as the rough hemp bit into her flesh.

"So sorry," he said. "But I am afraid I can't have either one of you ladies running off to tell everyone my secret."

Delia tried to assure him that she did not even know what his secret was, would swear not to tell anyone anything—at least not until she was well clear of him. But with his silk handkerchief stuffed in her mouth, Delia could do no more than issue a few unintelligible moans.

Still smiling, Lord Walsing shook his head at her. "Alas, Miss Renwick, why could you not have remained at home today?"

Delia was asking herself the same question.

"And after I spared your life last night. I could have killed you, you know. But when I realized it was you instead of Fanny, I stopped choking you."

He straightened up, sighing. "Now you have made everything so much more difficult. One fatal accident is easy to do, but two at once!"

As he rubbed his chin, thinking, Delia felt Fanny beside her galvanizing into a fit of panic. The girl whimpered, squirming about to no purpose.

Delia attempted to remain calm, seeking an avenue of escape. If only Walsing would leave them alone for a time. Delia might manage to cut her bonds on the sword that lay forgotten at his feet.

Then he snapped his fingers, grinning down at them. "I have it. A fatal coach disaster. That sharp curve, the ditch just on the other side of the park. Two young ladies out tooling about the countryside; you, Miss Renwick, such a careless whip."

Delia glared at him. She was excessively good with the reins.

"And you have even thoughtfully provided the gig." Walsing chuckled.

"Yes," a familiar deep voice said in steel-edged accents. "We can use it to convey whatever remains of your carcass when I am done with you."

Walsing jumped, then spun around to stare at the open door. Delia saw Miles's tall frame silhouetted on the threshold.

"Mmmmm-mmmmm," she squeaked, joyous tears of disbelief starting in her eyes.

But in one quick, fluid gesture, Walsing retrieved the sword from the floor. The wicked blade gleamed even in the chapel's dim light.

"Three fatal accidents!" He sighed. "This is becoming dashed awkward."

Delia's heart froze, her eyes fixed on Miles, expecting any minute to see him come rushing to meet his death. And she had provided Walsing with the weapon!

But her cousin moved cautiously. He stepped inside, slowly circling Lord Walsing. His lordship peered in that direction, his muscles tensed, sword poised ready to swing. Delia groaned, writhing against her bonds. She could not lie here idle while Miles was slain before her eyes. Mustering all her strength, she rolled forward and crashed into Walsing's legs. But at that split second, Miles leaped forward. Her assault on Walsing had the effect of putting him off balance, giving him added momentum in lunging toward Miles. The two men collided, Walsing nearly succeeding in burying the blade in Mile's skull.

Miles recovered and seized Walsing's arm. They grappled for the sword. Although Miles was clearly stronger, Walsing clung to the weapon with a frenzy born of desperation. Her screams trapped behind the silk handkerchief, Delia employed both shoulder and knee in inching her way toward the struggling men. She positioned herself so that when Walsing was

318

forced back, he tripped over her legs. Miles crashed over on top of him, nearly falling onto the blade held between the men.

"Delia," he grunted. "Stop . . . helping."

Gasping as Walsing's foot caught her in the ear, Delia worked her way from beneath the flailing legs of the men. Rolling over, she maneuvered herself into a kneeling position. She squeaked as she saw that Walsing was forcing the curve of the blade upward toward Miles's throat. The cords on his neck tensing, Miles strained back from the sharp steel. Never loosening his grasp on Walsing's wrist, he began pressing the arm back toward the floor.

His chest heaving, Walsing went suddenly limp as Miles pinioned the hand holding the sword. But in the next instant his lordship's knee flashed upward, catching Miles between the legs.

His eyes flaring, Miles swore, tumbling off Walsing. Delia watched in terrified astonishment as he doubled over. It had not seemed to her as if Walsing could have kicked him that hard. But Miles's face turned white with an agony she could not begin to comprehend.

His lordship paused to catch his breath. In that split second, Delia acted without thinking, flinging her body forward to trap Walsing's sword arm beneath her. She hoped her action would give Miles the time he needed to recover from the blow. Still grimacing, he moved slowly, trying to get to his feet.

Walsing dealt Cordelia a vicious blow to the temple, knocking her away from his arm. With a triumphant grin, he staggered to his knees, squinting at Miles. He raised the sword. Sprawled behind him, her head throbbing, Delia heard Walsing mutter, "Now!" With a muffled cry of terror, she closed her eyes, unable to watch. A loud crack resounded through the room and something thudded hard upon the earthen floor.

Delia moaned low in her throat, not moving. Turning her head aside, she still dared not open her eyes, certain she would find Miles carved in half by that dreadful sword. The silk cloth at last slipped from her mouth, permitting her to sob. "Oh, Miles, Miles. My love. I wish I were dead!"

"Most unfortunate, my dear." Miles's voice panted close to her ear. "For I fear his lordship is no longer able to oblige you."

She had scarcely a moment to emit a startled squeak of joy before a pair of warm lips ruthlessly took possession of her own. Miles! There was no mistaking his kiss.

319

Delia's eyes fluttered opened, her mind whirling, as giddy from the embrace as from her flood of relief.

"But—but ..." she sputtered when Miles paused long enough to permit her to speak. "You were down. I—I saw him kick you. You seemed in such pain."

Miles grimaced before flashing his wicked grin. "No lasting damage, I assure you."

But—but where was Lord Walsing lurking? she thought with a returning surge of fear. When Miles began to undo her bonds, Delia twisted her neck until she could see a form slumped on the floor beyond his shoulder.

Walsing! The sword yet rested against his open palm; his eyes closed, his golden head tilted to a very odd angle, his classically molded nose shifted to the other side of his face. He was no longer smiling.

Chapter 11

"And Miles laid Lord Walsing out with one blow!" Cordelia demonstrated by clipping one fist to her own delicate chin.

Settled opposite her on the parlor settee, Aunt Violet and Rosamund heaved admiring sighs into their teacups. Delia had spent the last quarter of an hour regaling them with the same account she had rendered to her papa earlier, of her harrowing experience, of Miles's gallant rescue of her in the nick of time.

Papa had been quite overset by the tale. Delia had never seen her mild-mannered father look so furious, so vengeful against Lord Walsing for daring to threaten his only child.

"The pernicious villain. Oh! 'I would have him poisoned with a pot of ale,' " Papa had shouted.

It had taken Delia the better part of the afternoon to calm him enough so that he had resumed his studies in the library. No sooner had she seen him safely bestowed with his books when Rosamund arrived and Delia was obliged to recount the morning's adventures once more.

Basking in Rosamund's and Aunt Violet's solicitude, only one thing marred Delia's satisfaction. The hero of her tale was not present. Miles had not yet returned from delivering Walsing up to the local constable and Frances Pryce back to her aunt. Delia's lip curled in scorn as she recalled how Fanny had blubbered all over Miles when he untied her. The little craven! After trussing Walsing up, they had discovered that Fanny had used the opportunity provided by the fight to inch her way out of the chapel door, bent on saving her own neck.

Delia stared out the parlor window at the shadows lengthening across the stone fence. It seemed to be taking Miles an extremely long time, she thought. If Lord Walsing had not been out so cold, she might have dreaded that the villain had somehow managed to overpower Miles and escape.

Aunt Violet clucked her tongue. "My poor Delia. Two such dreadful experiences within twenty-four hours. You have been notoriously abused, child."

Delia shrugged aside Aunt Violet's sympathy, her own fears a fading memory. Instead of recollecting how her life had been in peril, her thoughts were full of how Miles had behaved afterward. When he had summoned one of the Walsing grooms to drive her back to Rose Briar Cottage, Delia had clung to him, trying to recall the words of the apology Walsing's attack had driven out of her mind. She had made a mess of it, completely jumbling her words until she was all but incoherent. Miles had said little, but the tender way he had lifted her into the gig, the warmth in his eyes, spoke volumes. "We'll talk later," he had whispered. "I have much to say to you, but not here."

Delia had been nigh light-headed with hopeful expectation ever since. Rosamund's voice recalled her to her surroundings. " 'Tis still quite incomprehensible to me, Delia. Why should Lord Walsing behave so? Why would he want to kill Fanny?"

Delia could think of any number of good reasons, but since she did not know the exact one, she remained silent.

Aunt Violet said, "I do not understand it, either. A gentleman like Lord Walsing! How could he behave so!"

"Ah, but if he were not Lord Walsing?"

At the sound of Miles's voice, all three women whirled around to look at him as he stood upon the threshold. Delia half rose from her chair, her pulses fluttering. But Rosamund and Aunt Violet were already chorusing greetings to Miles as if he were a conquering hero.

Aunt Violet hugged him about the neck. "Oh, Miles! Miles, my dear, brave boy!"

Rosamund blushed, even daring to plant a kiss upon his cheek. "Sir Miles, I cannot thank you enough for preserving the life of my dearest friend."

Miles smirked, clearly enjoying himself. He arched an eyebrow at Delia, extending his arms as if inviting her to take her turn. Take her turn, indeed! Scowling at him, she sank back against the cushion of her chair.

Nothing daunted, he took up a position before the center of the fireplace, looking so complacent that Delia longed to tweak his nose.

"Whatever did you mean about Lord Walsing?" Aunt Violet asked as she and Rosamund settled themselves back breathlessly upon the silk-striped divan.

"Yes, do tell us, Sir Miles," Rosamund urged.

"I am sure Delia has already told you most of it." Miles regarded Delia with infuriating condescension. "All that she knows, of course."

Delia stared at the tea tray, unwilling to give him the satisfaction of seeing her appearing about to burst with curiosity just as the others were. After tormenting them further with his silence, Miles said, "Alas, ladies, 'tis my sad duty to inform you that the paragon of good looks you have all been worshiping is not Lord Walsing. He is a rank impostor."

"No!" Aunt Violet and Rosamund exclaimed together.

"Yes, I am afraid so." Miles rubbed the knuckles of his right hand. "The fellow was, er, ah, induced to make a full confession. He was actually the real Peter Walsing's valet."

"Impossible!" Aunt Violet said. "Surely Lady Herkingstone would know her own nephew."

Miles shook his head. "That is a point I checked with her ladyship only this morning. Her nephew was raised entirely in America. She never set eyes on him, nor did her late brother ever think to send a likeness of the young man. Therefore, when the news of his lordship's inheritance reached New York, 'twas a simple matter for the valet to steal the family records and pass himself off as the heir."

Delia could no longer keep silent. "Then what became of the real Lord Walsing?"

"We don't yet know." Miles gave a rueful frown. "Nothing would persuade the villain to tell us that. I fear that further investigation will reveal that Lord Walsing met with an untimely accident."

Aunt Violet sighed. "I might have guessed that anyone with that handsome a nose could not be a true Walsing."

"But poor Fanny must have recognized the impostor at once." Rosamund's brow clouded with bewilderment. "Why did she never say anything?"

"I am afraid 'poor' Fanny had designs of her own," Miles said dryly. "She was extorting money from the fake Walsing as the price of her silence. I believe the foolish chit even cherished hopes of becoming Lady Walsing through him."

Although Rosamund and Aunt Violet looked deeply shocked,

Delia crowed in triumph. "I always knew there was something sly about that girl."

"Such a judge of character you are, my dear Cousin," Miles said. "I daresay it was the same keen perception that prevented you from ever having been taken in by such a pretty fellow."

Delia blushed, then glowered. It was most unhandsome of Miles to remind her that she had once been so foolish as to fancy herself enamored of Lord Walsing.

"And, pray tell, sir," she said acidly, "when did you become so much more perceptive than the rest of us that you suspected Lord Walsing was a fraud?"

Miles stroked his chin as if searching his memory. "I believe I had my first inkling that something was 'rotten in the state of Denmark' . . ." At the sound of Delia's indrawn hiss, he quickly amended his remark. "Er, that something was amiss when I noticed how dashed queer Walsing acted when Fanny Pryce introduced herself as an old acquaintance from America. I also found it strange that a man reputed to be a skilled marksman could obviously not see much farther than the end of his aquiline nose, despite how he tried to disguise the fact."

"Yes, I remember that, too," Delia interrupted excitedly. "I overheard Lord Walsing talking to Squire Newbold while I was waiting for you to fetch me punch. The squire was very put out that Lord Walsing would never go shooting."

She subsided when Miles folded his arms, waiting much like a stern parent would for an unruly child to become quiet so that he could continue. "Then, on the night of the play, Fanny was shoved down a flight of stairs, a fall that could have broken her neck. Shortly thereafter, Delia was nearly strangled; Delia, whom to a man of Walsing's limited vision could easily be mistaken for Fanny. To the best of my recollection, I could not remember seeing his lordship in the ballroom after he gave up his seat to my cousin Walter. The fellow was also conspicuously absent during the search for Delia's attacker."

The other ladies applauded Miles's clever deductions, but Delia interrupted, speaking in deeply aggrieved tones. "If you guessed that Lord Walsing was my attacker, why did you wait so long to do something about that horrid man, so long that I was almost killed again?"

Miles eyed her sternly. "Because I had no proof of what would seem an extremely wild accusation, not even after I talked with her ladyship this morning. I called upon Mrs. Forbes-Smythe in an effort to wring the truth from Fanny, but she had never returned from Walsing Manor. In any case, I never imagined you would go haring off about the countryside, totally unaccompanied. If I hadn't chanced upon young Tom Leighton and learned where you had gone, if I hadn't spotted where you left the gig . . ."

Miles left the grim sentence unfinished. Delia's indignation softened when she saw how shaken he looked at the mere thought of what might have happened to her.

"It has all been too dreadful," Rosamund said. "Such wickedness! What will be done with that horrid man and Fanny?"

"Fanny has already managed to slip away from her aunt's house, absconding with the better part of that lady's jewels. I expect when—if—Mrs. Forbes-Smythe recovers from her shock, she will set the Bow Street Runners after Fanny. As for the erstwhile Lord Walsing with his penchant for strangling . . . He will face a very stout noose unless Lady Herkingstone manages to get at him first."

Miles chuckled. "I do not know what enraged her ladyship more when she learned the truth. The prospect that her own nephew had likely been murdered or that some low-born scoundrel had dared to pass himself off as her relation."

Even Delia had to laugh at that. When Miles had finished all of his explanations, the room fell quiet. Delia's cheeks waxed hot as she felt the other two ladies staring at her and Miles, making little attempt to hide their smiles. Rosamund exchanged a glance with Aunt Violet. Then the two women both found excuses for abruptly quitting the room.

When the parlor door closed behind them, Delia's gaze locked with Miles's deep brown eyes. He cleared his throat, then stopped. It had all seemed so easy when he had rehearsed his speech during the ride back to Rose Briar. Would he ever forget the way Delia had sobbed when she thought Walsing had killed him? Miles's heart had flooded with joy, knowing that despite their bitter quarrel of the evening before, despite how his words had hurt her, she had forgiven him. Why then did all the tender words he wished to say, asking her to be his wife, freeze upon his lips? He could think of a hundred marvelous ways Shakespeare would have expressed his love, none of which would be acceptable to Delia. Smacking his fist against his hand, Miles took a nervous turn before the hearth.

Delia was disconcerted to find that he suddenly appeared as tongue-tied as she. She averted her eyes, staring down at her toes. The silence stretched out unbearably. Good heavens! Did the man never mean to speak?

"Delia." The very softness of his voice startled her. "The time has come again for me to bid you farewell."

Farewell? The hopes that were causing her heart to pound so fast plummeted. "M-more business?" she quavered, scarcely trusting her voice.

"Yes, I have recently purchased a home and must see it prepared for the coming of my bride."

Delia's head jerked up. She stared at Miles, feeling utterly betrayed.

"The chief problem," he said, tracing one finger thoughtfully along the stone edge of the mantel, "the chief problem will be finding a place to hide my copies of Shakespeare. My betrothed positively loathes the man and I fear I could not trust her near my folios."

"Your betrothed?" Delia's heart skipped a beat, although she felt a twinge of indignation over Miles's teasing. "Pray tell, is she anyone with whom I happen to be acquainted?"

Miles smiled, his half-hooded eyes dancing with mischief. "Mayhap you do. Shall I describe her to you? She is about the same height and coloring as Miss Frances Pryce. Ah, but her eyes! There lies the difference. You should see how they dart lightning whenever—"

"Oh, you—you insufferable rogue!" No longer able to contain herself, Delia leaped at him. "How dare you assume that I will marry you when you have not even troubled yourself to ask! Of all the abominable conceit. The unmitigated gall!"

Miles covered his ears. "I should have kept that silk handkerchief by me. Fortunately, I have other methods much more effective."

He seized Delia hard against him. Her struggles to escape were futile, so she was forced to be content with glowering at him. "Oh, no, you don't. You're not going to cozen me with a kiss this time. I—"

Miles silenced her with his lips. From the first touch of his mouth on hers, Delia knew she was lost. Her resistance grew weaker and weaker until she sank against the muscular width of his chest, her arms stealing around his neck.

"Villain!" she complained as Miles proceeded to kiss first one of her eyes, then the other.

"Blackguard!" she mumbled as his lips moved on to brush against the tip of her nose. "You—you . . ."

"Varlet?" he suggested, nibbling at the corner of her mouth.

"That, too." She sighed. She turned her head so that he was obliged to kiss her full on the lips again, sending delicious ripples of warmth coursing through her veins. She moaned a protest when he began to draw away.

"If you truly insist, my dear, I can go down on one knee and make a formal declaration. I am sure some appropriate quote will come to mind."

Delia's response was to tighten her grip. Standing on tip-toe, she captured his lips again, making certain that nothing came into his mind at all except the thought of kissing her. She raised no objections whatsoever when he seated himself on the wing-backed chair and drew her onto his knee.

Delia nestled her head against his shoulder, hearing something crinkle inside his coat pocket. "Oh, I nearly forgot," Miles said, raising his lips from where he had buried them amidst her curls. "Your betrothal present."

She reluctantly shifted away from him long enough so that he could draw forth a crumpled piece of parchment. Delia had more interest in trailing a line of kisses along his jaw than on reading the paper. Miles's eyes clouded in blissful distraction, then he shook his head, sternly demanding that she examine the sheet. Snuggling against him, Delia attempted to focus on the dark lines of ink.

Her heart skipped a beat. She bolted upright. "Miles! This— this is the deed to Renwick Manor. Where did you get it?"

" 'Tis customary to receive a deed when one buys an estate."

"You b-bought Renwick Manor. B-but how could you?"

"With money," Miles said, beginning to nuzzle her ear.

"Are—are you not rather poor?"

Miles laughed. "Well, I am not exactly well-heeled. But my father did leave me a respectable competence and I am an exceedingly thrifty fellow." His expression grew solemn for a moment. "Of course, I will not be able to offer you the sort of luxurious existence that you might have enjoyed as the mistress of an estate like Walsing Park."

Tears prickled behind Delia's eyes, the deed dropping from her fingers. "Oh, Miles, you needn't have done this. I would have been content to live with you even in—in a tent on the banks of the Avon."

"If 'tis all the same to you, my love, I would still prefer Renwick Manor. We could even fix up a suite of apartments for your father and your Aunt Violet if they should wish to leave Rose Briar."

Delia's tears brimmed over. She hung her head, feeling completely humbled. All those unkind thoughts she had had about Miles when he had been away so long before, and he had gone to recover her childhood home. So generous, so patient. How very seldom Miles had grown angry despite all that she had done to torment him. How could he possibly wish to marry her? She felt so undeserving.

She sniffed, gazing at his dark head bent over her hand. "Miles, are—are you truly sure you wish to m-marry me? You—you know what a dreadful t-temper I have."

He pressed a kiss into her palm that set her tingling with a sudden rush of heat. "I shall manage, my dear. ' 'Tis a world to see how tame . . . a meacock wretch can make the curstest shrew.' "

All thoughts of her own unworthiness quite popped out of Delia's head. The man was incorrigible! Completely out of hand, and they were not even wed yet! But Delia found it extremely hard to be vexed with him, not when he looked at her so, as if no woman had ever graced the earth before but she.

"I have my own theories about *The Taming of the Shrew*," she said softly. "About why Petruchio was able to conquer Katherina."

"Pray enlighten me, sweetheart."

"Love," she said, staring deep into his eyes. "Love is the only thing that can tame the fires in a woman's heart."

"Then, my darling, you will never want for that." As if to offer proof of his words, Miles kissed her again. She was still locked in his arms when the parlor door opened. Both of them were far too preoccupied to notice Walter Renwick enter, the open folio in his hand.

Since Delia had grown so much more reasonable about Shakespeare of late, Renwick had wondered if she might care to hear his latest reflections why Hamlet had not married Ophelia. He halted on the threshold, staring at his daughter ensconced on Miles's knee.

Mr. Renwick had no difficulty in interpreting the scene before him. The corners of his mouth upturned in a broad smile touched with a slight hint of melancholy. His little girl. So he must perforce surrender her to Miles after all. He had nigh given up hope. Such a perfect match, but he would miss his Delia.

It would be only himself and Violet left in the parlor of an evening. He cocked his head to one side as a thought occurred to him. Of course, there was that intelligent little woman, Miss Letitia Pym. Letty, he believed he had heard her called. Mr. Renwick slicked back the ends of his ruffled hair. Yes, Letty. She might be quite amenable to calling of an evening to listen to his Shakespeare.

Renwick glanced one more time at Delia and Miles, marveling at how long they could kiss without coming up for a breath of air. Discreetly backing out of the room, he snapped the book closed, his lips tilting into a broad smile. Od's bodikins! For some things even Shakespeare could wait.

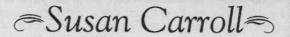

ᴥSusan Carrollᴥ

Two-time winner of Best Regency from the Romance Writers of America

Published by Fawcett Books.
Available in your local bookstore.